Praise for Lenora Worth
and her novels

"There is a wonderful warmth about this story, with characters who make the reader feel at home."
—*Romantic Times BOOKclub* on
BEN'S BUNDLE OF JOY

"[Lorna and Mick] are likeable characters, sharing some great scenes. She with her French temper and he with his quiet understanding."
—*Romantic Times BOOKclub* on
WHEN LOVE CAME TO TOWN

"Lenora Worth delivers a great story with strong, believable characters. Combine an intense romance with solid faith and you have A RELUCTANT HERO. I highly recommend it."
—*Inspirational Romance Page*

"An inspirational romance and mystery thriller rolled into one.... For a sweet, heartwarming story that is full of suspense, I recommend AFTER THE STORM."
—*Romance Reviews Today*

"As a curl-up-by-the-fireplace-and-escape-from-the-hustle-and-bustle read for the Christmas holidays, these agreeable novels meet expectations."
—*Publishers Weekly* on
ONCE UPON A CHRISTMAS

LENORA WORTH
Ben's Bundle of Joy

&

When Love Came to Town

Steeple Hill®

Published by Steeple Hill Books™

STEEPLE HILL BOOKS

Steeple Hill®

ISBN-13: 978-0-373-65264-8
ISBN-10:   0-373-65264-X

BEN'S BUNDLE OF JOY AND WHEN LOVE CAME TO TOWN

TABLE OF CONTENTS

BEN'S BUNDLE OF JOY   11

WHEN LOVE CAME TO TOWN   267

Books by Lenora Worth

Love Inspired

The Wedding Quilt #12
Logan's Child #26
*I'll Be Home for
   Christmas* #44
Wedding at Wildwood #53
His Brother's Wife #82
Ben's Bundle of Joy #99
The Reluctant Hero #108
One Golden Christmas #122
**When Love Came to
   Town* #142

*Something Beautiful #169
*Lacey's Retreat #184
***The Carpenter's
   Wife* #211
**Heart of Stone #227
**A Tender Touch #269
†A Certain Hope #311
†A Perfect Love #330
†A Leap of Faith #344

*In the Garden
**Sunset Island
†Texas Hearts

Steeple Hill Books

After the Storm #8
'Twas the Week Before Christmas
   "Once Upon a Christmas"

LENORA WORTH

knew she wanted to be a writer after her fourth-grade teacher assigned a creative writing project. While the other children moaned and groaned, Lenora gleefully wrote her first story, then promptly sold it (for a quarter) on the playground. She actually started selling in bookstores in 1993. Before joining Steeple Hill, Lenora wrote for Avalon and Leisure Books.

Married for thirty years, Lenora has two children. Before writing full-time, she worked in marketing and public relations. She has served in her local RWA chapter and as president of Faith, Hope and Love, the inspirational chapter of RWA. She also wrote a weekly opinion column for the *Shreveport Times* for five years, and now writes a monthly column for *SB* magazine.

BEN'S BUNDLE OF JOY

For you were once darkness, but you are light in the Lord. Walk as children of the light.

—*Ephesians* 5:8

To Anne Canadeo, with gratitude and appreciation

Chapter One

Deep within the still, peaceful confines of the old church, he thought he heard a baby's soft cry. Glancing up, Reverend Ben Hunter decided he must be imagining things. He was alone in the church, alone with the brilliance of stained-glass windows on a crisp, sunny October morning, alone with his own unvoiced thoughts and unanswered prayers. It was too early in the day and way too quiet for any of his overly protective members to be paying a visit to the sanctuary of The Old First Church of Fairweather, Minnesota.

At least he hoped so.

Ben liked being alone. Not that he minded having to deal with his congregation and their joys and concerns on a daily basis, but he craved the peace and solitude of his private early-morning devotionals here in the church that he'd called home for the past three years. But was this really his home? Would it ever be?

He didn't get a chance to ponder that particular prayer request. The cry came again, this time impatient and almost angry, but still soft, like the mewling of a kitten.

Lifting his athletic frame off the aged pine pew in the middle of the small church, Ben shook his head as he followed the sound toward the back. "Not another kitten. Emma, Emma, when will you stop trying to push pets off on me?"

He knew the church secretary, Emma Fulton, meant well. Emma was a social butterfly. She liked being the center of attention, and she liked having people and pets around all the time. So, naturally she thought Ben needed the same in his life—for companionship. Which meant she was constantly trying to fix him up with either blind dates or abandoned animals. Ben didn't know which was worse—the setups never panned out because he usually never heard from the ladies again, and because he couldn't turn the animals away, he was slowly collecting a small zoo. At least the animals took a liking to him, even if none of the single women in town did.

"I can't take any more strays, Emma," he said, his voice echoing over the cream-colored walls and vaulted, beamed ceiling of the antique church. He half expected the plump secretary to jump out from behind a pew, singing one of her favorite hymns. As he reached the back of the church, though, Ben stopped and stared into the sturdy cardboard box someone had left on the pew. This was no ordinary stray.

This one was human. A baby. A tiny newborn baby lay kicking and whining in the box, mounds of blankets encasing the ruddy little body.

"Well, hello there," Ben said, glancing around to see if anyone would come out and lay claim to the infant. "How did you get here, little one?"

This time the baby's cry grew louder, more demanding. Not sure what to do, Ben reached down and lifted the infant out of the box, careful to keep it wrapped in the protective blue blankets someone had left with it. As Ben lifted the child, a note fluttered out from the folds of the blanket.

Sweeping a hand down to catch the note, Ben held tight to the baby in his arms. "Let's see what this says."

Carefully Ben balanced the wiggling bundle in his arms, so he could unfold the note and read it over the cries of the baby.

"'Reverend Ben, this is Tyler. He is one month old. I know you will take good care of him.'"

Stunned, Ben dropped the note back into the empty box, then stared blankly down at the little baby boy in his arms.

"Tyler?" The infant answered him with a lusty cry.

"You're probably hungry...and wet," Ben said as he shifted the child in his arms. "And I don't have any food or diapers.'' Then, in spite of his concern, he smiled. ''But I certainly know someone who does.''

Sara Conroy glanced up just in time to see the tall man with the baby coming directly toward her. The man, handsome in a gentle kind of way, seemed frantic in his efforts to calm the screaming baby. Sara watched, somewhat amused, as he looked up, his incredible blue eyes latching on to her as he headed down the center of the tidy, colorful classroom. He walked carefully so as to avoid stepping on crawling toddlers in his haste.

''Where's Maggie?'' the man asked, his tone breathless in spite of the deep tremor of his voice. ''I need her, right now.''

Sara raised a hand, then tossed back her shoulder-length curly red hair. ''Hold on there, Daddy. What's the problem?'' Automatically she reached out to take the baby from him.

''This...'' the man said, gladly handing the infant over to her. Scissoring a hand through his curly brown locks, he said, ''I found him...in the church...a few minutes ago. He's hungry—'' here he wiped one hand down the side of his jeans ''—and very wet.''

Spurred into action, Sara glanced over the baby in her arms. ''You found him?''

Ben let out a long sigh. ''Yes. Someone left him on a church pew. I heard him crying—'' He stopped, his gaze shifting from the baby to Sara's face. ''I'm sorry,

I'm Ben Hunter. And you must be Maggie's replacement.''

"Sara Conroy.'' She nodded, then lifted her eyes to meet his. "Calm down, Reverend. He won't break, but we do need to check him over. And we'll have to call social services, of course.''

"Why?'' Ben watched as she gently settled the bawling baby down on a changing table, then moved her hands expertly over his little, thrashing body.

"Well, this child was obviously abandoned,'' Sara explained, concern for the baby evident in her words. "We have to alert the proper authorities.'' She automatically handed him a sanitized baby wipe to clean his hands.

Ben relaxed a little, then leaned into a nearby counter. "You're right, of course. There was a note. His name is Tyler and someone seems to think I can take care of him. Is he…is everything all right?''

"I think so,'' Sara said. At his doubtful look, she added, "I was a pediatric nurse back in St. Paul. He seems healthy—no fever, no signs of exposure or respiratory problems, but we should have a doctor check him out, just the same.''

Ben threw the wipe into a trash can. "I'll call Morgan Talbot. He's the local favorite with all the kids.''

Sara nodded. "Yes, I met Dr. Talbot just the other day.'' Glancing over her shoulder to make sure the other children in her care were safe, she buzzed one of the aides. "Abby, can you bring me a warm bottle

of formula from our extra supplies?'' Then, while Ben
called Dr. Talbot, she changed the baby's soiled diaper
and found an extra set of flannel pajamas the day-care
center kept on hand in a clothes bin. ''We'll get him
fed and quiet, at least. He'll probably sleep the morning away, poor little fellow.''

After hanging up the phone, Ben watched as Sara
Conroy went about her work, amazed at how calm and
collected she was. Even with a baby in her arms and
children pulling at her long denim skirt, she still managed to somehow keep everything under control.
Within minutes, she had Abby entertaining the older
children while she sat in a cane-backed rocking chair
and fed little Tyler.

''You look right at home here,'' he said a few
minutes later as Sara laid the contented Tyler down in
a nearby bassinet.

''I love children,'' she said, her expression growing
soft as she gazed down at the baby.

He couldn't help but notice how pretty she looked
with her red hair glinting in the bright sunshine that
streamed in through the big windows. She had a serene
smile, and her eyes were every bit as green as a Minnesota spring, but there was something else about Sara
Conroy. She had attitude. Big-city attitude. He could
see it in her stance, in the way she carried herself—a
little self-assured, a little hard-nosed and tough, maybe
a little cynical and wary, and a whole lot weary. Sara

Conroy would not take anything off anybody, he imagined.

Even a small-town minister who hadn't quite found his footing and certainly didn't want to part with his heart ever again.

"Well, you don't have to stare," Sara said, causing Ben to quickly glance away and then back, a grin on his face.

"Sorry, it's just…you're not from around these parts. St. Paul, did you say?"

"Yeah, but last time I checked, St. Paul women look and act pretty much the same as other women, especially when a handsome man keeps staring at them."

He actually blushed. "I'm sorry. It's…it's just been one of those mornings. First, finding the baby, then finding…you. Not your typical Monday morning."

She lifted a slanted brow. "You were expecting Maggie, right?"

He nodded. "Yeah. I forgot she's out on extended maternity leave. Doctor's orders. She can't risk losing that baby."

"That's why I'm here," Sara said, motioning for him to come into the little office just off the nursery. Turning as Ben followed her, she settled down in the desk chair and smiled up at him. "Have a seat. Less noise in here. We can talk while Abby reads to the children."

"Is that really why you're here?" he asked, surprising himself and Sara. "I mean, why would you give up being a pediatric nurse to work in a church day-care center?"

Sara took her time in answering. "I guess that's a fair question."

"But none of my business?"

"No, no." She held up a hand. "It's okay, really. It's just hard sometimes."

"Then you don't have to talk about it."

But she needed to talk about it and he seemed like a good listener. Being a minister probably made him an expert listener. And it certainly didn't hurt that he was intriguing in his shy, quiet way, and handsome in a rugged, unpolished way. Completely opposite from Steven.

Not wanting to dwell on her ex-fiancé and his many flaws, Sara shrugged then said, "My mother died recently. She had Alzheimer's and it was up to me to take care of her in her final days. Once it was all over, I realized I needed a break, something less stressful. Maggie suggested I come here, to take her place for a while."

He leaned back on a table. "I'm sorry about your mother. That must have been very hard on you."

"It was," she replied, some of the brightness leaving her eyes. "It wasn't easy, watching her deteriorate right before my eyes. But…we always depended on each other. She didn't have anyone else. It was up to me."

Ben reached out a hand to touch hers. "Sounds like you did need a break. Maggie is good at suggesting things like that. She cares about people."

"She saved my life," Sara said, then instantly regretted it. "I mean—she called me at exactly the right time. I was on my last legs. Just exhausted."

"Physically and spiritually," Ben added, his blue eyes filled with compassion and understanding.

"Yes, I suppose so." Refusing to give in to the luxury of self-pity, Sara stood up. "But I'm doing okay. I'm all settled in out on the lake and I do love the peacefulness of this place. Less hectic than the big city."

Ben lifted off the table to follow her out into the long, colorful nursery. "But not nearly as exciting?"

Sara's little bubble of a laugh magnified her dimples.

"What's so funny?" Ben asked, captivated.

"Well, Reverend, I'd say my first morning here has been rather exciting, don't you think?"

"Yes, I guess it has." He glanced down at Tyler's pink face. "He's a handsome baby, isn't he?"

"Beautiful," Sara said, the word filled with awe. "I wonder why someone would abandon him like that."

"I don't know," Ben replied. "And why with me, of all people?"

Sara gave him another direct look, again taking her time to answer. "Because, like the note said—whoever left Tyler with you thinks you can take care of him. And I think maybe they're right.''

''You think that—based on me rushing in here to hand this baby over to the first person I could find?''

''I think that—based on the concerned expression on your face when you brought him, the way you handled him and the way you looked down at him when we finally got him settled. I've worked with a lot of parents and children, Reverend, and it's taught me to be a pretty good judge of character.'' She lifted her head, then folded her arms over her leaf-patterned sweater. ''Besides, Maggie has already sang your praises. And that's good enough for me.''

Her smile was full of confidence and assurance. But Ben didn't feel so confident or so assured. ''We'll have to see about all of that,'' he said, looking up to see Dr. Morgan Talbot weaving his way through the toys and toddlers in the room. ''I don't want to disappoint you, or Maggie, but I'm not sure I'm up to taking care of an infant.''

Sara grabbed Ben's shirtsleeve. ''You're not thinking of sending him away, are you?''

Ben hesitated, then whispered. ''I just thought foster parents might be better equipped—''

Sara shook her head. ''They left the baby with you. You can't send little Tyler away without even trying to help him.''

Morgan came in, smiled at them, then went right to

Tyler's bed. "Well, well, Reverend, let's have a look at your little bundle of joy."

Ben glanced at his friend, then back to the red-haired, obviously determined woman flashing green fire at him. "I just don't know—"

"I'll help you," she offered, shocking herself in the process. "I'll help you with Tyler. You should keep him here, surrounded by people who care, until we can decide what to do about him. I'm sure social services will agree."

Ben could only nod. She certainly seemed determined to keep the baby nearby, but he wasn't so sure. He wasn't so sure at all. This was just one more burden, one more test, and he didn't think he could bear up underneath much more.

But Ben knew that God didn't always send His answers in the easiest, most convenient packages. Sometimes they came in the form of crying babies and red-haired women with attitude. Whether you wanted them to or not.

"The baby is in good shape," Morgan told Ben later as they both stood over the bassinet. "He looks completely healthy to me."

"That's a relief, at least," Ben said, one hand automatically touching the tiny fingers of the sleeping infant.

"What are you going to do about him?" Morgan asked, a faint smile on his lips.

"That's a good question." Ben let out a sigh, then glanced around the empty nursery. Sara and Abby had taken the other children outside for some fresh air before lunch and nap time. "I don't think I'm qualified to care for a baby."

"Someone obviously thought you were."

"Well, that someone obviously wasn't thinking this thing through." He shook his head, then turned to stare out the window where the children toddled here and there on the miniature playground equipment. "I've got a meeting with a woman from social services in a few minutes, to decide. Sara seems to think I should keep Tyler here for a little while at least."

"Sara?" Morgan glanced in the direction of his friend's gaze. "Oh, that Sara. She comes highly recommended, you know. A friend of Maggie's, I believe, from college. And fast becoming a friend of Rachel's, too. My wife met Sara after church yesterday when she went over to visit with Maggie."

"She's nice enough," Ben admitted, his eyes on the smiling woman sitting in a pile of leaves, surrounded by children. He had to smile when she let one of the toddlers drop leaves on top of her head. As she shook her long, wavy hair and laughed, the varying shades of red and orange foliage merged with the brilliant auburn of her shining curls. "Maybe she should take Tyler. She was a pediatric nurse, and she seems to love her work here."

"They didn't leave Tyler at her door, friend," the doctor reminded him. "They left the baby with you."

"So you're casting your lot with Sara?"

"I'm casting my lot with you, Reverend. I trust you to do what is best for this child. And for yourself."

Ben whirled to stare at his friend. "And what's that supposed to mean?"

"Oh, nothing. Nothing at all." Morgan grabbed his wind jacket and started for the door. "You've just seemed…well, a bit restless lately, Ben. Like you're not quite settled."

"I don't know that I am settled. Every time I think I've won the congregation over, something comes up and I'm right back in the middle of a dispute."

"Give them time," Morgan told him with a friendly hand on his arm. "Some of these members have been in this church for well over thirty years. They are definitely set in their ways."

Ben nodded. "And dead set against me and my newfangled changes. Last week, someone complained because I played the guitar during the service. Said he liked the pipe organ just fine, thank you very much. You'd think after three years—"

"Yeah, you'd think," Morgan said, grinning. "Three years is not much time, considering Reverend Olsen was their minister for most of his life—and thankfully, he never attempted to play any instruments. You've at least got him beat in that particular talent."

"He was a very patient man," Ben said as he waved Morgan out the door. "I'll be all right. Finding a baby at my door has just thrown me for a loop. Hey, tell Sara I'm going to wait in here for the police and social services."

"Okay." Morgan gave him a salute, then called, "How about a game of one-on-one this afternoon? I think it's my turn to win."

Ben nodded. "Okay, hoops on the church court, right after work."

"I'll see you then."

Ben turned back to the sleeping baby, taking the time to enjoy the quiet that had fallen over the usually noisy room. He closed his eyes and stood there for just a minute, a silent prayer forming in his heart. *Lord, show me what to do.*

Then he lifted his head, his gaze searching out the intriguing woman who'd already issued him a challenge. Sara glanced up at him, waved, then grabbed a cute little blond-haired girl and lifted her onto the tiny swing. Soon she had the child going back and forth in an arc of rainbow swirls. They sure made a pretty picture.

So pretty, that Ben had to look away. He'd often thought he'd have a family one day, but it wasn't meant to be. He was alone again, with not a sound to disturb him.

Except for the faint, rhythmic breathing of the baby someone had left in his care.

Chapter Two

"We really don't have much choice."

Betty Anderson looked at the crowd of people gathered in her office at The Old First Church Day-care Center, her reading glasses tipped precariously on the end of her pert nose. "I think Ben will make a fine temporary guardian for Tyler."

"I agree." The chief of police, Samuel Riley, a short, round man with white hair and a beard that always got him the part of Santa in the church Christmas functions, nodded his head so vigorously that his ruddy double chin rolled up against his chest. "Ben, with all this red tape we have to wade through with social services and child welfare, and given the fact that we've never had anything like this occur in Fairweather, I think you're the best candidate for taking care of the baby at this point—just until we can weigh all the facts and find out exactly what the proper procedure is around here.''

''It would only be for a few days, a week at most,'' Betty pointed out. ''And, Ben, you know we'll all pitch in. You can bring Tyler here every day during the week. Sara has already agreed to watch him for you—whenever you need her to.'' Her smile indicated she was immensely pleased with Sara's offer.

''I'll even go over the basics with you, step by step,'' Sara told him, that glint of a challenge in her green eyes.

''I appreciate that,'' Ben replied, his eyes touching on Sara Conroy's face as he sat back in his chair. It was late in the day and Tyler was safe in the infant room with all the other children. But it had been a long and trying day for Ben. Not only had he had to go round and round with the police, but the child welfare office in Minneapolis hadn't offered up much help, either. The closest available foster family they could come up with was in St. Paul. And everyone agreed that the baby shouldn't be carted off to the big city—not when he had a loving, supportive community of people right here, willing to help take care of him. The authorities had pulled what strings they could, to keep the child here.

But, ultimately, the responsibility rested with Ben. He didn't want to send the baby away any more than the rest of them. And he was fast losing the battle against his own insecurities and doubts. ''I'll need lots of help,'' he said at last. ''I don't know a whole lot about babies.''

''You can hold your own,'' Betty told him as she took off her glasses and came around the desk. ''I've seen you with the children right here. They love you.'' At his doubtful look, she added, ''You'll be just fine, Ben.''

''Okay.'' Ben scissored his fingers through his hair, then let out a long sigh. ''Guess I'm a temporary father.''

Betty patted him on the arm. ''I'll have Warren load a bassinet and all the other equipment to take to the parsonage. And I've already been to the grocery store—got you plenty of formula and diapers. And I even bought two of the cutest little outfits—nice and warm, with teddy bears and baseballs.''

''Thanks, Betty.'' Ben got up, then looked over at Sara. She sure seemed amused with all of this. ''Well, time to pay up, Miss Conroy. Want to come to my house and show me how to mix up formula?''

''Does this count as our first date?'' she teased, in a voice meant for Ben's ears only.

''I didn't think you'd be interested in me, except in a strictly temporary guardian capacity,'' he shot back. ''Since you seemed so determined for me to take this foundling.''

Lifting her brows in surprise, she retorted, ''Maybe I just wanted an excuse to come and visit you, Reverend.''

She was rewarded with another blush. Not used to flirting, or being flirted with, Ben did manage a glib reply. "All you had to do was ask."

Sara laughed, then moved past him. "I'll follow you in my car."

"Do you know the way?"

"Julianne pointed your house out to me when we took a walk at lunch," she told him.

"And just so you'll know," Betty interjected, "Emma has already told Sara that you are single and in need of female companionship."

Ben groaned while Sara nodded, that amused look coloring her face. "And she grilled me, so I'll just go ahead and get the awkward questions out of the way. Yes, I'm single, but no, I'm not interested in any type of long-term commitments, and yes, I just want a little peace and quiet, but yes, I'm more than willing to help you with Tyler."

"So much for our first date," Ben said, an uncomfortable grin pinching his face. Somehow though, he felt disappointed that she'd answered all his questions before he'd even had a chance to ask them. Oh, well, that was probably for the best. He had a full plate— no time for starting a heavy personal relationship, and Sara Conroy struck him as a no-nonsense, tough-minded woman. It would be hard to win her over.

"You don't have to look so relieved," Sara said as they made their way up the hall to the nursery.

Ben felt sheepish and knew he was a coward. "I'm sorry. I've just got a lot on my mind."

"And becoming a temporary father hasn't helped?"

He stopped as they reached the room where the babies up to one year old spent most of their days while their mothers worked. It was a colorful, playful room with a painted mural of Noah's ark centered on one wall, and various other bright Biblical figures painted on every available surface.

The room was quiet now; most of the parents had already come to claim their little ones and the aides were busy cleaning up for the day. Outside, the burnished sunset that proclaimed Minnesota in the fall shined golden and promising.

"I'll take care of Tyler," he said, more to himself than to Sara. "I just wish I could help the person who left him here. Whoever did it, must have been so desperate, so alone. His mother is probably out there somewhere right now, wondering if she did the right thing."

Sara watched the man standing beside her, and felt a tug at her heartstrings that almost took her breath away.

Almost. Hadn't she just five minutes earlier told Ben in no uncertain terms that she wasn't interested in any kind of romantic relationship? Hadn't she pledged to avoid opening up her heart to that kind of pain ever again?

Remember, Sara, she reminded herself, time and circumstance can ruin any relationship.

That's exactly what had happened with Steven. She'd never had the time to give to him, to nurture what they had together, and because of the circumstances—her mother, his work—he'd taken a job in Atlanta, Georgia, far away from the cold winters of Minnesota and far away from what he'd termed her cold heart.

But this man, this man would understand why she'd had to sacrifice so much for her own work and her mother's illness. This man, this gentle, kind man, would do the same thing. He was doing the same thing by taking in Tyler.

Somehow, knowing that warmed her, melting away the layers of hardness she'd wrapped around her heart. But with that warmth came a warning—to take care, to be cautious.

Time and circumstance could once again bring her pain. She only had a little time here before she'd have to make a decision regarding her job back in St. Paul, and she wouldn't let the circumstance of an abandoned baby trick her into thinking she, too, could find a good life with someone like Ben Hunter.

Besides, the man was a minister, a preacher, a man of God. And she was definitely not preacher's wife material.

As she watched Ben lift baby Tyler out of his crib and bundle him in a thick cotton blanket, she regretted that. Ben would make the right woman a fine husband. Except her. Except Sara Conroy. No, she was too cynical, too burned-out and disillusioned for someone like Ben Hunter. She wasn't the right woman, and she had to remember that.

"I think I can remember all of this," Ben said hours later as he tucked the baby in, hopefully for a few hours of sleep at least. "Sterilize the bottles every night, mix the formula, put it in the refrigerator, heat it till it feels warm on my skin." He shook an empty bottle toward his wrist to demonstrate. "Feed him every three or four hours, regardless of what time it is, until he gets on a schedule. Change diapers as needed—what?"

Sara couldn't help the laughter bubbling over in her throat. But she couldn't possibly tell Ben that he looked so incredibly adorable, standing there in his flannel shirt and old jeans with a burp cloth slung over his shoulder and his dark curls all mushed up against his forehead, while one of the three cats he owned meowed at his feet. "It's nothing," she said. "You just look so helpless."

"I am not helpless," Ben retorted in mock defiance. "Well, not as long as you're here, at least."

She took another sip of her coffee, ignoring the little tremors of delight his innocent statement brought to her stomach. "Oh, I think you'll be just fine. From all the phone calls you've received, I'd say you've got more than enough help.''

"You're right there. My congregation has really surprised me with all their support. I was afraid some of them would frown on this—a single man taking in an infant. I'm pleasantly surprised, and very grateful.''

"Maybe you don't give yourself enough credit,'' she said as he refilled her coffee. "Of course, I've heard a lot about Reverend Olsen—hard shoes to fill.''

"He was the best. I still visit him in the nursing home and sometimes I bring him here, just to spend an afternoon with me. He is the wisest man I know and I respect his suggestions, even if I don't always follow them.''

"I see,'' she said, smiling back at him. "You want to do things your way.''

"Sometimes, but I find that I mostly have to do things His way.'' He pointed heavenward.

"An awesome task,'' Sara retorted, meaning it. She had long ago stopped trying to figure out God's plan for her life. Now she was taking things one day at a time.

"Do you plan to come to church, hear one of my sermons?''

The question, so direct, so sincere, threw her. "I...I probably will.'' Lowering her head, she added, "I haven't been very regular in my faith lately. In fact, I think I kind of gave up on it.''

"Losing a loved one can do that to you," Ben said, his head down, his whole stance seeming to go weary.

His tone was so quiet, so introspective, that Sara wondered if he'd suffered such a loss himself. Not wanting to pry, she stayed silent, helping him put away the many supplies required to feed and care for a baby. "I'm better now. I was bitter for a while—about my mother's illness, about life in general. And I hope coming here will help me to...to find some sense of peace."

He turned to her then, his gentle smile reminding her that although this man was different, a man of strong faith no doubt, maybe he was still just as vulnerable to pain and frustration as the rest of humankind.

Leaning close, he said, "I hope you find your peace here, Sara. This is certainly a good place to start."

Is that why he'd come here? she wondered. Before she could ask him to tell her, he lifted off the counter and turned away. "Let's sit down and catch our breaths."

Then he dropped the diaper and grabbed his own coffee cup, motioning for Sara to follow him into the tiny sitting room of the cottage he called home. The room, like many of the rooms she'd noticed in the charming, old house, was in a state of repair.

"Sorry about the boards and nails," he told her as he offered her the comfortable old leather armchair near the fireplace. "I fully intend to finish that wall of bookcases, and all the other work around here—someday. But I'm not the handyman type. I'll have to get Warren Sinclair to repair my repairs, I'm afraid.''

The small kitten that had been meowing at Ben's feet, aptly named Rat because he was a deep gray and tended to skitter like a mouse, hurriedly followed them into the room, then jumped up on her lap the minute she sat down.

Sara nodded as she glanced around the cozy room. Books everywhere—that didn't surprise her—and a few unpacked boxes coupled with very few personal touches. In spite of the volumes of philosophy and poetry and religious tomes, in spite of the clutter and typical male chaos, it looked as if Ben was just a visitor here—not really settled in yet. Maybe that was why he was afraid of taking on little Tyler. He wasn't ready for any permanent commitments, either.

Since she knew that feeling, she shrugged. ''I like it. It has potential.''

''Somewhere underneath all the old paint and leaking roof, and all my many messes, yes, there is a lot of potential for this to once again become a showcase.''

Sara thought the current occupant had a lot of potential, too, but she didn't voice that opinion. ''I'd better get out to the lake,'' she said instead. ''It's getting late and we both have an early day tomorrow.''

Ben held up a hand in protest. ''I could warm up

some of that stew Emma sent over. Or we could just go for the oatmeal cookies.''

"Reverend, are you stalling the inevitable?"

Ben lowered his head. "Yeah, I admit it. I'm terrified about being alone with that baby. What if I don't know how to handle his cries?"

"Your cats seem to be thriving—even if they are fur balls instead of humans. You must know something about nurturing babies."

He grinned, then rolled his eyes. "Emma thinks I'm the humane society. But taking care of little Rat and his fuzzy companions is a tad different from providing for a baby."

"Just hold him," she said on a soft voice, her eyes meeting his in the muted lamplight. "That's what most babies want and need the most."

"Most humans," he echoed, his voice warm and soothing, his eyes big and blue and vastly deep.

"Yes, I suppose so."

Because the conversation had taken an intimate twist, and because for some strange reason she herself felt an overwhelming need to be held, Sara placed the still-whining Rat on the braided rug at her feet and got up to leave. "You can call me, day or night."

"Even at 3:00 a.m.?"

Imagining his sleep-filled voice at three o'clock in the morning didn't help the erratic charges of awareness coursing through her body. "Anytime," she managed to say. Why did his eyes have to look so very blue?

"I'll hold you to that," he told her as he escorted her to the front door. "Drive carefully."

"I will. It's only a few miles."

"I'll see you tomorrow then."

"Tomorrow." She hurried out to her car, not daring to take a breath until she was sure he couldn't see her. What on earth had come over her, anyway? Her first day in a new town, her first day on the job, and the first eligible man to walk through the door already had her nerves in a shamble and her heart doing strange pitter-pattering things that it shouldn't be doing at all.

It's just the stress, she decided. She'd been through so much—first Steven's decision to transfer to Atlanta—with or without her, then her mother's inevitable death, then the hospital telling her she might want to consider an extended leave of absence because she was exhausted and not too swift on her feet. It had all been just too much for one person.

Maggie's call had come at exactly the right time, but now Sara had to wonder if she'd made the right decision, coming here. She only wanted to concentrate on the children in her care, enjoy the less stressful, much slower way of life here, go home each night to her quiet cottage, and stare out at the endless blue waters of Baylor Lake.

That's all she needed right now—time to decide where she wanted to go in her life, time to heal from the grief of watching her mother deteriorate right before her eyes, time to accept that Steven wasn't coming back for her and that she wouldn't get that family she'd always dreamed about.

If she let herself get involved with the town preacher, she wouldn't know any peace, none at all. But she could be a friend to Ben Hunter, and she could help him with little Tyler. That at least would ease some of her loneliness.

And his, too, maybe.

Ben's kindness, his gentle sense of nobility, had touched on all her keyed-up, long-denied emotions. That was why she felt this way—all shook up and disoriented. Throw in an adorable, abandoned baby, and well, any woman would start getting strange yearnings for home and hearth, strange maternal longings that would probably never be fulfilled. Any woman would feel completely and utterly lonely, sitting in her car in the cold.

"I'll be all right," she told herself as she drove toward the charming cottage she'd rented at Baylor Lake. "I'll be all right. I came here to find some time, to heal, to rethink my life. Not to get attached to a poetic preacher and a sweet lost little baby."

But somehow she knew in her heart that she had already formed a close bond with those two, a bond that would be hard to forget, even given time and circumstance.

Chapter Three

~~~

In a blur of baby, blankets and bags, Ben Hunter stepped inside the outer reception room to his church office, thankful that the cold morning air didn't have a hint of snow. That would come soon enough in November. And he couldn't imagine having to dress a wiggling, tiny baby in a snowsuit. It had taken him twenty extra minutes just to get Tyler in the fleece button-up outfit Betty had thoughtfully supplied.

"Oh, there you are."

Emma Fulton got up to come around her desk, her blue eyes flashing brightly as she cooed right toward Tyler. "Let me see that precious child, Reverend Ben."

Ben didn't hesitate to turn the baby over to Emma. The woman had five grandchildren, so she knew what to do with a baby.

"He had a good night," Ben said, letting out a breath as he dropped all the paraphernalia he'd brought along onto a nearby chair. "He was up around four, but other than that, we did okay."

"Of course you did," Emma said, still cooing and talking baby talk. "Even if the good reverend does look a little tired." Pointing her silvery bun toward the small kitchen just off her office, she said, "There's pumpkin bread."

"Bless you," Ben replied, heading straight to the coffeepot. "Somehow I didn't manage to get breakfast." With a grin he called over his shoulder, "But Tyler sure had his. That little fellow can go through a bottle."

"He's a growing boy," Emma replied as she danced a jig with the baby. "Oh, my, look at that. He's laughing. He likes his aunt Emma."

"Well, go ahead," Ben teased as he came back into the room with a chunk of the golden-brown bread, "tell him you were Strawberry Festival Queen in…what year was that, Emma?"

"Never you mind what year, kid. Just remember who you're dealing with here." Her smile belied her defensive tone.

"I always remember who's the boss around here," Ben admonished. Then when he heard someone clearing his throat in his office, he turned to Emma. "Visitor?"

"Oh, I almost forgot." She whirled with the baby

in her arms. "Finish your breakfast first. It's Mr. Erickson."

Ben immediately put down his coffee and the last of his bread. "Maybe he's heard something from Jason."

"Don't know," Emma whispered, her expression turning sad. "Want me to take Tyler to the nursery for you?"

"Would you mind?" Ben gathered the baby's things for her. "Tell Sara I'll be over in a little while to check on him and give her a report about his first night with me."

"I certainly will do that," Emma said, getting her smile back in a quick breath, her eyes perfectly centered on the baby.

Ben knew that look. Emma would try to match him up with Sara. Somehow, the thought of that didn't bother him nearly as much as it should—considering Emma had tried to match him up with every single woman in Fairweather, usually with disastrous results. With Sara Conroy, he couldn't foresee any disaster, other than the one in which he might lose his heart. And he wasn't willing to risk that just yet.

As he entered the quiet confines of his office, however, another type of disaster entered his mind. Richard Erickson stood looking out over the prayer garden, his hands tucked in the pockets of his dark tailored wool suit pants, his graying hair trimmed into a rigid style, just the way he ran the local bank and most of this town.

Ben dreaded another confrontation with the man, but his heart had to go out to Mr. Erickson. His only son, sixteen-year-old Jason, had run away from home several months ago.

"Hello, Mr. Erickson," Ben said, extending his hand as the older man pivoted to stare at him with a look of condemnation mixed with a condescending air.

The handshake was quick and unmeaningful, but Richard Erickson was too polite and straitlaced to behave without the impeccable manners that befit a descendant of the founding family of the town. Ben gave him credit for that much, at least.

"Reverend."

"What can I do for you this morning? Any word from Jason, sir?"

At the mention of his youngest child's name, Richard Erickson's whole demeanor changed. After having three daughters, his son, Jason, had been his pride and joy, and ultimately, the child of which he made the most demands and held the highest expectations.

His expression became etched with regret and pride. "No. I was hoping you might have heard something. He did call you before."

"You know I would call you immediately if Jason tried to contact me," Ben told him. "I'm sorry, but I haven't heard anything since the last call back in September."

"Are you sure you'd tell me if you did?"

Ben could see the hostility in the man's brown eyes. It still galled him that this man who contributed so much financially to the church, could not contribute anything emotionally to Ben or his ministry, or to his son Jason, for that matter. Yet Ben didn't have the heart to tell Richard Erickson that part of the reason his son was missing today was because of Mr. Erickson's cold, distant relationship with the boy.

Jason had confided in Ben, and he wouldn't break that confidence. Early on, right after Jason had left, Ben had tried to sit down with Richard and Mary Erickson and explain what Ben had told him. He'd gotten to know the boy pretty well, after serving as coach for the church basketball team.

But the Ericksons would not listen to Ben's concerns. They had told him in no uncertain terms that they blamed him for interfering in their relationship with their son, that Ben's influence had put newfangled notions in the boy's head and caused him to rebel.

Now, however, Ben was their only source of comfort, since Jason had contacted him on two different occasions after running away earlier in the year. For that reason, and for Jason's sake, Ben swallowed his own resentment and tried to counsel the couple—when they would let him.

Sensing that Richard needed to talk, Ben gestured to a floral armchair. "Please, sit down."

"I don't have much time," Richard said, but he did

sit on the very edge of the chair, his back straight, his expression grim. "I just wanted to tell you—if you hear from my son again, you have to let me know. My wife is beside herself—what with the holidays coming up and everything. And all our efforts to track him down have only brought us disappointment."

"I understand, sir," Ben said, his hands folded over his heavily marked desk pad calendar. "I will do whatever I can to convince Jason to come home. I hope you realize that."

"I realize," Richard Erickson said as he rose to leave, "that my son is deeply troubled and that I hold you partially responsible for whatever brought him to this extreme." He held up a hand then. "But I do appreciate your efforts on Jason's behalf, and in light of this new situation, I just wanted to remind you where your priorities should be."

"I'm afraid I don't quite understand," Ben said, getting up to follow Erickson out of the office. "What are you trying to tell me, Mr. Erickson?"

Richard Erickson stopped at the door, then turned to face Ben, the look in his eyes devoid of any compassion or understanding. "Taking in a stray baby, an orphan? Come on, Reverend, we both know that you have no business trying to take care of an infant. You should be concentrating on taking care of your congregation. I still get complaints about you, you know. And this latest development hasn't helped matters, not one bit."

Shocked and angry beyond words, Ben gripped the edge of Emma's desk in order to regain his composure. "You don't need to worry about Tyler, Mr. Erickson. I know what I'm doing and I don't intend to let taking care of this baby interfere with my work here. Rest assured, I know what my responsibilities are."

"Do you?" Erickson pointed a finger in the air. "If you had concentrated on preaching instead of sports, my son might be here today. But you had to form that basketball team, just to glorify yourself. You had to prove that you were the best in college, so you got these local boys all worked up about basketball and winning. Jason didn't have any complaints in life until you came along. Then all he could think about was practice. He was neglecting his studies, getting behind in school. He changed right before our eyes. And now you're planning on raising a baby?"

Ben couldn't believe the things coming out of Richard Erickson's mouth. The man had a skewered idea of what had brought his son to such desperate measures.

Hoping to set him straight, Ben said, "Jason had problems long before I came into the picture, sir. If you'd only listen—"

"I'm done listening to you, Reverend. And I have a good mind to call the authorities and tell them what I know about you. You are not fit to raise that baby, and by trying to prove yourself once again, you will fail. And this church will suffer even more for it. Maybe you should have thought about that, before you took on this new challenge.''

Ben looked up to see Sara Conroy standing in the hallway that led to the small narthex of the church. She must have come in from the other side, and from the frozen expression on her face, she'd obviously heard most of their conversation.

Feeling defeated, but refusing to give in to Richard Erickson's rigid attitude, Ben sighed, then asked God for guidance. The very thought of this man trying to have Tyler taken from him only reinforced Ben's close bond with the baby. "I can take care of that baby. I have plenty of people more than willing to help me through this.''

"I can change all of that easily enough," Erickson stated, the threatening tone in his words leaving no doubt that he would do just that.

"But you won't," Ben said, his own stance just as rigid. "You wouldn't do that to an innocent child, would you?" When the man didn't answer, he added, "Sir, you can do what you want to me, you can blame me for Jason's problems, too, if that makes you feel better. But don't do anything to jeopardize Tyler. He's very young and very alone right now, and if you interfere, he'll just be snatched away again. Do you really want that on your conscience?"

His words seemed to calm the older man. Richard Erickson looked up then and realized they weren't alone anymore. The manners set in immediately. As he lifted a hand to Sara in greeting, his whole expression softened.

"I've got too much to deal with as it is," he said at last, his voice low now. "But I'm warning you, you'd better watch your step. And you'd better hope I find my son soon."

"I'll pray for that day and night, just as I've been doing," Ben told him, meaning it. "If you need anything—"

"I don't." With that, Erickson nodded to Sara, then turned and headed out the door to his luxury sedan.

Sara took one look at Ben and headed straight to him. "You should sit down."

He didn't argue with her. Instead, he fell down into Emma's softly padded desk chair, sighed long and hard, then ran a hand through his hair with a groan of frustration. "Sorry you had to witness that."

Hoping to lighten the somber mood, Sara said, "Do you always win over your members in such a sure way?"

"Every last one of them," he told her, some of the tension leaving his face. Then he looked up at her. "Mr. Erickson doesn't like me very much right now. His youngest child, and only son, Jason, ran away from home earlier this year, and he blames me for it."

"You?" Shocked, Sara leaned against the corner of the desk, near him, her long khaki skirt rustling as she crossed her legs. "I thought your job was to save souls, not alienate them."

"Yeah, me, too, but it doesn't always go that way."

"Want to talk about it?"

He looked up at her again, taking in those glorious red curls and her mysterious green eyes. She had a few freckles scattered across her pert nose, but the rest of her skin was porcelain white and looked creamy soft. She wore a short, green-and-brown striped heavy cotton sweater that only brought out the red of her hair and the green of her eyes. And brought out the warmth in his heart.

"That's supposed to be my line," he told her by way of an answer.

"Which means you probably don't ever have a chance to vent your own frustrations, right?"

"I have plenty of chances," he replied, his hands resting on the arms of the chair as he leaned back to admire her. "I can talk to God anytime."

"Yeah, right."

"Did you just snort? Are you scoffing at me?"

"I'm not snorting or scoffing at all," she said, then smiled. "Okay, maybe I'm a little cynical right now. I know, I know—God is always there. But you look like you could use a real friend right now, a human friend."

"And you're offering to be that friend?"

"Yes, I guess I am." She pushed away from the desk, leaving a trail of flower-and-spice perfume in her wake. "You know, Emma told me that you wanted me to join you for a slice of her famous pumpkin bread—insisted I come right on over here." She headed into the kitchenette. "But I can't leave the babies with an aide for long. Now, do you want to talk to me about this or not. Time is precious."

Ben shook his head, laughing as he managed to finally get up out of the chair. "It will take a long time to explain what you just heard and saw."

"Well, sorry. Gotta go." She had her slice of bread and was already headed out the side door. "I guess you'll just have to bring Tyler out to the lake, for dinner at my place tonight. Say around six-thirty?"

Ben almost fell back into the chair again. This woman was different, that was for sure. And full of intriguing surprises. "Miss Conroy, are you asking me for a date?"

"No, Reverend Hunter, I'm just telling you I'll fix you dinner."

He tipped his head to one side, his smile changing into a grin. "That Emma—look what she's done now."

"Oh, you didn't really invite me for breakfast?"

"No, but I'm glad you came by."

"So, does that mean you'll come for dinner?"

"I didn't know nurses could cook."

"We're pretty handy with a microwave and a few written instructions," she said, giving him an impish smile.

"I'll be there," he told her as he walked her down the short hallway.

"With Tyler?"

"With Tyler," he said, then added, "if Richard Erickson doesn't have him taken away before sundown."

She heard the humor in his voice, but saw the concern in his eyes, too. "He wouldn't do that, would he?"

"He would and he could. The man is very bitter right now and he'd do just about anything to have me removed from this church."

"We'll just have to say a prayer that he doesn't follow through on his threats, right?"

Ben grabbed at his chest, an expression of mock surprise on his face. "You—you're going to pray for me?"

"Hey, I still talk to God on occasion, even if I don't think He's really listening."

Ben touched her arm then. "He always listens, Sara. You have to know that. After all, He sent you to rescue me this morning, didn't He?"

"That was Emma's doing," she said, acutely aware of the clean, fresh smell of baby lotion mixed with aftershave that lifted out around him. "And remind me to thank her later."

"Are you sure it was all Emma's doing?" he countered, holding the door for her, but not letting her pass just yet.

"No, I'm not sure of anything right now, except that I need to get back to work. I'll see you tonight, Rev."

Ben watched her walk across the yard toward the day-care center, her straight skirt swishing, her long booted legs carrying her on her merry way. He didn't know if God had sent Sara to him, but she had come just in time, he decided.

Because she was right. He could use a friend. He was blessed with several well-meaning friends here in the church and he appreciated how Emma and Betty stood by him and fought for him, but he needed someone to share quiet moments with, someone he could really open up to and talk with. And Sara Conroy fit the bill—almost too perfectly.

Yet, she'd set the ground rules, and as long as they stuck by them, they'd both be okay. She was willing to be his friend, and she was willing to help with Tyler. Surely there could be no harm in that.

Ben decided he did need her help—he needed Sara to show him how to be a good surrogate dad to Tyler. And he wouldn't lose Tyler. Richard Erickson's threats had made Ben even more determined to keep the baby safe and near. Somehow he had to show Jason's bitter father that he was fit to take care of the little baby, and fit to take care of this congregation, too.

And somehow he hoped God would hear all of their prayers and show Jason Erickson the way back home again.

Chapter Four

"So, because you stepped in and tried to counsel this boy, his father now blames you for his running away?"

Sara held her fork on her plate, her gaze falling across Ben's troubled face. He'd just told her, between bites of salad and spaghetti, about Jason Erickson and his prominent, immensely wealthy family.

"That about sums things up," Ben replied as he snagged another crusty piece of French bread then dipped it into the sauce on his plate. "And maybe Mr. Erickson is right."

"I see," Sara replied, laying her fork down to stare over at him. "So now you're beginning to blame yourself, too? Ben, from everything you just told me, it sounds as if you did all you could to help this boy. It's not your fault he felt forced to run away from home."

Ben dropped his bread on his plate, then sat back in his chair with a long sigh. "But did I cause this? I've asked myself that same question over and over in the last few months. I encouraged the boy to come out of his self-protective shell, to open up to me, and I also encouraged him to get involved with the church basketball team—something his father apparently didn't approve of at all."

"But you have to remember that by doing those things you opened up a whole new world to Jason. It sounds as if he needed an outlet—precisely to keep him out of trouble and give him some confidence, and you gave him that outlet."

Ben gave a little nod of agreement and straightened up in his chair. "He loved the game and he had a natural talent for it. But he'd been struggling in school and I'm afraid all the practices and the heavy schedule did make matters worse. I tutored him, but—"

"But—nothing," Sara said, getting up to refill their water glasses. As she walked by the coffeepot, she flipped the On button and started a fresh brew for later. "Something else must have triggered his leaving. I can't believe a few bad grades would make him do something so desperate."

Ben leaned back in his chair again, and Sara watched as he surveyed the quaint little kitchen decorated with various antique cooking utensils and dozens of potted plants which she hoped she could keep alive through the winter.

"His grades had actually improved a little. And he was trying so hard to please his father and still maintain his own identity. I just wish I knew what really happened."

"When was the last time you saw him?"

"In April of this year. He came by the office to do some homework, but his mind wasn't on it. He seemed distracted, worried. I tried to find out what was wrong, but he wouldn't talk and I just thought he was nervous about the history test he had the next day." Rubbing a hand across his chin, he added, "But I've talked to him on the phone a couple of times since then. He won't contact his parents, so I've tried to encourage him to let me help him, but he refuses to tell me what's going on. I should have tried to help him, make him tell me what was wrong, way back when I had the chance."

"You had no way of knowing," Sara said as she set a plate of cookies on the table, then indicated to Ben to take one. "Emma sends her love along with her special tea cakes."

That perked Ben up. "I've had her tea cakes," he said as he snared one and bit into it. "Mmm, good."

"Let's take these delicious cookies and our coffee into the den," Sara told him, hoping to take his mind off Jason. "That way we can check on little Tyler, too."

Ben followed her, carrying the plate of cookies. "He's sleeping away. I think he likes the fire."

Sara smiled down at the baby. They'd fixed him up a blanketed bed on a deep arm chair near the fire, safe with pillows all around. "He does look content. You apparently did a good job on your first day as his guardian."

"I was a nervous wreck," Ben admitted as he settled down on the matching floral couch, then glanced over at the sleeping baby.

As she sat down in another armchair, Sara had to admit it felt good, having them both here in her new home. It didn't seem nearly as lonely tonight.

The room was long and narrow, with a dozen or so paned windows that allowed a sweeping view of the lake down below the tree-shaded hills. In the summer, the windows could be thrown open to the fresh country air, but tonight Sara had them shut tight against the approaching chill of winter.

Ben looked at Tyler, his expression thoughtful and hopeful. "I think that's why I'm determined to help this child—after all of this with Jason, I mean. I let Jason slip away, but maybe this…maybe this is another chance for me, having Tyler to look after."

Sara's heart went into another telltale spin. Oh, she didn't want to feel these things she was beginning to feel. But Ben Hunter looked so sweet, so scared, so lost, sitting there with the firelight reflecting in his blue eyes. Funny, how she'd always assumed ministers just had pat answers for every situation, that they coped above and beyond anything ordinary humans had to endure. But being around Ben Hunter had taught her that even a man of God was still a human being, with feelings and emotions just like anyone else.

Yet, this particular minister did his very best to shield the rest of the world from his own innermost thoughts and torments. Which was why she was worried about him now.

She could tell by the way he talked about the baby, that he was already forming a strong bond with little Tyler. What would happen when the authorities made a decision regarding the baby? What if Ben became too attached to the little boy?

"Ben, you realize you might not have Tyler for very long, don't you?"

"Oh, sure," he said, but it sounded hollow in the silent room. "Don't give me that doubtful look. I know I won't be able to keep him. But at least while he's here, I can give him all the love and nurturing that I've got."

"And you've sure got a lot, from what I can tell."

He looked up at her then, his cookie in midair, his expression warm, his eyes questioning. "How do you know that? We've only known each other a couple of days now."

Sara shifted in her chair, wishing she'd learn not to blurt out whatever popped into her head. "Well, you seem to have a good rapport with your congregation, Mr. Erickson aside. And I feel as if I knew you already, before I even met you, thanks to Maggie's accurate description.''

Yes, Maggie had told her Ben was handsome and sensitive, a good minister. Maybe that was why Sara seemed so attracted to him—she'd come into this with already-high expectations. She shrugged, uncomfortable with the whole conversation. ''Emma thinks you hung the moon, and Betty is always singing your praises.''

There. That explained it. Everyone thought Ben was perfect, so naturally, Sara would just *assume* that he was. She'd been brainwashed, obviously. Surely there was a flaw hiding behind that captivating grin and those incredible blue eyes.

His gaze didn't waver. ''They have both been a tremendous help to me, that's for sure.''

Because he was staring at her with that bemused, confused expression plastered across his face, because the room was growing exceptionally warm, Sara hopped up. ''Want some more coffee or more cookies?''

''No, I want to know why you think I'm such a lovable guy?''

Flustered, she sank back down on the overstuffed chair. ''Well, because…you're a preacher. Isn't lovable a prerequisite?''

''I suppose, but I've known some cold, unlovable ministers in my time.''

Seizing on that, she threw out a hand. ''There, you

see! You obviously aren't one of those. You know how to connect with people, draw people out. I'm surprised you're still single.''

Her soft, mortified moan only made Ben laugh. ''You like me, don't you?''

Sara hung her head, hoping her mop of curls would hide the red in her face. ''Of course, I *like* you. You've been a good friend, and you've made me feel very welcome here. And since we've agreed to share the responsibility of taking care of Tyler—''

''That would naturally make us have to stay in close contact, right?''

''Right—so that's why I'm just…glad that you're—''

''Such a lovable guy?''

''Yes, exactly.'' She slapped her palm on her lap, her gaze centered on the fire. ''It would be hard to maintain a relationship—I mean, a friendship—with someone who was distant and uncaring.''

The bemused expression shifted into something more confident and self-assured. ''So, we've agreed that we'll share in Tyler's well-being, and we've agreed that we have some sort of relationship—I mean, friendship—developing here.''

She squirmed, straightened a stack of magazines on the table, then crossed one booted leg over the other one. ''Yes, I think we can safely agree on those two things.''

Ben took a bite of his cookie. "Well, I'm glad we got that settled."

Sara looked up at him at last, and seeing the amusement in his eyes, ventured a nervous smile herself. "I feel like a complete idiot."

"Why? Because you had to admit you like me? I'm flattered, of course, but I promise I won't fall at your feet with undying gratitude and embarrass you any further."

"Thanks for that, at least." She got up to stir the fire, which was blazing right along with no intent of going out—just like the one burning in her belly. "Ben, I was engaged—"

He sat up, another cookie uneaten in his hand. "Are you about to tell me you're not ready for anything long-term and heavy?" In spite of the lighthearted nature of his words, Sara sensed the seriousness in his eyes.

"Yes, that's exactly what I'm about to tell you. Steven and I were a couple for years, but...for some reason, we never did really make a strong commitment to each other. We tried, but there was *my* work, and *his* work, and then when my mother got ill—"

"He didn't know how to handle it?"

When his tone became just as serious as his gaze, she turned to face him. "No, he didn't appreciate my long hours at the hospital, and my refusal to put my mother in a home."

"What happened?"

"He took a job in Atlanta, Georgia, and he gave me an ultimatum. Either come with him, or the wedding was off."

"So I guess I know the answer."

"Yep. Same old story, different chapter."

"You did what you had to do."

"That's a rather tired cliché, don't you think?"

"But an accurate one."

"I couldn't leave my mother."

At the anguish in her voice, Ben dropped the forgotten cookie back on the plate and came to stand by her in front of the fire. "No, you couldn't do that, and you don't have to explain that to anybody."

He wasn't exactly sure when his hand had moved up to her shoulder, but suddenly he was holding her, hugging her the way he'd hugged hundreds of suffering church members in a time of crisis. "I'm sorry, about your engagement, about your mother. But I'm not sorry you got rid of ol' Steven."

"Oh, really?" Because he held her face crushed against his sweatshirt, it came out muffled.

"Really. Because now you have a chance to get to know a lovable, *nurturing* preacher who needs a lot of help with a little baby boy."

"And his ego, too, apparently," she said as she raised her head, her expression dubious.

Ben looked down at her and felt his heart swelling with a certain need, a need that he hadn't felt or wanted to feel for a very long time. When had this solicitous hug turned into something more intimate, something more...rewarding?

"My ego *is* fragile," he said as his gaze touched on her shining, clouded eyes. Too fragile to tell her his own dark fears and secret regrets.

"Then you know none of this can last, right?"

"You mean, Tyler's being here, you and I being here, together like this?"

"Yes."

The one word held all the defeat he felt in his soul. Yes, he knew this couldn't last, and he didn't really want it to last, did he? This was too close to being perfect; too close to being exactly as he'd envisioned his life so long ago. But he'd envisioned this dream with another woman, and she was gone now. He couldn't bring himself to tell Sara about Nancy just yet. Because he wasn't accustomed to baring his soul to anyone other than God, the pain of losing his own fiancée three years ago was his to bear alone.

"Yes," he echoed, his gaze searching her face, "I know this is all very temporary. I'm not holding my breath, waiting for any sort of commitments, just dealing with what the good Lord has thrown my way."

"You sound so resigned."

He backed away then, sweeping a hand through his hair. "Yes, I guess I am resigned. I've learned the hard way that sometimes the very things you think you want and need, the things you think you can't live without...well, sometimes those very things can be taken from you in a heartbeat."

He glanced over at Sara. The expectant look on her face scared him, forcing him to put a different spin on his own self-pity. "I've seen it so many times—losing someone you love is never easy and there are no easy answers. We tend to lash out at God, because we expect Him to give us answers. But, in the end, we have to wait and pray and hope we find our own peace of mind."

"That's so true. It was like that when I lost my mother and Steven, too. I felt so alone."

Relieved that she seemed satisfied with his pitiful ramblings and gentle platitudes, Ben turned back to her then, his words full of compassion and the trace of bitterness he couldn't hide. "Maybe we should just enjoy our time together and let it go at that."

"Maybe," she replied, the one word full of questions.

Ben didn't miss the disappointment in that one word. He felt that same disappointment in his heart.

But disappointment was so much easier to deal with than real pain.

Ben entered the Book-Stop, a combination bookstore and café located directly on the green in beautiful downtown Fairweather. Intent on finding a book on infant care, he smiled and waved at Frank Wren, the owner, and Maggie's anxious husband.

"How's Maggie?" Ben asked as he made his way to the long wooden counter where Frank was taking inventory of some paperbacks.

"Any day now, Reverend," Frank said in his fast-clipped Minnesota accent. "My wife is ready to have this baby."

"We're all praying for you," Ben told the nervous father-to-be.

But who could blame Frank for being nervous? After trying for five years to have a child, Maggie and Frank had just about given up, and then there had been complications throughout the pregnancy. This child was truly a blessing.

Frank nodded, then replied, "And I'll do the same for you. How's your little one?"

Touched that Frank had referred to Tyler as his own, Ben grinned. "He's amazing. I've only had him a week, but I think he's grown a few inches already. And that's why I'm here, Frank. I need a book on babies."

Frank chuckled, then pointed to a row toward the back of the store. "Got lots of those, but, Rev, they don't make an accurate instruction manual for children. That's what Maggie is always telling me, anyway."

"She would know," Ben said, shaking his head. "She's certainly helped take care of most of the children in Fairweather. And now, her own. She'll be a good mother."

"That I know." Frank pointed back to the shelf. "C'mon, let's see what we can find."

Ben followed Frank's stocky, fast-walking figure to the back of the store. It was late afternoon and he had to get back in time to pick up Tyler from the church nursery. And see Sara, of course.

Like it or not, he was growing closer to Sara Conroy each and every day. Maybe because she was helping him take care of Tyler, and because they worked in the same building, they just naturally ran into each other. Maybe because he liked her, a lot. Maybe because she was pretty and charming and a straight-talker with no secrets to guard.

Well, maybe a few.

Sara was a complete mystery, a mystery that Ben found himself wanting to explore more and more. So he also found himself coming up with little excuses to visit the nursery.

Well, he had to check on Tyler, didn't he? The little baby had become a big part of his life. And he looked forward to taking Tyler home each night, to cuddling with him in the big leather chair by the fire, to telling him stories of the Bible and God's amazing work. A baby, Ben had found out, was easy to talk to, to share secrets with, to open up your heart to. And so was Sara Conroy.

What would he do when they were both gone from his life?

"How 'bout this one?"

Ben looked up to find Frank staring at him, a fat book in his hand.

"That one looks good," Ben said, not even bothering to read the title. Didn't he know Maggie was right? There were no concrete answers to raising a child.

"Of course, you have the best book of all already," Frank told him as they headed back up to the front of the shop.

Still distracted by thoughts of Sara, Ben said, "I do?"

"You do. The Bible, Reverend. All you need to teach a child is right there." Frank pointed to his own worn Bible, lying on a big desk behind the counter.

Ben patted his friend on the arm. "You're right, Frank. And thanks for reminding me."

Frank rang up Ben's purchase. "Want a cup of coffee, some biscotti?"

"No, I have to go pick up Tyler."

Frank grinned. "Well, tell her I said hello."

Confused, Ben lifted a brow. "Excuse me?"

"Sara." Frank winked. "Tell her I said hello. Maggie's wanting to have the two of you over to dinner, but Doc Talbot told her to stay off her feet."

Groaning silently, Ben could only smile. "That's nice of Maggie, but Sara and I...we aren't—"

"A couple?" Frank looked downright disappointed. "That's not what I've been hearing."

"Emma?"

Frank didn't have to acknowledge his sources. Ben knew how much his well-meaning secretary had riding on this match. And it didn't help that Betty Anderson backed her up all the way, and that they both watched a tad too intensely every time Sara and Ben were in a room together.

Not to mention Rachel and Morgan, Julianne and Luke, Warren Sinclair and lately, even Reverend Olsen—the whole town was way too involved in Ben's social life.

Thank goodness the annual Fairweather Harvest Celebration was coming up in a few weeks—planning for that should keep them occupied. They all needed a distraction, to take the heat off *his* back.

Just as Ben started to leave, the phone rang, giving him that much-needed distraction so he wouldn't have to answer any more of Frank's pointed questions. While Frank spoke into the receiver, Ben glanced through the book he'd just purchased, then waved goodbye.

"Rev?" Frank dropped the receiver to come spinning around the counter on one foot. "It's Maggie. It's…the baby." His eyes widened, his next words coming out in a breathless amazement. "The baby is coming."

Ben went into action, since Frank looked helpless. "Come on. I'll drive you. Where to? Is she at the hospital?"

"No, she's at home. We'd better hurry."

"Okay. I'll call Sara from the car and tell her to meet me at the hospital with Tyler. We'll get Maggie to the hospital."

Frank looked doubtful. "I'm scared, Rev."

"Hey," Ben told him as he ushered the excited man out the door, "remember the advice you gave me."

"The Bible," Frank said, a calming sigh moving over his flushed features.

"That's right." Ben gave instructions to another clerk to close up the store, then hurried Frank to his car. "God will take care of everything, my friend."

"That's good," Frank admitted as he slid into the seat. "Since I seemed to have lost my ability to function properly."

"Don't worry. You're going to be a good father." Ben beamed at his friend, then cranked the car and zoomed toward Frank and Maggie's house. "A father. What a wonderful feeling that must be."

And then it occurred to Ben, he could be a good father, too. To little Tyler. Maybe he could go ahead and adopt the child. That way, he'd never have to suffer the pain of losing him.

Chapter Five

Emma and Sara met them at the hospital.

Emma immediately took charge of the one gurgling baby and all the anxious, joyful adults, sending Maggie and Frank off with the nurses, then turning to Sara and Ben. "You both need to be here for Maggie and Frank, so I'm taking little Tyler home with me. Sam and I will take good care of him."

Touched, but determined to keep Tyler near, Ben shook his head. "Emma, I can't let you do that. You've worked hard all day already."

"Excuse me," Emma replied, a hand on her hip. "I happen to love babies, and Sam has been asking to see Tyler. Besides, you can't keep him here."

"She's right," Sara told him as she smiled down at the wide-eyed baby. "He'd be better off safe and warm at Emma's house, than sitting here in his car seat in this drafty waiting room."

Ben ran a hand through his hair and let out a sigh. He'd never realized just what a tremendous responsibility taking care of an infant could be. "Okay. Emma, I appreciate it. I'll pick him up later."

"Take your time," Emma said, beaming as she began wrapping the baby back in his jacket and blankets.

"There's formula for two bottles in his bag," Sara told her. "But I had just finishing feeding him right before Ben called."

Emma lifted the car seat in her arms, then smiled reassuredly at Ben. "He'll be fine, I promise."

"Spoiled, is more like it," Ben said. With a lopsided smile, he watched as Emma hefted the baby back out the same doors they'd all just entered minutes before.

With Tyler in good hands, he turned back to standing vigil over Maggie. The nurses had rushed her away the minute Frank escorted her into the emergency room, but the couple had been out of breath and deliriously happy that their baby was finally going to arrive. Now came the waiting part.

Ben was glad to be here, to share in their joy, to offer up prayers of hope and acceptance, whatever the outcome. But he knew in his heart the outcome would be good. Maggie and Frank deserved this bit of happiness.

He looked over at Sara and wondered if he'd ever have the opportunity to rush his wife to the emergency room to give birth to a child. Would he ever even have a wife? Maybe that wasn't in God's plan for his life, but right now he did have little Tyler. And an opportunity to possibly adopt the baby. What would Sara think about this idea?

"Can I get you anything?" Sara asked now, bringing his attention back to the clinical buzz of the tiny, efficient county hospital that served several of the small towns around Fairweather.

"No, I'm fine. Just jittery, I guess. I'm used to christening babies, but this is the first time I've been so involved with a pregnancy and birth."

"I wondered—the way you were staring at me— you looked so serious, I thought maybe you needed to talk or something."

Ben shifted on his feet, looked out at the chilly wintry dusk. He wasn't quite ready to share his latest revelation about possibly adopting Tyler. He had to be sure he was making the right decision. And it was such a big decision. It would change his life forever. So instead of sharing his doubts and dreams with Sara, he focused on the event at hand. "No, I was just thinking how lucky Maggie and Frank are."

"Very." Sara came to stand by him, her gaze following his as he continued to watch the coming nightfall. "Are you thinking about Jason, out there all alone?"

He shrugged, then turned away from the window. "No, actually, I wasn't. Mostly I was being selfish." Then he looked over at her and indicated his head toward the double doors leading to the emergency room. "I want what they have."

Sara was so caught off guard, she had to grip the windowsill to keep from showing her surprise. How was it possible that at the very moment she'd been standing here, watching Ben and thinking how wonderful it would be to have a family of her own, he'd been looking at her and thinking the same thing?

She had to do something, say something, but he just kept standing there, watching her with those poetic, almost sad, all-knowing eyes, making it nearly impossible for her to catch her breath, let alone speak.

"I suppose we all want a family," she finally said, then wished she'd just gone for coffee instead. Wanting to fill the silence, she went on in spite of her better judgment. "I thought Steven and I would have children, of course. But we just kept putting things off— getting married, finding a home together. We couldn't even settle on a date for the wedding, and now look at me—I'm almost thirty and still as single as ever."

He did look at her, his intense inspection making her feel all warm inside, in spite of the coolness of the nearby glass.

"You still have time."

She shook her head. "Not at the rate I'm going."

He kept on looking, his smile appreciative. "You'd make a good mother."

Oh, he did have this way of just making a simple statement sound so enticing. Maybe it was that deep, throaty voice, or the masculine little catch in his words.

"Sure," she said, her skepticism obvious. "You're just saying that to be nice."

"Right, I do tell everybody that," he countered. "In fact, I just told Maggie that in the car when she was wailing and doing her breathing exercises. And I also told Frank that he'd make a good father, and come to think of it, he was wailing, too."

"Is there something about Fairweather?" she asked, relaxing a little from his teasing.

"That makes people wail, you mean?"

She shook her head again and smiled. "No, that makes people want to settle down and produce offspring."

He tipped his head, grinning over at her. "Yeah, there's definitely something about Fairweather. This town seems to bring people together. I think it has something to do with all those adorable children we take care of in the center."

There was just a hint of promise in his words, or maybe a hint of challenge. Wanting to know more about him, she said, "How long have you been here—three years, is it?"

"Yes. But sometimes it seems as if this has always been my home, or maybe the home I was always searching for."

"Tell me about your mother," she said, turning to

lean back on the windowsill. "Maggie talks about her a lot."

"My mother." He smiled, then looked down at his heavy leather ankle boots. "She comes to visit every now and then—just drops in like Mary Poppins, without warning—and she did take a liking to Maggie. She'd love to see me find just such a woman to settle down with."

So, they were back to that subject. Sara lifted off the windowsill to find the nearest chair, since she was feeling incredibly weak at the knees. Deciding to pick a safer subject to talk about while they waited, she asked him, "Ben, how…how did you find God?"

Ben's face lit up. Swinging over the chair across from her, he sat down and crossed his long legs at the ankles. "I think that was the other way around. I think God found me. My father died when I was small and my mother, Alice, was a college professor back in Madison. She tried to bring me up right, but I'm afraid I gave her a real run for her money."

Intrigued, Sara asked, "What did you do to torment your poor mother?"

He glanced out the window, rolled his neck to relieve the apparent tension centered there, then lowered his voice as he focused his attention back on Sara. "My senior year of high school, I got into some trouble. I guess I was rebelling against my lot in life—you know, no father figure and a mother who was constantly absorbed in her students and the world of academia. I fell in with the wrong crowd and got arrested for vandalism.''

Sara sat up. "No! You—I can't picture you harming anyone's property."

"Well, I did. Drove around crashing mailboxes, breaking windows, stuff like that."

"Ben!"

"I know. It was terrible. Luckily though, after a night in jail, I grew up pretty fast. Out of respect for my mother, no one pressed charges."

"So, you learned your lesson and...turned to God?"

He grinned, then threw his head back against the armchair. "No, not just yet. My mother turned me in to a higher authority than herself—our minister."

"Uh-oh."

"Uh-oh is right. I was terrified of Reverend Winslow. Especially when he explained in no uncertain terms that I would be a changed teen by the end of the summer."

"Penance?"

"In a way. He put me to work in a summer camp for underprivileged inner-city kids, kids who'd never had any of the advantages I'd had. It was a real eye-opener."

"And then you found God?"

He laughed, his eyes twinkling. "Do you want to hear the whole story, or not?"

Sara ran an impatient hand through her hair. "Yes. Tell me all of it."

"As I said, God found me. Up until that time, I'd only pretended to be a Christian, mostly to keep my mother off my back. I went to church, attended youth meetings, but it was an empty, unmeaningful existence. Then that summer, I saw what it was to be a true Christian. When I got back home, I enrolled in college, but continued to do volunteer work around the church, and I worked after classes for Reverend Winslow—odd jobs and helping out with the youth. That man saved me, in more ways than one."

Sara watched his face, saw the joy in his expression. At that moment, he looked so at peace, so completely confident in his faith. She envied that. "That's a beautiful story, Ben. When did you decide to become a minister?"

"My second year in college. Went on to divinity school, then became an assistant pastor at a small church near Madison."

"I see." Sara folded her arms in her lap, and growing bolder, decided to tease him a bit. "And how about your love life? Want to tell me about that, or were you too busy to date?"

The peaceful look was shattered. His whole expression changed, and the old bittersweet sadness returned to his eyes.

"I dated in college," he told her, his tone low and cryptic. "But that's enough about me. Your turn."

Shocked at his abrupt change, she didn't know what to say. "You already know my story—and Ben, I'm sorry if I seemed to be prying."

"It's okay." But he didn't elaborate. "Go on, talk."

"I told you, you already know all about my sad state of affairs."

"Yes, I understand about that. I'm asking you, when did *you* find God?"

Sara lowered her head, then glanced back up into his eyes. He definitely wanted to change the subject, take the spotlight off himself. Not knowing what else to do or say, she obliged him. "I think maybe I haven't found Him exactly. I don't know, I was raised to believe, to have faith, but lately—"

"Then, *He'll* just have to find *you* again, same way He found me."

Sara doubted she'd have the same experience as Ben. "Does it really happen that way, you think?"

"I know," he replied, confident once again. "If you let Him in, Sara, you'll know it in your heart. You'll realize He's been right there, all along."

She sat there, watching his face, wondering again about all the many facets of Reverend Ben Hunter. There had to be more to his story, but she wouldn't push him any further tonight. Ben seemed content to let others talk, while he did all the listening. Sara had to wonder if it was a natural trait, or one borne of some long-ago pain that had caused him to shut himself away from people. Maybe because his father had died when he was so young, or maybe for some other reason. And maybe he'd tell her one day.

For now, she was content to just sit there with him. Being near him gave her a sense of peace, of security, that she was unaccustomed to. It was a good feeling, but Sara reminded herself she couldn't get used to this.

Ben was a minister. He deserved someone who shared his same strong sense of faith. He deserved someone who had found God, not someone who couldn't even get her life in order, certainly not someone who'd just been dumped by another man because she couldn't make a firm commitment.

For the first time in a long time, Sara hoped Ben was right. She sincerely hoped God would find her again. She needed Him in her life now more than ever, to guide her through this maze of disturbing, exciting feelings she'd been bombarded with since first seeing Ben Hunter.

So she sat there, silent, smiling, and secretly asked God to show her the way, or at least to give her the strength to walk away—when the time came.

"I think it's time we had a prayer," Ben said to the group of relatives and friends of the Wrens gathered in the waiting room outside the maternity ward. Two sets of anxious grandparents-to-be got up from their chairs to stand with Ben and the others who'd come to lend their support.

Betty Anderson stood with Warren Sinclair, her

soon-to-be husband, while Julianne and Luke O'Hara waited beside Rachel Talbot. Morgan, being a doctor, had gone back to check on the progress of the birth.

He came bursting through the doors then, a big smile on his face as he pulled his wife into his arms. "It's a girl. Elizabeth Anne. And she's just about perfect."

"And how are the proud parents?" someone asked.

"They are...beaming with joy," Morgan said. "Maggie came through like a trooper. And Frank, well, at least he didn't faint."

"Oh, what a relief," Betty said as she hugged Warren close. "Praise God."

Julianne smiled over at her husband. "How wonderful."

"Definitely time for a prayer," Ben reiterated.

Sara had been standing apart from the tight-knit group, not sure how to handle this. Should she join them, or just stay here and lift up her own thanks that her friend's baby was healthy?

Ben seemed to sense her hesitation. Holding out a hand, he called to her. "Sara?"

She looked into his eyes and felt as if she'd come home.

"Pray with us."

It was a statement, unflinching and unquestioning, as if he had no doubt whatsoever she'd want to be a part of this.

Sara moved into the little circle of friends and

watched as they all joined hands. Humbled, she took Ben's hand in her own, acutely aware of the strength and warmth in his gentle touch. Julianne took her other hand, squeezing it briefly in an age-old symbol of understanding and camaraderie.

Then Ben's deep, emotion-packed voice filled the small waiting area.

"Lord, we thank You for the miracle of this birth, and we welcome little Elizabeth Anne Wren into the world. And we promise, as Your servants, Lord, to watch over this child, to cherish her, to teach her by example about Your great love and Your saving grace. We ask that You continue to protect her and that You continue to bless her family. We ask all of these things in Your name, Lord. Amen."

Sara looked up, her eyes misty, and found Ben's gaze centered on her face. His eyes appeared misty, too. But his smile was so rich, so promising, that she knew something wonderful was happening here tonight. Her heart picked up its tempo, her soul opened and filled with an amazing sense of happiness and fulfillment. It had been such a very long time since she'd held anyone's hand and prayed.

"Thank you." They all turned to find Frank Wren standing there in hospital scrubs, tears streaming down his rugged face. "Thanks to all of you. You all mean the world to us and we are truly blessed to have so many good friends here tonight to share in our joy."

After that, Sara stood back watching as everyone

began hugging everyone else. Before she knew it, she was being hugged herself. They each pulled her close, murmuring endearments, spouting happiness. Then she looked up to find none other than Ben Hunter waiting his turn.

He pulled her close, crushing her against the scratchy wool of his navy blue sweater. She wanted to stay there forever.

Letting her go, he looked down at her. "Thanks for being here. I know it will mean a lot to Maggie."

"She's been a good friend," Sara replied on a voice thick with emotion. "I'm so happy for her."

"Tyler will have a playmate," Ben said, assurance in the statement.

"For a while at least," she replied, worried again that they'd both become too attached to the infant.

Ben glanced back down at her. "I'm beginning to think there's something to this fatherhood thing."

"Frank sure looks pleased as punch."

"It's a good night—even if we have been here for hours."

Thinking that would be a good excuse to leave before she did something crazy like cry, Sara nodded. "It is late. I guess I should get home."

"Want me to drive you?"

"That's sweet, but I have my car right outside."

Since he was still holding her, a hand on each shoulder, she didn't force herself to move. Instead, she stayed in his arms a minute longer, then said, "We'll come back and visit Maggie tomorrow, when she's rested.''

''Yeah, and see that new daughter.''

Sara patted him awkwardly on the back. ''You'd better go get Tyler.''

She watched as he nodded. ''Children are a big responsibility, aren't they?''

''They certainly are.''

He let her go then, but turned just as she was about to say her goodbyes to the rest of the group.

''What?'' she asked, bemused by the sparkle in his eyes.

''Oh, nothing. In spite of the responsibility...I still want what they have.''

With that, he glanced over at Frank, smiled and waved good-night to Sara.

''Me, too,'' Sara whispered later as she headed out to her car, parked near the entranceway. ''Me, too.''

Had God truly found her again, and brought her here to find the home and hearth she so craved? Or would she be disappointed yet again?

Or had she, in search of that elusive dream, not only found God again, but something else just as precious, too?

As she cranked her car and pulled it around, she glanced back at the wide doors leading into the hospital. Ben was there, watching her safely home.

She sighed and smiled. For so long now, it had

seemed she'd been lost in the darkness, unsure which way to turn.

Maybe tonight, at long last, she'd found her way, and a light to guide her there.

Chapter Six

"We need volunteers to help with the Harvest Celebration," Julianne O'Hara told Sara a week later, her brown eyes sparkling. "And I think you'd be perfect."

Sara gave her friend and fellow day-care teacher a wry smile. "I'm sure you think that. Just like you think Ben and I have a—what did you call it—a thing going on."

"Well, you do." Julianne tossed her long blond hair over her shoulder and took a sip of her hot herbal tea.

They were enjoying a quiet lunch hour while all the children took their much-needed afternoon naps. Since Sara had temporarily replaced Maggie, Julianne had taken her under her nurturing wing and they'd become fast friends. Sara enjoyed their daily luncheon chats and had grown fond of her new friend, if not a tad envious of Julianne's glowing happiness at having found love, and an adorable set of four-year-old twins, with Maggie's brother, Luke.

"Oh, you're still in the newlywed stage," Sara retorted. "You see everything with overly romantic eyes."

Julianne leaned forward on the small table centered in the kitchen down the hall from the classrooms. "I can see perfectly fine, thank you."

"Yes, with rose-colored glasses."

"I don't wear glasses, but I'd have to be blind not to notice the way Ben watches you whenever you walk into a room. During church Sunday, I think he wasn't preaching to anyone but you."

It had seemed that way, Sara thought now, since he seemed to glance in her direction more times than she cared to remember. The message, however, *had* echoed her own feelings the night Maggie had given birth to little Elizabeth Anne.

"He's just trying to win me over to a higher source," she replied, memories of Ben's moving service making her smile. "He is a powerful speaker, though."

"Yes, all that talk about walking in the light, being children of the light—Ephesians. It was a good sermon, but Ben seemed a bit distracted." Her grin indicated she thought Sara was the culprit.

Sara, however, didn't want to take any credit, even though her friend's observations hit very close to right on the mark. "I think you're wrong. He's probably just preoccupied because of Tyler and because Jason is still out there somewhere.''

Julianne settled back in her chair, nibbling a handful of grapes, her expression turning serious. ''You might be right. Ben takes everything to heart. He loves his congregation and he has been so worried about Jason. They were close, you know.''

Sara nodded. ''He told me. It's really a shame the Ericksons have been so stubborn about this, blaming Ben, when clearly he was only trying to help.''

''I hope that sermon got through to them,'' Julianne said. ''They sit there on the front row, acting as if they own the church, and they expect all of us to jump just because they've got so much money.'' Shrugging, she added, ''I don't mean to sound so judgmental, but they won't budge from their high-handed attitude. They need to reexamine this whole situation with Jason. Ben is not to blame here. But he insists that we all need to pray, not only for Jason, but for his parents, too.''

Sara got up to rinse her soup bowl in the sink. ''Regardless, Ben appreciates your support, I'm sure.''

Julianne finished her tea, then got up, too. ''Well, I mean it. Ben is a good person. And that's why I'm so glad you've come into his life.''

''Oh, we're back to that.''

''Mmm-hmm. Sara, he was lonely. And…well, I have to tell you a funny story. After I broke up with old what's-his-name—before I met Luke, of course—Emma tried to fix me up with Ben.''

Interested in spite of herself, Sara felt a stab of jealousy. "She did?" Then she grinned. "Obviously, that match-up didn't work out."

Julianne's laughter bubbled over so loudly, she had to catch herself so she wouldn't wake the children. "It was a disaster. Don't get me wrong, Ben and I hit it off right away, but it was a brother-sister type thing. No sparks, no fast-beating hearts, just…an immediate friendship."

Julianne's description was very accurate. Sparks? Fast-beating heart? Julianne might not have fallen for Ben, but Sara had all the symptoms, all right. Glad that Ben was so brotherly to Julianne and realizing what *she* felt toward him was definitely not sisterly, Sara tried to sound sincere. "How sweet."

"You sure looked relieved."

"I'm just surprised. Ben doesn't talk about his past relationships much."

"No, I don't suppose he would," Julianne countered. "He helped me get over my fear of dating again, but he never really opened up about Nancy. Of course, Emma told me the whole story. I think she's secretly repeated it to everyone in town."

"Nancy? Who's Nancy? What story?"

"Oops." Julianne glanced around. "I shouldn't be gossiping about our minister, but you have a right to know, to understand what he went through."

Concerned but curious, Sara held up a hand. "Maybe you'd better not tell me—"

"No, let me, before Emma corners you and embellishes the whole thing. Ben met Nancy Gately in college. They were engaged and had planned to marry after Ben settled into his first church. But…three years ago, right before he came here, Nancy was killed in a car wreck on the way to work. She taught first grade, and some impatient driver pulled out right in front of her, just a few blocks away from the school."

Gasping, Sara found the nearest chair. This certainly explained Ben's reluctance to talk about his past, and it also explained the sadness that sometimes shrouded him. "Oh, how horrible. How horrible for Ben, and the children she taught. She must have been a very special person."

"Ben loved her so much." Julianne grabbed a tissue from her pocket and dabbed at her eyes. "I always cry when I think about what that man's been through. And after he's stood by all of us—Morgan and Rachel, Luke and me, Maggie and Frank—and soon, he'll be marrying Betty and Warren. He's always performing weddings or baptizing babies around here. That has to be so hard on him, since it's so obvious by the way he's taken to little Tyler that he'd love to have a family of his own, too."

Remembering Ben's words to her at the hospital— *I want what they have*—Sara had to clear away the lump in her throat. "And he's so gentle, so kind. He's like a rock."

"Except when it comes to his own loneliness," Julianne told her. "I think that's why Emma is constantly trying to find him the perfect partner."

Sara got back up then, her head quickly clearing. Now, more than ever, she was convinced she didn't have a future with Ben Hunter. The man was obviously still grieving over the tragedy of losing the woman he loved.

Giving her well-meaning friend a determined look, she said, "Well, none of you should pin your hopes on me. Besides the fact that I'm not cut out to be a preacher's wife, I don't know how long I'll be here and I don't know where I'm going next."

Julianne regained some of her teasing spunk then, a thoughtful expression brightening her pretty face. "Well, one day at a time, sister. I've lived here all my life and I didn't know where I was headed until I met Luke. Now I have a wonderful husband and an adorable little boy and girl to love. Ben hit it right on target with that sermon. We have to come out of the darkness sometimes."

Sara felt as if everyone in this town knew she'd had an epiphany at the hospital last week. But instead of annoying her, this only brought her a sense of comfort. "Coming here has helped me a lot, but sometimes I still feel as if I'm walking around in this heavy fog searching for…I don't know what."

Julianne drooped a slender arm across her shoulder as they walked out of the kitchen together. "Well, high time you found your way out of that fog. And you can start by helping out with the Harvest Celebration. Oh, Sara, you'll have so much fun. We have a big fair right in the center of town—with food and crafts and artwork, music and singing. It's a great time to share our blessings and get in the mood for the holidays.''

Thinking she'd need the distraction herself, Sara bobbed her head. "Okay, sign me up. I'll be glad to help out."

"Great." Julianne smiled as she scooted toward the hallway. "I'll tell Emma to put you in charge of one of the craft booths."

That should be safe enough, Sara decided as she headed back to relieve the aide watching over her sleeping babies. Surely she wouldn't have to be around Ben too much if she was busy selling pillows and quilts.

Holding a quilt that smelled faintly of baby lotion mixed with Sara's flowery perfume, Ben stood over Tyler, watching in amazement as the infant slept soundlessly in his little crib in the day-care center's nursery. Without consciously thinking about it, Ben took the whimsically patterned quilt and tucked it around the baby's chubby midsection.

"He's such a good baby," Sara said, her whisper filling the still room with a lyrical echo.

Ben turned to find her watching him. How long had she been standing there, and how was it that when she entered a room, even a room deliberately darkened for rest time, she automatically brightened everything around her? Noting the ornate silver clips that held her flaming hair off her face, and the brown wool jumper that flowed to midcalf around her slender form, he once again realized that he'd taken a keen liking to Sara Conroy.

"He has a good caregiver," he replied, waiting as she drew close. "And a pretty one, too."

"Yes, he tells me that everyday."

She didn't look at him. Instead, she kept her eyes on the baby. But Ben thought he saw a faint blush on her creamy cheeks.

"Oh, and what else does he tell you? Hope he hasn't divulged all my secrets."

He didn't miss the trace of concern, and maybe a little hesitancy, crossing her face. But the expression quickly changed to another wry smile. "I'm afraid you have no secrets, Rev. Word is out on you."

"I imagine you're right," Ben said, hoping against hope that Emma hadn't been innocently telling Sara the story of his life. Testing her, he asked, "And just what do you think you have on me, anyway?"

Sara squinted, as if debating whether to tell him or not. Then she watched as Tyler made a gurgling sound and sighed contentedly. "Oh, only that you love Emma's tea cakes, but you have to play basketball to burn up the extra calories and that you're a hardworking, considerate man who cares about your church."

Feeling anything but, Ben shrugged. "Other than my penchant for cookies, you've obviously gotten the wrong impression about me."

"Oh, no. I think I have the right impression."

Hoping to deflect some of her high praise, Ben twisted his face into a grimace. "But…that sounds so…so boring. I'm sure Tyler told you all about our dashing escapades—how we slay dragons and chase the bad guys when we're alone at home, how we help Noah build that ark all over again and follow Moses through the desert. That's why he's sleeping so hard right now. He's tuckered out from all that noble manly action."

Her laughter sounded like the wind chimes someone had hung in the picnic area out on Baylor Lake— delicate, dainty, highly feminine. Ben had to inhale to find air in the suddenly too-warm room.

"You wouldn't be telling tall tales, now, would you, Preacher?"

"Not me."

They stood silent for a moment, each looking down at the baby.

"He's so adorable," Sara said in a whisper. "How could anyone abandon something so precious?"

Ben watched the sleeping baby, then whispered an opinion. "Desperation. That's the only answer I can come up with." He reached out a hand to touch Tyler's own tiny hand. "I've been thinking…if no one comes forward to claim Tyler...I'm thinking about maybe adopting him.''

Sara lifted her head, her gaze falling across Ben's face. Seeing that he was serious, she thought about what Julianne had just told her and her heart went out to him all over again. He was lonely—that much she could see. And having Tyler in his life would certainly fill that empty void Nancy's death had caused. But what if things didn't turn out the way he hoped? He'd be devastated all over again.

When she didn't answer immediately, Ben turned away from the sleeping baby, his gaze centered completely on Sara now. ''You don't look so sure about what I just told you.''

Glad that she was learning to think before she spoke, Sara wondered if she should tell him her doubts. ''I—I just don't want you to get your hopes up. We still don't know what will happen with Tyler.''

''No, but so far I'm it. I'm his only hope. And look how he's thriving. Being here, surrounded by love. He'll automatically have an extended family—a large, nurturing family. It's the best place for him.''

''You might be right,'' she said, wishing that she could be a part of Tyler's life, too. ''He's doing great and I can't think of a better place for him to be raised.''

''Well, you did encourage me to take on this little task.''

''Yes, I certainly did do that.''

"But?"

She hated to be blunt, but it wasn't in her nature to dance around reality. "But being a single parent might work against you, Ben. The authorities frown on that, you know."

He nodded, then scissored a hand down his face. "I've thought about all the things working against me. Short of marrying in haste, I can only hope I'd get endorsements from the congregation."

"I have no doubt about that," Sara told him. "Most of them are behind you one-hundred percent."

"But you're still not so keen on this? Why would you push me to keep him, if you don't think I have a chance of adopting him?"

Touching a hand on his arm, Sara said, "Personally, I'm very keen on you raising Tyler. I wouldn't have insisted that you take him if I didn't feel very strongly about it in my heart. I just think it would be a big responsibility, a major undertaking, to keep him for a lifetime. You work long hours and you're called out at all hours of the day and night. A lot of people depend on you already. There are so many things to consider."

"You're right." Looking defeated, he turned to leave. "Speaking of which, I have to get to the hospital right now, to check on some of my elderly church members."

Sensing his disappointment, Sara followed him.

"Ben, don't give up on this. I'm sure we can weigh all the pros and cons and find a solution."

"There's only one solution as far as I'm concerned," he told her. "I want to keep Tyler with me."

After Ben left the nursery, Sara went back to stand over Tyler's crib. As much as she wanted things to work in Ben's favor, she also worried that he might be in for a fight, and that maybe, just maybe, he wanted Tyler for all the wrong reasons. Yet, she *had* been the main one to talk him into keeping the baby. If she'd known then what she knew now, she might not have insisted so much. If things fell through and he lost Tyler, he'd probably resent her for forcing him to bond with the baby, and he'd have to suffer yet another emotional loss.

Maybe she needed to examine her own motives a little better. She could have taken Tyler, yet she'd encouraged Ben to do it. Maybe because she was afraid *she'd* be the one left out in the cold? Maybe because Ben was the better choice, the strong minister with real friends who'd help him in any situation.

She'd never had that, never been a part of something so rich and so strong. Until the other night in the hospital, when she'd felt as if she truly had found a home. But that might have been a one-time deal, brought forth by an outpouring of emotion and the birth of a child. It might not happen that way again.

Yet, as she stood there, Sara couldn't help but have a little daydream of her own. For just a minute, she

imagined herself in the picture with Ben and Tyler—
the three of them together as a family. But just as
quickly as she conjured up that beautiful image, she
pushed it away, reminding herself she didn't have
what it took to be a minister's wife, and Ben might
not be ready for any kind of permanent commitment.
Yet...he'd said he wanted what Maggie and Frank and
the rest of their friends had.

Ben wanted a family.

And so did she.

What a shame they couldn't pull it off together.

Reaching out to touch Tyler's pink cheek, she whispered, ''You and the good reverend might enjoy slay-
ing dragons and building arks, but I think I could get
used to plain old boring myself.''

She thought she saw Tyler smile in his sleep.

Chapter Seven

❧

"What are you smiling about?" Sara asked Maggie a couple of weeks later as they entered the social hall of the old church.

Maggie set down the large chicken casserole she'd brought to serve at the Harvest Celebration committee meeting, her blue eyes bright with amusement.

"Oh, nothing. It's just good to see you looking so rested and relaxed. You look two shades better than when you arrived on my doorstep all those weeks ago."

Sara inclined her head and shot her friend her own smile. "Well, no wonder. Everyone around here has pampered me beyond end. Food, cards, telephone calls—I don't have time to feel sorry for myself."

"That old Minnesota spirit," Maggie replied as she dug through a drawer for a spatula. "Or that old thing called love, maybe?"

Sara busied herself with preparing for the meeting, her head down, her gaze fixed on the counter. "Yes, this town is full of loving, caring people. A far cry from the big city."

Giving her friend a sideways glance, Maggie said, "I was referring to one particular citizen of Fairweather."

Sara stopped smiling and groaned. "Not you, too. Does everyone in this town think I'm head over heels about Ben Hunter?"

"Did I mention Ben?"

Sara blushed, then hurriedly marched to the refrigerator to pull out the liquid refreshments. "No, you didn't, but we both know that's who you were talking about. And besides, Emma has that same smile plastered on her face every time I see her, too. And she's only too happy to ask me how things are going between Ben and me, that is when she's not trying to constantly throw us together."

"Well, how *are* things going?" Maggie ignored her obvious irritation as she concentrated on heating up her casserole.

Sara found the napkins and plastic forks, then pulled out the bread and cookies she'd brought to contribute to the casual meal. "Fine. Just fine. I'm helping take care of Tyler, of course. He's the best little fellow. I see Ben at work and we talk and I see him at church and we talk and—"

"Surely there's more?" Maggie's eyes widened as

she put her hands on her hips. "What about after hours?"

"I go straight home after hours."

"Running away to the lake, huh?"

"Now, what's that supposed to mean?"

"Well, I thought you were helping Ben with Tyler, maybe even after hours. Ben needs a woman's guidance with that little boy. That child is growing so fast, and little Elizabeth Anne is right behind him. They're probably in the nursery right now, comparing formulas. And Tyler's probably whining to his new best friend that his teacher won't even come and visit after dark, simply because she's trying so hard to avoid his foster father."

That brought a smile to Sara's face, in spite of her aggravation with her friend. "I do help Ben with the baby. I take care of Tyler every day, as you well know." Shrugging, she added, "And I'm not trying to avoid anyone. Ben and I have a working agreement that we're just friends. It's best that way, keeps things in the proper perspective. We're both too caught up in our own lives to get involved with each other."

"That's not what I want to hear," Maggie admitted. "I thought surely since you'd cooked dinner for Ben that one time and you'd been so *supportive*—"

"We're friends, Maggie. That's all. And that's the way we both want it, regardless of how the rest of Fairweather feels."

Maggie gave her a mock-nasty glare. "You don't have to be so defensive."

Slamming a cookie sheet loaded with bread into the oven, along with Maggie's casserole, Sara said, "Yes, I do. Everyone keeps pushing us together and I don't think either of us is ready for that yet."

"I'm sorry," Maggie said, coming to place a hand on her arm. "I shouldn't have teased you and I didn't mean to pry."

"It's okay." Sara let out a pent-up breath, then leaned on the long serving counter. "I care about Ben—a lot. But he's still grieving over Nancy and I think he's grasping for this perfect picture of a family. I don't want him to think I can be a part of that picture."

"But why couldn't you?"

Sara scoffed, then tossed her hair back. "Look at me. I came here burned-out and tired, completely disillusioned with life. I'm not the meek-and-mild preacher's wife type. And besides, who said I wanted to be that anyway?"

"You just did," Maggie replied sagely.

"No, I didn't."

"Yes, you did. Every time you deny something so adamantly, it only means you've been thinking about that very thing."

"Oh, you sound just like you used to in college, when you were sure I had a crush on a certain boy."

"And I was usually right."

Sara had to give her that. "Well, this time you're wrong. After Christmas, I'll be going back to St. Paul, anyway. I'm only staying on now because I want you to enjoy some time with your new baby."

"And I appreciate that," Maggie told her. "But a lot can happen between now and Christmas."

"Not if I don't let it."

"Stubborn."

"Pushy."

Maggie nudged her good-naturedly. "Still friends?"

Sara saw the sincere expression on Maggie's serene face. Reaching out, she hugged the other woman close. "Friends forever, in spite of your overbearing interference in my private life." Patting Maggie on the back, she grudgingly added, "And...thanks for caring."

"Always." Maggie smiled a bit too smugly. Then, as the other committee members started arriving, she busied herself with laying out the food.

Emma pranced in, resplendent in teal wool, followed by Betty Anderson with her daughter, Rachel Talbot, and Julianne O'Hara. In a few minutes, the other church members who'd volunteered to help had arrived and the meeting was about to get started.

"We're expecting one more person," Emma stated as she gathered her folders and charts, a practiced smile encasing her pink lips.

Just then Ben walked into the room and nodded a

greeting to all the people gathered around the long table, his gaze locking on Sara as he stood over the group.

Bidding her heart to slow down, Sara glanced up at him, hoping she didn't look as lovesick as she felt. Since everyone in the room was watching her, she gave a shaky little wave of the hand, tore her eyes away from the man who'd somehow managed to ingratiate himself into her whole being, then quickly looked down at the table in front of her.

"Hi, there, Reverend Ben," Emma said, beaming up at him. "We were just about to get started. I'll pass out your assignment sheets, then we'll eat Maggie's good-smelling casserole while we go over the details."

"Great," Ben said as he found a chair near Sara. "I'm starving."

Emma handed him a stack of papers. "Take one and pass them along." Then she gave a dainty shrug and sent Ben and Sara one of her best Strawberry Queen smiles. "Oh, and by the way, I've assigned you two to the craft booth. Hope you don't mind a four-hour shift together."

"Have you been avoiding me?" Ben asked Sara later as he bundled little Tyler, who'd just been handed over by a nursery worker, into his stroller and secured him with a thick blanket.

Because of Emma's fast-paced meeting agenda,

they'd had little time for any personal conversation, but the meeting was over now and everyone was ready to go home.

Sara glanced around to make sure the others weren't listening. Emma and Betty were deep in conversation with Rachel, and Julianne was holding little Elizabeth Anne and helping Maggie clean up. Most of the other members had left.

"I don't think so," she began, careful not to look at him for fear he'd see she wasn't being exactly honest. "We see each other every day."

Ben shot her a dubious look. "True. But you seem to be in such a hurry all the time. What happened to all those interesting conversations we had when you first came here?"

"Haven't we been communicating?"

"Depends on your definition of 'communicating.'"

Nervous and cornered, Sara tried not to squirm. Helping him to put on Tyler's bright red winter hat, she said, "Did you need to ask me something specific?"

Ben finished dressing the baby, then stood. "Yes. Why are you avoiding me?"

Pushing at her wayward curls, she gave him what she hoped was an honest look. "I've just been so busy—with work and…things. I've been going by to check on Maggie and give her some relief. Newborns can wear you out and new mothers need their rest."

"Yeah, I know all about newborns," Ben countered, his expression quizzical as he nodded toward wide-eyed Tyler.

"Do you think I've been neglecting you and Tyler?"

"Yes. Horribly. But I intend to make up for that. How about dinner soon? My place. I don't think I've ever told you, but I can cook a mean pot of Texas-style chili."

"Chili?" Sara laughed then, and immediately relaxed back into the old familiar banter. "Have you ever been anywhere near Texas?"

"No, but I have lots of reliable cookbooks. My mother gives me one just about every birthday—thinks a bachelor needs to learn to cook for himself."

"I have to meet your mother. She sounds like such a sensible woman."

"I'd like for you to meet my mother."

The banter was gone, replaced with something as warm and alluring as a mug of rich hot chocolate. The way he'd said that, his tone low and gravelly, promising and wistful all at the same time, told Sara that she'd just stumbled back into dangerous territory.

Hoping to get out safely again, she bobbed her head, then started collecting her stuff. "That would be nice."

"She usually comes for the Harvest Celebration. And she always comes for Christmas, since that's my busy season and it's hard for me to get away to go visit her."

"Then I look forward to seeing her."

"What about dinner?"

"Sure, I'd love to have dinner with your mother sometime."

"No, I mean, yes, that would be great. But what about my chili?"

Her immediate reaction was to make an excuse, but her heart wouldn't allow her to do that. So she caved in. "Is this chili safe for human consumption?"

"Barely, but that's beside the point."

She grinned then. "Oh, and just what is the point, Rev?"

"I miss you."

Sara had to swallow and catch her breath. Eating chili was now the farthest thing from her mind, but she did feel as if she'd gotten hold of some fire. Maybe it was the way he stood there, looking at her with those beautiful, poetic blue eyes, or maybe it was the way his voice carried to her ears only, so intimate, so cozy, so appealing.

"I haven't gone anywhere," she finally managed to say.

"Then it's a date?"

"When?"

"How about this Saturday? We can start early, maybe enjoy a walk in the last of the fall leaves before we head in to eat some spicy chili?"

That would mean two Saturdays in a row with Ben,

since Emma had given them the Saturday late shift at the celebration, too.

Searching for excuses to decline, she asked, "What about Tyler?" At least the baby would be a source of distraction.

"He can't eat chili just yet."

"No, I mean will he come along on this excursion through the leaves? It is awfully chilly some afternoons now. I could stay in with him, if you feel the need to kick up some leaves."

He shook his head. "Why would I want to go for a walk by myself? I'm sure he'll want a front-row seat, with me doing all the stroller pushing."

She giggled in spite of herself, then came up with another stalling technique. "And what do you plan on doing with him during the Harvest Celebration the next Saturday? Will he be okay while we work? If not, I can stay with him and arrange for you to have another booth partner."

"Sadie has the nursery shift that day."

Sara liked Sadie Fletcher, an older African-American church member who'd raised six children and was now working on spoiling about twice as many grandchildren—most of whom also stayed at the center. Sadie worked part-time in the day-care center and helped out with the church nursery on Sunday mornings, too. She was famous for her hugs and grandmotherly wisdom. And the children adored her. No way to change that arrangement.

Deflated, she said, "Oh, then he'll be just fine."

"And so will you," Ben told her, his expression quizzical. "You're out of excuses, Sara, so don't look so glum."

"I'm not glum. I'm just relieved to hear Sadie will be taking care of him. She loves Tyler."

"Everyone loves little Tyler," Ben replied, smiling down at the alert infant.

Glad to shift the subject matter away from her, Sara quickly agreed. "He's growing so fast."

"He is pretty amazing. But I worry that he gets passed around so much with all these sitters and day-care. You were right about that, but like most working parents, I don't have much choice." He ran a hand down Tyler's pink cheek. "To make up for leaving him so much, I just enjoy sitting at night and holding him."

Good. She'd diverted his attention away from their chili-cooking, leaf-tossing possible day together. Fortified, she kept talking about the baby instead.

"I'm sure he loves being held. And I think that's an important part of being a working parent. You have to spend quiet time with your children, let them know you love them."

As they headed out the door, Ben turned to lock things up. Everyone else had somehow managed to scoot, leaving them alone. A cold blast of air greeted them on the way to the parking lot. "Well, I'm just so blessed that we have one of the best day-care centers in the area right here at The Old First Church. Doubly blessed, since I get to visit with him and you at the same time.''

Sara chose to ignore that sweet remark. She couldn't afford to encourage this relationship, even though she reminded herself, she'd just agreed to having another cozy meal with Ben and Tyler. Thinking maybe she should come up with a more plausible excuse so she could refuse, she opened her mouth to speak.

But as she watched Ben fussing over the baby, the words died on her lips. She *wanted* to eat chili and walk through golden leaves with these two. She wanted to spend quiet time with them, away from the hustle and bustle of the nursery and Ben's hectic work schedule. She wanted to get to know Ben better, away from prying eyes and teasing remarks. She wanted these things in her heart, even while her head told her she shouldn't ask for them. So she just stood there, freezing.

Ben checked Tyler to make sure he was warm, then lifted the collar of his quilted jacket. ''Winter's coming.''

''That's for sure.''

He walked with Sara to her car, then turned as she bent to open the door, a hand on her arm. ''Sara, are you avoiding me because you don't agree that I should try to adopt Tyler? It does seem as if your attitude changed once I told you I was considering it.''

The doubt in his question, and his misunderstanding

as to why she'd pulled back from him, tore through her. She couldn't lie to this man, she couldn't hide what was in her heart. It wouldn't be fair to either of them.

"Ben...I didn't realize I was avoiding you. Okay, maybe I was being standoffish. I guess I just thought we both needed some time."

"Was I coming on too strong?"

"No, not at all. You've been such a good friend, but...it's important that we both understand that's all we can be. I just thought it best if I gave you and Tyler some breathing room."

He reached out to pull a strand of hair off her chin. "But we like having you around. Tyler talks about you all the time."

Sara lifted her head, the warmth of his finger brushing her cheek like a touch of flame against the bitter cold. "What does Tyler say about me?"

He leaned closer then, his eyes holding hers in the glowing security light from the churchyard. "That you always have a smile for him, that you smell like a spring garden, that your hair is full of sunshine and autumn, that your voice is as soft as a song."

Gulping in a breath, she whispered, "That Tyler sure has a way with words. Have you been reading poetry to him?"

"He's a very smart little fellow. And yes, sometimes late at night when we can't sleep, we read...everything from the Bible to Robert Frost or

The Odyssey. Or I play the guitar and sing off-key to him. He kicks up his heels to 'Just a Closer Walk with Thee,' but I think he really prefers 'Just As I Am.' He gets wide-eyed with excitement, just listening to the possibilities of life.''

Sara had to hide her sigh. A poetic, guitar-playing preacher who sang lullabies to an orphaned baby. Did she really think she stood a chance against these two?

Trying to sound rational and unaffected, she tugged on Tyler's wool booty. ''Well, he certainly looks wide-awake right now.'' She leaned down toward the baby, just to distract herself from the sweet image of these two sitting by a fire, taking a literary adventure to heart. ''But I can't resist giving him a good-night kiss.'' She did just that, laughing as the baby gurgled, before she turned to get in her car.

''Not so fast.'' Ben whirled her back around, his hand cupping her chin. Before she could take another breath, he gave her a quick peck on the mouth. ''I couldn't resist giving *you* a good-night kiss.''

With that, he let her go, stepped back, then grinned. ''I'll see you Saturday—come hungry.''

Sara didn't think that would be a problem. She yearned for a taste of something, but she didn't think food had anything to do with whatever it was.

Touching a hand to her lips, she watched as Ben walked the baby stroller the few blocks to his own house. Then she thought she heard him whistling, but it might have just been the wind.

* * *

Ben heard the phone ringing even as he jingled his keys in the front door. Pushing the stroller inside, he rushed to pick up the receiver, catching it on the fourth ring.

"Hello?"

"Reverend Ben?"

The voice was shaky and far-away sounding, but Ben recognized it immediately. "Jason?"

"It's me. How are things?"

"How are *you*, Jason? Where are you calling from?"

"That doesn't matter. I just…I just needed to hear a familiar voice."

Ben pulled Tyler's stroller along, then sat down in the armchair by the silent fireplace, one hand rocking the stroller to appease the infant as he tried to talk to the teenager. "Jason, why don't you come home? Your parents are so worried about you."

"Yeah, I'm sure."

"They are," Ben said, stressing the words. "I just talked to your father a few weeks ago. Why don't you call him?"

"No."

"Jason, you can't make it out there alone, especially with winter setting in. Let me help you."

"No, I just called to see how things are going with you. How's the team doing?"

Ben shifted, his head lowered. "The team's okay. We could use a good center, though."

"And the practices—are you still having regular practices?"

Hoping to hold him on the line, so he'd open up, Ben thought about all the familiar, everyday things he could tell Jason. "Well, yes. I've had to do some major juggling, though. Jason, you won't believe it, but someone left a baby in the church—about a month ago. A cute little boy. And I'm taking care of him."

Ben heard a sharp intake of breath, then silence. "Jason, are you still there?"

"Yes, sir. A baby? Wow. Do—do you know who the baby belongs to?"

"No. We can't seem to locate the parents, so we got it cleared for me to be his foster parent. I'm thinking about adopting him, though."

"You are?"

Hoping that talking about his own struggles would help the boy share his problems, Ben continued. "Yes. His name is Tyler and he's so beautiful, or handsome, I guess I should say. He has this bright fuzz of reddish-blond hair and big blue-green eyes. And he has the hands of a true basketball player."

Silence, then, "Sounds like you care about him a lot."

"I do. I sure do. He's both a blessing and a challenge."

Silence again.

"Jason?"

"Sir?"

"I could use some help—you know, someone to pinch-hit when I get busy. Why don't you come home and meet Tyler?"

"No. I can't do that."

Surprised at how shaky the boy sounded, Ben hoped he might be reaching Jason at last. "Why not?"

"Just can't."

Ben heard a sniffling sound. Tears misted over in his own eyes while he gripped the phone so hard, he was sure it would crack. "Jason, son, I've been praying for you to stay safe. And I'm praying that you'll find your way home. Do you hear me?"

"Uh-huh." More sniffles.

"Tell me where you are. I'll come and get you."

"No. Just…just take care of that baby, okay?"

There was a loud click, then the suspended silence of the dial tone ringing in Ben's ear.

He put the phone down, feeling more alone there in the darkness then he ever had in his life. Then he heard little Tyler gurgling.

Wanting more than anything to hold the child close, Ben lifted the baby out of his protective blankets and gently cradled the tiny bundle in his arms.

"Lord, please help Jason," he said into the night. "Winter's coming and he's out there, alone and frightened. Help him, Lord, to know that no matter what he's done, no matter the burden, You will bring him comfort and forgiveness. Bring Jason back to us, God.

Bring him back to us safe and sound. I ask this in Your name. Amen.''

Ben sat there for a long time, cooing to Tyler, then praying to God. He was afraid to let the baby go, afraid to put him down in his little crib. So he just sat there, holding on while Tyler took a bedtime bottle, then drifted off into a deep, peaceful sleep.

"Why can't we all sleep so peacefully?" Ben asked, his voice carrying out over the still night.

He looked around at his home. Rat lay curled on the couch, oblivious to any human suffering. And two more cats, aptly named Calico and Chubby, lay sprawled on the braided rug, probably wondering in their dreams why Ben hadn't come home to build them a cozy fire tonight.

Safe. Ben and his menagerie were safe.

He only wished he could feel the same way about Jason.

Exhausted, he finally got up to put Tyler to bed. As he stood over the little boy, he made a promise.

"I won't ever let that happen to you."

He hoped, prayed that God would see fit to help him live up to that promise. Now, more than ever, he realized the tremendous responsibility of raising a child. But he still wanted that responsibility; he still wanted to adopt Tyler.

Ben gave the baby a gentle kiss, then he went back into the sitting room and, clasping his hands together, he started praying all over again.

Chapter Eight

The next morning, after dropping Tyler off in the nursery, Ben hurried back to his office to call Richard Erickson. He dreaded making the call, but he had to do it. Regardless of their feelings toward Ben, the Ericksons needed to know that Jason was safe.

Mary Erickson answered on the second ring. "Hello?"

Ben cleared his throat and sent up a prayer. It was always hard, talking to them about Jason. "Mrs. Erickson, this is Reverend Ben Hunter. Can I come over to visit with you and Mr. Erickson before he leaves for the office?"

"Why? What's this about? Is it Jason?"

Hearing the panic in the woman's voice, Ben quickly reassured her. "Yes. I heard from him again, late last night. I thought you'd want to know."

"Of course."

She was sobbing so hard, Ben hardly heard her response. His heart went out to her. "I'll be over in about five minutes."

The phone clicked in his ear.

"Emma, I'm going to talk to the Ericksons," he said as he rushed past the startled secretary who'd just arrived for work. "I might be a while."

Emma bobbed her head in understanding. "I'll say a prayer for all of you."

"Good. We need it. Especially Jason. I'm very worried about him."

"Did you hear from him again?"

"Yes, late last night. He didn't sound so good, either."

Emma got up then, halting him with an waving hand. "I'm not one to spread gossip, as you know, but I heard something interesting the other day when I went to visit my sister in New Hope. I just forgot to tell you about it. I knew there was something important I needed to tell you."

Trying to be patient, Ben stopped at the door. "Emma, can this wait?"

Not in the least affronted, Emma said, "It's about Jason."

"What?"

"You remember that youth trip way back last year? The one where you took the kids to New Ulm during spring break?"

"Yes, I remember."

"Well, according to my sister, several of the youth from her church there in New Hope also went on the trip."

Ben nodded, wishing Emma could tell a story faster. "Yes, about four area churches brought their youth that weekend."

"Okay, well, one of the girls from Bertha's—that's my sister—have you ever met her—she's my *older* sister…"

"Yes, I think I have," Ben said, his hand moving to indicate she needed to bring things to a wrap.

"Anyway, Bertha said this young girl named Patty Martin—Mitchell, something like that—went on the outing with their youth. She wasn't a member, rarely came to youth meetings, but she went along on the trip. Well, apparently she took a liking to a boy from Fairweather—said his name was Jason."

Ben dissected what Emma was trying to tell him. "Patty met Jason Erickson on this youth trip?"

"I think so," Emma replied, bobbing her tightly bunned head. "But from what Bertha told me, I don't think his parents knew about the relationship."

Wanting to hear more, but concerned that the Ericksons were waiting, Ben waved his hand again. "What are *you* trying to tell *me,* Emma?"

"Well, Bertha and I got to comparing notes—you know about things that have happened recently—just talking, worrying, you understand."

"Yes, I understand," Ben said, his patience walking a thin line. "What did Bertha say?"

"Bertha said that Patty Martin ran away from home at around the same time Jason Erickson did."

Emma stopped for dramatic effect, her words knocking the wind right out of Ben's body.

"Do you think they ran away together?"

"I'm not suggesting that," Emma replied, holding up a hand, "but it does seem a mighty big coincidence, don't you think?"

"Mighty big," Ben had to agree. This certainly added a new wrinkle to the whole sad situation. Yet Jason had never mentioned this girl. "If this is the case, why haven't we heard about Patty before? Jason certainly hasn't mentioned being with anyone."

Emma clucked her tongue. "Patty Martin comes from a very troubled home—very poor. Apparently she's been in and out of trouble a lot. Her parents didn't even bother reporting her missing until months after she'd left. Said she'd done this before, but she always came back home. Just recently, her mother happened to confide in one of the women at the church that Patty had been secretly seeing a very wealthy boy from Fairweather—Jason, of course, and that he was the reason she ran away. Now Bertha says everyone in New Hope is talking about it, so naturally when we started putting two and two together—"

"Naturally," Ben finished, pinching the bridge of his nose with his forefinger and thumb, the beginnings of a headache working its way through his throbbing brain. "Sounds as if you and Bertha need to open a detective business on the side." Shaking his head, he added, "As for this girl's parents, honestly, I don't understand some people. They should have reported this immediately."

"Pray for them," Emma said. "From what I gather, they said good riddance to the girl." Giving a long-suffering sigh, she sat back down to get her workday started.

Ben envied Emma. She was so innocent, so content to do her work and help out here and there, and provide much-needed information in the giddy form of harmless gossip. She had no way of knowing that what she'd just told him would only add to the Ericksons' woes.

As far as Ben could tell, they'd never approved of any of Jason's friends. It wouldn't help matters to tell them that their son might have run away with a girl they didn't even know, a girl from what they would obviously term the wrong side of the tracks.

But how had he missed this? Ben wondered as he drove the short distance to the Ericksons' mansion. Thinking back, he didn't remember Jason hanging out with any one particular person on that spring retreat. But then, there had been well over fifty teenagers milling around on the scheduled tours of the quaint, historical town. It had taken all he and the other chaperones could do just to keep up.

I should have been more aware, he told himself as
he pulled his utility vehicle up the winding drive to
the Ericksons' gabled Victorian house. They'd blame
him for this, too, he was sure.

And they'd be right to lay blame at his feet.

"I don't believe you," Richard Erickson said a few
minutes later, after Ben had told him about his conversation with Emma. "My son would never run away
with a girl he barely knows. That's just not like Jason."

Mary, a petite woman with a soft brown pixie hair-
cut, glanced at her husband, her dark eyes red-rimmed
and watery. Then she turned back to Ben. "Did…did
he ever mention this Patty to you?"

"No, ma'am," Ben told the heartbroken woman.
"He's never mentioned anything about being with another person."

"It's all just a pack of lies," Richard said, jumping
up off the sofa in the formal living room to pace before
the enormous marble fireplace. "Emma needs to learn
not to listen to idle gossip."

"I couldn't agree with you more," Ben pointed out,
"but she's only trying to help. I intend to go to New
Hope and ask the minister there if this could be true.
If you'd like, I'll talk to the girl's parents, too."

Mary looked across at him then. "That would certainly help to ease our minds, Reverend. Thank you."

Ben looked around at the house, wondering how

any child could have a normal life in such a place. It was beautiful, full of priceless antiques and imported luxuries that had somehow survived centuries of Ericksons, yet it seemed to be missing that lived-in look most modern homes had. Everything about the Erickson household was stilted and formal, with no hope for straying away from that theme. And tiny Mary Erickson worked day and night to keep things proper for her demanding husband.

Sensing that Jason's mother needed his guidance, in spite of her husband's hostility, Ben nodded, then took her hand in his. "Mrs. Erickson, I will do whatever it takes to bring Jason home. I promise you that."

She clutched his hand as if it were a lifeline. "You were good to our boy. I don't think I ever thanked you for that."

"You don't need to thank him!" Richard shouted, a shocked expression on his face. "Have you forgotten that this man instigated the changes in our son? Jason was fine until we got a new minister. Reverend Olsen would have never encouraged Jason the way Hunter here has."

Mary let go of Ben's hand then to stare up at her husband. "Reverend Olsen is a good, decent man, but he had lost touch with the young people in our church."

"How can you say that?"

"I'm not disrespecting him," Mary said on a timid

voice, "but you can't deny that since Ben came here, our youth program has grown."

"That's because he lets them get away with foolish things. He encourages them in all the wrong areas."

Richard Erickson glared down at Ben, clearly intent on believing the worst. And right now, Ben had to agree with him. But he couldn't let that get in the way of helping Jason.

Ben stood then, a hand raised in the air to ward off any more attacks. "I'm not here to defend myself. I'm certainly not perfect, and I'll never be able to fill Reverend Olsen's shoes, but I love your son. I love all of the teenagers, the children, in my congregation. Right now, my only concern is to help Jason. Can we all agree on that, at least?"

Mary nodded her head, then reached for a fresh tissue. "Whatever you can do, Reverend, I'd appreciate it."

Richard didn't look so sure. Finally, with a defeated sigh, he sat back down on the sofa, his head caught in his hands. "I miss my son, Reverend. I've used every means available to try and find him, but I'm losing hope."

Ben reached out a hand to touch Richard Erickson's coat sleeve. "I understand, sir. And from what I've seen and read about teenage runaways, they go underground and watch out for each other by turning their backs on adults. Jason is out there somewhere, hiding away for some reason, and so far he's ignoring all our pleas and our efforts to help him. But I'm asking you not to give up hope. As long as Jason keeps calling me, we can know he's safe and I'll encourage him to seek help. Until he's ready to come home, I'll do whatever I can to help track him down.''

Mr. Erickson didn't pull away as he'd expected. Instead, he placed a shaking hand over Ben's, his eyes bright with tears he couldn't shed. ''I'll hold you to that promise, Reverend.''

Ben lowered his head, then gave the other man a direct stare. ''I promise. And I don't want you to give up on me, either. I'm still struggling here, each and every day, and I'll be the first to admit I've made some mistakes. But I've always had the best intentions regarding the children within this church. I want you to know that and...I need your prayers and your support.''

His words and his request seemed to filter through some of Richard Erickson's disapproval. The harsh planes of the older man's features softened ever so slightly. But he remained silent, his eyes still wary and uncertain.

''I'm counting on you,'' Mary offered. ''And I'll pray for you, too.'' Then she got up to come and sit by her husband, giving him a pleading look. ''Richard, could we stop blaming Reverend Hunter and work on seeking help for our son—together, the three of us?''

Richard's nod was slow and hesitant, but Ben could tell the man didn't have anywhere else to turn.

"Let's pray," Ben suggested.

With that, Mary placed her hand over her husband's, then reached out to Ben. "Reverend?"

Ben put his hand over their clasped ones, then turned to the Lord for the answers they all sought...

A few minutes later, he left the Ericksons', feeling as if he'd just somehow survived a very hard-fought test. Now he had to live up to the promises he'd just made.

And he would—somehow.

"I appreciate you going with me," Ben told Sara as they headed out of town toward New Hope.

It was a brilliant, cold but sunny Saturday morning, making the unpleasant trip bearable at least.

"I don't mind a bit," Sara told him, turning in her seat to check on little Tyler. The baby was happily kicking in his snug car seat. "This is just all so very sad."

Ben's face reflected that sadness.

He'd told her all about the entire situation late yesterday afternoon, when he'd come by to pick up Tyler. And before she'd been able to stop herself, Sara had volunteered to ride over to New Hope with him, to find some possible answers to all his questions regarding Jason and Patty.

Now she was glad she'd insisted on coming along. Yesterday he seemed to be carrying the weight of the world on his broad shoulders, and today he wasn't much better. He definitely needed a friend, and since most of his male buddies were now happily married and busy with their new families, that left Sara.

Again, she had to wonder if God had brought her to Fairweather for just such a reason. But that would be too much to ask—finding the perfect man in the perfect little town. And a baby to love, too.

I won't get my hopes up, she told herself as she glanced out at the rolling Minnesota countryside. She'd just concentrate on lending Ben support and encouragement, to help him through this rough spot. Besides, she didn't want to spoil this nice drive by fretting over her place in this world.

"I just about missed fall," she stated now, hoping to keep the conversation light. "Look at those trees. There is nothing like fall in Minnesota."

All around them, the brilliant orange, russet, gold and brown of fall lifted out, the trees so thick with foliage they looked like a patterned quilt.

Ben kept his eyes on the road, but nodded. "Yeah, and I'm just sorry I had to cancel our walk."

"That's okay. Driving's just as nice. It's breathtaking."

He lifted his head. "It's a shame we have to even make this trip. I wish I could make Jason see that he needs to come home."

Sara looked over at Ben's profile, well aware that he wasn't even seeing the glorious tapestry spread out around them. His face showed the strain of worrying about the runaway. "Did you get any sleep last night?"

"Not really." He chanced a glance at her, then brought his attention back to the curving road. "I—I just feel somehow responsible for all of this. I've gone over everything in my mind, but—"

"It's not your fault, Ben," she told him, wishing there was a way she could help him believe that. "I mean, you're only one man, and you've tried to be the best counselor, the best example a man could be to the youth in your church."

"But that's just it—I'm supposed to lead the members of my church, set an example for them. What if I set the wrong example? What if I did put ideas into Jason's head?"

"By offering him guidance and friendship, by teaching him how to be a better basketball player?" Sara shook her head, causing the hood of her parka to shift against the seat. "No, I'm telling you—I believe you did the best you could. Isn't that all any of us can ever do?"

Ben's smile didn't lift the darkness in his eyes. "Thank you," he said, his gaze falling across her face.

Giving him a sideways glance, she said, "For what?"

"For believing in me."

Suddenly aware that she'd been a bit fierce in her defense of him and his obvious abilities, Sara glanced back out the window. But she wasn't embarrassed; she did believe in Ben. As any friend would. "And why shouldn't I?"

He shrugged. "That's the part I don't get. You aren't even a member of my church—yet. But you seem to have more faith in me than a lot of my own church members."

Realizing she was slipping back into the danger zone, Sara shrugged back at him. "You know, I worked in a big city hospital for several years. I saw all kinds of people coming through those doors—all kinds of parents, good and bad, some caring and loving, some uncaring and brutal. It forced me to become a very good judge of character." She was silent for a minute, then she added, "And it made me cynical and jaded, too. I came here with an attitude. I was broken, tired, disillusioned in both spirit and body."

"But now?"

"But now, I—I feel better every day." She swallowed, held her breath, then said what was in her heart. "And—you're part of the reason I can say that now."

He looked surprised, but pleased. "I've helped you?"

"You've helped me. So you see, you aren't so bad."

"Maybe not."

"I know not."

"Does this mean you *really do* like being with me?"

She liked the genuine smile breaking across his face

to erase the worry lines she'd noticed earlier. But she wasn't about to admit anything close to her true feelings. "This means I'm willing to eat your chili."

"It's a start," he told her, his eyes holding hers. "If we get back home in time for me to cook it."

"If not, we'll just grab a burger," she told him.

"Now Tyler might go for that. I think he's just about ready to move up to some solid food soon."

"He does have an appetite."

As if knowing they were discussing him, Tyler made a gurgling giggle, then kicked his booties high in the air.

Sara laughed, turning to grab a kicking little foot. "You are so adorable, and you know it, don't you?"

The baby gave her a toothless grin, then in typical baby fashion, settled back with droopy eyes to take a little nap.

Sara had never felt so content, so settled herself. This could be habit-forming, this hanging out with Ben and Tyler. Her heart lurched strangely at the thought of having to leave them and go back to the city. But soon...

She decided not to dwell on that right now. This day was too beautiful for regrets and worry.

All around them, golden leaves emerged over the narrow road to form a brilliant canopy. The sky was a rich, promising blue.

Too promising. Too hopeful. Sara sat back in her corner of the sturdy vehicle, afraid to cast a glance over at Ben for fear he'd see what was in her heart. This shouldn't feel so right, so good. But it did.

So she enjoyed the silence, the soft music from the radio and Ben's soft gaze on her face each time she glanced up at him.

A few minutes later, however, they pulled into the parsonage near the church where Emma's sister was a member. Ben had arranged to talk to the pastor at home.

"Okay, here we go," he said as he shut off the engine. "Maybe we can find out something about Jason and Patty."

"I'll watch Tyler," Sara told him. "I'll push him around the yard in his stroller while you talk to the pastor."

"Okay, but don't get too chilly."

"We'll be fine," she assured him. "He's all bundled up and the sun's out."

Ben helped her with the baby's stroller, then headed to the wooden-framed white house while she cooed to the now wide-awake baby. Then he turned at the steps.

"Sara?"

"Hmmm?"

"Nothing. I'm just glad you came."

"Me, too," she told him as she urged him on.

Ben knocked on the heavy wooden door, then stepped back to wait. An older man came out on the porch, then smiled and shook Ben's hand.

"I'm Reverend Harry Brooks. Glad to meet you at

last, Ben. I've heard good things about your church in Fairweather.''

''Thanks,'' Ben said. ''I appreciate your agreeing to meet with me.''

''No problem.'' Reverend Brooks glanced out toward Sara and Tyler, his smile as warm as the sunshine. Then he nudged Ben on the arm. ''Well, son, don't make your pretty wife and that cute little one stay out in the cold. Bring them on in by the fire.''

Sara watched as a surprised Ben turned from the polite minister to her. Something in his eyes caught at her soul and held her there, like a freeze frame from a movie.

In that gentle, coaxing voice she knew so well, she heard him say, ''Maybe it is time they both came in out of the cold.''

With that, he motioned for her.

Sara had no choice but to follow him into the house.

She noticed he didn't bother correcting Reverend Brooks. He didn't tell the man that she wasn't his wife and Tyler wasn't his child.

So she did. ''I'm just a friend—Sara Conroy—and this is little Tyler. We're taking care of him…for someone else.''

''What a pity,'' Reverend Brooks said, shaking his salt-and-pepper head. ''You three look like you belong together.''

Sara didn't have to look up to see what Ben was

thinking. She could feel it in the way he was watching her.

And she wondered how such an innocent assumption, coming from a complete stranger, could feel so wonderful and so painful all at the same time.

Chapter Nine

"Okay, so we know that Patty Martin left home at the same time Jason Erickson did."

Ben stood over the stove at Sara's cottage, absently stirring the bubbling chili he's spent the better part of the hour putting together. His mind whirled and bubbled just like the hearty mix he'd fixed for dinner. Now he wasn't so sure he could even eat the chili. Somehow, over the course of the afternoon, he'd managed to lose his appetite.

"Yes." Sara nodded beside him as she finished up the salad she'd created for the meal. "And we now know that what Emma told us was true—Patty and Jason had some sort of relationship going on."

"A secret relationship," Ben replied, picking up a dish towel to wipe his hands. "How am I supposed to tell the Ericksons that their son had been writing letters to this girl, meeting with her on weekends, sending her e-mails? How do I tell them that Jason had fallen in love, but felt forced to keep that love a secret from his own parents?''

''It won't be easy.''

''No, especially when you compare the two families.''

They'd also gone by the address Reverend Brooks had given them to see if they could talk to Patty's parents. The rundown little house was a testament to a gloomy existence, and Patty's parents hadn't given them much hope. They'd been tight-mouthed and condemning about their daughter, and didn't seem in the least concerned about her whereabouts.

''She'll turn up when she gets tired of having too much fun,'' Fred Martin had told them, a cigarette dangling from his cracked lips. ''She thought she'd hit pay dirt this time, though. A rich boy.'' With that, the man had huffed, coughed, then turned to go back into the dilapidated house.

His wife, who worked as a cashier at a nearby convenience store and looked aged beyond her forty or so years, hadn't offered much hope, either. ''We did everything we could for Patty, but she was too hardheaded to listen to us. I was married and had babies by the time I was her age. She'll learn soon enough.''

Ben had gotten the impression that Patty's mother had suffered more than she'd let on herself. He didn't want to call it abuse, but both he and Sara had noticed the bruises lining the woman's skinny arms. He had to wonder if that was one of the reasons Patty had left home.

"I don't think Patty has had much positive reinforcement," Sara said now, shaking her head in wonder. "We never know how lucky we are to have good, solid parents until we're too old to appreciate it, do we?"

Ben shook his head. "I'd like to know the whole story regarding that family, though. I'm glad Reverend Brooks is keeping an eye on Patty's mother, for her own safety."

"Yes, but there's only so much he can do. Mrs. Martin will have to be the one to get away, if she is being abused. That could explain why Patty left, at least."

Ben stood silent for a minute, making a mental note to stay in touch with Reverend Brooks to see what else they could do. It had been a long day and he was exhausted, soul-weary. But at least he was with Sara now. She certainly brightened the gloom surrounding their mission.

He watched as Sara finished up her handiwork then put away the rest of the lettuce and other salad fixings, enjoying the way she hummed when she sliced cucumbers, enjoying the way her long wool skirt swished around those adorable flat-heeled boots she liked to wear.

He was so very glad she'd gone with him today.

She'd been right there, by his side, coaxing Reverend Brooks, asking the questions Ben couldn't seem to voice when they'd come face-to-face with Patty's parents. She'd helped him through this, and now they were back here, at her little house, watching as dark clouds rolled in out over Baylor Lake while Tyler slept peacefully in his portable bed nearby. It had been her idea to come here to fix dinner.

"The lake has a way of soothing your soul," she'd told him on the way back to Fairweather.

So a couple of hours ago, they'd picked up the necessary supplies and headed out here. With a few minutes of daylight left and the earlier sunny day being replaced by what promised to be a winter storm, Sara had urged Ben out the door. "Go take a long walk, and relax. I'll feed Tyler and get him to sleep for you."

She'd been right, of course. The lake waters had glistened like teardrops underneath the looming gray-blue clouds, and Ben had had a long talk with God, asking, hoping, praying for guidance and strength.

Sara was good for him, Ben decided as he watched her going about her work. She made him see things so much more clearly. He was beginning to depend on her.

Now she turned to give him her complete attention, and his heart did that little dance that it always did whenever he went into the day-care center to visit with Tyler. His Sara dance—a little flutter of beating pulse that only she could bring out. He had to hold his heart in check, just to hear what she was saying to him.

"Ben, you have to be honest with the Ericksons. You owe them that. They won't like hearing what we found out, but at least they'll know Jason isn't out there alone."

"I know," he replied, wishing they had a better topic of conversation, "but it's only going to hurt them worse. They didn't have a clue—none of us did—that Jason and Patty were serious about each other. Certainly not serious enough to run away together."

"When it comes to teenagers, who does have a clue?" she asked, throwing her hands up. "You remember being one, don't you?"

He gave her a sheepish grin then. "Oh, yeah. I gave my mother lots of sleepless nights. And I'm amazed I didn't do something stupid like run away myself."

Sara bobbed her head in agreement. "Me, too. My mother and I used to really go at it. Now, I only wish she were here to fuss at me, tell me my hair is too wild, my clothes are too radical." She stopped, sucked in a breath, wrapped her arms across her waist. "Seeing these two very mixed-up families has made me realize just how much I miss her and how blessed I was to have her."

Ben saw her expression change, the tears misting over in her eyes. "Have you even given yourself permission to grieve?" he asked gently.

Sara looked at him, surprise clear in her eyes, then whirled as if searching for something to do. "No, I guess I haven't really thought about it. This may sound cruel, but I was...relieved when she finally died." She turned to him then, a pleading look in her eyes. "I just wanted her to find some peace, some control, someplace safe and away from that terrible sickness."

Ben had her in his arms in two long strides. "Sara, here I've been whining all day about my problems, about Jason and Patty, and this has obviously upset you, too. I'm sorry."

"Don't be silly," she said, clearly mortified that she'd been about to cry. Sniffing loudly, she tried to laugh. "I'm a big girl. And I'm okay. It just hits me at the oddest moments."

"Well, let it hit you," he coaxed, lifting her chin to look into her incredible eyes. "But remember that your mother is safe now, and warm, and she's not suffering anymore. She's with God. I know that sounds pat and condescending, but you have to know she is at peace."

"I know that. I believe that with all my heart. But I sure do miss her."

"Do *you* need to go for a walk out by the lake?"

She smiled then, taking what little control he had left completely away. His heart was doing the Sara highstep again.

"No, I'm just fine standing right here."

"Are you sure you're all right?" he asked, wanting to make her feel better.

"I'm fine," she told him again. "I've had lots of long walks out by the water, believe me. It does help matters, doesn't it?"

He nodded. "Makes you feel closer to God."

"I guess that's it," she agreed, not bothering to move out of his embrace. "I've never felt so close to God. Being here in Fairweather, with so many good people to lend support, has truly helped me to put my faith back in the proper perspective."

"And what about me?" he asked, his voice betraying him.

"What about you?" She looked up, her eyes wide with wonderment and…maybe just a little doubt.

"Have I helped you to put things into perspective?"

She lifted a hand to his face, her touch warm, her eyes as deep and rich as a forest. "No," she said bluntly. "You've put my whole system into this…this out-of-control tailspin. I don't know about you, Rev."

"I know about you, though," he said, more than pleased that she seemed to be having some of the same symptoms as him. Then before she could bolt out of his arms, he leaned down to kiss her. His hand still held her chin; her hand still rested on his jawline. The chili still bubbled away on the stove, and outside, the winter wind picked up to rattle branches against the many windows.

Sara's sigh filled the tiny kitchen, making Ben smile

into her lips, her warm, welcoming lips. He lifted his head then. "Was that a protest or a promise?"

She looked up at him, her face flushed, her hair mushed, and gave him a crooked little smile. "Depends. Will your chili have the same effect as your kisses?"

"Oh, you mean that slight burning sensation all the way to the tips of your toes?"

"Did I say that?"

"You didn't feel that kiss all the way to your toes?" He feigned confusion. "It's always worked before."

She pulled away then, playfully slapping him on the shoulder. "Either way, I think I'm in for some major heartburn."

Ben let her go to catch his own breath. Well, *he'd* certainly felt that kiss. No amount of chili, spicy or otherwise, could ever compare to the slow burn he felt right now, just looking at her.

Heartburn. Was that what she thought he'd cause her?

She might be right. And he was sure his own heart would suffer in the process.

But he'd sure like to take that risk.

Sara was standing at the windows, apparently trying to distance herself from him as much as she could. She turned then, her eyes lighting up. "Ben, it's snowing."

He came to stand by her. "So it is." Then he looked over at her, saw the delight in her eyes, saw that something else he couldn't put a name to just yet. "First snow. First kiss—if we don't count that little peck I gave you in the church parking lot."

"Who's counting?" she asked, a soft flush of color brightening her cheeks.

"That was just a rehearsal for this," he told her, kissing her again for emphasis. Then he lifted his head so he could gaze down into her eyes. "We could have lots of firsts, you know."

"Like our first chilifest," she said, whirling by him, trying to escape, no doubt.

"Come here," he said as he pulled her back around. "The chili isn't quite ready yet."

"Oh, really? Smells ready to me."

"In another kiss or two, it should be just about right." With that, he tugged her close again. "Let's practice on that heartburn some more."

"So you're telling us that his kisses are right up there with four-alarm chili?" Julianne grinned, then glanced over at Maggie, a twinkle in her eyes. "Who knew old Reverend Ben could set such a fire in a girl's heart?"

Maggie chimed right in, whispering so they wouldn't disturb the babies. "Well, Julianne, you had your chance. But you got stuck with my charming brother Luke instead. Disappointed?"

"Never," Julianne replied, sticking out her tongue.

Then she glanced up. "Where's Rachel, anyway? Don't people at city hall get a lunch break?"

"I thought we were talking about Luke," Sara told them as she poured another round of hot tea.

They'd all agreed to meet at the center for a quick lunch, since time was precious for all of them and they had some last-minute details to go over for both the Harvest Celebration and Betty and Warren's upcoming wedding.

"We were talking about *Ben,*" Maggie reminded her, her grin as wide as Julianne's. "Does this mean you might consider staying on after Christmas?"

Before Sara could assure her friend that she had no intentions of remaining in Fairweather, Rachel Talbot came bouncing into the room, clearly out of breath. "Did I miss anything?"

"Just that Ben and Sara shared a kiss—during the first snowstorm the other night," Julianne proudly told her.

"No?" Rachel fell into a chair and grabbed a fresh apple muffin. "Did you two bring on all that fresh snow and then melt it right away again?"

Sara groaned, then sank into her own chair to glare at the other overly interested women sitting around the table. "We didn't bring on anything—"

"Except kisses spicier than four-alarm chili," Maggie reminded her.

"That's not what I said. How'd you two wrangle

this out of me, anyway? We were talking about the arts-and-crafts booth, remember?''

''Yes, and I said that you and Ben would be forced to endure four long hours of agony together,'' Julianne happily reminded her. ''And then you said, 'Yeah, and after that kiss the other night—'''

Sara groaned again. Why had she blurted that out? Maybe because kissing Ben had been on her mind since the snowstorm, and maybe because she was worried about being in a tiny booth with him for four hours. ''Right.'' Turning to the confused but highly interested Rachel, she said, ''And then they made me tell everything. They threatened to wake all the babies if I didn't spill the whole story.''

''Horrid women! And I missed it.'' Rachel placed her elbows on the table, her gaze cast on Sara. ''So you'll just have to tell it all over again.''

''No.'' Sara got to up to go check on Tyler. He'd been a bit fussy all morning. She was pretty sure he might have an ear infection. After checking his diaper, she picked up the baby and brought him over to the corner where all the women were seated.

Rachel automatically pulled up a rocking chair for Sara. ''Ben Hunter is a fine man. Aren't I always saying that?''

Maggie cooed at Tyler. ''Yes. And we all agree.''

Sara looked up from Tyler's cherubic face to find three women smiling smugly at her. With a long sigh, she whispered to the baby, "I think I'm outnumbered here."

"Definitely." Maggie bobbed her head. "If you let him get away—"

Just then, the man of the hour walked into the semi-darkened room.

Sara took one look at Ben, then shot a warning glare at her friends. Of course, he looked so handsome standing there in his flannel shirt and jeans. The only time she'd seen him look better was on Sunday mornings when he wore his suit and tie, then donned his robe to deliver the sermon.

He immediately headed to the corner, his gaze moving over each of the amused women. "Ladies, did I interrupt something important?"

"Don't answer that," Sara warned under her breath, all the while rocking Tyler with a serenity she didn't feel.

"You sure did," Julianne retorted, obviously enjoying herself. "Sara was just telling us how much she enjoyed…your…er…chili the other night."

Ben laughed, then cautiously glanced at Sara. "I'm glad she survived my cooking."

"Oh, she survived all right," Maggie told him, her smile completely composed. "Remind me to get that recipe."

Now that they had him flustered, Ben looked even more adorable. Rubbing a hand over his ever-tousled curls, he backed toward the door. "Something tells me

I don't want to know what's really going on here.''
Sending Sara a baffled look, he said, ''I just came in
to check on Tyler. Is he still fussy?''

''He's a little cranky,'' Sara told him in her best
professional voice, ignoring the giggles and sighs all
around. ''I'm just getting him back to sleep.'' Her concern for the baby overriding her friends' teasing looks,
she added, ''You might want to schedule a doctor's
appointment. I think he has an ear infection.''

Ben shot across the room then, to touch Tyler's rosy
cheek. ''No fever, at least. I'll call and make the appointment for this afternoon.''

Sara nodded, lifting her gaze to Ben. ''And I'll try
to keep him comfortable until then. Don't worry.''

''I'm not. I know you'll take good care of him.''

The room grew silent as they eyed each other. Sara
couldn't help but remember how sweet Ben's kisses
were. And from the way he was gazing down on her,
she felt as if he was remembering, too.

Sara looked up to find her friends enthralled with
the whole exchange. Sending them another warning
glance, she spoke at last. ''I'm going to put him back
down in a bit, see if he can rest.''

''Then I'll leave you to it.'' Ben glanced around,
and seeing the interested expressions on the faces of
the women sitting at the table, blushed, then backed
even farther out of the room. ''Ladies.''

''Bye, Ben.''

The chorus of goodbyes reminded Sara of long-ago

spend-the-night parties. Had all of her grown-up friends gone completely daft and reverted back to adolescence?

Rachel poked Maggie. "Yeah, right. Came by to check on Tyler."

"More like, to check out Tyler's efficient, lovely caregiver, I'd say," Julianne whispered, giggling in spite of herself.

"Would you all just drop this," Sara said, half irritated, half elated. "You'll give Ben the wrong idea."

"Or the right one," Maggie said, a warm look passing through her eyes. "I'd be so happy if you two—"

"Well, we aren't," Sara said as she shifted Tyler in her arms. "We're just friends."

"Why?"

The chorus again.

"Because..." She knew there were several very valid reasons why she and Ben couldn't be together, but for some strange reason they all seemed hard to voice right now. "Because I can't stay here, because he's still grieving over Nancy—he can't even bring himself to talk to me about that, even after I poured my heart out to him about losing my mother—and because I'm worried that he's getting too attached to Tyler and that he might get too accustomed to me being around to help him out, then we'll both be gone out of his life and, I don't want to put him through that again."

"Nice speech, but what about you?" Maggie asked gently.

"What about me? I'm fine."

"Are *you* afraid of getting too attached?" Her gaze drifted down to the baby Sara held tightly in her arms.

Sara looked around at the now-silent group of friends. It had been a long time since she'd felt she could trust anyone, but in spite of their good-natured teasing, she knew she could trust this group with her innermost feelings.

Taking a deep breath, she blurted it all out. "I'm afraid it's too late for that, ladies. I'm already way in over my head. And way too attached to the good reverend and his precious little bundle. There, satisfied?"

To her surprise, none of them laughed or made any teasing remarks. Maggie reached across the table to touch Sara's arm. "We're on your side, you know that."

"We sure are," Rachel said, her expression sincere and warm. "We'll pray that God sends you the answer, whatever decision you make."

Julianne sniffed, causing them all to glance up in alarm. "It's just so…sweet," she said, wiping away a tear. "And…I'm very emotional right now." Then she gave them a shaky smile. "I hear that happens to pregnant women a lot."

Realizing what her friend had just said, Maggie gave a little squeal of delight, then quickly covered her mouth with her hand. "Are you going to have a baby?"

Julianne bobbed her head. "Yes. I'm three months pregnant."

Rachel shot out of her chair, giving Julianne a tight hug. "Oh, Julianne, I'm so happy for you. And I guess that means I can share my news now. I'm going to have a baby, too."

Julianne got up to hug Rachel. "How wonderful! Maybe we'll go into labor together."

Rachel nodded, tears cresting in her eyes. "I'm not quite three months, so let's keep it quiet for a while. But I stay hungry, which is why I can't stop eating these apple muffins."

After hugs all around, tears of joy and many thanks for all their blessings, Sara watched her glowing friends, then held Tyler even tighter. "Two more babies for the nursery. I'm so excited for both of you."

Maggie followed suit. "Me, too. More playmates for Elizabeth Anne."

Sara smiled in spite of the little twinge of regret that nettled its way into her heart. "That's wonderful news, especially for you, Julianne. You thought it couldn't happen."

"Not to me, anyway," Julianne said between a fresh batch of tears. "But it did. So you see, Sara. Nothing is impossible."

"That's right," Maggie reminded her. "We might

not get the answers we want, but God will show us the way.''

"He certainly has with Morgan and me," Rachel reminded them, her expression full of serenity.

"'Cast all of your cares on Me,'" Sara said, remembering one of her mother's favorite Bible quotes from 1 Peter. "Thank you, all of you, for caring.''

"We do," Maggie told her. "And so does God.''

After baby talk, wedding talk and final plans for the weekend festival, the women finished their meeting, then all got back to their jobs, leaving Sara still rocking little Tyler.

And that's how Ben found her a few minutes later. She didn't see him at first, because she had her head bent close to the baby. Listening and watching, he realized she was humming and singing to Tyler, a beautiful lullaby about ponies at the fair.

Ben stood there, taking in the beauty of woman and child, his heart doing its little dance, his soul opening up with a breathtaking clarity. Was there a more beautiful sight in all of God's world?

Sara's burnished curls clung to her cheekbones and her neck, and Tyler's pink little face looked contented, rested, as if the baby knew he was exactly where he should be. So trusting, so precious. Such a perfect picture.

Ben thought of Nancy. Why couldn't he remember her face? Why couldn't he remember her laugh? He'd thought he'd never be able to get her image out of his mind. It troubled him that now Sara's image was slowly replacing that of the woman he had loved and planned to marry. But…maybe that was God's way of telling him he had to let go and move on.

And here was his chance. Here, sitting in this very room, was a woman and a child, and a chance for happiness.

Did he dare tell Sara that he was beginning to fall in love with her? Did he dare hope that Tyler could truly become his child?

As if sensing the intrusion, Sara looked up then, a little rush of breath leaving her, a surprised expression shining in her eyes. "Ben?"

"Is it safe now?" he said, amazed that he could even find coherent words.

"Very safe." She lifted out of the chair to place the now-sleeping Tyler back in his bed. Her movements were so maternal, so natural. She had a way with children. She also had a way with preachers.

"How's he feeling?" Ben asked on a whisper.

"He seems less restless now. Were you able to get an appointment?"

"Yes. That's why I'm here. Around three."

"I'll have him ready for you."

Then she turned to face Ben. "Is everything all right?"

"Everything is…just fine," he told her.

And yet, that statement wasn't completely honest. Everything wasn't just fine.

Watching her here with Tyler, seeing her in the role of nurturer and surrogate mother, Ben felt as if he'd let go of something he'd been holding on to for a very long time. That something was his heart.

And it both thrilled and terrified him.

Chapter Ten

"You've lost weight. You're way too thin."

Ben's mother stood in the middle of the town square, ignoring the festivities around her while her sharp eyes stayed centered on her son.

Ben looked heavenward, took a deep breath, then grinned down at the petite but tough woman who'd given birth to him.

"Nice to see you, too, Mother."

Alice Hunter waved a hand in dismissal, then reached out to hug him, her light wool cape fluttering around her elbows. "How have you been?"

"I'm doing okay," he told her as he leaned over the booth railing to return his mother's hug, all the while aware of Sara's amused curiosity.

His mother wore a bright green wool fedora over her short, clipped gray hair, making her look more like an Alpine hiker than a college professor.

Ben and Sara were in their assigned booth and the Harvest Celebration was in full swing. Thankfully the weather was holding out and the late fall day had been nice in spite of the cold temperatures. Bundled in lightweight jackets and coats, citizens moved along the town square and mingled in the open shops along the way. Swenson's Bakery was doing a brisk business and Ben already had two sandwiches from Olaf's Deli for Sara and him to munch on later.

In typical fashion, his mother hadn't announced when she'd be arriving. She'd just shown up and walked around greeting people she knew until she found her son.

"Been busy?" Alice asked now, her gaze moving from the attractive offerings inside the craft booth to the woman helping her son hawk them. Before Ben could answer, she extended a tiny, veined hand to Sara. "Hello. I'm Alice Hunter, Ben's mother. My son seems to have lost his tongue."

Ben strangled back a protest, then said, "I fully intended to introduce you two—this is Sara Conroy. She's working in the day-care center until Maggie comes back from maternity leave."

Alice continued to hold Sara's hand. "Well, so this is Sara. Very nice. So glad to meet you, and so glad Maggie finally had that baby." Then she turned to her son. "Now tell me about you—a foster father? When do I get to meet my foster grandchild?"

Ben gave Sara an amused look, then said, "Tyler

is in the church nursery with Sadie. You know Sadie. You met her last time you came for a visit.''

"Oh, yes.'' Alice nodded, then fidgeted with a lovely wedding ring quilt hanging nearby. "Sadie has the best remedy for a cold. It's some kind of spicy tea she got from her Cajun cousin way down in Louisiana. It'll cure what ails you. Do you have any of that available today?''

Sara looked around the booth. "I'm afraid I don't see any Cajun tea, Mrs. Hunter. But we've sold out of a lot of our most sought-after items. I can ask Sadie if she has any stashed away.''

"I'll ask her myself,'' Alice told her, her tone firm and no-nonsense. "When I go to meet little Tyler.''

"He's been sick with an ear infection,'' Ben warned. "Don't juggle him too much.''

"I believe I know how to handle a baby, dear,'' his mother said, a wry smile on her face. "But I promise I'll be gentle.''

Dropping her head, she gave Sara a direct look over the rim of her bifocals. "Ben's mentioned you in his letters and phone calls. He told me you were pretty, and I tend to agree.''

Sara shot Ben a surprised look, so he shrugged and said, "Well, it's the truth.''

Alice watched them with all the harshness that being a college professor dictated, as if she were analyzing them both for some sort of dissertation. Then with a slight smile and a wave of the hand, she turned.

"Going to get settled in at the parsonage. Key in the same place?"

"Yes," Ben replied, shrugging silently to Sara. "How long are you planning on staying?"

Alice kept walking away. "Depends," she called over her shoulder. "I'll see you later, son." Then to Sara, "Good to meet you, Miss Conroy."

"You, too, Mrs. Hunter," Sara called, waving to the woman's back. Then she turned to Ben with a long-winded sigh. "Wow, your mother is formidable, to say the least."

Ben ran a hand through his hair, then groaned. "That was her intimidating professor attitude—all five feet, four inches of it. She was scoping you out, sizing you up."

"I could tell. Do you think I'll get a passing grade?"

Ben gave her a mock-professor type look. "Depends," he said in a low, scholarly voice.

Then they both burst out laughing.

"Want some hot chocolate?" he asked Sara, wiping tears of laughter from his eyes while he still chuckled.

"Yes. I need some fortitude after that encounter."

Grinning, he turned and produced a thermos and the deli bag from Olaf's. "Our dinner."

Sara clapped her hands together. "Oh, I'm starved. This booth working sure brings on an appetite."

Ben motioned to the two stools they had set up in

the booth. "Well, let's sit and enjoy this before my mother comes back to dissect our relationship."

Right now, they were between customers, and the handmade quilts surrounding the booth on all sides provided a cozy privacy and a good cover from the crisp late-afternoon wind. Inside the booth, they offered everything from homemade jellies, jams and famous Fairweather maple syrup to decorated wreaths and hand-carved trinkets. Now they were down to a few items.

In the square, the local high school band played a merry polka tune that had everyone tapping their feet, while the food booths continued doing a brisk business by offering everything from fresh-baked apple and pumpkin pies to trout dinners and sausage on a bun.

And all around, the crimson and golden colors of fall, coupled with the remains of the early snow they'd had the other night, merged to form the perfect backdrop of towering maples mixed with birch, pine and aspen trees.

Sara munched the fat sandwich Ben had handed her, then took a long sip of the creamy hot chocolate. "This had been fun," she told him. "I'm tired, but it's the kind of tired that makes you feel good at the end of the day."

Ben held his own cup of cocoa in his hands. "Life's like that around here. Not too fast-paced, but when we get together for a celebration, we always have a good time."

"I never had time for anything like this in the city," Sara replied, her tone pensive. "It was all work, then home to relieve my mother's sitter."

"It must have been hard, working with those tiny babies every day, then having to turn around and tend to your mother."

Sara looked down at the sandwich she held on her lap. "Yes. Some nights, I'd fall into bed, exhausted, only to be wakened by my mother having a nightmare or wandering around the house, bumping into things. I never really could sleep soundly. I was always worried she'd fall and hurt herself."

"I can't imagine seeing my mother like that," Ben said, his expression full of understanding. "As you just witnessed, she's a character, sort of a human dynamo. It would be hard to watch, hard to accept her as anything but the independent, stubborn mother I love."

"I guess it depends on the person, too," Sara told him. "My mother never was very strong, and she seemed to go downhill after my father died."

She watched as Ben sat silent for a minute, hoping he'd open up to her in the same way she'd shared things with him. Since their time together out at her cottage on the lake, he'd seemed quieter, maybe a little distant. Or maybe she was imagining things. Maybe she'd even imagined the wonder of their shared kisses. She'd certainly tried to put all the strange new feelings bubbling up inside her out of her mind.

But here she sat, closer than ever to the man who'd changed her whole perspective, her whole outlook on life, in a matter of a few weeks. Yet that man couldn't seem to trust her with the secret hurts from his own past. And she couldn't seem to bring herself to confess to him that she already knew everything she needed to know about him. She just wished Ben could let someone share his burdens, the way he took on those of everyone else.

"Why are you staring at me?" Ben asked now, wiping a hand across his chin. "Do I have some of Olaf's famous hot mustard sauce on my face?"

Sara laughed, then shook her head. "I'm sorry. I guess seeing your mother has just made me wonder about you—you know, you as a little boy, in high school, those wild college days—"

"Hey, I attended seminary—that didn't get any wilder than a late night studying the gospels, trust me."

He was using another diversion technique, but Sara pressed on. "So…tell me about Ben Hunter anyway. Or do I have to ask your mother?"

He looked genuinely concerned then. Taking a napkin out of the sandwich bag, he wiped his hands then gave her his full attention. "Do not ask my mother anything. She'd tell you way more than you ever wanted to know."

"Why don't *you* tell me?" Sara asked, her tone completely serious.

"Why is it so important that you know?"

"Because…we're friends. And you know everything about me."

That silence again. Then Ben glanced up at her, his eyes holding hers. She could almost see the questions forming on his forehead. Could he trust her? Could he make her understand that he liked her, cared about her, enjoyed her company, but he was still hung up on the woman he'd lost, the one woman he'd planned a life with?

She waited, not making it easy for him, since he'd turned her life inside out. Sara needed to know, needed to hear the words from him.

Ben reached a hand out to her. "There's a lot you don't know," he said, his voice low and serious. "And maybe it is time I told you some things about my past."

Sara took his hand, held it in hers, remembering his kisses, remembering what a good and decent man he was. "I want to know, Ben."

But it wasn't to be. In the next instant, she looked up to find Richard and Mary Erickson standing at their booth, their frowning faces indicating that they did not approve of their minister holding hands with a woman in public.

"Mr. Erickson," Ben said, standing to extend his hand to the other man. "How are you, sir?"

"How do you think?" Richard Erickson replied, barely acknowledging the handshake. "After everything you told us during our last meeting, you should know we're no better off than we were before you went to New Hope."

Sara saw the disappointment come over Ben's face. He'd told her about that last meeting with the Ericksons. After he'd explained to Jason's parents that there was a good possibility that Jason and Patty had run away together, based on the information Reverend Brooks and Patty's parents had given him, the Ericksons had once again turned hostile, blaming Ben for bringing Jason and Patty together in the first place.

"I guess you haven't found out anything more," Ben said, his gaze falling on Mary Erickson. "Mrs. Erickson, I wish there was something I could say—"

"I've got private detectives and the police looking into the matter," Richard retorted, interrupting with a hand in the air. "I suggest you stay out of it from now on."

"You know I can't do that," Ben told the stubborn man. "I have a responsibility to Jason."

"You *are* responsible for all of this," Richard said, his eyes blazing with anger. "You've done quite enough already."

Mary looked as if she were about to cry. "Reverend, I do appreciate your going to New Hope. At least now we have a little more information. And I can rest a little better, thinking maybe Jason's not alone out there."

"No, he's never alone," Ben told her. "God is

watching over him and I pray that God will lead him home again.''

Richard snorted, then shook a finger at Ben. "My son is out there with some girl we know nothing about, doing things we surely don't approve, and all you can say is that you pray God will lead him home. You'd better do more than that, Reverend. You'd better pray that I don't have you kicked out of the church.''

Sara stood up then, anger clouding her better judgment. "Excuse me, but don't you think you're being a little too harsh on Ben? He's done everything in his power to help find Jason and I believe he did a good job in counseling your son before he ran away.''

Richard turned on her then. "And just who do you think you are, telling me all of this? You weren't even here when this man put all these notions into my son's head.''

"No, I wasn't here,'' Sara replied, her voice calm in spite of her fast-beating pulse. "But I've been here long enough to see that Ben Hunter is a good minister and that he cares about children. He would never purposely do anything to bring Jason to destruction.''

"It's mighty noble of you to stand up for him,'' Richard told her, "since it's obvious you two are carrying on just as much as my son and this—this girl he took up with.'' He jabbed a finger at Ben. "And him trying to raise a baby, too. All he's done is pass that child around from church member to church member. That's not the kind of role model I want for my son—

not him, and certainly not you, either, since you seem to be just as liberal-minded as him.''

"That's enough," Ben said, clearly frustrated. Running a hand through his hair, he let out a long breath. "Mr. Erickson, Sara Conroy and I are just good friends. She helps me out with Tyler and she works in the day-care center. I won't allow you to slander her, no matter what your opinion of me may be."

"He's absolutely right," came a tightly controlled voice from behind them. "My son does not need the likes of you telling him how he should be conducting his private life."

The Ericksons whirled to find Alice Hunter standing there looking for all the world like a mother lioness protecting one of her cubs.

"Hello, Mary," she said sweetly, her eyes flashing at Richard. "I'm so sorry about Jason. You know, when Ben was that age, he went through a rather bad period. Did not listen to me, and refused to follow my authority. I sent him to our minister and I haven't regretted doing it, not once. I'm praying that your Jason will come to his senses and return safely to you, but in the meantime I won't have you putting all the blame on my son."

Richard turned to face her, his face red with rage. "*Your* son is trying to raise some foundling baby and he's carrying on in public with a woman. Doesn't that sound out of sync with being a man of God?"

"Sounds right in sync to me," Alice said on a huff.

"He's taken in a child that needed help, and he's found a lovely woman to spend time with, all the while maintaining his church responsibilities and dealing with the likes of you. I'd say he's doing a pretty good job, too."

"Mother, I don't need you running interference for me," Ben said, a hand up to halt Alice.

Sara noticed that Alice seemed ready to continue her lecture. In spite of the uncomfortable scene in front of her, she had to smile. A mother's love was an awesome thing.

"You're right, son, you don't," Alice told him. Then turning to Mary, she asked, "Could we go have a good hot cup of tea, dear?"

Looking shocked, Mary glanced at her husband. "I...I don't know."

"You look as if you could use a friend," Alice said, taking the woman by the arm. "Richard, Mary is going with me for a while. You don't mind, do you?"

Richard Erickson looked as if he'd been hit by a truck. "I'm going home," he said to everyone in general. "Mary, you know where to find me."

With that, he turned and marched away, scattering fallen leaves all around his feet as he hurried off.

"I think the festival is just about over," Alice said. "Ben, why don't you close up and take Sara and Tyler home?"

"Thanks, Mother," Ben said grudgingly. As he watched his mother guiding the dazed and confused

Mary Erickson off, he let out another frustrated sigh. "Great—I have to have two women fighting my battles for me now."

"We did it because we believe in you," Sara told him. "And because you're caught in a very awkward position, being the minister. You couldn't very well deck the man."

He shook his head. "No, that would be just the ticket he needs to get rid of me for good."

"Okay, then stop beating yourself up. You handled the situation well enough, and being a macho man wouldn't make things any better." Touching a hand to his arm, she added, "You certainly came to my rescue fast enough."

Ben lifted his head, his gaze meeting hers. "I won't let him think anything bad about you."

"Oh, right. But it's okay for him to think the worst of you."

"He might be right there."

Her hand still on his arm, Sara shook her head. "No, Ben. He's upset, bitter, grasping for somewhere to lay the blame, but I think in his heart, Richard Erickson is so full of guilt, that he feels it necessary to hide behind blaming you. But you are not to blame here."

Ben put his hand over hers, then lifted her hand to his mouth so he could kiss it briefly. "I appreciate the vote of confidence. But maybe...maybe both Mr. Erickson and I are to blame here. Neither of us saw the warning signs, neither of us knew Jason had a girlfriend. Maybe we both blew it.''

"It's going to work out," Sara told him, trying to reassure him. "You've certainly taught me to believe that no matter what, God has a plan for all of us."

"Do *you* really believe in *me?*" Ben asked her then, his heart in his blue eyes.

"I do." She just wished *he* believed in her enough to trust her, and to let her help him get over his own grief. He'd come so close to telling her, to sharing all of his burdens with her, but now she didn't want to press him. Not after that terrible scene with Jason's father.

"Let's go home," Ben told her, his whole attitude changing from lighthearted to disheartened right before her eyes.

Silently they cleaned up their booth, then secured the rest of their wares for the owners to claim later.

Just as they were about to leave, Ben caught Sara by the sleeve of her sweater. "Hey, I almost forgot."

She turned in surprise to find him holding a small white box. "What's this?"

"I—I bought it for you, before the mad rush. Actually, I special-ordered it about a week ago."

Touched and curious, Sara took the box. "Can I open it?"

He managed a lopsided smile. "Sure."

She lifted the lid off, then let out a gasp of delight. A dainty necklace lay nestled in the fluffy cotton of the box. Holding it up, Sara surveyed the necklace in the glow of the sunset. It looked like carved wood— tiny colorful beads that formed a chain, with a beautiful wooden cross hanging at its center. In the center of the cross was a small, beautiful dark-veined stone that curved inward in the middle.

"One of our Native American church members carved and designed this by hand," Ben explained. "The stone comes from the bluffs overlooking the Mississippi River—granite and limestone, I think. It's sunken in like that because it's a worry stone." He took her thumb and placed it in the center of the stone, then pressed her hand underneath to hold the cross. "See, you can rub it while you're worrying over something, or praying about something."

Amazed that her thumb fit perfectly over the stone, Sara held it, rubbing the polished veins. It felt warm and comforting against her skin. "It's beautiful, Ben," she told him, the lump in her throat making it hard to speak.

"I thought you could wear it to remember that you're not alone."

"I have my rock," she said, touching on the smooth stone. "Thank you."

"You're welcome." He leaned close to steal a quick kiss. "You do have a rock, you know. God has always been right there with you."

Sara nodded, then placed the long beaded chain around her neck. It fit perfectly against her skin. She understood what Ben was saying. Since coming here, she'd found God in everything, from the soothing blue waters of Lake Baylor to the enchanting, calming blue of Ben Hunter's eyes.

She'd found her rock all right, in God, and in the man who'd just given her this beautiful cross necklace.

The man she was falling in love with.

Chapter Eleven

"Son, I've fallen in love with Carl Winslow and we're getting married next spring."

Alice Hunter took another sip of her breakfast coffee, then went about buttering her toast with dainty efficiency while Ben tried not to choke on his wheat cereal.

"Reverend Carl Winslow?" he squeaked, knowing it was a redundant question.

Alice fussed with Tyler. The baby had just finished a big breakfast bottle and was now content to gurgle and kick in his sturdy carrier while the adults finished up.

"Do you know another Carl Winslow?"

"No, Mother. Of course not." He waved a hand, then caught his breath. "This...this is a surprise."

"Yes, it was to me, too," Alice said, her gaze turning dreamy. "But you know how that goes, son. One day you're going along, perfectly content with your little life, then boom, something happens to make you see things in a completely new light."

Ben glanced over at his mother, making sure she wasn't sleepwalking. Yes, he certainly could relate to that kind of boom. He'd felt the same way since Sara Conroy had shown up in his own life.

Right now, however, he didn't have time to dwell on how much Sara had affected his life. Now he really needed to understand the news his mother had just dropped on him. "I guess so, since you've known Carl Winslow for about twenty years now, and since you purposely sent me to him that summer so long ago for guidance. You two have always been friends, Mother. Remember? Just friends?" Eyeing her sharply, he said, "Did you get hit on the head?"

"No, nothing like that." Alice actually giggled, then cooed to Tyler. "More like I got hit in the heart."

Ben felt aggravated that his own mother had found someone to share her life with, while it looked like he'd remain a bachelor the rest of his days. Squinting to hide the very real resentment he felt, he pushed away his jealousy and gave his mother what he hoped was an encouraging smile. "Mother, you're going to have to catch me up on things."

"There's not much to catch up," Alice replied. Dusting toast crumbs off her hands, she leaned forward. "Carl and I just suddenly realized we'd both been alone long enough. I lost your father a long time ago, but it took me many years to let him go. And Carl lost his sweet Janey ten years ago. We were both so busy trying to ignore our grief, that we forgot to celebrate life.'' She shrugged, an eloquent, dainty lifting of her tiny shoulders. ''And now…well, we're both headed toward retirement and I guess the loneliness finally got the best of us.''

''So you're marrying Carl Winslow for companionship?''

''No, I'm marrying him because he's a fine, good man and I love him. And I hope you'll approve and give us your blessings.''

Ben looked up then to find his mother watching him, her expression hopeful. Alice Hunter had never asked for anyone's approval; she'd just lived her life in a way that always warranted instant approval. Her value system was as intact as her grading system— and both tough to argue with. Now it humbled Ben to see that his strong, independent mother was asking, hoping for his support.

And here he sat, feeling sorry for himself instead of rejoicing because his mother had at last found someone to grow old with, someone to love and share her wonderful, incredible life with. Mentally kicking himself for being so selfish, Ben immediately changed his attitude. He wouldn't begrudge his hardworking mother any happiness. She deserved so much more; Alice Hunter relished life, loved the Lord and understood things about people that most never took the time to see. Ben wanted to share in her joy, not crush it with harsh words or his own bitterness.

He got up to come around the breakfast table. "Of course I approve, Mother," he said as he leaned down to give her a hug. "I love Carl Winslow. He's been like a father to me, and we both know he saved me from myself long ago. If you two can find some happiness together, who am I to judge? I can't think of a better person for you to spend your golden years with."

Alice hugged him so tightly, she cut off his breath, but Ben didn't complain. It felt good to be hugged.

"They will be golden now," she told him. "I just wanted you to understand."

"I do. It's a surprise, though. You never even mentioned that you two were…close."

"It took me a while to admit my feelings," Alice said. Then she asked, "Speaking of which…how do you feel about Sara Conroy?"

Ben sank back down, then gave Tyler a bewildered look. Alice Hunter didn't carry on a conversation in the normal way. No, his mother had to keep throwing him for a loop, sending him surprise after surprise by bluntly changing the subject with the same economic speed in which she granted grades on term papers. Never a dull moment, and he wouldn't have it any other way. Only, right now, he wished he could have it another way. He didn't know how to answer her question, and he surely didn't enjoy the all-seeing glare of her intense, questioning eyes.

"Don't get all pensive on me," Alice said, her sharp gaze centered on her son. "Tell me."

Ben leaned back in his chair, then crossed his arms over his chest. "Would you believe we're just friends?"

"No."

"Would you believe me if I told you I don't know how I feel about Sara?"

"No."

"Okay. I give up. Why don't *you* tell *me* how I feel about Sara?"

Alice bobbed her head, then adjusted her reading glasses. "Okay. I think you've fallen in love with her, but you've got so much else to deal with right now, you don't have time to pursue her properly. You don't have time to court her, woo her, show her how much you've come to appreciate her. You're worried about Jason Erickson, about raising little Tyler, about maintaining some sort of control over your flock, and you probably think that Sara just considers you a friend. You also probably are feeling a little guilty because you've refused to so much as look at another woman since Nancy's death. And because of that, you can't bring yourself to even tell that nice girl that you care about her."

Ben scratched his head, then stared across the table

at his smug mother. "Are you by any chance a college professor, 'cause you sure are smart."

"Just logic and deduction, son," Alice said on a soft voice. "And a mother's eyes. I saw the way you looked at her during the Harvest Celebration, and the other morning in church. Your father always had a special look, just for me. I saw that same kind of look in your eyes when you glanced at Sara."

"You and half the town," Ben said on a huff. "I'm surprised Emma hasn't rented a billboard proclaiming that I'm in love with Sara Conroy."

"Are you?"

"Would you believe me if I denied it?"

"No. But I do believe that, like your mother, you're so busy ignoring your grief over Nancy you won't allow yourself to even consider loving another woman." Taking his hand in hers, Alice looked into her son's eyes. "Don't wait too long, Ben. Life is a gift, a gift that should be shared with someone special. I think Sara is special to you, but you're afraid to admit it."

Ben got up to empty the soggy remains of his cereal. "You're right. She is special. She's different. Funny, loving, very outspoken—just like someone else I happen to love." He pointed a finger at his mother then. "I think I'm falling in love with Sara, but she doesn't know. At least *I* haven't told her."

"And why not?"

Ben stood there staring out the window, watching

as the wind blew maple leaves across his backyard. "I don't think she's ready for anything further. She just came out of a bad relationship. Her fiancé dumped her and moved away."

"That is sad, but you can change all of that. You two look so lovely together, and she seems to genuinely care about baby Tyler."

At the mention of his name, the baby squealed in delight and kicked his booties high.

"She does love Tyler," Ben agreed, turning to play with the woven tie on Tyler's colorful sweater suit. "I just don't know how she really feels about me. When we're together, everything seems so right, but when I try to take things to a new level, she backs away."

"She's scared. You're both scared," Alice said, coming to stand by him. "I know it was tough when you lost Nancy, but maybe this is a second chance for you. After all this time, maybe you've been hit in the heart, too, son."

Ben turned and hugged his mother close again. "You're right about that. And it hurts."

Alice patted her son on the cheek with maternal force. "It's not supposed to hurt, Ben. It's supposed to feel good, wonderful, right. And you'll never experience any of those things if you don't tell that woman how you feel about her."

"How do you feel about all of this?"

Ben looked down at the man sitting in his office,

then shrugged underneath the heavy black material of his robe. He was about to marry Betty Anderson and Warren Sinclair, and he'd gone out to the Fairweather Retirement Center to pick up Reverend Olsen for the occasion. On the ride back into town, Ben had told his friend about his mother's upcoming wedding plans, as well as all of his many other concerns right now. It had felt good to be able to share his burdens with someone who wouldn't judge him or condemn him. Reverend Olsen always just listened and offered gentle advice. Which was exactly what Ben needed right now.

Now the two of them were about to enter the church for the current nuptials and Ben had never felt so miserable in his life.

"I'm happy for my mother and Reverend Winslow," he said in an honest voice, "but…I guess I just worry about her. She's been on her own for so long now."

"Your mother is a smart, self-assured woman," Reverend Olsen told him in his leathery old voice. "She knows what she's doing, son."

"Yes, she's always known what she's about," Ben replied. "She's a scholar, but she relies on *this* book first and always." He picked up his Bible then and offered a hand to the older man. "I wish I could say the same for her son, though. I rely on my Bible, but I'm not sure what I'm all about."

Reverend Olsen started to stand, his bent form slow

in raising from the chair. But his crystal-blue eyes were as sharp as ever. "Troubles?"

Ben shook his head. "Just self-pity, I'm afraid. It seems everyone around me is getting married. And here I stand, still alone. Maybe that's God's plan for me, after all."

The older man gave him a knowing smile. "The good Lord can only guide you so far, son. It's up to you to go out and look for a helpmate."

Ben had to laugh at that. "I guess I can't expect someone to just show up on my doorstep and say, 'Here I am,' now can I?"

Reverend Olsen shuffled toward the door. "You mean, no one like that has come along lately?"

Ben didn't miss the teasing note in the old man's words. Letting go of an edgy sigh, he held the door. "Have you been talking to Betty and Emma?"

A deep chuckle filled the quiet room. "Well, they do come by and visit me from time to time, and we do tend to catch up on the news. You've been very busy lately."

"You mean because of Tyler?"

"Yes, with a baby to take care of and…from what I hear, a very nice young lady to court."

"Court? That's the exact word my mother used. Sara and I are not courting."

"Then what are you two doing?"

"We're friends. Just good friends."

The reverend turned as they approached the side

doors to the sanctuary, where even now the guests were arriving and soft music played in honor of the happy couple. "The best marriages start out as just friendship, Ben."

Ben stopped and looked down at his wise mentor. "You do have a point."

"Unlike most of my sermons, huh?"

"You preached some of the best sermons I've ever heard."

"And you are a good preacher yourself," Reverend Olsen told him, reaching up like a father to straighten his young charge's white stole. "You're just lonely. That's your problem, son."

"So everybody tells me," Ben replied. "Oh, well, now is not the time to bemoan my forlorn love life. We've got a wedding to attend."

"So we do." Reverend Olsen lifted a shaking, gnarled hand. "See you at the reception."

Ben gave Reverend Olsen a quick wave, then stepped into the little annex where Warren Sinclair and his best man, his son-in-law, Kenny, were waiting. Reverend Olsen's words rang in Ben's head as he wished Warren well and assured him the wedding would go off without a hitch.

The best marriages start out just as friendship, Ben.

The same thing had apparently happened to his mother. She and Carl had started out as friends and now they were in love. It made Ben pause to think about his feelings for Sara.

Could that be the answer he'd been seeking so hard?

Could friendship make a good match? His friendship with Sara was strong and complete, no doubt there. And while he could admit to himself that he loved her, he knew she might not be able to return that love. But could she settle for being his wife—out of friendship, for companionship? And for Tyler's sake?

The matter was certainly worth pursuing. And the idea perked him up considerably. Grinning, he slapped Warren on the back. "Don't look so anxious. Your bride's going to show up."

Kenny teased his father-in-law good-naturedly. "Yep, I've never seen such a big, strapping man look so much like a whipped puppy."

Warren let out a shaky breath, then rubbed his chin. "I feel like a pup—a lovesick pup." Then he smiled, the warmth of that smile transcending any physical discomfort. "But it's worth every minute of suffering through this, boys. Take it from me, finding the right woman is worth the agony."

Ben felt a familiar wrench of pain in his own midsection. He wanted to know that certain agony. He wanted a wife of his own. And now he thought he might have just found a way for that to happen—if he could also find a way to get Sara to agree to marry him.

"The wedding was beautiful," Sara told Ben much later as they stood with the other guests in the fellowship hall next to the old church.

The sanctuary had been decorated in all the colors of fall. Since Betty Anderson was the outdoors type and enjoyed fishing and hunting as much as her groom, they'd agreed they wanted as much of the outdoors inside on their wedding day as possible. The effect, while different from any wedding theme Sara had seen, had turned out quite lovely.

They'd used salmon-colored rose trees decorated with twinkling lights on each side of the altar, and the centerpiece had been a large cornucopia—Emma's idea of symbolism for their overflowing love and many blessings—filled to the brim with golden, burgundy and russet mums and lots of fresh greenery. The whole church had smelled as fresh as the great Minnesota woods surrounding Betty's beloved home out on Baylor Lake.

"Betty sure made a striking bride," Ben said now, his gaze following the happy couple as they laughed and talked to Reverend Olsen.

"She sure did." Sara couldn't help but feel a tug of regret and envy. She wanted to tell him he'd made a striking minister, in his dark robe with his hair glistening in the candlelight. But that would have been too sappy and intimate. Best to stick to safe subjects, such as the happy bride and groom.

Betty looked so radiant in her cream-colored wool suit and the triple strand of pearls and matching earrings Warren had given her, and the groom, in his dark wool suit, his graying hair clipped close to his head, didn't look half-bad either. They made a wonderful couple.

Sara longed for the day she would walk down the aisle. She was beginning to think it would never happen. Then she looked up to find Ben watching her, and blushed down to her toes.

"What's the matter?" she asked, noticing the bright gleam in his eyes. "You look as if you have a secret."

"Maybe I do," he said, his grin taking her breath away. "You know, I was in a rotten mood before the wedding. These past few weeks since my mother informed me she was getting married, all this worry about Jason, Tyler being up most nights with that tenacious ear infection, everything—it has all taken its toll. I whined to Reverend Olsen and as usual he put it all in perspective for me."

"So now you have a goofy grin on your face and an interesting gleam in your eyes. Whatever did that man say to you?"

Ben shook his head. "Ah, now, I can't reveal my private conversations with my mentor, can I?"

"Why not?"

"I don't want to give it away just yet."

Sara lifted her head to stare over at him. "Well, all right, then. I won't make you bare your soul. But whatever you two discussed, it's had a definite effect on you. You look positively giddy."

"Weddings do that to me," Ben told her, a hand on her arm. "Let's go sample that black forest cake on the groom's table."

"But we've already sampled the white chocolate wedding cake. You had two russet candy roses and a sugar-coated maple leaf on the side, remember?"

"Yes, and they were incredibly delicious. Mrs. Swenson hasn't lost her touch with icing."

Sara had to laugh. "Good thing you still play basketball on a weekly basis."

He patted his stomach. "I try to stay in shape, in spite of all the good cooks around me."

"And you being single and all, they just can't help but spoil you. I admire women who can cook, though. I'm afraid the man I marry will either have to cook for himself or starve."

Her smile died on her lips as her eyes met his. The look he gave her had nothing to do with food. And neither did his next words, spoken in that deep gravelly voice.

"The man you marry will be fortunate, regardless of how you cook his food."

Sara swallowed, suddenly feeling too warm in her light green wool dress. Glancing around the crowded room to hide her turmoil, she mustered a nervous chuckle. "You think so?"

Ben gently nudged her chin around with one finger, forcing her to look at him. "I'm sure of it. Food is easy to come by. Finding a soul mate is what's hard in life.''

Sara tore her gaze away from Ben to search out Betty and Warren. ''*They* sure look happy, don't they?''

''Yes. God led them straight to each other.''

She ventured another glance at him. There it was. That same knowing look—that secretive, almost smug look. What did he have in mind? Her heart hammered a message to her notion-filled head. Maybe Reverend Ben Hunter had some ideas about them—about her and him and this whole marriage thing. No, that would be crazy. That would be impossible. Yet the look on his face seemed so hopeful, and the way he kept staring at her. There was something different about Ben today, something more intimate and personal.

Quickly Sara again went over the list of reasons against such a match. She wasn't preacher's wife material, she couldn't even cook—and Ben wasn't over his first love. He couldn't even bring himself to talk about that with her. No, she was reading him all wrong. He was just in a silly, romantic mood because of the wedding.

That had to be it.

And yet her heart soared with the hope that maybe Ben was beginning to have real feelings for her. That they might have a chance, after all. In spite of all the obstacles she saw in their way, Sara couldn't help but hope.

Maybe Ben Hunter had fallen in love with her.

Chapter Twelve

Ben stood by the windows of Betty and Warren's big, rambling house, looking out over the snow-covered hills that led down to Baylor Lake. A few more weeks and they'd be able to ice-skate down there. Soon, Betty would have Warren out ice-fishing, and he'd heard them talking at the dinner table about getting in some skiing now that the powdery snow was settling in for the winter.

Everyone had a life, but the minister of the church.

No, that really wasn't fair to Tyler. The baby had become Ben's life, and while Ben in no way resented having the child to care for, he only wished he had someone to share his newfound joy with. He loved little Tyler, loved watching the baby grow and change almost on a daily basis. Tyler had just had his three-month checkup and, in spite of the bout with ear infections, he seemed to be thriving. Ben had realized during that checkup that he didn't even know the baby's birthday.

Maybe that was why he felt in such a state of limbo, as if his life had suddenly gone still and he didn't know where to go from here. That, and trying to make two very important changes in his life—he wanted to adopt Tyler and he wanted to marry Sara. Yet here he stood, as frozen in place as the lake waters surrounding the dock just below the trees.

Ben closed his eyes and relived the last few weeks since he'd gotten the notion in his head to ask Sara to marry him. Never one to rush into a situation, he'd thought his plan through a thousand times, and a thousand times more he'd decided it was too risky, too foolish to even hope that Sara would agree to marry him based on friendship alone.

He now knew he was in love with her, completely, without a doubt. He'd prayed about it, asked God to give him the courage to approach her about this marriage, asked God to help him get over her if she refused his offer and left Fairweather, but he'd gotten no answers, no signs as to what he should do next.

Sara remained a constant in his life, a friend he knew he could count on, but she hadn't tried to take things beyond that. She'd helped with Tyler, sitting with the baby during the roughest times, her patience and skills leaving Ben wondering how he would have ever managed without her. Still, she'd given him no signs of taking their relationship beyond friendship.

And he'd gotten no signs about Jason, either. The boy hadn't called in weeks, and Richard Erickson's private detectives hadn't found a trace of his son or Patty Martin. Ben was so worried about his young friend. Christmas was coming, and the thought of Jason being away from his family and friends during this most holy of seasons nearly broke Ben's heart.

Then there was the matter of little Tyler. Ben had officially applied to adopt the little boy, but the red tape of not knowing his parentage was stalling the whole process. At least he could still be a foster father to Tyler, until the state decided what to do about the child.

Ben said another prayer, hoping his worst fear wouldn't come true. What if someone else adopted Tyler? What if the state refused Ben's petition, because he was single? Or what if the real parents came forward and contested the adoption? So many questions, so much to struggle with, when he should be standing solid in his faith. Ben just didn't know where to turn anymore.

The scent of Sara's soap-clean floral perfume drifted to Ben's nostrils and he turned to find her standing there beside him with a large mug of hot chocolate. "Betty sent this. She noticed you'd left the meeting, and suggested I come and find you before the fur starts flying."

He took the warm mug, then shrugged, his face twisting in reference to the need to soothe ever-battling committee members. "I'm sorry. I needed to stretch my legs. I love the Christmas season, but it's a busy time for the church. I wanted to find a quiet moment and get in the proper state of mind. I won't let my dark mood put a damper on our Christmas bazaar and all the holiday traditions my church holds so dear."

Sara wrapped her fingers around her own mug of hot chocolate. "I thought you seemed a little down. Anything I can do to help?"

If only she knew, Ben thought, his smile self-deprecating. "Will you stay through the holidays?"

He enjoyed the way she blushed and started fidgeting with her unruly curls. "I hope to."

Ben saw that hope in her green eyes. In moments such as these, he could almost believe Sara might have feelings for him, too. But he couldn't be sure.

They'd spent Thanksgiving together, along with Maggie and Frank and most of their relatives. Ben's mother and Reverend Winslow had come for the event, too. They hoped to be back for Christmas, since it was easier on Ben to keep little Tyler in his own home, and as Alice had told him, "We're free to travel when the mood hits us."

"Are you still concerned about your mother?" Sara asked him now, bringing his thoughts back full circle.

"No." He took a sip of the rich cocoa, then shook

his head. "They are so happy, and they're good for each other. As I've told you, Reverend Winslow was like a father to me."

Sara patted him on the arm. "And now he can be your father in every sense of the word."

"Yes. I've been blessed with a wonderful, if not a bit eccentric, mother, and now I'll have someone else I also hold dear to lean on, turn to when I'm in doubt."

"Do you still have doubts?" She set her empty mug on a nearby Victorian table. "About God, I mean."

Ben couldn't resist taking her hand in his. "Never about God, but sometimes about myself. I want to keep Tyler with me, and I'm working toward that, but it doesn't look so good." He dropped his hand away, then looked out toward the lake waters. "You tried to warn me not to get too attached. But I'm afraid it's too late. I think it was too late the moment I heard Tyler crying in the back of the church."

Needing to see her reaction, he ventured further, his gaze sweeping over her face. "I'm attached to Tyler *and* to the woman who's taken care of him since the very first day. I don't know what I'm going to do when both of you are gone."

He saw the confusion, the hesitation in her expression. "You don't know yet if you'll lose Tyler. Where's that faith you're always telling me I should have?"

He gave her a wry smile. "I have the faith, but I

can't make the system work for me if there's a better home out there for Tyler. That wouldn't be fair to him.''

''You'd let him go, for his own sake.'' At his slow nod, she added on a tremor, ''Ben, there is no greater love than that. Maybe that's why someone left him with you in the first place, because they loved him enough to give him a better home, a better life.''

''I just wish I knew who that someone was, so I could convince them that I'll always take care of the gift they bestowed on me.''

''You love him.''

''I do love that little boy,'' he told her, the catch in his throat making it hard to speak. ''And yes, I'd have to let him go if I thought he'd be better off somewhere else, with a loving, *complete* family.''

She pushed at a wayward curl. ''It makes me so angry—the way the authorities think you might not be suitable to raise Tyler. You're a minister. Doesn't that count for something?''

''In the eyes of the law, that's just a title. They have to weigh everything.''

''Well, it stinks.''

He laughed then at her self-righteous indignation, even while his heart was slowly melting into little puddles of longing. ''I'll miss you, Sara.''

The look she gave him was full of longing, too. And yet she held back, hesitant, her whole expression filled with a questioning doubt. "St. Paul isn't that far," she said. "You can come to visit me in the big city."

"Sure." Ben tilted his head, watching her as she took their mugs. "You know what I think?"

"What?"

"I think I might not ever see you again, once you leave Fairweather."

"What makes you think that?"

He had to find out the truth, had to see if he could bring himself to suggest that she stay. "You seem to have this shield up around you. Sara, you've been a good friend to me, but I know that's all you can ever be. I just wish…I wish we could have gotten closer."

"Ben, we are close," she told him, her eyes glistening. "But I never gave you any false promises. I tried to be honest with you, tried to make you see that all I can offer is friendship. You will always have that."

"It's a start," he said, more to himself than to her.

Why wouldn't she take things any further with him? Hadn't he shown her that he could be trusted? He had a sneaking suspicion she didn't want to get any closer to him because he was a minister. Maybe Sara wasn't willing to turn her life over to God in the same way Ben had. Maybe she didn't want to get involved with someone who always had to put others first—sometimes before his own family.

But he couldn't believe that in his heart. He'd seen Sara with the children at the center. She was more than willing to put others first. She did so every day. And she'd certainly put her mother first, sacrificing both her career and personal life to help a loved one. Sara was capable of being a minister's wife—unless she didn't think so herself.

Ben watched as she headed back into the den where several church members were going over the Advent schedule. Sara had only come to this meeting as a favor to Betty, to help out with serving the refreshments and entertaining any children who'd tagged along—again an example of her willingness to be helpful.

As Ben stood there, his mind raced with the possibilities of being with Sara. If she was afraid of not measuring up, that would explain her deliberate efforts to hold him at arm's length. Maybe he could convince her otherwise. And maybe he could convince her that starting a marriage as friends wouldn't be such a bad thing.

But first he had to find some quiet time to talk to her about his idea, his hope that they might get married.

It did seem that they only managed to get together at church functions or at work. Too many distractions. That brought another idea to mind. They'd never really had a real date. Both his mother, Alice and his friend, Reverend Olsen, had suggested Ben needed to "court" Sara. Maybe he should try doing just that, before she did head back to St. Paul. If he gave her the option of marrying him, it might help solve her future, too. She only wanted friendship, but marriage would bring both of them companionship, too. It was worth a shot.

Feeling immensely better, Ben lifted up a prayer of thanks then strolled back into the den, where a lively bickering session over how to conduct the Christmas Eve services was taking place.

"Here's our leader," Betty said to the lady who'd just raised her voice to be heard, her tone just below a huff. "Let's let Ben decide which music we should use."

"'Joy to the World,'" Ben said immediately, bringing all the fussing to a halt. "'Joy to the world, the Lord is come. Let earth receive her King.'"

Betty shot him a grateful grin. "Certainly one of my favorites. Any other suggestions?"

"How about 'Peace on Earth'?" Ben gave the group a lopsided smile. "And especially, peace between committee members."

Everyone laughed then, breaking the tension between the several domineering, well-meaning church members who always wanted to control everything.

Ben leaned his hands on the back of a floral armchair. "We have many beautiful songs that we traditionally sing on Christmas Eve. So let's get serious about this. While we want the music for this special service to be beautiful, let's remember what's really important. We are celebrating the birth of the Savior,

Jesus Christ. The songs don't matter so much as the singers. We need to rejoice and lift our voices high, and we need to remember why we're singing in the first place.''

Several hearty amens followed Ben's minisermon. Those who'd been arguing the loudest now looked a little more humble. Within a matter of minutes, the matter was settled and several traditional favorites had been selected.

"Got it," Betty said, slapping a hand on her pleated wool skirt after she'd recorded the decision. "I'll give this to Emma to type up for the weekly bulletin. Thanks, Ben."

Ben searched out Sara, who sat rocking Tyler in a oak chair in the corner. She looked as beautiful and maternal as ever. Again he was struck by the perfect picture the woman and child made. And he realized his life wouldn't be complete until they were both in it permanently. On the way home, Ben intended to ask Sara Conroy for a date.

Then, on that date, he intended to ask her to marry him.

Sara checked her makeup one more time, then stood staring off into space, her fingers automatically searching out the cross pendant she wore around her neck. The worry stone centered in the middle of the large wooden cross had sure come in handy lately. Tonight

Sara had practically rubbed the polished stone down to a nub.

She didn't know why she was so nervous, but she'd changed clothes at least five times, finally settling on a long, high-necked flared brown wool jersey dress with tight sleeves. The color matched the beaded work in the necklace Ben had given her. And tonight it seemed especially important that she wear the necklace—for hope, for courage, for the strength Ben had assured her the necklace would bring.

She and Ben were going on a date. A real, honest-to-goodness date. Sadie was staying with little Tyler, the weather was brisk and cold, the night clear and bright—no storm predictions, and Ben had had no major crises this week at work. A perfect evening.

Or at least she hoped it would be perfect.

It was two weeks before Christmas. Maybe that was why Sara felt so keyed-up. She'd be leaving Fairweather soon, so she knew this might be the last time she and Ben would have to be alone together. It would be strange, being with him without Tyler. The baby had always served as a gentle buffer against any further intimacy, any further delving into the past or venturing toward an uncertain future.

In all the rest of the times they'd shared, they'd usually been surrounded by co-workers or members of the congregation. No chance to develop a close relationship, other than the mutual friendship they'd both acknowledged. And that had been just fine with Sara, until she'd fallen in love. Ben was right; she'd used everything and everyone as a shield to keep from getting closer to him. She just couldn't bear to fall in love with him and know he'd never be able to return that love.

Now she had to admit she was in love with him. But she still wasn't sure about how he really felt. At times it seemed as if he might feel the same; other times she thought he was just being a good friend, as he'd promised.

Remembering the last time she'd seen Ben, Sara felt the familiar tightness in her heart. She'd only gone to Betty's planning session as a favor to her temporary boss. Betty had insisted they could use Sara's help with the children and that she'd come in handy helping keep things in order as far as food and drink. Sara, not having anything to occupy her once she went home to her own little cottage not too far from Betty's big house, had agreed to help out. Knowing Ben would be there had helped in that decision, she had to admit. She liked being in the same room with him, and she loved taking care of Tyler. Plus she was almost certain Betty knew these things, too, and had wanted to bring them together. Fairweather was full of well-meaning matchmakers.

She could never tell Ben, but she'd become attached to him and Tyler, too—even though she knew Ben's attachment to her was strictly on a friends-only basis—in spite of her imagining otherwise. At Betty and

Warren's wedding, she'd hoped things might be changing for Ben and her, but in the weeks since, things had remained the same.

Sara didn't have the nerve to make a move, to tell Ben her true feelings. But now the thought of leaving was tearing through her soul, making her think crazy thoughts. Making her wish she could be all the things Ben needed her to be.

"Just stop," she told herself now as she ran a hand through her upswept riot of unruly curls. "You can be his friend. You can support him in his efforts to adopt Tyler, but that's it. You can't be something you weren't meant to be. No matter how much you want it in your heart."

Sara held her fingers to her cross. She loved her necklace, wore it every day. It was always there, reminding her that she wasn't alone. Reminding her that Ben cared about her...and that God did, too.

She left the bedroom, pacing the small living room until she found herself standing by the windows, looking out toward the frozen lake waters. Over the trees, a million stars twinkled toward her, assuring her that heaven wasn't so far away after all.

Sara stared up into the night sky, then spoke out loud. "Dear God, I know You're up there. You've always been there. And even though I haven't turned to You a lot lately, I'm turning to You now. Ben says You will listen, no matter how long it's been since I prayed. I'm praying now, Lord, for something, something to help me find the strength to go, to leave Fair-weather. Help me to make the right choice. Help me to find the strength to walk away from Ben and Tyler. I can't seem to find any other way.''

She stopped, her heart racing, her mind whirling.

At least they had tonight. She'd enjoy this quiet time with Ben, cherish it as a sweet memory. She'd appreciate the moment, rejoice in her newfound friend. That would have to be enough.

She didn't deserve to ask for anything more.

An hour later Sara sat with Ben in a secluded restaurant out on the lake. They had a corner table, complete with a spectacular view of the winter wonderland spread out before them. The trees glistened a shimmering gray-blue in the moonlight, while the night sky looked like a dark sheet of navy satin set against the pearly white snow. Out on the wide pier, a brightly lit star shone in white-gold colors, reminding all patrons of the season.

"Ben, this is so nice," she said, gazing across the small round table at him. He looked handsome in his dark wool jacket and white button-down shirt, with the intimate candlelight playing across his face. "And the menu—everything sounds great. I'm hungry."

"They're popular for their steaks and seafood, so order whatever your heart desires. The dessert is good, too." He grinned then waved a hand at the window. "Tonight, the sky's the limit."

"Did you get a bonus?" she teased, her nervousness subsiding just a bit.

"No, but I've got a little tucked back in savings. And since I rarely indulge, I'd say we're entitled."

"It is Christmas."

"Yes, and over the next few weeks I won't have much time to enjoy a quiet dinner such as this one."

"Then I'm all the more pleased you wanted to share it with me."

He grinned again, sapping her calmness in much the same way the winter wind was sapping the stark tree limbs lining the lake. Then he leaned forward, his eyes as velvet-blue as the night. "Did I tell you you look really pretty? I like your hair up like that."

Sara grabbed her cross, rubbing the stone for all it was worth. "It didn't want to cooperate, so I just pulled it up with a clamp."

"I like your uncooperative hair."

"Thank you."

"I see you're wearing the necklace."

Realizing she'd been clinging to it for dear life, Sara dropped her hand in her lap. "Yes. I've had several compliments on it. I tell everyone who asks about it to go to your friend and get one for themselves. Hope he sells lots of these."

Ben shook his head. "I doubt that. It's one of a kind."

"Really?" Shocked and touched, Sara reached for her necklace again. "He only makes originals?"

"He made that one especially for me, or rather for the special one-of-a-kind person I wanted to give it to."

Sara felt tears pricking at the back of her eyes. "Oh, Ben. That's the sweetest thing anyone's ever done for me. I'll cherish it always."

He took her hand in his. "Just remember what that necklace represents."

"I will, I promise. I'll remember everything you've done for me, too."

"I haven't done anything. I just enjoy being with you, and I want you to understand how much my faith means to me. It's my life."

"I do understand," she told him, her fingers touching on his. "And I appreciate what your faith has taught me about my own. I'm stronger now, from having known you."

"Don't make it seem so final."

"It's not final. We'll stay in touch, I hope."

"I'm planning on that."

She wondered about his smile. It was the same smile he'd given her at Betty and Warren's wedding. She didn't want to misinterpret anything though, so she just accepted it as part of Ben's charm.

The dinner progressed with good food and soft, uninterrupted conversation. The restaurant staff knew exactly when to bring the food and exactly when to leave them alone. When dessert and coffee arrived, Sara felt a sense of regret. This wonderful night would soon be over.

But she soon found out Ben had other thoughts.

He finished the last of his Italian cream cake, then took both of her hands in his. "Sara, there's something I'd like to talk to you about."

The look was back—the expectant, hopeful look. Sara's heart turned to snowflakes inside her chest while her mind battled hope against hope. "Go ahead."

"We're friends, right?"

"Of course."

"And we're compatible."

"I'd say so."

"And you love Tyler as much as I do, right?"

"You know I do."

"And we're both lonely, stuck in limbo, wouldn't you say?"

"I guess so." Wondering where all of this was leading, she laughed shakily. "What are you trying to tell me, Ben?"

Ben lowered his head, closed his eyes, then took a long breath. "I'm making a mess of this, but I've given it a lot of consideration and thought. I think I've found a practical solution that will benefit both of us. We make a good team, we'd make good parents for Tyler, and while we haven't taken things between us beyond friendship, I think we should...I think we should consider getting married."

The silence that followed Ben's proclamation sounded like a snow-covered night—stark, cold and brilliant.

Sara went through an entire gamut of emotions, starting with surprise, followed by elation, then finally, hurt, indignation and resignation. Ben Hunter had just asked her to marry him.

But he'd never once mentioned that he loved her and wanted her to be his wife.

Chapter Thirteen

Ben waited, his heart skipping a beat as he watched Sara's face. Her first reaction gave him hope, but then her expression changed from open and happy to a pale blank sheet that rivaled the snow lining the window seal.

"Well, what do you think?" he asked, a sinking feeling centering in the middle of his stomach. "It's a practical solution, don't you agree?"

Sara lifted her chin, her eyes misty and wide, a frown creasing her brow. "Practical? Is that your idea of marriage, Reverend?"

Ben knew from the tone in her voice that this wasn't going the way he'd planned. "No. I mean, yes...in this case, yes. We're friends, but a marriage based on friendship can work. At least I think it can."

"You think it can?" She looked away, out over the

snow. Then in a soft voice she said, "I thought all marriages were supposed to be based on love."

Ben didn't speak at first. Should he tell her that he did love her? No, not now. Now she'd just think he wasn't being honest, that he was trying to make up for this big, big mistake. Letting out a breath, he said, "That's true, but a lot of marriages start out with friendship. That's how Betty and Warren started, and now my mother and Reverend Winslow."

"So you decided to throw in with them and take a chance on me?"

"Sara, don't look so sad. Even though you've made it clear that we're just friends, I thought because you care about Tyler and because you're alone, too…I thought you'd at least consider this."

"You don't want to know what I'm considering right now," she told him, her eyes blazing such a deep green, Ben had to blink. "But I'll tell you exactly what I think about your 'practical' solution. I think you only want me as your wife to help you adopt Tyler. I think you only want me as your wife to help your standing within the church. And I think you don't even begin to know the meaning of all those vows you have couples repeat when you perform wedding ceremonies."

Before he could gain the breath to speak, she held up a hand and continued. "Betty and Warren Sinclair are so in love, they light up a room when they enter it. All of our friends are that way, too. In love, Ben. They love each other. They were friends of course, but they were in love before they ever agreed on marriage.''

"Luke and Julianne were friends," he interjected in a rush, "and they agreed to get married just so the twins could have a mother."

Sara scoffed. "Whether either you or Luke realize it, Julianne was half in love with that man when she married him."

"She told you that?"

"She didn't have to tell me. I've heard how they met, what happened to bring them together. What is it with men? Don't you all realize a woman today would never enter into a marriage if she didn't have true feelings for the other person?"

"Well, do you have feelings for me?"

Sara threw her hands up in the air, then sat silent for a long time, as if weighing that particular question. "Right now I don't know how I feel about you. But my answer to your well-thought-out proposal is a big, loud no."

Ben lowered his head. "I'm sorry. I just thought—"

"No, you didn't think," she retorted, anger and hurt bringing out a deep flush against her alabaster skin. "You seem to have forgotten that I was engaged—to a man who couldn't make a firm commitment to me, to a man who wanted everything his way. To a man who left me when the going got tough. Do you honestly think I'd rush into a marriage now...just for convenience?"

Ben didn't know what to say, how to repair the damage he'd just done. Of course Sara wanted a firm commitment. She wanted more than he had to offer, and she wanted to be able to give her heart completely, which meant she didn't care about him enough to go into a marriage just for the sake of friendship and companionship.

"I guess not," he finally said, his eyes downcast. "Sara, I'm so sorry."

Pushing her chair back, Sara stood. "I'd like to go home now."

Ben reached out a hand to her, gently grabbing her slender arm. "Sara, wait. Let me explain."

"I've heard that line before."

"But...you don't understand."

He'd tell her. Just tell her outright that he loved her. But she didn't love him. She couldn't love him and that was why marriage to him sounded so distasteful. And she'd accused him of some very conniving things. But he had hoped marrying her would help him with the adoption, and having a wife would improve his standing in some people's eyes. While her accusations hurt, they did hit close to home. But he'd never meant it to sound that way.

Telling himself Sara was just upset and that she didn't really believe those things about him, Ben decided he'd done enough damage for one night. Now he'd probably never be able to tell her how he really felt.

Because of her bad experience, she couldn't trust anyone right now. He should have seen that, but he'd been so wrapped up in solving his own dilemma, he'd never stopped to consider how cold and calculating this would seem to Sara.

"I understand more than you'll ever know," Sara said as she swept by him, heading to the front of the restaurant.

Ben hurriedly paid the check to the overly interested hostess who'd been watching the whole scene, then made a mad dash to catch up with Sara.

She was already at the car, waiting, her head down, her arms wrapped against the thick wool of her coat. Ben stopped just before he reached her, wishing he could take back his harebrained plan and just pull her into his arms and tell her what was really on his mind. But it was too late for any declarations of love and truth now.

Silently he opened the car door for her, then drove the short distance around the lake to her cottage. Before he could get out of the car to help her, Sara shot out of her side, then hurried to the front door. "Good night, Ben," she said over her shoulder.

Ben got out and stood there, the slamming of the door echoing through the trees around him with a finality that left him searching for answers and wondering why he'd acted so stupid.

He'd ruined it for both of them. Not only had he managed to mess up the marriage proposal, but he'd probably just lost the best friend a man could ever ask for.

Looking up at the brilliant blanket of stars winking back at him, Ben had never felt so alone in all of his life.

"I hate to leave you like this, Betty," Sara told her supervisor bright and early the next Monday, "but...I have to get back to St. Paul. Right away."

Betty took off her bifocals and leaned back in her desk chair. "Sara, what on earth's happened? You weren't in church yesterday. Is everything okay?"

Seeing the wary concern in Betty's hazel eyes, Sara flinched then looked away. "I—I wasn't feeling very well. And now...well, I'm afraid I can't finish out the next couple of weeks. I won't be able to stay through Christmas. I'm sorry."

Betty made a noise that sounded like a frustrated grunt. "Why don't you tell me what's really going on."

Sara couldn't hide her emotions. She'd tried all weekend. Staying shuttered in her cottage, she'd drank gallons of coffee and stared out at the lake, all the while wondering if she'd been too hasty in turning Ben down.

She'd been so angry, so hurt, that she'd said some things she didn't really mean. She could tell she'd hurt Ben, too, by saying those things. He at least wanted to marry her, even if it was for all the wrong reasons.

Or was it for all the right reasons? Little Tyler needed
a mother, and Ben needed a helpmate. And she needed
both of them in her life because she loved them both
so dearly.

Sara just didn't think she had the courage or fortitude to be either a mother or a helpmate right now,
though. Because...she couldn't settle for a man who
could only offer her friendship, no matter how tempting it would be to fall into Ben's arms. No, if she
accepted and married Ben, he'd soon know the truth.
She wouldn't be able to hide her feelings and he'd
realize she loved him. That could make things awkward, since he obviously couldn't return that love.

"Honey, you look as if you could use a good cry,"
Betty said now as she came around her desk to place
two firm hands on Sara's shoulders. "What happened?"

Sara had fought against the pain, the humiliation,
all weekend, but now, with Betty's maternal instincts
forcing the issue, she could only slump against the
other woman, gulping hard to hold back the inevitable
tears.

"Okay, okay." Betty hugged her close, rocking her
as if Sarah had just lost a loved one. "Come on over
here and sit down on the couch. Then you can explain
everything." She pulled Sara along with her, her hand
squeezing Sara's in reassurance. "And it won't go any
further, I promise."

As if to prove her point, Betty closed the door to

the long hallway, effectively shutting away the bright chatter of toddlers and the occasional cry from one of the babies.

Sara sank down on the overstuffed love seat near the window of Betty's spacious office. "I do need to talk to someone. I guess I need some advice."

"That's part of my job," Betty said, a concerned smile crossing her lips. "But that's also part of being a friend, too. You know, Sara, you've come to mean a lot to all of us around here. Particularly our minister."

Sara gritted her teeth, fighting back the tears. "Are you so sure about that?"

"Ah, Ben." Betty shook her head. "So we get to the gist of the matter. Did you and Ben have a fight?"

Sara shifted, then wiped away an annoying tear. "More like a battle—a strong battle of wills."

"Do you want to talk about it?"

"He asked me to marry him," Sara blurted out, tears rolling down her face.

Betty clapped her hands together. "Well, that's great news. So why are you crying and telling me you have to leave Fairweather?"

Sara shrugged then wiped at her red-rimmed eyes. "Because…because he doesn't love me. He only did it for…for practical purposes. He thinks we're a good team, that we'd be good for Tyler, that it would be a benefit to both of us. A benefit—he makes it sound like an insurance policy!"

"Oh, boy." Betty settled down beside Sara, then took one of her hands in her own, rubbing it as to put the warmth back in it. "Not exactly roses and candle-light, huh?"

Sara shook her head. "He took me to a romantic dinner out on the lake. We talked, laughed—we had so much fun. Then he asked me to marry him."

"So far so good. But...something was missing?"

Sara bobbed her head. "Yes, a very big something. Love! I want someone to love, not someone to be my best buddy."

Betty nodded her understanding. "Well, Ben is an honorable, caring man. I'm sure he thought he was doing the right thing."

"Right for him, maybe, but not right in my mind. I can't stay here, Betty. I can't face him. I tried so hard to avoid getting too close, getting attached to him and Tyler, and now look at me. I'm a mess."

"You're in love," Betty stated, slapping a hand on her navy flared skirt. "Happens to the best of us."

"Well, why did it have to happen to me? I didn't want it to. I wasn't ready for this. It's like being blind-sided."

"Yeah, that's love all right. A glorious thing."

Sara wiped away her tears, then glared up at Betty. "Not when the man you love can't even bring himself to talk about his past relationship. Betty, Ben's still grieving over Nancy, and he...he hasn't even been able to talk about her with me. He doesn't love me.

He can't love anyone else until he comes to terms with her death. I can't imagine being married to someone who pines away for a lost love. It wouldn't be fair to either of us.''

"You have a good point there," Betty agreed, her tone soothing. "If Ben Hunter has a flaw, it's that he's so busy listening to other people's problems, he's managed to hide his own. He stays busy to block out his grief, and that's caused him to be a little tight-lipped and guarded about his personal life.''

Sara felt like one of the toddlers being efficiently placated. "Then you agree he needs to deal with Nancy's death before he can love anyone else?"

"No, I didn't say that. I just said you have a good point. But honey, I think you're missing one really important issue here. Ben Hunter is a man in love.''

Sara brought her head up then, her eyes widening as she stared at Betty in disbelief. "Not with me."

"Yes, with you. That poor man's got it so bad, he doesn't know if he's coming or going. He just doesn't know how to convey that to you.''

"I don't believe that," Sara said, jumping up to pace the room. "I think Ben cares about me. And he's been a good friend. He's taught me to turn to God in times of need, and to forgive myself for my shortcomings. He's a wonderful person, but until he comes to me himself and tells me that he's over Nancy, until he can bring himself to share that part of his past with me, I won't believe he could ever love me. I have to hear it from him, Betty. I have to know that I'm the one he loves.'' She stopped ranting, then turned to face the other woman. ''Besides, it doesn't really matter anyway. Look at me—do I look like I could possibly be a minister's wife?''

''You look as good as any minister's wife I've ever seen,'' Betty told her. Getting up, she grabbed Sara by the shoulders again. ''That's just downright silly, worrying about that. The good Lord knows you're only human, Sara. None of us is perfect. None of us is above reproach. We just get up each day and do the best we can, with the talents and the guidelines God gave us. And we pray about the rest.''

Sara's sigh shuttered out of her body. ''Then pray for me. Pray for Ben. I love him so much, but I can't marry him.''

''I will pray for both of you,'' Betty told her. ''But Sara, think long and hard before you walk away from Ben Hunter. You should tell him how you really feel. You two have a real chance at happiness here, and if you throw that chance away because of pride and misunderstanding, it might be the biggest mistake of your life.''

''It was all a big mistake,'' Ben told Morgan and Luke as they watched the boys' basketball team running through a practice drill in the church gym. ''I messed up, big-time.''

Morgan and Luke exchanged knowing glances as

swiftly as they exchanged the basketball back and forth between them.

Morgan caught the ball, then held it near his stomach with one arm. "Well, my friend, I have to admit your intentions were honorable, but it sounds like you went about it all wrong."

Ben nodded, then turned to Luke. "But you didn't love Julianne when you two got married. You wanted a mother for your children."

Luke shrugged, then sighed. "Well, I told myself that at the time, but let's face it—Julianne and I were attracted to each other from the first, just like you and Sara. And I think she was more receptive to the idea because I had children and she didn't think she'd ever be able to have any of her own."

"That's changed now," Morgan said, grinning as he tapped his friend on the shoulder. "We're both in the family way, in a big way."

Ben felt that familiar tug of envy, coupled with joy for both of his friends. They'd announced earlier that they were going to have new babies in their households in a few months. "I'm happy for both of you, by the way, even if I've managed to ruin my own chances at being a husband and father."

Luke grinned right back. "A lot of things have changed now. But Julianne and I soon realized we loved each other. Maybe from the beginning."

Morgan glanced over at Ben, then tossed him the ball. "Which is the case with you and Sara, I believe."

Ben shuffled, dribbled the ball, then tossed it back to Morgan. "I know how *I* feel, but Sara doesn't love me. She's made that clear. And she also made it very clear that she won't marry a man she doesn't love. She has always stressed that we can only be friends, and now I guess I won't even have her friendship to count on."

"Do you love this woman?" Luke asked in a mock-stern voice, his eyes twinkling in spite of the serious question.

Before answering, Ben blew the whistle, then called to the boys. "That's enough for today. Go shower and get home. Be on time for warm-up before Friday's game."

"He's stalling," Morgan said as he watched the stomping feet of sweaty adolescents roar by like a herd of gazelles.

Ben waited until the locker room door banged shut, then turned back to his friends. "I didn't want the kids to overhear. Everyone around here's already involved enough in my personal life as it is."

"Which is why we're waiting for an answer," Luke told him, tapping a sneakered foot in impatience. "But I think we all already know the answer."

Ben hung his head, then lifted his gaze to his friends. "Yes, I love her. But I didn't have the nerve to tell her that."

Morgan poked Ben in the stomach. "Well, tell her now. I mean, what can be worse at this point? Letting her leave thinking you only wanted to marry her for—what did you call it?—'practical purposes,' or asking her to stay because you really love her and want to make a life with her and Tyler?''

"I vote for the second choice," Luke said, adding his own encouraging poke to Morgan's. "If you don't tell Sara the truth, she might leave for good and you'll never know what might have been."

Ben looked up then, a shining light of realization clicking on in his head, in his heart. "What might have been? Ever since Nancy died, I've asked myself that question at least ten times a day. I think I've been so worried with *what might have been,* that I've failed to see the possibilities of what *could be.*"

Morgan and Luke glanced at each other again.

"I think he's catching on," Luke stated, nodding his approval. "You know, Reverend, you preach a mean sermon, but you don't follow your own advice."

Ben lifted the basketball toward the nearby net, making a perfect free throw shot. "Well, I intend to do just that from now on."

"Two points." Morgan hooted, then slapped Ben on the back. "Go for it."

"I am," Ben told them. "I'm going to tell Sara the truth, and place the rest of it in God's hands."

"Now you're talking," Luke replied, his grin back.

Ben looked up at his buddies. "Thanks. I really appreciate both of you listening to my sob story."

"Don't make a habit of it," Luke told him, grinning. Then with his expression changing, he added, "You've helped both of us through some tough times, Ben. It's only fair that we do the same for you—when you'll let us."

Ben laughed then. "I'll have to remember that sometimes the preacher himself needs to hear a good lesson on life."

"That's what we're here for," Morgan said as they headed toward the locker rooms.

Just then they heard the door opening on the other side of the gym. All three men turned to find Emma rushing toward them, her heels clicking on the polished wood, a look of concern on her face.

"Reverend, come quick," she called, her voice breathless and shrill. "It's Tyler. Something's wrong—he's sick. Sara says we need to rush him to the hospital right away."

Chapter Fourteen

"Morgan, you have to tell me what's going on in there."

Ben paced the small area just outside the emergency room, still in his sweats and sneakers. Sara sat in a chair beside the room where they'd taken Tyler earlier, and all around, anxious church members stood in clusters, supporting Ben in his time of need.

Morgan, who'd driven Ben and the baby to the emergency room and asked his fellow pediatricians if he could help with the examination, had now come out of the examining room, his expression grim.

Morgan placed a gentle hand of restraint on Ben's arm. "They're doing everything they can to bring the fever down, but Ben, I have to be honest with you. They think it might be meningitis."

Sara jumped up, a hand going to her heart. "I was

afraid of that. I've seen it too many times. The rash, the high fever.'' Her voice became shaky. ''And when I couldn't get him to respond, when he wouldn't wake up, I just knew.''

''You did the right thing, alerting us,'' Morgan told her. ''We got him here quickly for treatment and that could very well make all the difference.''

Ben grabbed his friend's arm. ''You mean, that could save his life? Is Tyler going to die, Morgan?''

Morgan glanced from one anxious face to the other. ''I don't want to mislead you. It's serious. But Ben, we have advanced treatment and medication now that we didn't have years ago, and as soon as we can determine whether it's bacterial or viral, we'll be able to help him more.''

''How will you do that? How soon will we know?'' Ben ran a nervous hand through his hair. ''What are they doing in there?''

''They're going to do a spinal tap,'' Morgan explained.

Ben didn't miss the look Morgan gave Sara. ''Is that painful? Will it hurt him?''

Sara spoke at last. ''He has to lie completely still, Ben. It's just a prick, but it looks much worse to those watching than it feels for the baby.''

''I want to go in there,'' Ben said, heading for the room.

Morgan pulled him back. ''I don't think that's a very good idea. We don't know how contagious this is yet. The doctors know what they're doing, Ben. He'll be just fine.''

Ben turned to Sara. "Then you go. You're a nurse. You're trained for this. Sara, please, go in and hold him while they do the test.''

Sara shot Morgan a misty-eyed look. "Will it be okay?''

"Sure." Morgan nodded, then indicated his head toward the room. "I'll go back in, too. Together we'll make sure Tyler doesn't have to suffer any undue pain.''

Ben felt Sara's hand on his arm. "Ben, is that all right with you?''

Seeing the doubt and concern in her eyes, Ben regained some of his composure. As scared as he was, he didn't want to worry Sara. She loved Tyler, too. "Of course. Thank you.''

"We'll take good care of him," Morgan told him as he guided Sara into the room.

Ben stood watching her walk away, thinking how happy he'd been just over an hour ago. His decision to tell Sara the truth had been liberating, setting him free from three long years of guilt and isolation. He'd realized so much, standing in that chilly gym with his friends, the sound of kids playing basketball all around.

He now knew that as much as he loved Sara, he'd been holding part of himself away from that love— out of respect for Nancy's memory. He'd believed that it would be dishonorable to love someone else, when he'd never quite gotten over losing her. But Ben knew Nancy would be upset if he didn't find someone to share his life with. She'd been that kind of woman— giving, nurturing, putting others above herself, so much like Sara, yet so different, too.

Ben had attempted to keep that part of Nancy alive, by trying to be all the things she'd expected him to be, all the things that had made her proud of him. But all of his efforts had been a sham, really, because he'd guarded his heart to the point of becoming a kind of detached observer. Until Tyler. Until Sara.

He didn't want to be an observer anymore. He wanted to participate in life—good or bad.

No, to turn away from a chance at happiness wouldn't help to honor Nancy's memory, it would just make him even more bitter and lonely, and that would be a disgrace to her spirit, her love, everything they'd shared together.

After talking to his friends, and now with Tyler so ill, all of Ben's worries, his fears about loving too much had been washed away. He did love too much, so much that it hurt to think of life without Tyler and Sara. If only he'd had the courage to tell Sara the truth the other night, things might be so different right now.

Now, though, he wouldn't be able to tell Sara about his revelation, about how much he wanted to make her his wife. Now he had to put Tyler first.

"Dear God, he has to be all right."

Ben didn't even realize he'd said the prayer out loud until he turned to find Betty's hand on his arm.

"Here, Ben, take some coffee. You look drained. Want me to send Warren to the cafeteria for some supper?"

"I can't eat," he told her, accepting the coffee if only to warm his cold hands. "He has to be okay, Betty. That little baby's been through so much, and…"

"Don't think about it," Betty told him. "God will see us through this, Ben."

"But what if he dies?"

Betty patted him on the back, her touch gentle and motherly. "If Tyler dies, we'll just have to accept that God needed him in Heaven more than we needed him here on earth."

Shocking himself and Betty, Ben said, "I don't know if I can accept that. I don't know anymore, Betty. Maybe this is my lesson, for being so callous, for being so smug in my advice, when I didn't really even begin to know what I was talking about. Why would God send that little boy to me, then turn around and take him away?"

Ben saw the anxiety in Betty's hazel eyes, saw the uncertainty in her expression. "I don't have an answer for that," she told him, her voice soft but firm. "But we're going to think positive, and hope we don't have to wonder why."

Ben slumped into a nearby chair, his every prayer

centered on Tyler. He was so grateful for Sara being here. Just knowing she was in there with Tyler, soothing him, talking to him, made Ben feel better.

He glanced around, amazed at the support Tyler was receiving from the church. Betty and Warren, Luke, Sadie, Emma, Maggie and Frank, and several other church members had all poured in, and now were keeping a constant vigil. Julianne and Rachel had stayed at home with the twins, Rachel's daughter, Lindsay, and Maggie's little Elizabeth Anne. Since they didn't know what Tyler had yet, Julianne and Rachel couldn't expose their unborn babies to a risk. Luckily none of the children in Julianne's class had been exposed.

Ben closed his eyes, sending up a prayer of thanks. This community always pulled together, helping each other when times were tough. He'd seen that all this year, from last Christmas, to Lent, then the beautiful Easter service last spring, to the tornadoes of this summer, and in the many festivals and celebrations, to the times they'd all gathered right here in this hospital to celebrate births and mourn deaths.

But Ben couldn't—wouldn't—mourn the death of one so young, so innocent, so treasured.

He prayed silently now, his eyes shut to the pain. When he felt a warm hand in his, Ben opened his eyes to find Sadie kneeling beside his chair, her thick sable-colored curls framing her ageless face.

"Keep praying, Reverend Ben," she said, her dark

eyes bright with assurance, her grip on his hand tightening. "We're all here."

Ben glanced around to see his friends and fellow church members joining hands to form a circle. He felt both humbled and blessed to know that these people cared about Tyler and him so much. So he stood, holding on to Sadie's sturdy, steady hand on one side, and Betty's firm grip on the other. Then he opened his heart and prayed out loud.

"Dear Lord, please help us to understand. Help us to bear the burden. Help little Tyler, God. He's an innocent, brought to us through Your grace and assurance. And he's taught all of us so much—how to love unconditionally, how to overcome our own burdens and troubles and put others' needs before our own. This baby has brought our church together and brought this ministry the support and love that You've taught us to give. Lord, I ask in Your Name, please protect, watch over, heal…my son. Amen."

Ben smelled the fragrance that always brought him joy, then opened his eyes to find Sara standing there in front of him in hospital scrubs, her hand reaching for his, her eyes bright with glistening tears.

"They just finished the spinal tap, Ben," she said, her voice so soft, so gentle, he thought maybe he was dreaming. "We should know something soon."

While they waited for the results of the test, the doctors went ahead and put Tyler on antibiotics. Almost certain it was meningitis, they didn't want to take any chances. The night dragged on and soon the group of watchers dwindled, but Ben and Sara stayed near Tyler's bedside.

Although they didn't talk much, the silence was not entirely uncomfortable to Sara. She didn't press Ben for conversation. He seemed centered on watching over Tyler, centered in prayer and meditation. Out of respect, she allowed him his silence. Out of pain and fear, she refrained from voicing her own thoughts.

But Sara refused to leave. She wanted so much to take Ben in her arms and tell him how much she truly loved him, but now was not the time. Now they could only wait and hope. And if the worst happened, she'd be right here. Ben needed to know that she wouldn't desert him even during the darkest of times, even if he couldn't share his worst fears with her. After all, wasn't that the truest measure of unconditional love?

The dawn came. Tyler had survived the night. And Sara had learned the greatest lesson of all.

"He had a cold and then he had a couple of ear infections," Sara told Maggie early the next morning. "That's why he was fussy all those times. I knew that, but I never thought about the possibility of meningitis. I should have monitored him better."

"You had no way of knowing it could turn into this," Maggie said. "Morgan told us last night that meningitis develops within twenty-four hours. So, none of us could have predicted this.''

Sara took the bag of cinnamon rolls Maggie had picked up at Swenson's Bakery, laying them on a nearby table. "But yesterday, I was so…distracted. He was fussy again, and I tried to comfort him, but then—'' She closed her eyes, remembering how still Tyler had been when she'd gone to get him ready to go home with Ben. So quiet, so still, so burning hot with fever. "I've never been so scared in all of my life. He could have died.''

Maggie took Sara's hand in her own. "Well, he didn't. And Morgan said the fever seems to be slowly going down. The first night is always the most critical, and he made it through.''

"The longest night of my life,'' Sara told her, glancing up to where Ben sat sleeping in a nearby armchair. Motioning toward him, she whispered, "He's exhausted, but he won't leave. He's paced the floor most of the night—that is, when he wasn't in there, watching over Tyler. He loves that little boy.''

"And you love both of them,'' Maggie stated, a compassionate expression crossing her face. "Why don't you tell him? He could use some good news right now.''

"I can't,'' Sara whispered, afraid Ben would wake. "Not now. Maybe not ever. We had a terrible fight the other night and I've made such a mess of things.

I've hurt him with my angry words and awful accusations.''

Thankfully Maggie didn't push her for details. "I'm sure Ben knows you didn't really mean anything bad you might have said."

"No, I didn't mean any of it. It's just so hard. I need to talk to him, but he's got enough to deal with without me handing over all my baggage, too."

Maggie wrapped a comforting arm around Sara's shoulder. "Well, at least you're still here. That shows him you care."

"I couldn't desert him and Tyler, not when I was the one responsible for Tyler's well-being. If I hadn't been so upset and miserable yesterday, I might have seen this sooner. But I was too busy wallowing in self-pity."

"Stop blaming yourself," Maggie admonished. "Stay here as long as you need to. I can pinch-hit for you back at the nursery. And Sadie's offered her help, too. She's there right now, taking in the early arrivals. Morgan's going to stop by there, to check out the babies who were exposed to whatever Tyler might have."

"I didn't even consider that," Sara said, a long sigh moving through her body. "I'm sure Betty has that well in hand, though."

"She's like a drill sergeant—and I'm sure all the other babies are just fine. Betty has always abided by the strictest of sanitary rules, anyway. And Morgan will spot anything unusual in the other children.'' She sighed, then patted Sara's hand. ''Betty will mainly want to keep the other parents from going into a panic.''

''And you'll be there to help, too.''

''Yes.'' Maggie gave her a reassuring nod. ''I kinda miss the old place, anyway.''

''Are you sure you don't mind?''

''Very. Especially since Betty told me you might have to leave town earlier than expected. This will give me a chance to polish up my rusty skills.''

Worried that Betty had broken her pledge to keep Sara's explanation confidential, Sara gave Maggie a worried look. ''I hope you understand.''

''Not really, and no, Betty didn't bother explaining the details, but since you just told me Ben and you had a disagreement, I get the distinct impression it has to do with the adorable man sleeping in that chair over there.''

''It's all so complicated,'' Sara admitted. ''But I can't leave Ben now. And I certainly won't leave until I know Tyler is going to be all right.''

''We're all praying for that,'' Maggie said, raising up out of her chair. ''Now, I'm going to work and you try to get some rest. And call us as soon as you hear anything different, good or bad.''

''I will.''

After Maggie left, Sara sat there in the silence of early morning, watching Ben as he dozed. She loved

him so very much, and this latest crisis had only reinforced that love. Sitting here now, she made a silent
pledge to God.

*Let me have one more chance, Lord. Let Ben ask
me again—to marry him. This time I'll say yes, because I can't live without him in my life. That's all I
ask—one more chance. This time I won't be too harsh
or hasty in giving my answer. This time I'll say yes.
Please, Lord.*

Silently she prayed for Tyler and Ben, asking God
to help them both. And if God saw fit to take Tyler
home, she would be here to help Ben through the pain
of losing the child they'd both come to love so much.

After all, she thought, tears of happiness and despair
streaming down her face, God had found her again
and brought her here. She couldn't leave. She didn't
want to leave. She felt that now with such assurance,
that it made all of her doubts and fears seem small
and insignificant.

Touching on the cross necklace Ben had given her,
Sara once again found comfort in the polished stone
of her worry rock. The Lord was right there with her;
He'd been there all along, in her heart. All she had to
do was reach out. She was willing to do that now.
Willing to take a risk on being a minister's wife, no
matter how hard that task might be, willing to take a
risk on helping Ben adopt Tyler, no matter the outcome.

And somehow she had to make Ben see that she

loved him, that she could help him get over Nancy, that she would try her best to be a proper wife to him. In time, maybe he would come to love her just as much. They could have a good life together, if only God would give her another chance to make it so.

"When Tyler is better," she said to herself as she dried her tears. "When Tyler is better, I'll tell Ben the truth."

With that thought in mind, she sat there, clutching her hand to her necklace, her eyes never leaving the man across the room.

Ben woke with a start, his head and heart pounding protest throughout a body that hadn't enjoyed sleeping in a cramped chair all night. Sitting straight up, he remembered why he was here.

Tyler.

Tyler was very sick.

And where were all the doctors?

Glancing around, he saw Sara curled up in a chair across the room, her hand wrapped around her cross necklace, her eyes closed in either sleep or silent prayer. The early-morning sunshine streaming in through the wide glass doors highlighted her like a spotlight.

And that glowing light shone bright and clear to Ben.

She was beautiful. Her dark red hair, tousled by a night spent in such a state, shimmered down her neck and around her shoulders like burnished copper. Her skin, so pale, so dotted with cute freckles, looked alabaster and fragile, like fine porcelain. Her hands, so dainty, so strong, held tight to the thread of her faith.

She'd stayed.

She hadn't abandoned him.

For the first time in many hours, Ben felt a new hope. Everything would be all right. Tyler would be fine. And then Ben would go to Sara and ask her to marry him again.

Only, this time, he'd make her see that he really meant it. He'd ask her because he loved her with all his heart and he wanted her in his life forever. He'd ask her because she would make a wonderful mother for Tyler, because she loved the baby as much as Ben did. He'd ask her because he no longer had a choice in the matter. Because he was in love. And he now had the courage to tell Sara that.

Lifting his sore, twisted body away from the chair, Ben swept a hand through his hair, determined to find Tyler's doctor to see how the baby was doing.

He didn't have to search long. One of the pediatricians came toward him, a tight-lipped smile plastered on his face. "Ben, we got the results back. It's viral meningitis, which, while it is serious, isn't nearly as serious as bacterial meningitis."

Ben let out a quick breath of thankfulness. "So that means he's going to be all right?"

"I think so, but we're going to have to wait and

see. The antibiotics are just a precaution, but they really can't help viral meningitis. It has to run its course. And his fever is down this morning, so we expect a complete recovery. He'll just need a few days of quiet and rest.''

"Thank you, Doctor," Ben told the other man, shaking his hand. "Can I see him now?"

"Sure. In fact, he'll need loved ones around to comfort him. He's going to feel pretty uncomfortable over the next few days. Which is why we'll want to keep him here for a while longer.''

"I understand," Ben told him. "I won't be far away.''

"Neither will I," Sara said, coming up behind Ben. "We can take turns. Want me to take the first shift?"

Ben thanked the departing doctor again, then turned to Sara. "Thank you, I'd appreciate that. But you've already been here all night. You look tired. Are you sure?''

Sara touched his arm. "I'm very sure. I can get some rest sitting by his bed, while you go home and get a shower and check in at the church. I'll be fine. Maggie brought me some breakfast earlier, and Betty called to say she'll bring us some more provisions at lunch.''

Ben took her hand, holding it between them. "Sara, I really appreciate this—I mean, after the other night—"

Sara put a finger to his lips. "We're not going to

talk about the other night. Right now, Tyler is our main concern, okay?''

He looked down at their joined hands. ''You're right. I hope the worst of it is over.''

''Now that the doctors know what it is, they can treat it accordingly,'' she told him. Then, ''Ben, I'm so sorry—I should have been more aware. I should have done more for him.''

''Hush,'' he said, unable to resist taking her in his arms. Hugging her close, he whispered, ''You have given Tyler the best, the very best care, in the world. If anyone's to blame here, it's me. I was responsible for his well-being, but I passed him around like he was a toy, letting others take care of him when I should have been there.''

''You've been a good foster father,'' Sara said, lifting away from him to gaze up at him. ''Don't ever doubt that. These things just happen sometimes. We have to hope that it's a mild case and that he'll pull through with flying colors.''

Ben nodded, then touched a hand to her cheek. ''When this is all over, we need to get a few things straight, all right?''

''All right.''

She smiled up at him, giving him renewed hope. Her eyes were a bright, shining green, expectant and sure.

Ben's heart soared. Maybe, just maybe, Sara would reconsider and marry him in spite of his shortcomings.

Maybe everything would turn out all right for them after all.

Emma came bustling through the doors then, her gaze searching out Ben. "Oh, there you are. Thank goodness I found you. How's Tyler?"

Ben told her what they'd just heard.

"Thank the Lord." Then she touched a hand to her upswept hair. "Ben, I forgot to tell you in all the excitement. Last night Jason Erickson called right before closing time, looking for you."

Ben lifted his head, then gave Emma an encouraging nod. Hoping she had her information right, he asked, "What did he say?"

Emma looked a bit confused, then replied, "He said he needed to talk with you, and I told him you were here—that you'd had to rush little Tyler to the hospital." Shrugging, she added, "It was the weirdest thing. He kept asking me what was wrong with the baby. He seemed really upset, maybe because he couldn't talk to you."

"Probably," Ben agreed, wishing he hadn't missed Jason's call. "Thanks, Emma. Did he give any indication as to where he might be?"

She shook her head. "No. He just sounded so…agitated, and then before I could talk to him any further, he hung up on me. My heart goes out to that boy."

"Mine, too," Ben replied, a new source of worrying

clouding his earlier hopes. "Maybe he'll call back. I sure hope so. If he's in trouble, he'll need us more than ever."

A couple of hours later, Ben found out just how much Jason needed help. Ben had just returned to Tyler's room, after spending a couple of hours at the church, fielding concerned phone calls and checking in with Emma to make sure she had his pager number, so if Jason did call again, he could reach Ben at the hospital.

He and Sara were standing on either side of Tyler's crib, talking quietly while Tyler slept. The fever had gone down, but Tyler was still fussy and listless, so the doctors were being cautious and watchful.

Ben was trying to convince Sara to go home and get some real sleep, when the door burst open.

Ben and Sara both looked up in surprise to find Jason Erickson and his parents standing there. The look on Jason's face shocked Ben into action.

"Jason?" Ben crossed the space between them to embrace the teen. Although skinnier and haggard-looking, Jason was as handsome as ever, his light brown hair clipped and jutting around his frowning face, his blue eyes bright with a frantic, worried light. "Thank goodness you're home."

But Jason didn't seem to even hear Ben. His eyes were centered on little Tyler. Pushing past Ben, the young man reached the small bed, then glanced across at Sara with a wild gaze. "Is he all right? Is Tyler going to be all right?"

"We think so," Sara told him, wondering why the baby's situation had affected the teenager so much.

"You have to be sure," Jason said, turning to Ben as tears streamed down his face. "Reverend Ben, you have to make sure he's going to be all right."

Clearly confused and concerned, Ben glanced at Richard and Mary Erickson. They looked drained and pale, but as stern and unyielding as ever.

"He insisted we bring him here," Richard tried to explain with a shrug and a sigh.

"What's going on?" Ben asked, his gaze moving from them back to Jason. "Jason?"

Jason whirled away from the bed, his contorted expression showing all the misery in his soul. "Please, don't let him die." Then he fell against Ben, grabbing Ben's shirt with clenched, white-knuckled fists. "Tyler belongs to Patty and me. He's my son, Reverend Ben. Tyler is my son."

Chapter Fifteen

Ben felt as if he'd been physically hit by a fist right in his midsection. Standing back, he held his hands up to Jason, taking the boy by the arms to stare down into his face. "What did you say?"

Jason sniffed back a sob, then gave Ben a wide-eyed look. "Tyler is my son. That's...that's why I had to run away. I had to take care of Patty. She was pregnant."

Richard Erickson huffed a long breath, then slowly shook his head, his expression filled with shock. "I can't believe this is happening—not to my son. Jason, did you forget everything your mother and I taught you?"

Jason whirled to glare at his father then. "No, Father, I didn't forget, and I knew you wouldn't, either. I was afraid, so I ran. I tried to do the right thing, only everything got so mixed up."

Ben looked at Sara. The same despair he felt centered like a heavy stone in his own heart, was reflected in her eyes. All of his earlier hopes now seemed as remote as what Jason had just told him.

Needing to hear the whole story, Ben motioned to the Ericksons. "Let's find somewhere to talk, somewhere private."

"We don't have anything to discuss," Richard told him, his tone stilted, his eyes blazing. "Come on, Jason. We're taking you back home to explain this."

"No, Father," Jason said, a fresh batch of tears cresting in his eyes. "I need to tell Reverend Ben everything, why I couldn't tell him before. I—I had to come home to see if Tyler was going to live. I was so afraid God was punishing him, because of my actions."

Mary rushed to her son, taking the boy in her arms. "Oh, no, no, baby. God wouldn't do that. You can't believe that. Tyler is an innocent child."

"Your son needs help," Ben told Richard Erickson, his own heart filling with such a deep pain, it hurt to take a breath. "Can't you see what he's been through?"

Erickson nodded slowly, then turned toward the door like a sleepwalker.

Ben lifted his head toward Sara.

"I'll stay with him," she said, her expression worried. "Ben?"

He pivoted at the door, one hand on Jason's arm.

"I'm so sorry. I'll pray that everything turns out all right."

"Thank you."

Ben knew what she was trying to convey. If Tyler was an Erickson, what chance would Ben have of adopting him now?

After one of the nurses had escorted them into a private conference room down the hall from the hospital nursery, Ben shut the door and turned to the three people clustered around the small table. "Let's sit down."

Mary slumped into a chair, with Jason soon following. Ben watched as she grasped her son's hand, her misty gaze reassuring Jason, even while her lips quivered.

Richard Erickson let out another sigh, his features as gray and as pale as stone. Finally he threw his expensive overcoat on a nearby chair and sat down.

Ben found a chair and settled wearily into it, his gaze fixed on Jason. "Jason, why don't you start at the beginning. Tell us everything and don't be afraid. We're not here to judge you."

Jason shot his father a look that said he wasn't so sure about that, but he swallowed back his obvious fear and started talking, his voice shaky, his movements nervous.

"Patty and I met back last year when we all went on that youth trip—remember?"

Ben nodded. So far, Emma's story had been accurate. "Why didn't you ever tell me about her?"

Ben again glanced at his father. Shrugging, he said, "At first, we were just friends. But then, the more we talked…well, Patty seemed so interested in me, and she was so sweet, so alone. We really liked each other." Gaining strength, he said, "I didn't want anyone to know about us though, especially my parents."

Richard started to speak, but Ben held up a hand. "Let him explain, Mr. Erickson."

Jason lowered his head, then placed his hands together on the table. "Patty was from another town, so we couldn't really see much of each other at first. I e-mailed her a lot. One of her friends had a computer, so she'd send me messages that way. Then I called her some, too. We started getting together—she had to sneak out and…so did I."

Richard pounded the table with a curled fist, but he kept quiet, his glaring eyes never leaving his son's face.

"I knew you wouldn't approve," Jason finally said, staring across at his father. "That's why I didn't tell anybody, not even Reverend Ben. She wasn't the kind of girl you wanted me to date."

Mary held Jason's hand again. "What kind of girl is Patty?" she asked, her words hesitant and whisper soft.

"She's poor," Jason explained. "Her mother's had a hard time, and her father beats both of them."

Mary gasped, while Richard pursed his lips and looked down at his shoes. "Well, you're right about that. While I feel for the girl's plight, we'd never allow you to become involved with someone such as this. There are much more suitable girls for you, when the time comes for that sort of thing."

His every word indicated that he didn't think this was the time. On a softer note, he added, "You're still so young, Jason. How could you let something like this happen?"

Jason appealed to his mother then. "I know what we did was wrong, but I loved her, Mother. I mean, *I* thought we were in love. But things got so complicated. I didn't know what to do."

"You slept with her!" Richard got up to stomp around the room. "Son, you know we taught you better!"

Jason jumped up, too. "Yes, Father. You taught me right from wrong, but I was confused and lonely and Patty seemed to really care about me. She listened to my dreams. She understood how lonely I was. I thought she really cared about me. I can see it was wrong, so wrong, but it was too late. She got pregnant."

"So you decided to run away together?" Ben urged Jason back down. "Why didn't you come to me?"

"I wanted to," Jason told him. "But I knew what would happen. I knew you'd want me to tell them."

He pointed toward his father. "I didn't want to disappoint *him.*"

Mary put a hand to her mouth. "Oh, Jason. Don't you know we would have helped you?"

Jason lifted his chin, his eyes on his father. "No, I didn't know that. I was so scared, so ashamed, I figured you'd be so disappointed in me, you'd probably turn me out anyway."

"*I* wouldn't have done that," Mary told him, her look defiant and tragic.

"I was ashamed and confused, Mother. So I decided to take Patty away, so we could have our baby together. I had some money from my savings account and my allowance money. I thought that would get us started. But Patty had other ideas."

"What kind of ideas?" Richard asked, whirling around to grip the back of his chair.

"She knew my family had money, so she kept insisting that I bring her back to Fairweather. But I told her we couldn't come back here. So we decided to run. She knew a few people in the city, so we headed there first. We stayed in shelters here and there, under different names, and we got help from a few homeless people. I even found some work, just to get money for food and hotel rooms, but it was hard, living that way."

Mary started sobbing, but Richard just stared down at his son, his obvious disappointment throbbing right along with the pulse in his jaw. "I can't believe—"

"I couldn't believe it, either, Father. But I tried to take care of Patty. But it just got worse. We fought constantly, and I soon realized that she didn't feel the same way about me. She didn't have any money, and she didn't have a good family life. She thought because I was rich, I could change all of that. She thought my life was perfect, compared to hers."

"A gold digger," Richard shouted, his face turning beet-red. "You let a little gold digger entice you, and now look where it's brought you."

Jason ran a hand through his hair, then shouted back at his father. "Patty wasn't like that, at least not at first. It's just that she's never had all the luxuries I've had, and she couldn't understand why we couldn't come back here and eventually get married—raise the baby here."

He raised his face toward his father again. "I couldn't make her see that I had disgraced the Erickson name, that I'd never be welcome in my own home again. So we fought all the time before the baby was born. Then after Tyler came along, it got even worse. We had to have formula for the baby, we had to keep him warm and dry. We were running out of options."

He let out a long sigh, then sniffed again. "But in the end, Patty gave up the idea of having a better life with me and she did the only thing she could do. She brought Tyler here to Reverend Ben."

Ben looked up in shock. "You mean, *you* didn't bring Tyler to us?"

"No." Jason shook his head, then looked back down at the table. "We were staying in this shelter near St. Paul. Patty had Tyler in a free clinic, but we left before they could find out our real names and track down our relatives." He slumped over the table, his head in his hands. "It was hard on the baby. Hard on all of us. I wanted to come home, to bring Tyler home, but I was so afraid and mixed-up. We found a temporary shelter and decided we'd try to find work— enough to earn the money to maybe come home.

"For a while, things were okay. We saved up some money, but one day I woke up and Patty and Tyler were gone. The shelter supervisor gave me a note from Patty that said she'd taken Tyler to a safe place and that she was going to Wisconsin to live with her sister. She'd used all of the money to get away." He turned to Ben then. "I called you a few days later, and that's when I found out you had Tyler. I can't tell you how thankful I was for that."

"I remember the call," Ben said on a quiet note. "I just wished you'd told me that Tyler was your son. I would have come and brought you home." Reaching out a hand, he touched Jason's arm. "Jason, I'm proud of you for trying to do what you thought was right, but I'm sure glad you're home and safe."

Richard sent his chair crashing against the table. "You're proud! That's typical of what I'd expect from you, Reverend Hunter. Condoning the boy for his sinning ways. Well, I'm not so proud. I'm not so proud at all.''

Jason stood up then, his own rage spilling forth. ''No, Father, you were never proud of anything I tried to do. That's why I knew I had to get away.. And all this time you've blamed everyone else for this.'' He held up a hand, tears brimming in his eyes again. ''Will you please listen to *me?*''

Richard could only nod his head, his hands still gripping his chair, his eyes blazing his indignation.

''After I found out Tyler was safe with Reverend Ben, I made a promise to God. I promised to work hard to get enough money to come home and face the consequences of my actions, just the way you and Reverend Ben have always taught me to do. I called Reverend Ben and I wanted to tell him everything, but I knew Tyler was better off with him. I also got in touch with Patty at her sister's house, and she told me she didn't want to raise Tyler, that she wasn't ready to be a mother yet. She said that she remembered me talking about Reverend Ben and how he'd forgive anybody and give them a second chance, just like Jesus did. So that's why she brought Tyler to him.''

He stared up at his father again. ''Patty did the best thing. I mean, she could have dumped Tyler on *your* doorstep, or she could have demanded money from you, but she didn't. In spite of everything, she loves Tyler, too, and she knew he'd be safe with Reverend

Ben. She's agreed to sign away her rights, and her sister is backing her on that.''

Richard threw up his hands. ''So we're forced to deal with this scandal on our own.''

Mary stood up then, her slight frame shaking. ''*This* scandal happens to involve your son and your grandson, Richard. Or have you even stopped to think about that? Tyler is an Erickson. And he is our grandchild.'' Gaining stamina, she glared at her husband. ''Can't you be thankful that Jason is home again? Can't you see past your reputation and what others might judge, to realize that God had brought our child back to us? Or do you want Jason back out there, alone and afraid, simply because *you* can't deal with the scandal?''

Shocked at his diminutive wife's outburst, Richard sank down in his chair again. ''Mary, please don't cry. What am I supposed to do about this? Would somebody please tell me?''

Jason sat back down, too. ''I'll tell you what I want, Father. I want Tyler to stay with Reverend Ben. I already know Reverend Ben wants to adopt him, and I'm willing to let him.''

Richard Erickson looked at his son, disbelief evident on his face. ''You can't be serious. Let *him* adopt *my* grandson? That's ludicrous and completely out of the question.''

Ben spoke then. ''It wasn't so ludicrous a minute ago, when you were worried about the scandal. Would you really rather put Jason and Tyler through this, than see me raising that little boy? Do you dislike me so much?''

"He doesn't care about me or Tyler," Jason interjected, pointing a finger at his father. "He just wants to control things, like he's always done."

"That will be enough!" Richard shouted, banging the table again.

"No, Father," Jason said, his voice calm now. "I don't mean to disrespect you, but it's not enough. It's never been enough. Do you know how many times I longed to play catch with you in the backyard? Do you? But Ericksons don't play catch—not dignified enough. Do you know how many times I wished you'd let me call you Dad instead of Father? But we have to be formal about everything, including our titles for each other. And you never once came to watch me play basketball, did you? No, you always had a meeting or a dinner engagement. You didn't have time to see me wasting my time, as you used to tell me. Can't you see, Father? I don't want Tyler to grow up that way. I want him to be able to play baseball or basketball, and go on field trips and...I want him to be able to call someone Dad."

He stopped, caught his breath, then shook his head. "I am responsible for my actions. I chose to be with Patty. But now I see that I made a big mistake. But Tyler shouldn't have to suffer because of that mistake. I'm not ready to accept the responsibility of being a father, but I can accept the responsibility of making sure Tyler is safe and loved. I want Reverend Ben to go ahead and adopt him.''

Lowering his head again, he said on a soft voice, ''And maybe someday, I can explain to Tyler why I had to let him go—that is, if God sees fit to let him live. That's why I had to come back. I just felt so responsible, like God was teaching me a lesson.''

Ben grabbed Jason then, pulling the boy into his arms, his own eyes burning with unshed tears. ''No, Jason. Don't think that. God isn't trying to get even with you. You made a mistake, but you've more than owned up to that mistake. Tyler won't suffer—we have to believe that. He's already better. The doctors told me that earlier this morning. We have to pray that he'll pull through and be on the mend soon.''

Jason clung to Ben's sweater. ''Are you sure?''

''I'm sure.'' Ben glanced over the boy's head to his parents. They looked old and tired, completely at a loss as to what to do next. ''Whatever we decide regarding Tyler, I want all of you to know that I love him and I want to raise him as my own. And right now, I only want him to be well again. Will you pray with me, for your son and for Tyler?''

Mary bobbed her head, then dabbed at her eyes. Lifting her gaze to her husband, she sent him a pleading look. ''Richard, please. God has been so good to our family and now, He's brought our son home and given us the gift of a grandchild, too. Please pray with us.''

Richard sat still for a moment, his expression grim, his lips set in a tight line. But finally he reached out a shaky hand to his wife. "I don't know…how to deal with this. Mary, help me. Help me, please."

Tears fell down Mary's cheeks as she took her husband's hand in hers, then turned to her son to grasp his hand on the other side. "With God's help, we'll make it through this, Richard. You know that in your heart. Jason is a good boy, and he's home now. Whatever led him to this, we now have a chance to make things better between us."

He nodded, then cast a hard glance at his son. "Jason, you've made some harsh accusations toward me here today. Son, I never realized how much I've hurt you and I'm sorry. I always did what I thought was best. I worked hard to provide for my family and I tried to raise all of my children with the proper values and in the Erickson tradition. I don't know where we went wrong, but…I am glad you're home again."

Jason bobbed his head, unable to speak. Ben took his hand as they formed a circle around the table, then he reached out a hand to Richard Erickson. "Let's pray."

Reluctantly Richard took the hand Ben offered and silently lowered his head. Then suddenly he glanced up. "Wait, Reverend."

Ben held his breath, wondering what Richard Erickson would demand now. "Yes?"

Richard's eyes filled with tears. "After we pray… could we please see our grandson?"

Ben had to swallow back his own tears. "Of course."

It was a start. Ben lifted up a prayer of thanksgiving and forgiveness…and hope.

Chapter Sixteen

"**W**ow. I never would have dreamed in a million years that Tyler belongs to Jason Erickson."

Betty Sinclair shook her head, then glanced around at the group of teachers she'd assembled for the weekly staff meeting. "The Lord sure does work in mysterious ways."

Sara took a sip of her hot tea, then nodded. "And let's hope that the Ericksons consent to this adoption. They could really make things ugly for Ben, if they put their minds to it. So far, though, they've been very cooperative. They've visited Tyler at the hospital almost every day."

Maggie leaned forward in her chair. "Ben told me they're going to counseling with Jason. That should help them get through this rough spot. Maybe Richard will finally soften up toward his son a little when he realizes the rest of us aren't going to turn away from any of them.''

Betty checked her notes, then looked up. ''No, they need us now more than ever. I think that man's realized he could lose Jason forever, if he doesn't at least make an effort to change his harsh, condemning nature. Richard is a good man, just a bit too controlling. We're just going to have to pray really hard that he's learned a thing or two about turning control over to God, and we're going to have to show him by example that we can forgive and lend our support to his family during this crisis.''

Sara spoke up again. ''Jason is adamant about Ben adopting Tyler, so I don't think there will be a problem. Ben hopes to set up some sort of visitation rights with the Ericksons, since they are the baby's grandparents. He told me about it last night at the hospital.''

''That is good news,'' Betty replied. Then getting down to business, she added, ''And we're thrilled to announce that all of our children have been checked out thoroughly—no signs of meningitis. Seems the precautionary medicine and all of our disinfecting efforts have paid off.''

Julianne breathed a sigh of relief. ''Does that mean I can come back to work now?''

''Yes.'' Betty beamed a smile toward her. ''You and your pregnancy are safe. And Tyler is on the mend. Just got a report from Sara regarding that cutie-pie.''

Sadie, who'd been asked to sit in on the meeting since she'd been substituting so much lately, laughed a throaty chuckle and gave Sara a big-eyed smile. "And what else does Miss Sara have to report?"

"That's about it," Sara told the group. "As you all know, I'll be leaving at the end of the week."

"Right before Christmas?" Sadie looked crestfallen. "You'll miss the bazaar and…you have to stay for the Christmas Eve service."

"I don't know—"

"She's being stubborn," Maggie interjected, nudging Sara with her elbow.

"I'm being practical," Sara replied, uncomfortable with this whole business. "Can we get on with the official meeting?"

"Testy today, aren't we?" But Betty took the hint and started going over the schedule.

Which gave Sara time to think about the last few days. After Jason had announced that he was Tyler's father, things had come to a standstill for Ben and Sara while they concentrated all their efforts and energy on seeing Tyler through his sickness, and helping Jason to get back in his father's good graces. Thankfully the baby had pulled through like a trooper and was now headed toward a full recovery. And Jason was home for good, coping, and visiting Tyler every day.

But where would Tyler wind up? And where did that leave Sara's relationship with Ben? He was worried; she could tell that. She'd relieved him at the hospital, taking the afternoon and early-evening shifts so he could catch up on his work. But they'd had little time for any personal conversations, what with the constant interruptions by doctors and nurses, and well-meaning, concerned friends.

Maybe that was just as well. Maybe the best thing she could do now was go, before she opened her heart up to another rejection. Ben would be just fine. He'd have Tyler.

And she'd be left with nothing, no one. She'd waited, hoping Ben would talk to her, ask her how she felt about his marriage proposal. But she'd given him an answer already, in no uncertain terms. Why should he ask her again? He had no way of knowing she'd had a change of heart, after all.

"Don't polish that shiny stone into a hollowed-out hole," Sadie told her, her dark eyes full of compassion and understanding.

Sara hadn't even realized she'd been clutching her cross necklace. Quickly dropping her hand, she said, "I've got a lot on my mind. Sorry."

"Don't apologize," Sadie said. "You're going to be okay, Miss Sara Conroy."

"You're sure about that, huh?"

"Very sure." Sadie touched a finger to Sara's necklace. "He's watching over you."

Confused, Sara asked, "God, you mean?"

"God, and Ben Hunter," Sadie replied, then chuckled. "And let me tell you something, sister, that is one mighty powerful combination."

A few days later, Sara remembered Sadie's words to her.

One mighty powerful combination.

That was so true.

Until she'd come here and met Ben and found her faith again, Sara hadn't had anything powerful in her life. Oh, she'd had her work, but it had consumed most of her energy, leaving little time for her own nourishment of the soul. And she'd had her mother, but her mother's illness had taken over that relationship. She'd had Steven, but their commitment hadn't been strong enough to survive anything more than a day-to-day existence. And throughout all of it, Sara had thought she'd been in control.

But she hadn't been. She'd only been half-alive, going through the process, doing her duty. She hadn't really been living. Until now.

No, Sara hadn't known the power or the joy of love until she'd found Ben, and Tyler, and God.

Or as Ben had told her, God had found her.

Only, now it was Christmas Eve and she'd be leaving soon. She'd agreed to spend Christmas with Maggie and her family, only because she couldn't bear to spend that special day alone in the city. With Tyler well and out of the hospital, there was really no reason for Sara to hang around after the holidays, but oh, how she dreaded leaving.

Now as she stood looking at several half-filled boxes, torn between packing them and unpacking them, she wondered if she'd have the strength to attend the Christmas Eve services a couple of hours from now. It might be the last time she'd ever see Ben or Tyler.

All week long, she'd waited, hoping Ben would come to her, talk with her. He'd said they had some things to discuss. Had he had a change of heart? Had he decided he no longer wanted her in his life?

Sara automatically headed toward the windows so she could watch the wintry dusk fall like a velvety blanket over the white woods surrounding the lake. A soft snowfall rained down on the forest, reminding Sara of glistening frozen tears. It was a beautiful, peaceful night. A silent night.

Sara stood there, listening to the silence, her heart opening to God's grace. "Help me," she whispered. "Show me what to do next."

She waited, wondering if God sent signs or announced His grand plans. But the silence continued.

And in that silence Sara thought back over her life, searching, hoping, until at last she found her answers.

At last she understood completely.

Turning back to her boxes, she set about her work.

Ben checked his watch, then turned in the car to make sure Tyler was snug in his seat. He was so glad the baby had been released from the hospital a few days ago with a clean bill of health.

And just in time to spend his first Christmas at home, with Ben.

"Hope we make it, little fellow," Ben told the baby.

In a little over an hour or so, he had to deliver the Christmas Eve sermon. Not too much time, but he'd make it if he hurried. Only, he didn't want to hurry in this. It had to be right this time.

Pulling the vehicle up close to Sara's door, Ben ran around to get Tyler, making sure the baby was well protected from the delicate snowflakes falling all around them. It was Tyler's first outing since coming home, and although the doctors had assured Ben the baby was completely well, he didn't want to take any chances.

But he had to see Sara.

Such a beautiful night. So still and silent. It was as if the whole night was waiting, waiting for the miracle of Christmas.

Ben wanted to spend this night with those he loved the most in life—Sara and Tyler.

"It's now or never, son," he told Tyler as he cuddled the baby close. Tyler gurgled and cooed his agreement.

Taking that as a sign of encouragement, Ben knocked on the door.

* * *

Sara heard the knock, and startled, dropped the bundle of clothes she'd had in her hands. When she opened the door and saw Ben standing there with Tyler in his arms, a fierce joy lifted her heart to a gentle humming.

"Come in." Touching a hand to Tyler's cap, she blinked back tears. "Oh, Ben. He looks so rested and well. I'm so glad."

"Me, too. We wanted you to be the first to see that he's healthy and happy again."

Sara took Tyler from him, hugging the baby close to enjoy the scent of baby powder mixed with Ben's distinctive spicy aftershave. "Tyler, I'm so glad you're all better."

Turning to Ben, she motioned him inside the room. "So what brings you two out to the lake? I thought you'd be getting ready for the main event."

"We came to ask you to ride to the church with us." Ben's happy expression immediately changed as he glanced around the room, the smile on his face slicing into a frown. "Have we interrupted your packing?"

Sara's gaze flew to his face. "Ben, I—"

Ben held up a hand. "Sara, before you tell me that you're leaving Fairweather, I think there are a few things we need to get straight."

"All right, but—"

"Please?" Ben interrupted with the same hand, held even higher. "I really need to talk to you."

She motioned to the couch, afraid to say anything more. "Let's sit down, then."

After getting Tyler settled between them with a rattle, she offered Ben something to drink. But he refused. The serious look on his face didn't give Sara much hope.

"What's wrong, Ben?"

"Everything," he said, his voice so soft she had to strain toward him. "I messed up big-time, Sara. But I'm here to make things right."

"Oh?" Hope was back, bright and shining.

Ben gave Tyler a lopsided smile, then looked at her, his eyes so open and honest she wanted to cry.

"I never told you about Nancy, did I?"

Sara shook her head, suddenly realizing that the secret she'd longed to hear from his own lips no longer mattered. "Everyone else did, but not you."

He nodded slowly, understanding dawning in his eyes. "And you never questioned that?"

"I felt you'd tell me when the time was right. At least that's what I hoped."

He reached across Tyler to take her hand in his. "The time is right. I loved Nancy with all my heart."

"I know," she said, dreading his next words. "I understand, Ben. Really, I do."

"I think you do," he replied, his hand squeezing hers. "But I've been so unfair to you. I loved Nancy so much, I thought I would dishonor that love if I gave in to my feelings for you."

"I know," she repeated, bracing herself for the pain of his rejection.

She didn't want to hear him say that he would never be able to love anyone else. So she decided to say what was in her heart, simply because she had reached the point of no return. She had no other choice, no other options. She was going to see this through, and she wouldn't give up without at least being honest.

Sara held his hand tight to hers, taking that final leap of faith. "But I love you anyway."

The look of surprise on Ben's face was classic. He looked both relieved and confused, and completely lost. "You do?"

"Yes, Ben. I love you. I loved you when you asked me to marry you, and that's why I turned you down."

He also looked dazed and defeated. "Okay. So you love me, but you can't marry me? Is that why you're packing to leave?"

Sara looked around at the boxes, half empty, half full, depending, she supposed, on how you looked at things. "No, that's why I'm *unpacking*. I decided just a little while ago to stay and…fight for our love. I realized that I've always given up on things too soon. I gave up on my work because the hospital insisted I needed to, I gave up on Steven because he gave up on me, and I gave up on my mother, because I got too tired to fight her disease. But I'm not going to give up on you and Tyler. I love you, Ben."

The smile on Ben's face told her everything she

needed to know. With a shaky chuckle, he said, "So…if I were to get down on my knee—" he did just that "—and present you with this ring—" he pulled out a black velvet box and opened it to reveal a small, perfectly rounded diamond. "This time you'd agree to marry me?"

Sara gasped, her hand going to her cross necklace, her eyes brimming with tears. "Yes, I would. I would agree to marry you, to love you always, to be a mother to Tyler, to be the best preacher's wife I can be. I'd agree to just about anything, as long as you'd offer to love me."

Ben reached for her hand, then placed the ring on her finger. "I'm offering, then. I love you, Sara. And I loved you the night I asked you to marry me—the first time."

"You did?"

"Yes, I did. I had to work through a lot of things in order to reach that conclusion, but in the end, my love for you won out over all my doubts and my guilt about Nancy. I was just too afraid to tell you that then."

"Oh, Ben. What took you so long?"

Tyler let out a string of gurgles then, his eyes bright with the innocence of a child as he focused on something outside, beyond the long row of windows.

They both turned to see a brightly lit star shining off the dock across the lake.

"It's our star," Ben told her, his voice low and gravelly. "From the restaurant, remember?"

"I remember," Sara replied. "It's the Christmas star. They turn it on every night at dusk."

Ben leaned over to kiss Tyler, then he kissed his future wife. "'And a little child shall lead them.'"

Sara smiled as she pulled him to her. "I'm so glad God found me and brought me to Fairweather."

Epilogue

Ben stood at the altar with Sara, both of them smiling down at the eight-month-old baby they'd officially adopted a week earlier. The week before that, they'd said their marriage vows right here in The Old First Church, in a beautiful springtime wedding, with both Reverend Olsen and Reverend Winslow officiating.

Both reverends were back today, too. Because on this Easter Sunday, Tyler was being christened. And all around him were the people who would promise to be examples in his life, to guide him, love him, cherish him in God's holy name.

That included Richard and Mary Erickson and their son, Jason. Jason was back in school now, with tutoring from Ben and several other church members to help him catch up on his grades. He'd soon be looking toward college.

The adoption had gone through without any problems or disputes. The Ericksons had visitation privileges with Tyler, and that included Jason. Ben didn't know what the future would bring, but if Jason one day decided to tell Tyler that he was his biological father, Ben would back him and trust that God would guide them through it.

Patty was back in school, too, and still living with her sister. She'd kept her promise and signed the papers without question. She told Ben that she loved Tyler enough to give him to someone who could love him and help him grow and flourish. Tyler had changed her life, and now she was working hard to make that life better, and she was encouraging her mother to seek help, too.

Ben thanked God that he now had Sara and Tyler in his life. They were a family at last and settled into a routine with Sara working part-time at the hospital and Ben getting back full-time to his own job, and Tyler being spoiled with love from all quarters. But today brought yet another blessing to their joining.

Ben listened as the christening ceremony continued. Maggie and Frank had agreed to be Ben's godparents, and the rest of the congregation now pledged to watch over the baby and teach him in the ways of Christ.

After the ministers sprinkled Tyler's head with holy water, Reverend Winslow handed Tyler over to Ben, then stood back with his own bride of one month, Alice, to admire their new grandson.

"Show him to the people," he told Ben, urging him around.

Ben grinned, then took Tyler in his arms to walk out into the congregation while Sara beamed and wiped tears from her eyes.

"Everyone, I'd like you to meet our son, Jason Tyler Erickson Hunter," Ben said, pride evident in the words.

Then he walked back to Sara, leaning over to kiss her on the cheek. Tyler, tiring of all this fuss, and eager to go back into his mother's arms, let out a yell of protest at being ignored while Mommy stared lovingly into Daddy's eyes.

As everyone laughed, Ben handed the baby to Sara, then headed to the podium to deliver the Easter sermon, his heart full, his faith overflowing.

"That's our Tyler," he told the congregation. "He's our little bundle of joy. And what better way to begin the topic of today's sermon. It's about another little boy, born a very long time ago...."

*   *   *   *   *

Dear Reader,

Being a part of this series was such a joy for me. At first it was hard bringing to life characters that someone else had created, but the more involved I became with Ben and Sara and little Tyler, the more fun I had.

I learned so much from this story and these characters. Being a Christian sometimes means that others think of us as picture-perfect, almost above reproach. But we're not. We're just humans who struggle every day with right and wrong, good and bad, grief and joy. But we know that we have someone to turn to, in the good times and the bad.

Sara learned that lesson when she saw just how much she'd been missing without God's guidance in her life, and Ben had to remember that not only was he a minister to serve God and others, but he had to also minister to himself. They both stepped out of the darkness and into the light, and together they found their joy. I hope this story brings you a little bit of lightness and joy.

Until next time, may the angels watch over you while you sleep.

Lenora Worth

WHEN LOVE
CAME TO TOWN

You shall hide them in the secret place of
Your presence, from the plots of man;
You shall keep them secretly in a pavilion....
—*Psalms* 31:20

To my niece Rhonda, with love
And…to all the Hildas of the world

Chapter One

〜

"Boys, we've got ourselves one big mess here."

Mick Love looked around at the devastation and destruction, wondering how anyone had survived the predawn tornado that had hit the small town of Jardin, Louisiana, more than twenty-four hours ago. He understood why his friend at the power company had called him and his crew to come to the rescue.

Due to a nasty storm churning in the Gulf of Mexico, a series of powerful thunderstorms had rolled through most of Louisiana, leaving enough damage to tie up the local power companies for days to come. Both the governor and the president had declared the state a disaster area, so utilities workers from Texas and Mississippi had been called in to help.

Apparently, Jardin had been one of the worst-hit spots this side of the Mississippi River. Trees were down all across the tight-knit rural community, causing power outages and damage to many homes and businesses. This particular spot had suffered some of the worst damage Mick had seen. Just two days ago, the vast acreage had been breathtakingly beautiful, an historical showplace that attracted hundreds of tourists during the spring and summer when its gardens were in full bloom.

But not today. Today, the fertile, riotous gardens looked as if they'd been trampled and smashed by a giant's foot, the tender pink- and salmon-colored azalea blooms and crushed bloodred rose petals dropped across the green grass like torn bits of old lace. Heavy magnolia branches and limbs from the live oaks, some of them hundreds of years old, lay bent and twisted, exposed, across the lush, flat lawn. And everywhere, broken blossoms and hurled bushes lay crushed and bruised amid the split, shattered oaks of Bayou le Jardin.

Bayou le Jardin. The Garden in the Bayou, as some of the locals liked to call this place. Mick glanced back up at the house that stood towering over him like something out of a period movie set. Right now, the white-columned, pink-walled stucco mansion with its wraparound galleries and green-shuttered French doors looked as if Sherman himself had marched right through it. Shutters and roof tiles dangled amid the rubble of tree limbs and broken flower blossoms. A fat brown-black tree limb had just clipped one of the dormer windows on the third floor, taking part of the roof with it.

And yet, the house had somehow survived the wrath of the storm. Mick had to wonder just what else this centuries-old house had survived.

No time for daydreaming about that now though. He had work to do. Lots of work.

"Okay, let's get this show on the road," he called, issuing orders as he pulled his yellow hard hat low on his brow, his heavy leather work gloves clutched in one hand. "This won't be easy, but we've got to get these trees off those lines and out of this yard and driveway."

Soon, his crew was hard at work, cutting and removing some of the smaller limbs. These great oaks shot up to well over forty-feet high, and some of the limbs measured wider than a man's waist. Luckily, though, only a few of the thirty or so huge oaks had suffered damage. And most of those were in the back gardens.

Deciding things were well under control here, Mick headed around the front of the huge house. He wanted to see what needed to be done with the few broken limbs along the great alley of oaks that lined the driveway up to the house from the Old River Road that followed the Mississippi River.

In the back gardens, people were buzzing around here and there. Utility workers, concerned tourists and employees of the popular bed-and-breakfast—all hurried and hustled, some of them underfoot, some of them offering to help out where they could.

But now, as Mick came around the corner and into the long, wide front yard, he looked up to see one lone figure standing a few feet away, underneath the canopy of the double row of towering oaks.

Right underneath a broken limb that was hanging by mere splinters from a massive tree.

Mick squinted, then waved a hand as he ran toward the person—who looked like a teenager, decked out in jeans and a big T-shirt, an oversized baseball cap covering his head. That cap wouldn't help if the limb fell on him.

Which is why Mick waved and shouted. "Hey, little fellow, be careful out there. Watch for those limbs—"

The wind picked up. The hanging limb moved precariously, then with a shudder began to let go of the branch to which it had clung.

Mick didn't even think. He just dived for the tiny figure in front of him, knocking the boy and himself to the wet ground as the limb crashed to the very spot where the teenager had been standing.

Winded and angry, Mick turned from the still-shaking leafy limb, tickling and teasing just inches from his feet, to the body crushed underneath his, fully prepared to tell this interloper to save himself and everyone else some grief by getting out of the way.

And looked down to find another surprise.

This was no boy. No teenager, either. The cap had

fallen off in the scuffle, only to reveal layers of long, thick red-blond hair. And incredible eyes.

Green. A pure and clean green like freshly mowed grass—and they looked every bit as angry as Mick felt. Maybe even more angry.

''I'm not a 'little fellow,''' she said in a voice that moved between southern sultry and cultured classy. ''And I'd really appreciate it if you'd get off me. Now.''

Mick rolled away as if he'd been burned by a dancing electrical wire. ''Sorry, ma'am,'' he said, his Mississippi drawl making the words sound too slow to his own ears.

Then he glanced over at her, watching as she sat up and lifted that veil of hair off her shoulders. It rippled and fell in soft strawberry blond-colored waves and curls down her back.

Regaining some of his anger, he said, ''Well, you should have enough sense not to stand underneath a broken limb like that, little fellow or not.''

Blowing red-gold bangs out of her mad green eyes, the woman got up and brushed off her bottom, then grabbed her bright purple-and-yellow LSU baseball cap, her eyes flashing like a lightning bolt. With a long sigh, she tried with little success to pull all that hair up into a haphazard ball so she could put her hat back on. Finally giving up, she let her hair drop back down her back, then plopped the hat against her leg in frustration. "I was surveying my property. And just who are you, anyway?"

Her property. Mick gave her the once-over again, then grinned. "Don't tell me you're Aunt Hilda? Hilda Dorsette?"

"Hardly," she replied in a haughty tone, still flapping her hat against her damp jeans. An expression bordering on arrogant moved across her delicately freckled face. "I'm Lorna Dorsette, her niece. And I believe I asked you first."

"So you did," he said, still grinning, his heart still beating hard after that near collision with the limb. Or maybe because of the beautiful, petite woman standing in front of him. Extending his muddy hand, he said, "Mick Love."

She ignored his hand, then glanced at his hard hat, which had landed on the ground a few feet away, her neck craned as she read the bold black lettering stamped across the front. "Love's Tree Service?"

"That's me. Claude Juneau called us yesterday. Said you had some major tree problems out here."

She relaxed a bit, then nodded. "Claude and his crew took care of the worst of the power lines, so we do have electricity now, at least. But they had too much to handle to bother with the tree limbs. He said he'd have to call in reinforcements from Mississippi."

"That'd be me," Mick said, extending his hand again in what he hoped would be forgiveness. "I'm sorry I knocked you down, Miz Dorsette."

"It's Lorna," she said, returning his handshake with a firm, no-nonsense grip. "And I appreciate your concern." Glancing over at the jumbled mass of branches and leaves behind him, she added, "I didn't realize the limb was so badly broken."

"Could have been worse," Mick replied, as they turned to head back toward the mansion. "The backyard sure is bad off. It's gonna take us a few days to get it cleared up."

Lorna nodded again. "When I heard your trucks pulling up, I threw on some clothes and came out to supervise." She stopped walking, then looked up at the house. "But the sight just made me so sick to my stomach. I had to find a quiet spot."

To compose herself, Mick reasoned. Lorna Dorsette didn't strike him as the type to burst into tears, but he reckoned from the flash of anger he'd seen in her eyes earlier, she'd gladly throw a fit or two. Yeah, she'd probably just grit her teeth and keep on going, telling everyone exactly what she thought. Even through a disaster such as this. What, besides being a glorious redhead, had made her so strong-minded? he wondered.

"I understand," he said. "These spring storms can really do some damage, and this one was a doozy. It's hard to look at, when it's your own place."

She turned back to him then, her face composed and calm, shimmering from the building early morning humidity. "Yes, but we're blessed that no one got hurt or killed—some did in other parts of the state. We've mostly got property damage. That, at least, can be repaired.''

Mick didn't miss the darkness in her eyes. Or the way she'd almost whispered that last statement. Curious, and against his better judgment, he asked, ''What exactly were you doing out there underneath those big old trees?''

Lorna put both hands on her hips, then gave him a direct look. ''Praying, Mr. Love. Just praying.''

That floored him. The intense honesty in her eyes left no room for doubt. And made Mick feel foolish. Most of the women he knew rarely prayed. This woman was as serious as the big trees shading them from the sun. And apparently, just as rooted. A provincial country girl. Quaint and pretty. And toting religion. Double trouble.

Which only made Mick, the wanderer, the unsettled bachelor, doubly intrigued.

When he didn't speak, she lifted her head a notch. ''Do you pray, Mr. Love?''

''Call me Mick,'' he said, all of a sudden too hot and uncomfortable to be reasonable. ''Does it matter if I do or don't? I'll still get the job done.''

Her smile made him edgy and immediately put him on alert. ''Yes, it matters. Aunt Hilda will have you out in the garden in a heartbeat, reciting the 'Lord's Prayer' if she finds out you don't pray.''

''Oh, I see.'' He laughed, relieved to see that she

had a sense of humor right along with her sense of piety. "So you pray to impress your aunt?"

"No, I pray to remain close to God," Lorna explained, slowly and in that voice that poured like soft rain over Mick's nerve endings. "We have a tradition here at Bayou le Jardin. We take our troubles to the garden. And there we walk and talk with God. It's based on my aunt's favorite hymn."

Okay, so he'd just stumbled on a praying, hymn-singing, petite redhead with eyes that looked like green pastures. But Mick couldn't help being cynical. "Well, that's nice, but what did God tell you to do about these broken limbs and destroyed property?"

She smiled at him then, and brought his heart hammering to his feet. "He told me He'd send you."

Floored, dazed, winded, Mick couldn't think of a snappy reply. Until he remembered he'd saved her butt from that limb. That gave him some much-needed confidence.

Glancing up at the gaping open space where the limb had once hung, he said, "And just in the nick of time, I do believe."

Lorna only smiled and stared. "That remains to be seen, but yes, I guess you did come to my rescue back there."

"And don't you forget it," he retorted, glad to be back on a human level of understanding. All this business about walking and talking with God made him jumpy.

"Oh, I won't." She marched ahead of him around the corner, her faded navy tennis shoes and frayed jeans making a nice melody of sounds as she walked.

The nice melody ended on the next beat, however, when she groaned and whirled to glare up at Mick. "Just what in blazes are your men doing to my beautiful gardens, Mr. Love?"

"Lorna's out there pitching a fit," her older sister Lacey said as she watched from the open dining room doors. "Think I should go play referee?"

Hilda Dorsette reached for her silver-etched walking cane, then slowly made her way to the French doors leading out onto the flat stone gallery. Without a word, she watched as her great-niece went nose to nose with the handsome man named Mick Love. Then she chuckled. "Good thing he's wearing that hard hat. He'll need protection from Lorna. She sets such high store in those live oaks."

Lacey shrugged, her floral sundress rippling as she moved away from the window. "He'll need more than a hard hat if he damages those gardens. I'll be right there with Lorna, fighting him."

Hilda gave Lacey a fierce stare. "The man came here to do a job, dear. The gardens are already damaged beyond repair from the storm. What more can he possibly do? He's trying to clear things up."

Lacey heard her sister's raised voice coming through loud and clear from the many open doors and windows. "But you know Lorna thinks she has to be the one in charge. She's obviously upset because his crew with all that big equipment has just about mashed what little garden we have left."

"The garden will grow again," Hilda replied. "It always does."

Lacey turned back from checking the urn of strong coffee Hilda had suggested they brew for the workers and few remaining guests. "Lorna needs to get in here and see to breakfast. They'll all be hungry."

"Rosie Lee has breakfast well under control," Hilda reminded her over her shoulder. Even as she said the words, they could hear dishes rattling in the large industrial-sized kitchen located off the main dining room. "Lacey, calm down. We're all going to make it through this."

"I'm calm," Lacey retorted, then rubbed her forehead to ward off the headache clamoring for attention. "I'm calm, Aunt Hilda."

But she knew in her heart that she wasn't calm. How could any of them be calm after surviving the intensity of that storm? No wonder Lorna was taking out her anger on the very man who'd come to help them. It was Lorna's way of dealing with the situation, of finding some sort of control over the chaos. Because they both knew only too well that, in the end, they had no control over either joy or tragedy.

When her baby sister's heated words turned from English to French, however, Lacey knew it was time to take the matter into her own hands. "I'm going out there," she told Hilda as she brushed past her. "I'll drag her in here by her hair if I have to."

Hilda stood leaning on her cane, her chuckle echoing after Lacey. "Maybe our Lorna has finally met her match."

Lacey didn't find that so amusing, but it would serve Lorna right if this Mick Love brought her down a peg or two. Lorna loved to boss people around, and she loved being the center of attention. Lacey was used to reining in her firebrand little sister, and, truth be told, she was getting mighty tired of it. How their brother Lucas could just take off and paddle away in his pirogue, heading out into the swamps and leaving Lacey to cover things, was beyond her. But then, she was the oldest and used to handling things.

"Lorna, we can hear you all the way to the river," she said now as she made her way through branches and bramble.

Lorna turned to find her big sister standing with her hands on her hips, that disapproving look on her lovely face. Lacey, looking so cool and collected in her sundress and upswept hair, only added to Lorna's aggravation. "Well, I don't care who can hear me. This man and his big machines! Look what they're doing to the garden, Lacey. *Je voudrais—*"

Mick held up a hand. "Don't start that French again. If I'm being told off, I'd like it in plain English, please."

Lorna ground her teeth and dug her sneakers in for a good fight. Deep down, she knew she was making a scene. Deep down, she realized she was still in shock from the storm and the tremendous damage it had left in its wake. Deep down, in the spot where she'd buried her most horrific memories, in a place she refused to visit, in the dark place she denied with each waking breath, her emotions boiled and threatened to spill forth like a volcano about to erupt. And the storm and Mick Love had both provoked that hidden spot, bringing some of her angst right to the surface. It didn't help that she'd purposely gone out underneath the trees to find some semblance of peace, only to be broadsided by both a limb and a handsome stranger. It didn't help that she hadn't even had her coffee yet.

She let out a long-suffering sigh, then returned to English. "I would like…" She stopped, took time to relax, find control. "I would like for the past day or so to go away. I want my trees back, I want my garden intact again."

She couldn't stand the sympathy she saw in Mick Love's deep blue eyes. So she ignored it. And the way the memory of his hands on her, his body falling across hers to protect her, kept coming back to bother her when she only wanted to take out her anger on someone. Anyone. Him.

"I can't fix your garden until we get these trees out of here," Mick told her, his hands held out palm down, his head bent as if he were trying to deal with a child.

"I understand that," Lorna said, trying to be reasonable. "But do you have to stomp and shove everything that is still intact. Look at that big truck over there. They pulled it right up on top of that camellia bush. That bush has been there for over a hundred years, Mr. Love."

"And if you let me do my job, I guarantee it will be there for a hundred more years, at least," he told her, all traces of sympathy gone now. "How can you expect us to clean this up, if we don't get right in there on top of those trees and limbs?"

"It's a reasonable request, Lorna," Lacey said from behind her, a firm grip on her shoulder. "Come inside and get something to eat."

"I'm not hungry," Lorna huffed back. Her sister, always the mother hen. "But I could use a cup of coffee."

"Then let's find you one. And you, too, Mr. Love," Lacey said, her voice so cultured and cool that Lorna wanted to throw up. Whereas Lorna pretended to be calm and in control, her sister's serene countenance was no act. Lacey had it down pat. She never wavered. She never threw fits.

Lorna tossed her scorn back in Mick Love's face, daring him to make nice. She had only just begun to make a scene.

He didn't seem willing to take that dare. Eyeing

Lorna with those arresting blue eyes, he said, "I don't think—"

"I insist," Lacey said, shooting Lorna a warning glare. "Come onto the gallery so we can talk. I want you to meet our aunt Hilda, anyway. You can explain to all of us exactly how you plan on clearing away all this debris."

"Would that calm *her* down?" he asked, glaring at Lorna.

Lorna didn't flinch, but that heated blue-velvet gaze did make a delicate shudder move down her spine.

"I think the coffee would help immensely," Lacey stated, pinching Lorna to make her behave. "And some kind of explanation would certainly put all of us at ease. This has been so traumatic—we thought surely we were going to be blown into the swamp. I think we're all still in shock."

"Obviously," Mick replied, his gaze shifting from Lorna to Lacey.

Lorna watched as Mick listened to her sister. Oh, he'd probably fall for Lacey's charms, bait and hook. Lacey did have a way of nurturing even the most savage of beasts. And Lorna had a way of sending men running. No, she didn't send them running, she just sent them away. Period.

Oh, she didn't need this right now. The bed-and-breakfast mansion was booked solid for the spring season, and the Garden Restaurant located out back was always busy. But what choice did she have? They had to get things cleared up.

Feeling contrite, Lorna turned back to Mick. "I'm sorry. I'm at a loss as to what to do next, and I took it out on you. We do appreciate your help."

Mick's expression seemed to relax then. He had a little-boy face, tanned and energetic, playful and challenging. Mischievous, as Aunt Hilda would say.

And tempting. Very tempting. Like a rich pastry, or a fine piece of ripe forbidden fruit.

"Apology accepted," he said. "And coffee would be most welcome."

"Then come on inside," Lacey told him, giving Lorna a nudge toward the gallery.

"Let me just talk to my men a minute," Mick replied. "I'll be right back."

Lorna watched as Mick instructed one of the men, his hard hat in his hand. He had thick, curly ash-brown hair, sunny in spots and as rich as tree bark in others.

"Don't break a stitch staring at him," Lacey warned.

"Don't pop a button telling me what to do," Lorna retorted.

Then she gasped in surprise. The man Mick had been talking to headed to one of the big white equipment-laden trucks they'd pulled into the backyard— the truck parked over the camellia bush.

"He's moving the truck," Lacey whispered. "Lorna, do you see?"

"I have eyes," Lorna stated, her hands on her hips, her brow lifted. Her heart picking up its tempo.

She looked from the groaning, grinding truck to Mick Love's gentle, gracious eyes. And felt as if the storm was still raging around her.

She had eyes, all right. But she could see right through Mick Love's kind gesture. Kindness always came with a price, didn't it?

And Lorna had to wonder just what Mick Love expected in return for *this* kindness.

Chapter Two

$\sim$

He had expected the strong coffee. Louisiana was famous for that. And he had expected the house to be big, cool and gracious. It had once been a plantation house and now served as an historical bed-and-breakfast vacation spot. But what Mick hadn't expected was the fierce intelligence and remarkable strength of the three women sitting out on the gallery having breakfast with him.

Nor had he expected to be extremely smitten by the very one who'd chewed him out in two different languages not an hour ago.

But then, Mick was beginning to expect the unexpected at Bayou le Jardin.

"Have your men had enough to eat, Mr. Love?"

He glanced over at Hilda Dorsette. The breakfast of French toast, biscuits, ham, grits and eggs, and fresh fruit had been more than enough. "Yes, ma'am, I think they've eaten their fill. And we sure appreciate your giving us breakfast. We cranked up in the middle of the night to get here by daylight."

"Well, we appreciate your willingness to help out," the older woman replied as she watched several of the workers going about their jobs.

Mick gave a slight nod while keeping a watchful eye on the bucket trucks. As he watched the rookie named David spike a tree so he could climb it, he added, "Claude Juneau and I go way back. I didn't mind helping him out one bit. Just sorry for the noise and clutter."

"What noise? What clutter?" The teasing light in her eyes made Mick relax, even as another chain saw cranked up and went to work on cutting up a big limb.

Mick figured the noisy wenches, stomp cutters and wood chippers would frazzle anybody's nerves. But Hilda Dorsette sat sipping her coffee as if she had heavy equipment in her fragile garden every day of the week.

Mick liked Aunt Hilda. She was plumb, petite and no-nonsense. And she was the mayor of the nearby town of Jardin—another unexpected revelation. Dressed in a bright salmon-colored casual top and a sturdy khaki flared skirt, she looked ready to take on the day. With her coiffured silver-gray hair and bright blue eyes, she was a charmer. And shrewd, too.

"I'm glad you took the time to explain the work

you're doing," she told him. "I've heard of tree services and tree surgeons, of course. We've had a local tree expert watching over our great oaks for years now. But I never knew utility companies rely on companies such as yours to help them out of tight spots."

With that statement, she finished the last of her coffee, then set the delicate china cup down on its matching saucer. "Since we seem to be in your capable hands, I'm going to leave the girls in charge while I let Tobbie drive me into the village to see what else needs to be done there. I'm sure the Mayor's Office will be hopping with activity again this morning, and my assistant Kathryn is already there waiting on me. We have to coordinate the Red Cross efforts and make sure everyone is fed and sheltered. So many people lost everything." She shook her head, then rose from the white wrought-iron chair. "I am so very thankful that Bayou le Jardin only lost trees and some of the storage buildings. It could have been much, much worse."

Mick got up as she did, helping her with her chair. "I understand, Miz Dorsette. You've got your work cut out for you."

"And so do you, son." She glanced at Lorna when she said this, then turned to give Mick a knowing look.

He didn't miss the implications. Hilda Dorsette figured he'd get the job done, if he could just convince her niece to stay out of the way.

He sat back down, hoping to do just that. Glancing

from Lacey to Lorna, he said, "So, do you two ladies have any more questions or concerns?"

Lacey smiled over at him. "I don't. I'm sure you know what you're doing. I think the best thing we can do is leave you to your work."

She got up, too, and again Mick did the gentlemanly thing by helping her with her chair. Lacey seemed a tad more centered and serene than her younger sister. Her smile was politeness itself.

"I have to walk down to the shop and make sure what little damage we received falls under the insurance policy."

"What kind of shop do you run?" Mick asked, once again amazed at the Dorsette women. Except for Lorna. He wasn't sure what she did around here, except pray and tell people off in French.

"Antiques," Lacey explained. "The Antique Garden, to be exact. You passed it when you came in through the gate. It used to be the overseer's cottage. We get a lot of business during the tourist season."

"I don't know a thing about antiques," Mick said. "I move around way too much to set up housekeeping."

He didn't miss the way Lorna's eyebrows lifted, or the little smirk of disdain on her pert face. He guessed someone as countrified and dour as Miss Lorna Dorsette didn't cotton to a traveling man too much.

"That's a shame," Lacey replied, her skirts swishing as she went about cleaning the table. "I love old things. They keep me rooted and remind me of where I came from.''

Mick didn't need anything around to remind him of where he'd come from. That's why he kept on moving. But these lovely ladies didn't need to hear that particular revelation. He sat silent, well aware that he should just get back to work and forget about trying to impress the Dorsette sisters.

Lacey bid them good morning, and that left... Lorna.

He didn't have to look at her to know she was impatiently tapping a foot underneath the round wrought-iron table. Too much caffeine, he reasoned. And he couldn't resist the grin or the sideways look. ''Uh... and what do you do? How do you stay occupied?''

Lorna tossed her long flaming hair over her shoulder, still staring daggers after her ethereal sister. ''Oh, not much,'' she stated as she waved a hand in the air. ''I guess you could say I'm the chief cook and bottle washer.''

Another surprise. ''But I thought Rosie Lee was the cook. And a mighty fine one, at that.''

Mick had first met the robust Cajun woman when the trucks had rolled up over two hours ago. Apparently, she and her equally robust husband, Tobbie, helped out around the place. While Rosie Lee had introduced Mick to Emily, their teenage daughter and Tobias, or Little Tobbie, the youngest of the six Babineaux children, Big Tobbie immediately began assisting Mick's crew in setting up. Then Rosie Lee and Emily had given everyone coffee to get them started, while Little Tobbie had badgered Mick with questions about all the big equipment.

"What's that do?" the black-haired eight-year-old had asked, pointing with a jelly-covered finger to one of the bucket trucks.

"That, my friend, lifts my men up high, so they can get to the trees," Mick had explained.

"Can I have a ride?"

"Hush up," Rosie Lee had told her youngest son. "That little imp will drive you crazy, Mr. Love."

Rosie Lee had jet-black hair which she wore in a long braid down her back, and a jolly personality, which caused her to chuckle over her words. At least *she* was cheerful and down-to-earth. Rosie Lee had given him extra French toast loaded with fresh strawberries. They had bonded instantly.

But Lorna now only gave him a sweet smile that clearly told him he was way out of his league. "Rosie Lee works for me. And she is a very good cook. She and Tobbie, and their entire family for that matter, have been working for us for more than twenty years now. But I do most of the cooking for our guests, and I run the restaurant out back. It was once the carriage house and stables." She stopped, took a sip of coffee. "We had to shut it down, though. The storm damaged part of the roof, and we've got a major leak in one of the dining rooms.''

Mick turned to squint into the trees. ''Just how many places of business do y'all have around here?''

She actually almost smiled. ''The house, the restaurant and the antique shop. Oh, and our brother Lucas has his own business on the side.''

''What side would that be?''

She shrugged, causing her hair to move like a golden waterfall at sunset back around her shoulders. ''You never know with Lucas. He does a little trapping here, a little singing and saxophone playing there, and a little crop dusting whenever someone calls him, but mostly, he does whatever he pleases, whenever the mood strikes him.''

''A trapping, singing, crop-dusting Cajun?'' Mick had to laugh. ''I'm getting a good picture of your family, Lorna. You pray and stomp. Lacey smiles and flutters. And you just explained Lucas—he likes to play. And I guess Aunt Hilda is the sensible glue that holds all of you together, huh?''

He'd been teasing, but the serious look in her eyes stopped the joke. ''Did I say something wrong?''

''No,'' she replied, shaking her head. ''You hit the nail right on the head, especially about Lacey and Lucas, and even me, I guess—although I don't always stomp around. Aunt Hilda *is* the backbone of this family, this entire town. You see, we've lived with her since we were children. After…after our parents died, she took us in.''

Mick wasn't grinning anymore. "That's tough, about your parents. I didn't mean to make fun—''

Lorna held up a dainty hand. "It's all right, really.''

But he could see that darkness in her eyes, a darkness that took them from bright green to a deep rich shade of sad. And he could also see shards of fear and doubt centered there, too, as if it wasn't really all right at all.

Wanting to say something to replace the foot he'd just extracted from his big mouth, Mick said, "Well, Hilda Dorsette seems like a good woman. And this is certainly a beautiful place.''

"Yes, to both,'' Lorna replied, drumming her fingers on the table again. "Which is why I overreacted earlier. I just hate to see any part of Bayou le Jardin destroyed, and I guess I felt helpless. So I took it all out on you and your men. But, hey, we can't change an act of God, can we.''

"No, Mother Nature doesn't discriminate.''

"And God always has His reasons, I suppose. Aunt Hilda says we should never question God.''

Mick watched as she jumped up—didn't even give him a chance to help her out of her chair. Did she resent God, then, for taking her parents? No, she'd said she prayed to Him. But…maybe even though she believed in God, she still had some harsh thoughts holed up in that pretty head of hers. And since she couldn't take everything out on God, Mick Love would probably come in handy.

He was getting the picture, all right.

And he'd have to tread lightly in order to avoid this cute little woman's wrath. Or he'd have to flirt with her to take her mind off her troubles.

Either way, his time at Bayou le Jardin surely wouldn't be boring. Not one little bit.

"We've still got a little bit of cleaning up to do in the rear gardens," Mick told Lorna hours later, as they stood beneath the remaining live oaks in the backyard. "Then tomorrow we can start on that big one by the back gallery. I'm afraid there's not much to do for that one but cut it down and break up as much of that massive stump as possible. Even your expert landscaper Mr. Hayes agrees with me there."

Lorna placed her hands on her hips, then looked over at the tree that had clipped part of the roof during the storm. The tree looked as if someone had taken its trunk and twisted it around until it had reached the breaking point. "Yes, I suppose if you did try to salvage what's left, it would only be misshapen and mainly a stump with twigs sprouting from it." She shook her head. "That tree has been there for centuries."

"I know," Mick said, taking her by the arm to guide her around broken limbs and torn roof tiles. "I've always loved trees."

Lorna glanced over at him. He was filthy dirty from stomping around in mud and bushes all day, but he still had an air of authority about him that dirt and sweat couldn't mask. He'd worked side by side with the ten or so men on his crew, issuing orders in a clear, precise way without ever raising his voice or exerting power. She certainly couldn't fault him—he'd done a good job of clearing up the debris.

But he sure could use a shower.

Glad she'd had one herself and even more glad she'd changed into a flowing denim skirt and printed cotton scoop-neck T-shirt, Lorna told herself to stop being silly. It had been a very long time since she'd taken time to dress for a man. She wasn't about to start now. But she had washed her hair, just in case.

Just in case of what?

Wanting to get her mind off Mick Love and back on business, she asked, "Is that why you became a forester, because you like trees?"

Mick shook the dust and dirt out of his tousled hair, then smiled over at her. "Yeah, I guess so. I grew up in rural Mississippi—nothing but trees and kudzu. I used to climb way up high in this great big live oak out in the woods behind our house and pretend I was Tarzan."

Lorna laughed out loud. "Did you swing through the kudzu vines and yell like Tarzan?"

He actually blushed, just a faint tinge of pink against tanned skin and dirt smudges. "Yeah, and I beat my chest, too.'' Then he demonstrated, his fist hitting his broad chest as he made a strange and rather loud call.

''Hey, boss, stop trying to impress that pretty woman and tell us it's time to call it a day, please.''

Mick and Lorna turned to find Josh Simmons, Mick's assistant and crew foreman, laughing at them from the corner of the house.

Josh stepped forward, his hard hat in his hands, a big grin on his chocolate-colored face. ''Miz Dorsette, that's the only way he knows how to attract females.''

Mick groaned. ''Yeah, and sometimes it only brings out the wrong kind.''

Lorna could understand that. Even pretending to be a savage, Mick Love made her shudder and wonder. He was definitely all male, and every bit as tempting as any Tarzan she'd ever seen at the movies. And he was as tanned and muscular as any outdoorsman she'd ever been around.

Stop it, Lorna, she told herself. Then to bring her simmering heart back under control, she asked, ''Where are you and your crew staying?''

Mick looked surprised. ''Hadn't really thought about that. Is there a hotel around here?''

Lorna scoffed, then waved a hand. ''We *are* a bed-and-breakfast, Mick. Why don't you stay here?'' And wondered immediately why she'd just invited the man to stay at her home.

''But that would be way too much trouble,'' Mick

replied, his blue eyes skimming over her face, her hair. "I don't want to be a bother."

"Nonsense," Lorna exclaimed. "Most of our guests have checked out because of the storm, anyway." Trying to hide the fact that his eyes moving over her made her feel like a delicate flower lifting to find the sun, she turned to Josh, instead. "We have several guest cottages around the bend in the lane. The storm missed them—just some minor repairs. They sleep six to a cottage, so you and your men can take the first two. They're clean and waiting, and they have bathrooms and everything you need to be comfortable. Breakfast is at the main house, and the restaurant should be open again in a day or so. We'll furnish all of your other meals there, free of charge. And if we can't open up again, don't worry. Rosie Lee and I will see to it that you're fed properly."

"We couldn't—"

"Mick, you drove for hours to come here and help us—I insist."

They stood there, staring at each other. Lorna knew she'd just issued more than an invitation for a place to stay. And so did Mick Love. At least, the expectant look in his eyes gave her that impression.

"Well, what's it gonna be, boss?" Josh said, a questioning gaze widening his face. "These fellows are dirty and hungry and about to fall asleep in their boots."

Mick looked back at the trucks, where the men sat

gathered and waiting for his next order. Then he turned back to Lorna. "Are you sure?"

"Very sure," she told him, wishing that were true. Having Mick Love underfoot day and night meant having a big complication in her life. And she didn't need any complications right now. As far as men were concerned, anyway. She'd had enough of those to last a lifetime. But then, she couldn't send the man away. Not after the hard work he'd put in cleaning up the gardens. And there was still lots of work ahead.

"It just makes sense," she said aloud, but more to convince herself than Mick. "How long do you think you'll be here?"

Mick wrinkled his nose, which made him only look more adorable. "At least a couple of days, maybe all week."

"Then it's settled. I'll have Rosie Lee get the keys and some fresh towels, and Tobbie can show you to the cottages."

"Okay," Mick said. "Thank you."

"Don't mention it. We owe you our own thanks."

After finding Rosie Lee and telling her what needed to be done, Lorna watched as Mick and his men followed Tobbie to the cottages. She could handle this. She could handle having him around for a couple of days. Soon, this mess would be cleaned up, and he'd be gone, and life would return to normal.

Then Lucas came strolling up, a lopsided grin on

his handsome face. "*Chère,* you look tired. Long day?"

Lorna nodded her head, then frowned up at him. "Yes, long day. And where have you been?"

Her brother shrugged, tipped his black curly haired head. "Never you mind. I had things to see about."

Lorna knew she wouldn't get anything more from Lucas. He was either playful or moody, depending on which way the tide was flowing.

She hurried ahead of him. "I want to survey the damage once more before dusk. Since you didn't take the time this morning to see for yourself, you can come with me or not. It doesn't matter to me."

"Little sister isn't pleased with Lucas," he said, his long fingers, touching her on her chin, trying to tickle a smile out of her.

Lorna refused to give in to her brother's charms. She was furious with him for staying away all day. Just like Lucas to slink off and hide from his responsibilities. Or maybe he just couldn't face the natural disaster that had almost destroyed his beloved Bayou le Jardin. He'd been up before any of the rest of them, and gone by sunrise.

Lucas was always full of surprises, so she wouldn't put it past him to have been off helping someone else get through the devastation of the storm, rather than face his own close brush with mortality. Lucas laughed at death, had stood out on the gallery in the wee hours, daring the storm to pass over Bayou le Jardin. And had probably been just as scared and worried as any of them. But he'd never come out and admit that, of course.

Well, this storm had rattled all of them. Lorna offered a prayer for peace and calm. She just wanted things fixed and back to normal. After everything she'd been through leading up to her return to Bayou le Jardin, she now liked "normal."

But then Lucas grabbed her by the hand, his next words really taking her by surprise. "Oh, by the way, I just ran into Mick Love. Seems like a nice enough fellow. I invited him up to the house for supper."

And that's when Lorna Dorsette realized her life might never return to normal again.

Chapter Three

〰

"I can't believe Lucas asked the man up here for supper. I was fully prepared to send something down to Mick and the rest of his crew."

Lorna flounced around in the big kitchen, worrying over the thick, dark shrimp-and-sausage gumbo she and Rosie Lee had been preparing all afternoon. After stirring the gumbo yet again, she opened the door of one of the two industrial-sized ovens to make sure her French bread was browning to perfection.

"Will you relax," Lacey told her from her spot across the kitchen. "Lucas probably heard about the ruckus between Mr. Love and you this morning, that's all. Knowing Lucas, he deliberately invited Mick here just to get on your nerves."

Lorna whirled to glare at her sister. Why did Lacey always looked so pulled together, when Lorna felt like a limp, overcooked noodle? In spite of the cool night, the spring humidity and the heat from the ovens was making her sweat like a sugar-cane farmer, while it only made her older sister glisten like a lady.

Blowing hair off her face, she said, "Well, *you're all* getting on my nerves. You with your smirks and teasing remarks, Lucas with his shenanigans—and now I've got to sit through supper with Mick Love hovering around. I just want to curl up with a good book and then sleep for twelve hours, but I've got the restaurant repairs to worry about and a million other things to keep me awake." *Never mind Mick Love,* she thought to herself.

Lacey finished putting ice in the tall goblets Rosie Lee had lined up on a serving cart, then turned to her sister. "Well, you can prove Lucas wrong, you know. He just likes to shake things up, then sit back and watch the fireworks. So, don't give him anything to watch."

Lorna lifted her chin a notch. "You might be right there. If I act like a perfect lady, using the impeccable manners Aunt Hilda instilled in all of us, then Lucas will be sorely disappointed and Mick Love will be put in his place."

"And just what is his place?" Lacey said, lifting her perfectly arched brows. "I think Lucas is right, if he did figure this out. I think Mick Love gets to you."

"Don't be a dolt," Lorna retorted. "I simply meant

that Mick Love is here to do a job, and that should be that.''

''You'd think.''

''And what's that supposed to mean?''

''If the man has no effect on you, why are you so nervous? You're jumping around like a barn cat.''

''I'm perfectly fine,'' Lorna retorted again. ''And if everyone around here would just mind their own business—''

''Have we ever?'' Lacey shot her a tranquil smile, then took the tea tray. Pushing through the swinging door from the kitchen to the formal dining room, she called over her shoulder. ''Better take a deep breath, sister. Mr. Love just walked in the back door.''

''Easy for you to say,'' Lorna mumbled, after her sister was well out of earshot. ''Nothing ever ruffles your feathers. Smooth as glass, calm as a backwater bayou. That's our Lacey.''

She'd often wondered how her sister got away with it. Lacey held it all together, no matter what. She was the oldest, had witnessed the death of their parents. Lacey had saved Lucas and Lorna from a similar fate by hiding them away, but none of them ever talked about that. Ever.

Especially Lacey. She kept it all inside, hidden beneath that calm countenance. And she'd done the same thing when she'd become a widow at an early age, and through all the other tragedies in her life since.

She'd even remained calm during the thrashing of the storm, never once moaning or whining or worrying.

Lacey had herded the few terrified guests—an older couple staying in the downstairs blue bedroom and a set of newlyweds staying in the honeymoon suite on the second floor—down into the kitchen root cellar along with the family, soothing them with soft words all the while, telling them not to worry.

Lorna had done enough of that for all of them, she supposed. But she hadn't whined aloud. She'd pleaded and prayed with God to spare her home and guests, to spare her town, from any death or destruction brought on by the wailing tornado bearing down on them.

Even now, she could hear the wind moaning, grinding around the house.... Wind that only reminded her of that other night so long ago.

"Hey, need any help here?"

Lorna pivoted so fast, she knocked a wooden spoon off the counter. She turned to find Mick standing there in clean jeans and a faded red polo shirt, a lopsided smile on his interesting, little-boy face.

He pushed still-wet hair off his forehead. "Guess I shoulda knocked."

Lorna held up a hand, willing it not to shake. "It's okay. You just startled me. I was thinking about the storm and remembering—"

He was across the spacious room in three long strides. "Are you sure you're all right?"

Anger at her brother for putting her in the position

of polite hostess, and a need to find control, brought Lorna out of her stupor. "I'm fine. It was just...so scary. I was concerned for our guests, of course. I'm not really afraid of the weather—they say the weather in Louisiana changes every thirty minutes and that does hold some truth—but this storm was different. It was so powerful, so all-consuming. And I just keep remembering—"

She just kept remembering another night, another dark, storm-tossed night long ago. A night she had buried in that secret place in her mind and soul. Was she confusing the two?

"I just can't get it out of my mind," she said, completely unaware that she'd spoken.

Until Mick took her trembling hand in his. "You survived a major catastrophe, Lorna. It's understandable that you might have some sort of post-traumatic reaction."

She had to laugh at that. Placing a hand over her mouth, she tried to stifle the giggles. Sometimes, she thought her whole life since her parents' death had been one big post-traumatic reaction.

Mick looked down at her as if she'd lost her senses. And she supposed she did look quite mad laughing at his very serious observation. "I'm sorry," she said, sobering and becoming quiet. And becoming so very aware of the man standing in front of her. He sure cleaned up nicely. And smelled like a fresh forest after a gentle rain.

To make amends for acting like an idiot, she said, "It's just been a rather long day, and I'm exhausted. We've had to cancel guest reservations for the weekend and send others away. None of us has had any rest since the storm hit, and it's only going to continue until we get this place cleaned up and open to the public again."

He guided her to a nearby high-backed chair, gently pushing her down on the thickly hewn straw bottom. "And it's understandable if you don't feel up to having company for dinner."

He rose to leave, but Lorna's hand on his arm stopped him. "No, stay." Then she jumped up, rushing past him to check on the bread. "I mean, we've set a place for you and Aunt Hilda is looking forward to talking with you. You can't leave now."

He leaned on the long wooden counter in the middle of the room, then looked at her in a way that left her senses reeling, in a way that made her think he could easily read her deepest secrets. Then he smiled again. "I guess that would be rude."

"Yes, it would. Just ignore me. I'm all right, really." Pushing at his arm, she said, "Why don't you go into the front parlor with Aunt Hilda and Lacey. I think my brother Lucas is there, too. I'll be out just as soon as I cut the bread."

"And you'll be okay?"

Lorna ignored the little spot in her heart that longed to shout for help, for someone to soothe all the pain and make her feel better. She didn't need, didn't want, pity or sympathy. And she couldn't bring herself to ask for comfort.

"I'm a big girl, Mick. I think I can manage through supper." She pointed a finger toward the swinging door. "But if you could tell Rosie Lee I'm ready to serve now..."

"Sure," Mick said, backing toward the door. "I saw her and Tobbie in the dining room. I'll get her for you."

"Thank you." Lorna watched him leave, then turned to the stove, letting out a long breath that she hadn't even realized she'd been holding.

She didn't understand why being around Mick seemed to turn her into a bubbling, blathering mess. She'd been in charge of her senses early this morning, even when he'd landed smack on top of her. Even when he'd saved her from that tree limb.

Saved her.

Lorna saw her distorted reflection in one of the wide, paned kitchen windows, and knew instantly what was the matter with her.

Mick had saved her life, or had, at least, thrown himself between her and danger. These strange, erratic stirrings deep inside her were only gut reactions to what he'd done. She felt gratitude toward him, and she didn't know how to express that gratitude.

"That's all it is," she told herself. "The man protected me from that giant oak limb.'' *And I didn't even bother to thank him.*

A voice rang as clear as a dinner bell inside her head. *And maybe...Mick Love saved you from yourself.*

It had been a long, long time since Lorna had allowed anyone else to be her protector. She'd never accepted that she needed rescuing, had never allowed anyone other than her immediate family close enough to see her fear. But because of what could have been a freak accident, because she'd been in the wrong place at the wrong time, Mick had gotten way too close.

Had he seen her fear? Was that why he seemed so solicitous of her? Was that why she felt so vulnerable around him?

''Leave it to me to do a foolish thing like stand underneath a broken limb.'' But then, she reminded herself, she always somehow managed to be in the wrong place when things turned from bad to worse.

Or maybe she'd been in the *right* place at the *right* time. Aunt Hilda always said God put people in certain circumstances to get them where they needed to be.

And Lorna had been in that place at that time, praying for something, someone to help her understand. She'd told Mick that God had answered her prayers by sending him. That much was the truth, at least. He'd come along exactly when she needed him.

That was a debt Lorna wasn't ready to accept or repay. Yet somehow, she knew she'd have to find a way to do just that.

Mick found Rosie Lee and Tobbie Babineaux busily setting up the dining room, little Tobias at their feet playing with a hand-held computer game. Mick watched as the couple laughed and worked together, side by side. He envied their easy banter and loving closeness. They were married with six children, yet the radiant smiles on their faces showed how much they enjoyed being together.

"Hello," he said as he strolled toward them, then touched a hand to Little Tobbie's arm in greeting. "You folks need any help?"

"Mr. Love," Rosie Lee said, laughing so hard her whole belly shook, "you the guest. We the workers."

Mick shrugged and laughed right along with her. He liked her strong Cajun accent. "Sorry. I'm just used to earning my keep."

Tobias immediately jumped up. "I saw you up in a tree. Don't you get scared, being way up high like that?"

"Nope," Mick replied, leaning over to ruffle the boy's shining black hair. "I'm so used to it, I don't even think about it."

Tobias's black eyes burned with questions. "I can climb way up high, too. Maybe I can be a tree man one day."

His mother groaned, then turned to her son. "You

stay out of Mr. Love's way, you hear? Don't go climbing any more trees, either. You almost got stuck the other day, remember?''

''I need me one of them buckets like Mr. Mick uses, I guess.'' Tobias grinned, then scooted away before his mother could grab him.

''I'm going out back to play,'' he called, already running out the open door.

''Don't bother Mr. Love's equipment,'' his father warned.

Mick grinned, then turned to Tobbie. ''I bet he's a handful.''

''Yep. And his older brothers just make it worse by teaching him their bad ways, too. Our house is always full of fightin' boys.''

''And a couple of quiet girls,'' his wife said with a grin and a nod.

Mick glanced around the beautiful room. ''Sure is quiet around here tonight.''

Tobbie winked at him. ''All the other guests gone and checked out. Storm got to 'em. So we gonna treat you like royalty—you and your men, that is.''

''Nah, now,'' Mick replied, holding up a hand. ''I'm just a regular joe—no prince. But I have to admit, I could get used to this. This place is amazing.''

Just like the women who run it, he thought to himself. Especially the woman now alone in the kitchen. The woman who didn't want him to see that she was still frightened as a result of the tornado.

But what else was scaring Lorna? He thought about asking Tobbie what had happened to Lorna's parents, but footsteps from the front of the house halted him.

"Hey, man, c'mon up here to the parlor," Lucas called from the wide central hallway, his cowboy boots clicking on the hardwood floors as he walked toward Mick.

"Coming," Mick said, lifting a hand to Rosie Lee and Tobbie. "Oh, Lorna's ready to serve now," he remembered to tell them.

Lucas had an accent similar to theirs, but a bit more cultured. Yet he seemed every bit as Cajun as the Babineaux, while his sisters seemed more refined and pure Southern. But then, this family was as mysterious and full of contrasts as the swamp down below the back gardens.

Maybe if he made small talk with her family, Mick would be able to get a handle on Lorna. He didn't yet understand why she brought out all his protective instincts, or why she fought so hard to hide behind that wall of control. He reckoned it had something to do with him falling headlong into her out there beneath the great oaks this morning.

Saving someone from near death did have a dramatic effect on a person. Didn't that mean he had to protect her for life now? Or was that the other way around? Did she now owe him something in return? That option was certainly worth exploring.

"How ya doing?" Lucas asked, as Mick approached him. "Want some mint iced tea or a cup of coffee? We've even got some kind of fancy mineral water—Lorna insists on keeping it for our guests."

"I'm fine," Mick replied, his gaze sweeping across the winding marble staircase. "Hey, this house is unbelievable."

"Nearly as old as the dirt it's sitting upon," Lucas replied, his grin showing a row of gleaming white teeth, his dark eyes shifting to a deep rich brown as the light hit them. "Been here for well over a hundred and fifty years, at least." He shrugged. "My sisters are the experts on the history of this old house. Me, I prefer hanging out in the swamps where the real history is found."

That statement intrigued Mick. "I bet you've seen some stuff out there."

Lucas nodded, then, with a sweeping gesture, announced Mick to his aunt and sister. "Mr. Mick Love, ladies." Then he turned back to Mick. "The swamp holds all of her secrets close, but I've seen a few of her treasures and a few of her dangers, yeah."

Mick thought that best described Lucas's sister, too. Lorna obviously held her secrets close. But Mick had seen something deep and dark and mysterious there in her green eyes. Something he wanted to explore and expose, bring out into the open. Which might prove to be dangerous, too. He worked too many long hours to even think about getting involved with a redheaded woman.

Glancing around the long parlor, he was once again assaulted by the opulence and old-world elegance of Bayou le Jardin. His gaze swept the fireplace, then settled on a small portrait of a dark-haired man and a beautiful woman with strawberry-blond hair, centered over the mantel.

"Our parents," Lucas told him in a low voice, his black eyes as unreadable as a moonless night. "They died when we were children."

Mick wanted to ask Lucas what had happened, but on seeing the look on the other man's face he decided that might not be such a good idea. Mick had lots of questions, for lots of reasons he couldn't even begin to understand or explain.

Right now, though, he had to remember his manners and make polite conversation with the Dorsette bunch. And wonder all the while why he was so attracted to Lorna.

"That was one of the best meals I've had in a very long time," Mick told Lorna later, as they all sat around the long mahogany dining table. "I don't get much home cooking."

"Oh, and why is that?" Aunt Hilda asked. She sat, stirring rich cream into her coffee, a bowl of bread pudding on her dessert plate. "And while we're talking, where did you grow up? Who's your family?"

Mick glanced around the table. Everything about Bayou le Jardin was elegant and cultured, down to the silverware and lace-edged linen napkins. And he was sure the lineage went back centuries, too. Aunt Hilda's question was typical of blue-blooded rich people. They didn't really care about you; they just wanted to make sure you came from good Southern stock. He didn't begrudge her the question, but he did find it pointed and obvious, and amusing. She wanted to know if she could trust him, count on him to do what was right.

Did he really want to tell these people that he'd grown up in a trailer park deep in the Mississippi Delta with an abusive father? Or should he just tell them that after his old man had drunk himself to death, his mother had changed from a weak, submissive wife into a strong, determined woman who wanted the best for her only son? Should he tell them she'd worked two jobs just to make sure Mick finished school and learned a trade? Or that she had died from a heart attack before she could enjoy his success? Should he tell them that he had no one to go home to, now that she was dead? And that the woman he'd planned on marrying had dumped him for someone else? That he'd left the Delta and had never looked back?

Mick looked at Lorna, saw the questioning lift of her arched brows, and knew he wasn't nearly good enough to be sitting at this table. So he simply said, "I was born and raised in Mississippi, and I still have a home there right outside of Vicksburg—that is, when I can ever get back to it."

"So you travel around a lot." This statement came from Lorna. She'd obviously already summed him up.

Mick glanced over at her without bothering to defend himself. She sat there, bathed in golden light from the multifaceted chandelier hanging over the table, her hands in her lap, her hair falling in ringlets of satin fire around her face and down her back. She was beautiful in a different kind of way. Not classic, but fiery and defiant. Mick couldn't explain it, but he could certainly see that beauty. And feel it. It washed over him like a golden rain, leaving him unsteady and unsure.

Wanting to give her a good answer, he went for the truth this time. "Yeah, we stay on the road a lot. We travel all over the state, and on rare occasions, such as this, we travel out of state. Do a lot of work in Alabama and Georgia, too. I reckon you could say we go wherever the work takes us."

"You probably keep steady," Lucas said, before taking a long swig of his tea. "There's always trees around."

"If you have your way, that is," Lacey interjected. "Lucas is a naturalist—the protector of the bayou." She grinned, but Mick didn't miss the pride in her eyes.

"Among my many other talents," Lucas said, his dark eyes twinkling with merriment.

"Yes, and if we could just pinpoint what exactly you *are* good at and make you stick with it, we might all be able to retire with a nice nest egg,'' Lorna stated, her attention now on her brother.

Lucas pumped up his chest. "Now, suga', you know I'm good at whatever I set my mind to.''

His sisters and aunt all laughed, then shook their heads. Soon, they were all talking at once, each giving pointed suggestions as to what Lucas needed to do with his sorry life.

Mick was just glad the conversation had switched away from him. Even if Lorna's gaze did drift back to him now and again.

Then Lucas made an intriguing remark. "Well, sister, you're a fine one to ask Mr. Love about traveling.'' He grinned toward Mick. "Lorna took off a few years back, traveled all over the world, settled in Paris for a while.''

"I went to cooking school,'' Lorna snapped as she stared hard at her brother.

"And now she runs a French restaurant out back and cooks good old Cajun, Creole and American food for the houseguests,'' Lacey explained with pride.

"She's a bona fide chef,'' Lucas replied with a wink.

Mick raised his tea goblet toward her in a salute. So she wasn't just a country bumpkin, all tucked away here on the bayou. He wondered why he'd even thought that. Lorna was as sophisticated as any French woman, and she could definitely speak the language—

very colorfully. Lifting his glass high, he said, "And I thought all the great chefs were men."

"No, men just like to believe that," she replied, her expression smug.

Mick decided there was probably much more to her travels, but he didn't press for the details. Yet.

When they'd finished their dessert, Lorna, Lacey and Lucas all helped with the dishes, while Aunt Hilda went up to bed on the third floor where their living quarters were located. Rosie Lee and Tobbie had eaten in the kitchen with Emily and Tobias. Emily also worked at Bayou le Jardin, but now they all chipped in to get the work done. Mick was amazed at the sense of family here, and the way the Dorsettes seemed to think of the Babineaux family as part of their own, even down to Little Tobbie running and playing throughout the vast mansion.

He'd never had that. He'd always been an outsider.

And soon, he'd be gone from Bayou le Jardin. Gone from the mystery and secrets of the swamp. Gone from the scent of azalea blossoms and wisteria sprigs on the night wind. Gone from the green-velvet gaze of a red-haired woman with a heart full of fire and a soul full of secrets.

Mick liked traveling around, liked being on the road. Liked running, always running from his past. But tonight, tonight, he felt a stirring that was as unfamiliar to him as crystal goblets and crisp linen napkins, as unfamiliar to him as polished wood and freshly cut flowers.

For the first time since he'd left that trailer park, Mick Love wanted to stay right where he was. Just for a little while.

Just long enough to find out all the secrets Lorna Dorsette kept hidden so well behind all that feminine fire.

He waited until everyone else had bid him good-night, then he turned to Lorna. They stood on the back gallery, where the moonlight played hide-and-seek with the Spanish moss in the great oaks, where the wisteria blossoms entwined around the stout gallery columns, showering them with delicate purple rain every time the wind lifted.

He didn't want to be away from her just yet.

"Show me the river," he said, reaching out a hand to her as he stepped out into the shadows of the damaged garden.

He watched as moonbeams hit her face, watched as tiny violet-colored wisteria flowers caught and held to her long hair. And again, he saw that distant, disturbing fear in her eyes.

But she took his hand and followed him.

Chapter Four

The big trees cast mushroom-shaped shadows in the moonlight. Lorna walked with Mick through the long front gardens, following the path she'd taken so many times over the years. The dirt and gravel lane was now littered with broken branches and split tree limbs. Thank goodness the storm hadn't taken any of the ancient oak trees completely down. With Mick's help, and their own landscaper, they should be able to re-shape those that had been damaged.

Lorna shuddered in spite of the mild spring night. She should have gone in to get her flashlight. Or better yet, she should have stayed inside tidying up the kitchen, making sure everything was set for breakfast. But then, she reminded herself, all the guests had checked out due to the storm, and she was turning away any reservations until things were back in tip-top shape. It was going to be a long week.

"You okay?" Mick asked. His words echoed over the silent countryside.

Lorna wouldn't tell him that she never came out here at night. That she never walked around the grounds alone at night, or that she always, always carried her powerful flashlight, even when someone was with her.

She took a deep breath. "Fine. Just tired. We're almost there."

The river was across the narrow country road, behind a dirt-and-grass levee that cows grazed on now and then. At this time of year, red clover bloomed profusely along the levee. Lorna could see the clover dancing in the moonlight. It looked like a flowing red scarf winding around the river.

Not wanting Mick to see her apprehension, she held tightly to his hand as he guided her over the cluttered pathway. She managed to let him go long enough to open the black wrought-iron gate that kept uninvited curiosity seekers away from the secluded mansion.

"Looks like the storm clouds are all gone," Mick said, as their footfalls sounded on the paved road.

"Yes, but the levee will be muddy still. So watch your step."

With a spurt of determination, Lorna pushed up the soft loam of the levee to distance herself from Mick, then stood on the crest to stare down at the black, swirling waters of the Mississippi River. "Maybe the spring rains will hold off for a while now. The river is just about overflowing as it is.''

Lorna had never realized how beautiful the river was at night. The soft gurgling sound of the tide sang a timeless song, while the buzz of mosquitoes hummed in perfect harmony. She could see fireflies lifting all around them, their flickering iridescent greenish glows like tiny lanterns in the dark.

Which only reminded her that she did not have her own lantern. But she held the panic at bay, determined not to show Mick her humiliating weakness.

Instead, she watched gladly as he trudged up the small incline, right behind her. He stood there a minute with his hands on his hips, then lifted his head to the sky. His silhouette was highlighted by grayish-blue moonlight, casting him in a dreamlike state.

Maybe she was dreaming. She still couldn't understand why she'd taken Mick's hand and allowed him to guide her out into the darkness. She'd only met this man early this morning, under the strangest circumstances, and now she'd walked through the moonlight with him. It had been a while since she'd been alone with a man. And she'd never brought anyone other than family out here to the river—and even then only in broad daylight. Usually their guests wandered around on their own, leaving Lorna to do her work.

What's wrong with me? she wondered now as she watched Mick through the veil of moonlight and shadows.

Her emotions were raw from the storm, her nerves were like stretched, tangled wires curling tightly through her body, and yet, for some obscure reason, she almost felt safe with Mick Love.

Even in the dark.

"Listen to the water," he said, his head down. "All that undercurrent, all that power. I've always been fascinated by nature."

"Is that why you decided to become a tree expert?"

"Probably. As I told you earlier, I loved getting lost in the woods when I was a child. There wasn't much else to do around the house, so I'd take off for hours on end, just roaming around, exploring, playing make-believe."

Lorna could understand that. "When we first came here, I did the same thing. Lacey and I would wander around the house, pretending we were princesses lost in a castle. When I saw this house and the land surrounding it, I thought I'd found a secret garden. It looked like something out of a fairy tale."

Mick turned then, to look back at the big house looming in the distance. "It's a beautiful spot."

"A safe haven," she replied without thinking.

The image of the great house glowing with yellow lights beckoned her, reminding her that she *was* safe here. It was an image that caused motorists to slow down and stop, inspired artists to keep painting, enticed photographers to take one more picture. From the narrow road, the house came into view around a winding curve, always catching admirers by surprise.

Lorna still slowed down herself to glance over at the panoramic view of the square, pink-walled house with the massive white columns sitting back behind the oak-lined driveway. And it still took her breath away.

"It's home," she said, a great well of love and gratitude pooling in her heart and bringing tears to her eyes. Once again, she thanked God that her home and family had been spared from the worst of the storm.

"How old were you when..." Mick paused, glanced down at the ground.

"When my parents were—when they died?" She had to close her eyes a minute. She still couldn't bring herself to say the word *murdered.* "I was six."

He turned to her, coming much too close. "That must have been tough."

"It was hard." She nodded, wrapped her arms across her midsection to hold off the night chill—and his nearness. Then she glanced back at the house, suddenly very sure that she needed to be back inside, near the warmth of her family, near the lights. "We'd better get back." She hoped he didn't hear the panic in her words.

Mick's expression wasn't hard to read, even in the grayish night. Confusion, coupled with concern. She'd certainly seen that look before.

"We just got here," he said through a flash of a

smile. "But...I can't really see much of the view in the dark, anyway." He leaned closer still. "Except your pretty green eyes, of course."

The flirtation brought Lorna out of her panic. "Did you bring me out here to the river to tell me that?"

He tipped his head to one side, sighed long and hard. "Actually, I don't know why I brought you out here. It was just such a beautiful night, and I felt like going for a walk. I like to walk."

"Me, too, but not at night."

Confusion again—but thankfully, he didn't ask for an explanation.

"And obviously not with someone you barely know."

"I'm fine with that—with you, I mean. Just...don't try anything."

He must have sensed her apprehension, but he didn't comment for a minute or so. He simply stood there, staring down at her. Then he said, "We can go back if you feel uncomfortable with me."

Lorna did feel uncomfortable with him, simply because he made her feel close to being...comfortable. That was almost as unnerving as being out here in the darkness. She was torn between the urge to enjoy the safety of his nearness and the urge to ignore that feeling and run toward home. But she couldn't explain that to him. So she tried to make excuses.

"I'm sorry. I'm so tired, and I've got to get up early

to talk to the insurance adjusters and contractors about the restaurant repairs.''

''Sure.'' He reached out to take her hand, tugging her arms away from her body. ''I'm sorry, too. I wasn't thinking, dragging you out here.'' Then he pointed toward the house. ''Which room is yours?''

Surprised, Lorna stood silent for a minute. Then she told him. ''It's on our far left, on the rear side of the house near where the tree clipped the roof. I have a view of the entire back gardens and the restaurant.''

''Do you ever come out on the gallery, to look at the stars?''

Such odd questions. ''Sometimes,'' she responded. *Sometimes, when I get up the courage.*

''Maybe I'll see you up there one night, then.'' He pulled her down the damp levee. ''Thanks for the walk. I needed it after that meal.''

''It was nice to just relax a bit,'' she responded, knowing that she wasn't at all relaxed. ''You and your men missed the worst of it—yesterday morning was total chaos. People wandering around, looking for pets, checking on relatives, digging through rubble for what was left of their homes. After we'd assessed the damage here and made sure all our guests were safe, we all went into town to help out there. It's going to take a while to get things cleaned up, but thankfully no one was killed.''

She didn't mention that she'd always remember the roaring rage of the tornado. She'd always remember the agony of being in total darkness while monstrous winds and pelting rains assaulted her home. She couldn't tell him that Lacey had held her hand, that Lucas had touched his fingers to her face there in the pantry, as they'd all three surrounded Aunt Hilda like a protective shield. She couldn't tell him that her worst memories had been trapped inside the silent scream that echoed in her mind over the roar of the storm.

They were alive; they had survived. She had to be thankful that her family had been spared. She had to calm the scream down again and regain control.

This innate fear she had tried so long to bury, this fear that the storm had brought hurtling back to the surface, was clouding her judgment. That had to be why she didn't want to let Mick out of her sight.

"Well, I'll do my part to help y'all out, I promise," Mick said, as they strolled back up the drive toward the house. "We can take a couple of extra days—the men won't mind one bit."

"Thank you," Lorna said, meaning it. She stopped just as they reached the back of the house. A beckoning light glowed from the wide foyer, but she held off a bit longer. "Mick, I didn't thank you—for saving me from that tree limb this morning."

"No thanks needed."

Lorna looked out at the back driveway, where the big trucks and heavy equipment had been neatly parked in a long row. Mick was organized to a fault; she'd give him that.

"Yes, I do need to thank you. It was rude of me not to, and even more rude of me to fuss at you and your men. I was just overreacting to the storm, I think."

"I understand," he said. "You don't have to explain."

"You probably get a lot of that, right?" Which was why he was being so gentlemanly and concerned, showing her extra attention, she reasoned.

He grinned, his white teeth gleaming like polished ivory in the moonlight. "Yeah, but never in French. I declare, I think I liked it."

"Oh, you haven't heard my best—I know a few choice phrases of Cajun French, too. Lucas taught me."

"About Lucas—he does seem a lot more Cajun than the rest of you. Why's that?"

Lorna shrugged. "When we first came here, Lucas was nine years old. For some reason, he immediately bonded with the Babineaux family. Since then, he's spent more time with them than he has with the rest of us. He's picked up their ways, which I guess is natural. Our father was Cajun and our mother was French-Irish. Lucas looks just like our father, and Lacey and I resemble our mother."

"Your mother must have been beautiful, then."

Lorna's heart lifted like the delicate wisteria vine on a nearby railing, taken by an unexpected wind. "She was very pretty, as you probably could tell if you saw the portrait over the fireplace in the parlor. Lacey looks more like her than I do. And acts just like her, too.''

"You and Lacey are both attractive women."

"How kind of you to say that."

She wanted to ask him which he found more attractive, but stubborn pride made her keep the burning question to herself. It didn't matter anyway, did it? Anyone could look at Lacey and see a pure lady. While it was obvious Lorna was a hopeless cause—half tomboy, half wild child.

"I wasn't being kind. You are a pretty woman, Lorna."

He stood there again, silent and staring. The man certainly didn't mind taking in his fill. Lorna tried not to fidget, but she wasn't used to this kind of attention from a good-looking stranger.

"Thank you," she managed to say, remembering how Aunt Hilda had taught her to accept a compliment with graciousness, not excuses and self-incriminating remarks. Yet Lorna found herself wanting to correct Mick. He didn't know her—couldn't understand that she doubted his sincerity.

He must have sensed her discomfort, though—yet again.

"Well, thanks for the tour. Good night, Lorna."

He turned to walk down the path leading to the cottages, his sturdy boots pushing at more broken branches.

"Good night. See you in the morning."

He waved, then headed off into the darkness.

Lorna watched him disappear from sight, then hurried inside to the welcoming light.

Mick went into the tiny cottage bedroom he was sharing with Josh Simmons and one of the other workers, the rookie named David. The kid was already sacked out in one of the small beds, his snores of contentment echoing through the cozy sitting room where Josh was relaxing in front of the small television, listening to the evening news on low.

Josh grinned then held a finger to his lips as Mick came into the room. "Boss, you wore that boy slap out."

"He'll get used to it," Mick said, settling down in one of the dainty armchairs to smile at his friend. "But he'll sure be sore come morning."

Josh rubbed his own neck. "Yep, I'm aching myself. But we put in a good day's work."

"With more to come tomorrow," Mick replied. "Did y'all get enough to eat?"

Josh moaned, then patted his flat belly. "Way too much. That Lorna and Rosie Lee, they can sure put on a spread. We ate out on one of the picnic tables— it was turned over from the storm, but we set it right."

Mick could just see Josh issuing directions. "It was nice of them to give us supper."

Josh grinned again. "And how was it up at the big house?"

Mick knew that teasing look. Josh was a real ladies' man himself, so he liked to watch when one of the other fellows got involved in a relationship. Mick needed to set his well-meaning friend straight, though.

"The food was great, the conversation sparkling in spite of all the talk about the storm. What else can I say?"

"And how was Miss Lorna Dorsette?"

Mick gave up. He couldn't lie to his friend. He rubbed a hand down the beard stubble covering his face. "She was just fine. We went for a nice walk by the river, but she did seem a bit skittish."

"Whoa, you're moving right along on this one," Josh said, throwing an embroidered sofa pillow at his boss. "No wonder the woman is skittish—she's having a really strange week, and now you come along."

Mick attempted to keep a straight face. "Hold on, now. I'm just being nice to a lady. We both know we don't get much of a chance to be around ladies in our line of work."

"No, more like old married women who want to boss us around and blame us for their dead trees and equally dead marriages."

"You sound bitter, my friend."

"Just smart. Single women don't seem to need trees cut down or stumps removed, know what I mean? They're out having fun, without us."

"Poor thing," Mick replied, throwing the pillow back at Josh. "You know, marriage and settling down aren't such bad things."

Josh raised a dark eyebrow. "Yeah, I know that—but this coming from a man who's said time and time again he'd never get hitched? Did a tree limb fall on your head, boss, or did saving the lovely Miss Lorna make you change your tune?"

"Maybe both," Mick admitted, grinning sheepishly. "No, I just mean that we're both put off about marriage because we've seen the bad side of things. My dad and his drinking, my breakup with Melinda. You and your brothers and sisters being moved from pillar to post—"

"'Cause my momma couldn't provide for us on her own," Josh finished. "Yeah, man, and we need to remember where we come from. And we need to keep the faith, as my dear momma would say." He waved a hand in the air. "This place is like something out of *Lifestyles of the Rich and Famous*. Not for the likes of you and me."

"Yeah, you're probably right, there," Mick replied. "I'm going to bed."

Josh got up, too. "Hey, man, I didn't mean to tell you what to do. Lorna is sure pretty, and we all could tell the sparks were flying out there between you two. I'd just hate to see you get in over your head."

"I get you," Mick said, nodding. "I'm just trying to help her—all of them—through a rough time. They seem like good people." He turned at the open door to the other small bedroom off the sitting room. "That's why I've been thinking I might stay on here a couple of extra days—send you and the men back to Vicksburg once we've cleared up the worst of it."

Josh's eyes opened wide. "Am I hearing right? Mick Love wants to stay in one spot longer than a day or two?" Then he raised a finger toward his friend. "Man, you got it bad. Go on now, admit it. You want to hang around here, and it ain't got nothin' to do with landscaping or clearing trees."

Mick let out a groan. "Okay, but if I promise to be a good boy and mind my manners, will you let me have some much-needed comp time?"

Josh nodded his head. "Boss, you can have all the comp time you want. You deserve a vacation—never knew you to even take one. Just be careful."

"I intend to," Mick answered. "Just doing my good deed for the week, Josh."

"Yeah, right." Josh brushed past him, still grinning. "I'm turning in. Hey, don't forget to say your prayers."

The lighthearted comment was just another reminder of Josh's firm faith. Even though he'd grown up in a large, poor family, his mother had always managed to get all her children to church each Sunday. Sometimes Mick thought Josh's gentle nudging was the only thing that kept him attending off and on through the years. Josh had enough faith for the both of them.

"I'll be there in a minute," Mick told him. "And I want the left bunk, okay?"

"Why, so you can stare out the window at that mansion up on the hill?"

Mick chuckled. "Yeah, something like that."

About a half-hour later, Mick was stretched out on the crisp white sheets of the old-fashioned brass bed, the window by his left side open to the fragrant night air.

And open to Lorna's bedroom directly across the garden and way up high on the third floor.

He lay there, staring up at that lighted window, wondering why Lorna Dorsette had gotten to him when so many other women had never been able to get near. Not even the woman he'd pledged to marry once, long ago.

Maybe it had been Lorna's green eyes, surprised and luminous, staring up at him when he'd pulled her away from that falling limb out in the garden. Or maybe it had been all that long red-blond hair toppling out of that ridiculous baseball cap. Or maybe it was just a physical attraction, plain and simple.

But no, there was something more, something he sensed there in the depths of her eyes. At times, she seemed almost like a little girl, her eyes full of fear. She tried hard to hide it behind all that polished control, but it was there.

And it made Mick want to get to know her, to protect her, to touch her. And not just physically. He wanted to see inside her, touch her heart.

"I'm getting downright sappy," he whispered to the darkness.

He thought about the long day—thought about Lorna and her family, devout in their faith, loyal in their sense of family and community. Those were things he'd never had, had tried to avoid all his adult life. Things that he didn't think he was anywhere near worthy enough to receive.

Now he found himself turning toward that single glowing light, wondering what it would be like to have faith in something, someone. Wondering what it would be like to be part of a big, loving family. That light beckoned him, called to him, as it flowed out into the night from atop a mansion Mick had no business dreaming about.

From the bedroom of a woman he surely had no business thinking about.

And yet, he did.

Sometime before dawn, he awoke and turned to look up through the trees, searching for Lorna's room there in the darkness.

He was surprised to see that her bedroom light was still on. Over the coming days, he'd discover that the light stayed on all through the night, always.

Chapter Five

Lorna stood surveying the damaged roof of the Garden Restaurant. The noise of beams being ripped from the ceiling only accented the memories being ripped from her heart.

Her three years of being back here at Bayou le Jardin had been filled with good memories. Peaceful memories. Quiet memories. She wanted to get that back. She didn't want the bad memories to take over again.

Turning to Lacey, she let out a long sigh. "I can't let this storm interrupt my life any longer. I sure hope the contractors can get this repaired in a couple of days."

Lacey placed a hand on her sister's arm. "Lorna, relax. They're working on the roof, and the rest of the damage is not that bad. Didn't they tell you they'd work 'round the clock to fix it?"

"Yes, they did. But I'm losing business and money. Not to mention having to deal with the insurance people."

Lacey nodded her understanding. "Why don't you leave this to the workers and come into town with me. We're taking sandwiches to help out the Red Cross."

"I know that," Lorna snapped, irritation at her sister making her harsh. "I helped fix the sandwiches early this morning."

"Then why don't you stop thinking about yourself and come with us to help the other people—the ones who don't even have a house to go back to?"

Lorna looked at her sister, then realized she was being a bit selfish. "Listen to me—whining as if I'm the only person in the world who's been affected by the tornado. Okay, I'll go with you. I guess this little problem *is* minor compared to what others have been going through."

"Precisely," Lacey agreed. "I know you're worried, Lorna. But we'll be okay."

"How's Aunt Hilda holding up?" Lorna asked, forcing herself to turn away from the construction work, only to be assaulted by the grind of chain saws and wood-mulching machines on the other side of the garden. "She seemed tired last night."

"She's exhausted," Lacey replied, as they headed back toward the mansion. "But she insists she has to be right there in the thick of the cleanup operations."

"The way I feel I need to be right here with my restaurant?"

Lacey grinned, lifting her voice over the roar of machinery. "Yes. I guess we are a stubborn, pushy lot, huh?"

"Don't I know it." Lorna glanced around as workers in hard hats moved hurriedly here and there. She automatically searched for Mick, then chided herself for doing so.

She hadn't seen him at breakfast, which had been almost a relief after last night. She hadn't slept very well, knowing he was down there in the cottage, knowing that he now knew where her bedroom was, that he hoped she'd come out onto the tiny alcove balcony like some lovesick teenager and pine for him. Or maybe the man was just flirting. Who knew?

"Mr. Love and his crew were up at dawn," Lacey said as she watched Lorna's face. "Surprising, since you and he went for such a long walk last night." Lifting a slanted brow, she added, "And...he must have really made an impression. You forgot your flashlight."

"The moon was full," Lorna retorted, not ready to explore her feelings for Mick with her overbearing sister. "I stayed close to Mick and everything was fine."

"Really?" Lacey looked doubtful. And concerned.

"Really," Lorna replied. "It's silly and hard to explain, but I felt...safe with Mick."

"That's not silly," Lacey said, her words soft with wonder, her eyes going tender. "That's amazing."

"Don't go reading anything into it." Lorna decided to change the subject. Nodding as one of the workers tipped his hard hat to them, she said, "They've certainly been working to get this place cleaned up."

Lacey took the hint, then bobbed her head. "See, they've managed to get the worst of the trees cleared away. And you'll be happy to know that most of the broken limbs will be recycled into mulch or, possibly used for firewood next winter. Nothing is going to waste around here."

Amid the noise of saws, grinders and shouting men, Lorna asked, "And what about the gardens? Has Lucas had a chance to talk to Justin yet?"

Justin Hayes was a very capable landscaper, if not a bit too possessive about the gardens. He watched everything from tender plants to the oldest trees with an eagle's eye. And he especially liked to keep an eye on Lacey. Which her stuck-up sister tended to ignore.

Justin wouldn't like having someone else messing with his landscaping. But Lucas knew how to handle Justin. They'd been fast friends since fourth grade.

"He's supposed to be talking with Justin right now, deciding what can be salvaged and what has to be pulled out," Lacey said.

Before they could continue the conversation, Mick walked around the white, octagon-shaped summerhouse in the back garden near the restaurant's entrance. "Morning, ladies."

Lacey sent Lorna a quizzical look, then turned to greet Mick. "Hello, Mr. Love. Did you and your men get breakfast yet?"

"Yes, ma'am," Mick said, his eyes coming to rest on Lorna's face. "Rosie Lee passed out biscuits and ham and lots of that strong coffee you folks seem to like."

"We can make it less strong—that is, if you can't handle it," Lorna said, a teasing smile creasing her face.

She felt much better seeing Mick in the light of day. It proved that he was just a man, after all, and not some sort of mystic hero she'd dreamed up in the dark last night, come to protect her.

"I like it strong," Mick replied, his blue eyes focusing on her again. "How's the restaurant coming along?"

"It's slow going," Lorna told him. "In fact, my sister just came to get me away—seems I'm putting my nose into the repairs and harassing the workers, so she's forcing me to go help the needy. To bring out my docile side, I imagine."

"Does she have a docile side?" Mick asked Lacey.

His smile made Lorna think of mystic heroes all over again. He looked utterly charming, standing there in his work clothes, with his hard hat riding low over his wavy hair and sawdust covering him from head to toe. He might be mystic, but he was also very modern, and very much a real man. And he was teasing her, flirting with her again.

"It comes out every now and then," Lacey explained, giving her sister's arm a playful tug. "Our Lorna needs to relax and let all the relief workers do their work. I hope she hasn't been in your face already this morning."

"No," Mick replied, still looking at Lorna while he took the time to remove his hat and shake some of the dirt and dust off it. "In fact, I missed her at breakfast."

"I'm standing right here," Lorna said through a growl of frustration. "Y'all don't have to talk about me as if I'm not around. Feel free to include me in on the conversation regarding my lack of tact and manners."

"Has she had her coffee?" Mick asked Lacey, pointedly ignoring Lorna.

"I think she needs a little bit more," Lacey replied, deliberately talking over her sister's head.

Lorna was about to burst into a tirade, when Mick turned to her. "I'll buy you a cup."

"I have to go with my sister," she replied too sweetly.

He glanced back over his shoulder. "How about I drive into town with y'all. I can leave Josh in charge here. I've been wanting to survey the damage there, anyway. I might be able to lend a hand myself."

"How thoughtful of you," Lacey said, nodding.

"Yes, how very thoughtful," Lorna echoed, sarcasm dripping from every word.

"I'm going to make sure Rosie Lee has the food ready, then I'll bring the truck around to get Aunt Hilda," Lacey told them. "Give me about twenty minutes."

"We'll be ready," Lorna said, wishing her sister would quit giving her those meaningful looks.

"You don't mind me tagging along, do you?" Mick asked Lorna when they were alone.

"Of course I don't mind."

She whirled to stalk into the summerhouse. The big rounded building boasted white wicker furniture with floral cushions and sheer white curtains that flapped in the breeze when all the French doors were thrown open. Lush tropical plants made the room look like part of the outdoors, which was why the summerhouse was such a popular extension of the restaurant. Several of the regular patrons often requested to dine at one of the more private bistro tables here.

Right now, Lorna only wanted to get the building back in shape, and put thoughts of Mick Love right out of her mind. But where to start?

Several hibiscus trees, some with bright pink flowers and others with rich reds, sat in clay pots all around the airy building. In one corner, a vivid orange bird-of-paradise plant hung over a white wicker breakfast table, while a moon vine—its white fragrant flowers now closed in a sleeping trumpet shape while they waited for darkness—clung to one of the intricately carved posts near the entrance way.

Lorna began picking up crushed hibiscus flowers. Someone had set the overturned pots back in their proper places and the muddy curtains had already been washed, bleached and hung back up, but the whole room still needed a good cleaning.

Mick's work boots clicked on the worn wooden floor.

"If you *don't* mind me being around, why are you in here attacking these poor plants?"

"I'm looking for dead-heads," Lorna explained, intent on doing something to stay busy. "The summer-house is a favorite spot for our guests, and as you can clearly see, the wind blew one big mess of pine straw and magnolia leaves in here. I'm just surprised the storm didn't lift the whole thing up and destroy it, too."

She went about her work as she explained this, picking dead blossoms off the hibiscus trees, bending to pick up wilted flowers, then tossing it all out when her hands got too full.

"Tornadoes are like that," Mick said as he put his hard hat down and stooped to help her. "All fury in one place, then hardly lifting a twig in another."

Lorna kept right on cleaning. She found the big push-broom one of Rosie Lee's daughter's had left out here yesterday and started moving it across the polished hardwood floor. The others had already taken the braided rugs up to wash and dry, too. The entire building had been filled with mud and dirt, the wind having blown right through the open doors and windows.

When she reached the main entrance door, she found Mick standing there blocking her way.

"Yep, tornadoes are a lot like women."

That remark, made with a smirk, brought her head up. "Are you comparing me to that storm that ripped through here?"

"Maybe."

"And why would you do that?"

"Maybe because you seemed like a whirlwind this morning yourself. Was it something I said?"

Lorna stood there holding the broom, her heart pumping as if she were indeed about to take off in a mad wind. "Actually, it's several things you've said, and it's the way you've been acting."

"Oh, and how's that?"

"You...you're deliberately flirting with me, teasing me. It's your fault if I'm acting like a cyclone. I don't understand what you're trying to prove."

"So...do you always go into a flying tizzy every time a man comes near you?"

She wanted to send the broom flying at him. Honestly, Lorna didn't know why she felt so scattered, so angry. Maybe because she liked order, and there didn't seem to be any here right now. "No, I do not. It's just that—"

He stepped closer, his hand coming down over hers to hold the broom handle between them. "It's just that you feel it, too, right?"

"Feel…what?"

"Us," he replied, his blue eyes the color of the bearded irises growing down near the swamp basin.

"Us?" She repeated the little word, understanding with a fast-beating heart its big meaning. "There is no 'us,' Mick."

"I think there might be, if you'll just relax a little bit."

"You can't be serious," she said, a tiny hint of breath escaping as she tried to find air.

But breathing was near impossible, with him standing there so close. She could see the sawdust in his hair, see the flecks of triumph in his eyes.

"I'm very serious," Mick replied, reaching up to pull a long strand of hair away from her flushed face.

"We've know each other—what, twenty-four hours?" Lorna asked, trying to sound logical. But it came out more like an awe-filled statement than a logical question.

"That's the strangest thing," Mick replied, his fingers moving through her hair as he placed the lost locks back on her shoulder. "It's weird, what with you telling me off all the time, but I just like being around you, Lorna."

"That's preposterous."

"You said you were praying. You said God sent me to you. What did you mean by that?"

She tried to move away, but his hand held her there. "I meant…I meant that we needed help, and God sent someone who could help us."

"But it's more than that, don't you think?"

Oh, she not only thought it. She knew it in her heart. She'd walked in the moonlight with this man, then gone inside only to feel empty and alone. She'd asked God to help her find her center again, to calm her fears as He'd always done. She'd asked God to let her see His reasoning for bringing Mick Love here. She wanted to understand why this man made her pulse weak and her heart race.

Had God sent Mick to her?

The way Mick stood looking at her now, she wanted to believe that. But then, she'd made so many mistakes before, with so many men. She'd always fallen in love much too quickly, only to realize too late that it wasn't right. So she panicked and pushed them away. Lorna never let things get out of control, out of hand, except in the love department—there she rushed headlong into disaster, only to bring things to a skidding halt before anyone could get too close.

But after Paris, after Cole had broken off their wedding, she'd been very careful around men. Or, at least, she had been up until now. Now, she had to keep things in perspective.

For the past few years, she'd been tucked away here, safe and content. She'd put any thoughts of love out of her mind, since her last relationship had ended on a very bitter note. Since then, she'd learned to stay in control.

But with Mick, she couldn't seem to find any control. And with Mick, things seemed different. Whereas before, she dated men to prove that she was capable of being intimate, of having a relationship, now she wasn't so sure about any of that. Now, she really didn't want her heart to talk her into anything she'd regret. Maybe that was the difference. Her heart was doing the talking now. Before, she'd always been impulsive, jumping into a relationship simply because she thought she *needed* to be in one. She had always thought being with a man was just the next logical step, but being involved had never seemed to work out logically. She'd learned that the hard way.

"I said, what do you think?" Mick asked again, bringing her out of her rambling thoughts.

"I think you are...*impossible*." She stressed the French pronunciation of the word.

"Don't go using that foreign language on me."

"Well, since you don't seem to understand English—"

He tugged her close, his hands pulling through her loosely braided hair. "I understand that I like being with you. I understand that you seem to like being with me. But other than that, there's a whole lot I don't understand. But I'm willing to stick around to find out the rest."

"Don't waste your time," Lorna told him. "I usually send men running in the other direction."

"I can't imagine why."

"See, there you go teasing me again." She managed to pull away this time, her broom intact. "Maybe I should explain how things work with me, Mick. I've been engaged…oh, let's see…three times. I called off two of them, and the last one jilted me at the altar. And in between, I've dated for a few weeks, maybe months, but then suddenly, each time, I decided I was tired of the relationship and sent my suitor packing. For some reason, in spite of my earnest prayers for God to send me someone to spend the rest of my life with, I can't seem to make the right connection."

"Well, maybe you've been praying for the wrong things."

That comment astounded her. "And what would *you* know about prayer?"

She regretted asking the question, especially when she saw the hurt and anger warring in his eyes.

"More than you might think," he told her. Then he leaned back against the door frame and crossed his arms over his chest. "I used to pray, every night in that matchbox trailer my mother and I called a home. I used to ask God to explain to me why my old man had turned out to be such a louse and why my mother had to suffer every day of her life. But I never got any answers to those prayers. So I quit asking and I quit depending on God to help me out. I struggled and I worked and I finally made something of myself—''

He stopped, took a deep breath, then threw up his hands. ''Look, just forget it, all right. It sounds like you've been burned just as badly as I have, and I sure don't need to be reminded of that. Or the fact that we don't have a whole lot in common. We're not the same, you and me. Not from the same stock.'' He shrugged, grabbed up his hat. ''I was just flirting. Just killing time with a pretty woman. I won't bother you again.''

And with that, he was gone.

Lorna stood there, flabbergasted, clinging to her broom, while the gentle morning breeze lifted the white lace sheers of the summerhouse and sent them trailing after him like a bride's veil tossed in the wind.

Chapter Six

Before Lorna could go after Mick to tell him she was sorry, Lacey came rushing down the winding garden path toward the summerhouse, her floral skirt lifting all around her slender calves as she ran.

"We have to go, Lorna. There's been some trouble in town. Several people were cleaning up some of the debris and…a building caved in. They think someone is trapped inside."

"Oh, no." Lorna dropped her broom, then hurried toward Lacey. "Where's Aunt Hilda?"

"In the truck," Lacey told her, tugging her up the path.

They met Josh Simmons on the way to the car. "Ladies," he said, tipping his hard hat, a wide smile on his dark face. Then he noticed their concerned expressions. "Something wrong?"

"Accident in town," Lacey said over her shoulder. "We have to hurry."

"I'll come, too," Josh told them. "Want me to get Mick?"

"We could use the help," Lorna called, hoping Josh would be able to find Mick. After their confrontation, she wasn't sure he'd stick around Bayou le Jardin much longer. Why had she said such hateful things to him, anyway?

Why, indeed? Didn't she always manage to send men running with a few choice words? Mick probably wouldn't be any different from the rest. Apparently, he'd suffered through some bad spots himself. Wondering about his comments—living in a trailer park, his father's wrath and...being of different stock—only made her want to get to know him better, to show him that she wasn't a blue-blooded snob. But Lorna knew she could never really explain herself to Mick. That would mean having to tell him about her many flaws, and that usually did the trick for her in the love department. Maybe it was for the best that he'd seen her callous side so soon. That way, they wouldn't start something they could never finish.

"I thought Mick was with you," Lacey said as she ran toward the utility vehicle they used to get around the vast property.

Lorna headed for the front passenger seat, knowing Aunt Hilda preferred the back seat. "He...he had things to do. I'm sure he and Josh will follow us."

As they both hopped into the truck, they heard Aunt

Hilda talking on her cell phone. "What do you mean? Why was Kathryn there? Oh, my. Oh, my. We're on our way."

"What's wrong?" Lacey asked, glancing in the rearview mirror as she cranked the big vehicle around, then took off down the winding gravel drive toward the old River Road.

"The building… They think Kathryn might be the one trapped inside." Aunt Hilda held a wrinkled hand to her heart. "She was helping a child look for her kitten."

"Kathryn?" Lorna glanced over at Lacey. Her sister shot her a worried, pale look that only mirrored the sick feeling in the pit of her own stomach. "Do they know for sure?"

"No," Aunt Hilda replied, shaking her head. "They only know she was headed in that direction…and then a few minutes later they heard a crash and the wall caved in. Oh, I've told Kathryn to be careful, to stay away from the clean-up efforts. Why didn't she listen to me?"

"Because she's a hard worker, and she loves animals," Lorna replied, turning to give her aunt a pat on the arm. "We'll find her, Aunt Hilda. Try to stay calm."

"I'm perfectly calm," her aunt told her. "But you both know how I feel about Kathryn."

Yes, Lorna knew how much her aunt loved her young assistant. Hilda Dorsette had been a mentor to Kathryn Sonnier since Kathryn's days in middle school. Kathryn was a beautiful African-American child who'd come from a poor family. Her mother had wanted Kathryn to have a better life than the one she'd had, so she had encouraged her daughter to do well in school. When Kathryn's teacher sent out a call for mentors to help some of her struggling students, Aunt Hilda had signed up right away. And since that day more than thirteen years ago, Aunt Hilda had seen Kathryn through high school and college, funding most of her endeavors in a quiet, behind-the-scenes way. And she had promised Kathryn a job when she finished college.

Kathryn had worked her way up from front-desk clerk to assistant to the mayor in just under three years. Aunt Hilda loved the young woman just as much as she loved all the Dorsettes and the Babineaux. And Kathryn felt the same way about Hilda. She was a good assistant, and the protector at the gate when it came to people harassing the small town's lovable mayor.

If anything happened to Kathryn...

"I hope she's okay," Lacey said, as if reading Lorna's mind.

Soon, they neared the small community that was located just around the bend from the bed-and-breakfast.

"It's the general store," Aunt Hilda said, craning her neck to see. "It got hit pretty bad—they had to condemn it. I don't know if Jesse will be able to re-build or not, and now this."

"She can't take much more," Lorna said underneath her breath to Lacey, as they pulled up to where a crowd was gathered in front of the damaged building.

Lorna hated seeing the distress in her aunt's sweet eyes. Aunt Hilda was their rock—she held them all together, just as Mick had suggested. Lorna had taken that for granted over the years, but since she'd come back home she'd learned to appreciate her aunt. Now, Lorna felt the fingers of her unnamed fears surrounding her again. What would they do if they lost Aunt Hilda?

Asking God to put that particular scenario out of her mind, Lorna instead concentrated on the matter at hand. They had to find out if Kathryn was in that building. And if she was, they had to save her.

Mick pulled up his Chevy pickup underneath a towering oak tree near what was left of the quaint little town square in Jardin. A road sign hung next to an historical marker citing the population as 1,003. Mick was only interested in finding one of those 1,000 or so people. Turning off the roaring motor of the truck, he scanned the crowd gathered at the dilapidated remains of what used to be Jesse's General Store of Jardin.

"Let's see if we can find Lorna and Lacey," he told Josh, as they hopped out of the big-wheeled truck, hard hats in their hands. They'd left the rest of the crew back at the mansion to clear away the broken limbs near Lorna's bedroom so the contractor could get to the roof and make necessary repairs.

"Yeah," Josh replied, squinting toward the morning sun. "They were pretty shook up when I saw them."

"I guess so," Mick replied. At least, he imagined Lorna was still shaken from their earlier conversation, and he was sure hearing about this accident hadn't helped matters.

And now that he'd blurted out the details of his measly life, he was also sure Lorna Dorsette would no longer have anything to do with him. He wasn't good enough for the likes of her. She was a lady, pure and simple, first-class all the way, while he was a first-class fool for even entertaining the notion of getting to know her.

And yet, he searched for her long red hair in the crowd. He wanted to help her. "There they are," he told Josh, grabbing his friend by the sleeve to urge him forward.

Lorna looked up. She was standing near the cave-in where several men were trying to dig through the rubble. "Mick," she called, waving a hand for him and Josh.

Mick hurried over, nodding his head to Lacey and Aunt Hilda. "How bad is it?" he asked in a low voice.

"Pretty bad," Lorna told him, her green eyes bright with fear and worry. "My aunt's assistant, Kathryn Sonnier, is down there. She went in after a kitten. They were bulldozing some debris close by, and the movement must have made the wall shift. She's alive—we've talked to her, but they can't seem to get to her, and she's been awfully quiet the past few minutes." She motioned toward the men. "We only have a volunteer fire department—they're all loyal and well-trained, but we've never had anything such as this. The National Guard hasn't arrived here yet, so all we can do is wait for the ambulance to come from Kenner."

Mick put a hand on Lorna's shoulder. "What can we do?"

One of the men, a robust fellow with a bulging belly, stood up and turned to Mick. Out of breath from trying to remove broken bricks and timbers, he said, "Well, son, you and your friend there are a might bit skinnier than the rest of us. We need someone to squeeze in there and help Kathryn up. We can get her out through this path we've cleared, but she thinks she broke her leg, and she can't find the strength to move. The whole thing isn't very stable, though. If we don't hurry, she might get buried in there."

"I'll go in," Josh said as he marched up to the other man. "I worked as a volunteer fireman a few years ago—before Mick gave me a job."

"Are you sure?" Lorna asked Josh.

Mick pushed his friend forward, hoping to lighten the concern in her eyes. "Look at him. Tall and lanky, and he can shimmy like a snake. We used to hide in the kudzu vines near the railroad tracks, and Josh always found the best hiding places."

Josh grinned. "And speaking of snakes, I saw a

few. But listen, we can talk about all of that later. Tell me what to do.''

The big fellow, named Ralph, proceeded to explain. ''We were tearing away the damaged walls from the video store when we heard the crash. We came right over and called out. That's when we found out from a little girl standing nearby that Kathryn was down there. But we can't seem to get in to see how badly she's hurt. We're just lucky the kid didn't go down in there with her.''

He motioned to the doctor, a feeble old man with a tuft of white hair combed at an exaggerated sideways slant across his ruddy brow. ''And Doc Howard ain't able to climb down in that mess.'' Then he turned back to Josh. ''If you can get in, then move the debris that's got her trapped or at least pull her out from it, we can send a rope and stretcher down to make a pulley so we can lift her up.''

''And I can give you instructions on how to splint her leg so she won't damage it further,'' Dr. Howard told Josh.

''Okay,'' Josh said, already stepping into the shadowy opening. ''I've set a broken arm before. A leg can't be much different.''

He got halfway down the hole, then called, ''Kathryn, can you hear me? My name is Josh, and I'm coming in after you.''

''Yes'' came the weak reply. ''Are you going to get me out of here?''

''I'm going to try,'' Josh told her, holding a hand

to his hard hat. "Just stay calm, honey. This might take a while, but I'm coming down there so I can get some of that mess off you and see how badly you're hurt."

"Okay." Then on a feeble plea, she added, "Please hurry."

Mick watched as his friend started pushing debris out of the way. "Josh, be careful."

Josh gave him the thumbs-up. "Hey, buddy, we been in tighter spots, don't you know?"

"I do know," Mick replied, trying to muster up a smile of his own. "Bring her out—and hey, don't flirt with her too much."

"Right," Josh said, just before he disappeared from sight down the V-shaped passageway between the collapsed wall and the remains of the building's foundation.

Mick looked up from the narrow opening to find Lorna's eyes on him. He thought he saw gratitude there, and maybe a little understanding. Then again, maybe it was just his imagination working overtime.

"Thank you for coming," she said, her whisper for his ears only. "Kathryn is a very special person. My aunt would be devastated if anything happened to her."

"Josh will bring her out," Mick told her, as they waited. "And I'm right here if they need me."

"You always seem to be in the right place at the right time."

"Or the wrong place at the wrong time, depending on how you look at things."

"I don't always see things so clearly," she replied. Then she turned away, her eyes moving over the collapsed building in front of them.

Was that her way of apologizing for her earlier harsh words? Well, she'd been right. He certainly wasn't an authority on religion and prayer. And he hadn't depended on God's help or strength for a very long time.

And Lorna seemed to thrive on those very things.

He wanted to ask her if she really did understand. Make her see that although he'd lagged behind in the faith department, he wasn't a bad person.

Mick didn't question her, though. Now wasn't the time. Instead, he just reached out and took her hand.

After a few minutes, he called to Josh. "Hey, man, what's going on down there? You're way too quiet."

He got a grunt in reply. "Tight space…can't talk right now."

Mick pulled Lorna with him so they could peer down the narrow opening. "It looks like the wall fell in right over some steps."

"The storage room," Lorna told him. "Jesse had a basement down below." Then she explained that Kathryn had probably been moving down the narrow basement stairs when the wall just to the left had given way. "They think a bulldozer moving rubble from the video store shook the wall and triggered the collapse, just as Kathryn leaned down the steps to look for the kitten.'' She shrugged, her green eyes like a dark, mysterious forest. "We found the kitten right away." She pointed to where a little dark-haired girl held tightly to the meowing cat. "And thankfully, Kathryn made the child stay far away from the building."

Mick nodded, then glanced around. "Where's that ambulance?"

"They're on their way," Lorna told him. "They have to come from Kenner, about fifteen miles away."

"Are any of your volunteers trained for a medical emergency?"

"They're all trained, but only one is in the best of shape to handle something like this—and he had to go out of town before the storm hit. He's been trying to get back, but…" She stopped, looked toward where Aunt Hilda was sitting on a chair in the shade with Lacey watching over her. "Our aunt is trying to obtain funds for a new fire station. We managed to get a two-man police department a few years back, but it's tough to get much else out here, so we have to rely on volunteers. They're pretty dependable, but they've never had to deal with something like this."

Mick nodded. "And they don't look as fit as big city firemen."

"No," Lorna replied. "They work hard and mean well, but we really need someone to come in and take charge, get them up to standard."

The small talk kept Mick sane, while the grunts and distant words of his friend drifted up to him now and again. Jesse, the owner of the store, and Doc Howard both kept calling out to make sure Josh was okay.

After what seemed like hours, they heard Josh's excited shout. "I've found her. Send down the rope and pulley. Might need a scoop stretcher—this space is tight—and the equipment to make a splint. Her leg is definitely broken."

The doctor and several other people went to work gathering the needed supplies and securing them onto a board that Mick helped to send down the narrow passage to his friend.

"Here it comes," Mick shouted to Josh. "Can you reach it?"

They heard a shuffling noise, then Josh called out, "Got it."

Mick breathed a sigh of relief, then wiped the dust from his perspiring face. "That Josh, always rushing in. He did that when we were growing up, too."

"You two grew up together?"

He glanced over at Lorna, ready to see scorn or condemnation on her face. Instead, he saw a questioning look, as if she really were interested in knowing. And she *should* know: She should see right away that Mick Love wasn't her type at all.

Even if Mick Love suddenly wanted to be the man of her dreams.

Knowing how upset she was, he decided to keep her distracted with mundane chitchat. That would help calm his own knife-edged worry, too, he guessed. He hoped. "Yeah, we lived in the same trailer park, near the Pearl River. Floods used to get us just about every spring.''

''We've had a few flood scares ourselves, living on the Mississippi,'' she told him.

Mick tried to compare living at Bayou le Jardin with living in a run-down trailer park. Flood or not, there was no comparison. He put that particular issue aside for now and continued the conversation on a low, even tone.

''Josh and I did everything together,'' he said, a flash of memory making him shake his head. ''Went to school together, then skipped school together. Got into all kinds of trouble. Until our mommas pooled their resources and put us in church each Sunday.''

He saw the surprise in her eyes, coupled with regret.

''It seems I misjudged you…before.''

''No, you pretty much nailed me,'' he replied, unsmiling. ''I haven't been very devout in my faith as an adult. Now, being a child was a different thing. My momma saw to it that I understood right from wrong.''

He grinned and was rewarded with one of her dazzling smiles.

''And did you see the error of your ways?'' she asked quietly and without judgment.

''Pretty much, but we kept getting into trouble. Josh comes from a big family, and I used to hang out at his house. His momma can sure cook.''

''Didn't seem to stick with him,'' she replied, nodding toward the hole Josh had disappeared down. ''He's in good shape.''

"He's very athletic."

"I guess you'd both have to be, what with the business you're in."

"Yep."

In spite of the easy banter, Mick could see the worry coloring Lorna's brilliant eyes a deeper shade of green. "They'll make it," he told her, pulling her close. "Josh knows what he's doing."

"I hope so," she said, turning to give her sister a quick smile. "My aunt isn't taking this very well. She's held up so wonderfully through all of this, but—"

Just then they heard a shout from Josh. And then a loud rumble moved through the broken building. Lorna rushed forward, but Mick held her back as the timbers and bricks around them seemed to shudder and sway, dirt and dust lifting up in a choking cloud that temporarily blinded them. Then a deadly silence fell over the shrouded mass of wood and stone.

"Kathryn?" Lorna shouted. When she didn't get an answer she leaned forward, closer. "Kathryn, say something!"

Mick stepped up, still holding her. "Josh, buddy, you'd better talk to me!"

Nothing.

Behind them now, Lacey stood holding Aunt Hilda's hand, waiting with a look of dread on her face as she tried to keep her aunt still and calm.

"We have to do something," Lorna said, clutching Mick, terror underscoring each word.

Mick acted on instinct and adrenaline. Pushing Lorna into the arms of the surprised doctor, he shoved on his hard hat, then pressed his lower body into the tight opening, calling to his friend as he went. "Josh, are you all right? Joshua Clarence Simmons, you'd better answer me. Right now, and I mean it."

Mick couldn't explain the sick feeling of dread, didn't stop to think about it. It moved like an electrical jolt through his entire system as he entered that dark, dusty hole. But he had to find Josh and Kathryn. Alive. He didn't even realize he'd started praying. But the words were forming in his head as quickly as the dust had formed on his body.

"Dear God, help them. Help me."

"Mick, don't go in there!"

Lorna's voice was the last thing he heard as he descended into the pitch-black alleyway of twisted metal and broken glass and boards, determined to find his friend and Kathryn.

And even more determined to get back to Lorna Dorsette once this was all over.

Chapter Seven

❧

He remembered a face. A face with long red-blond hair, and eyes the color of a summer meadow—green and lush, rich with hope and promise. He could hear her voice calling to him. Or was he just having a wonderful, peaceful dream.

"Mick, can you hear me? It's Lorna."

Mick opened his burning, heavy-lidded eyes to find Lorna bent over him, her long hair falling in gentle curls and waves around her face and shoulders, her perfume reminding him of magnolias and honeysuckle...a garden.

Bayou le Jardin.

Then the memories came swirling by like a black fog. He bolted upright, but his head hurt so badly, he couldn't see straight. Reaching up, he found a bloody knot the size of a hen's egg just above his right temple.

Lorna's arms on his brought him back down. "Take it easy, Mick."

"Where am I?"

"On a couch in Aunt Hilda's office at City Hall. You lost your hat and hit your head. Doc thinks you have a mild concussion. We really should get you to the emergency room."

"Where's...?" He couldn't form the words, so he just looked up at her, sure he'd see the answers he needed in her gentle face, but not sure he wanted to know them.

Then, because he was afraid of the news, Mick glanced out the door of the tiny office to a small reception area with two large ficus trees on each side of the glass doors. A sign on the wall gave directions to the mayor's office and the business office. Everything looked so normal. He could hear voices in another part of the building, a phone ringing off in the distance.

Then he looked back at Lorna. "Are they all right?"

"Josh and Kathryn are safe. They took them to the emergency room in Kenner. Mick, you saved their lives."

His throat felt as rough and dry as tree bark. But welcome relief flowed over him, causing him to relax back against the floral cushions someone had placed beneath his head. "Oh, yeah, and how'd I do that?"

Lorna sat down next to him on the wide vinyl couch, so near that a thick mass of her hair brushed

Mick's forearm, making him think of angel's wings and harp strings.

"We're really not sure," she said, her own voice shaky and strained. "One minute you were there, the next you were gone down that hole. We heard you shouting for Josh, then you called out to us that you'd found them. Josh was unconscious, but somehow, you got him out of the way, moved a timber beam off Kathryn, then lifted her, maybe dragged her to safety."

"But...her leg?"

"You didn't have time to worry about that. The building was very unstable. Her leg is broken, and she's got bruises and cuts, but she's going to be okay."

"And Josh?"

"He's all right, too. He'd just found Kathryn and was trying to set her leg, when the building gave way again. His hard hat saved him from having a concussion, too, according to Doc. But he threw his body over Kathryn's, so he's got a long gash on one arm and some cuts across his shoulder. They were concerned about him losing so much blood."

Mick looked down at his own shirt. It was stained a dark red. The memory of touching his friend, only to find him covered in blood, made him queasy. But he tried to sit up again. "I have to go see about him."

"Whoa." Lorna pushed him back down with surprising force for someone so petite and small framed.

"It's bad enough that you insisted the ambulance take them first, but you still need to be checked over."

She shook her head, obviously amazed at what he'd done. "You kept telling us you were all right, so we sent the ambulance away. Then you passed out on us when we were trying to check your head. So just stay put." She waited for him to settle down, then explained, "The only reason you aren't headed to the hospital yourself is that Doc assured me you'd be all right. But I have very strict orders to keep a close eye on you." She stayed right beside him, as if daring him to move. "As soon as you get your bearings, I'm driving you into Kenner to make sure Doc's diagnosis is correct."

"Good, then I can see Josh, make sure he's okay."

"That's fair enough," she replied, nodding. Then a worried look creased her brow. "Are you sure you're really all right? I mean, how do you feel right now?"

Mick couldn't begin to answer that question. She was too near, and he was still too shaky. But right now, this very minute, he felt as if a voice had indeed come to him and whispered in his ear. *"It's not your time, Mick. You have to do this. You have to save them and yourself."*

Had he imagined that, there in the dark bowels of that ravaged building? How had he managed to get Josh out of the way in spite of all the blood, remove that heavy timber beam, then get Kathryn hoisted onto the stretcher? He didn't even remember dragging her onto it there in the semidarkness and dust. How had he managed to do that, then get her up to safety?

"It's all so foggy," he said now. "I don't know what happened, really. I just remember thinking I had to hurry."

"You called out to us," Lorna said. She sat back, her arms wrapped around her midsection, her eyes wide with memories and anxiety. "Jesse and Ralph pulled on the stretcher rope, then Lucas showed up and helped them tug Kathryn up. She was lying across the board on her stomach, but you'd managed to get her broken leg up on the board so it didn't drag. Doc said that helped, but the pain caused her to pass out."

Pain. He did remember a burst of pain. "How did I hit my head?"

"I don't know," she replied, still clutching herself, staring down at a spot on the patterned carpet. "Probably some falling debris when you started climbing out. We kept hearing rumbles, things falling."

Then she looked back up and right into his eyes. "You scared me, Mick. I thought…"

"Shh," he said, taking her arms to pull her hands away from her body. Her fingers felt both icy and clammy. "It's over now. We're all safe. It's going to be okay."

"Thanks to you. This is the second time you've come to the rescue for us. I won't forget it."

His head was swimming again, but not from the concussion. This dizziness came from the look in

Lorna's eyes, that vulnerable look of a lost child, that confused and dazed look of someone searching for answers in the dark. That look that shattered him and battered him and made him want to pull her into his arms and hold her tightly.

Right now, their differences didn't matter. Right now, although he knew it was wrong, he didn't want to walk away from what he was feeling. He wasn't nearly good enough for her, would never measure up. And yet, he was willing to try.

He knew it would be tough. She'd told him about her other relationships. Engagements that had failed. And apparently, one trip to the altar that had turned out badly. She was trying to forget all of that, and in doing so, she was denying everything between them.

He didn't want her to forget. He didn't want her to deny. He didn't want her to forget *him* or deny *him*. Because he'd surely never forget her. And he could no longer deny his own erratic feelings.

And after being down in that dark, tight space with little air and little confidence, with his life flashing in slow-motion before him and his best friend bleeding and hurt, he knew that he had to have her by his side— somehow.

So he let go of her hand, then reached up a finger to touch her cheek. "Hey, you know something?"

Her eyes widened. "What?"

"When I went down there, I wasn't thinking about

anything in particular—I just had to help Josh and Kathryn.''

She nodded, her gaze searching.

''But I do remember this—I remember thinking that if I ever got out of there alive, I'd do something I've been wanting to do since the first time I held you in my arms.''

Her eyelashes fluttered against her cheeks. Letting her gaze drop, she refused to look at him. ''Oh, and what's that?''

''This—'' he said, as he lifted her head with his thumb. Then with his other hand, he pulled her head down. ''This—'' he repeated, the one word caught on a low, husky growl. Then he kissed her, his mouth lifting, then returning to hers until he'd settled his lips against hers in a gesture of pure pleasure and deep-seeded longing.

He was dizzy again, reeling in a sweet-smelling, soft-to-the-touch dream. A dream filled with moonlight and flowers and a river flowing nearby. A dream of her taking his hand in the dark and holding him forever.

Lorna sighed against him, kissed him back with the same softness and tenderness he'd seen in her eyes that first day. But he could feel the tentative fear he'd also seen like a dark aura surrounding her.

He wanted to capture that fear and turn it into something else. He wanted to change that fear to a steadfast joy. If he could kiss it away, he would. But he had a distinct feeling that it would take more than kisses to win this woman's heart.

So he stopped kissing her, then pulled her close and held her near his own erratic heart.

She sank against him, then sighed, content for now it seemed.

Or so he thought. She turned her head, her breath brushing on his ear like spring flowers moving in the wind, while her angry words rolled over him like a tide changing. "Don't ever do that to me again, Mick Love."

Lorna got up, seeking air, breath, control. This couldn't be happening. It was too fast, much too fast. Faster, quicker than any of her other so-called relationships. Her heart was beating too fast, her breath was coming too fast. And the kiss—oh, that had happened way too fast. And ended much too soon. But this had to end. Now.

Mick held her arm, wouldn't let go. "Are you going to deny this? That you've wanted the same thing since the day we met? Are you going to tell me you didn't enjoy that kiss just as much as I did?"

Lorna took one hand and daintily removed Mick's tanned, veined hand from her wrist. Then she lapsed into French. *"Cochon! Imbecile!"*

"Hey, it was just a kiss. No need for name-calling."

She turned then to see the hurt Mick quickly tried to erase. *"Stupide*—don't be stupid. I'm not talking about the kiss, and I'm not calling you names—those are aimed at me for being so foolish. What I was trying to say—'' She threw up her hands, ran them over her hair. ''Don't ever scare me like that again. When you went into that building, my heart stopped.''

The lopsided grin on his face made her heart stop all over again.

''Oh, that. It was nothing, really. Let's get back to the important stuff. So, you did enjoy the kiss?''

''*Now,* you find this amusing—*now,* after I was so helpless and horrified. Oh, you're impossible!''

''I think you've told me that before.''

Gaining strength with distance, she said, ''That's because it's true. You went down there, risking your life—''

''I had to help Josh.''

''I understand,'' she said, trying to find the words that would describe all the emotions she'd been through in the past couple of hours. ''I can't explain it,'' she said, throwing her hands up again. ''I can't explain this—'' she pointed to her lips, still swollen and tingling from their kiss ''—I can't explain this—'' she held her hand to her heart. Then she sank down on a nearby chair. ''I feel as if I'm the one with a bump on the head—and stop grinning at me!''

''I can't help it,'' he told her, still grinning. ''You are so beautiful. Especially when you've just been kissed.''

She got up to come and stand over him, wagging a

finger in his face. "Well, don't go getting any crazy ideas."

Mick grabbed her hand, urged her down onto the couch beside him. "Oh, I've got several ideas—some crazy, some completely sane."

Lorna inhaled deeply, bracing herself for another onslaught of gale-force kisses. "Put them out of your mind. I'm taking you to the hospital."

He let her go. "Yep, maybe I do need my head examined, at that."

She didn't miss the trace of sarcasm in his words. Did he already regret kissing her? Did she really, truly care?

She realized she did. And that put the tremendous, unnamed fear back in her heart, quickly replacing the wonderful sensations that being in his arms had awakened.

Wanting to get back to business and back in control of her senses, she said, "Lucas took Lacey and Aunt Hilda to the medical center in Kenner to be with Kathryn. Can you manage to walk to the front door and wait, while I pull the truck around?"

"I think I can manage that, thank you," he said, raising himself up off the couch. The effort caused his dark skin to turn pale, however. "Whew, I'm hurting in places I didn't even know I had, but at least the room isn't tilting and swaying anymore."

Not trusting him, Lorna took his arm. "You're obviously still in a lot of pain. You'll be sore and bruised for a while, no doubt." Then she softened her tone. "Here, lean on me."

Mick looked over at her, his blue eyes filled with an unreadable message—longing, a search, and finally, a resigned kind of quietness. But before she could prop him against a white column outside the front door of the small City Hall office, he grabbed her hand again. "This isn't over Lorna. Not by a long shot."

"It has to be over, Mick," she replied. "We both got a little carried away in there, that's all. Too much excitement."

"If that's what you want to believe," he replied, his eyes never wavering.

Lorna hurried to find the truck. *Lord, I don't know what's happening to me,* she silently prayed. *Help me. I'm so scared. I've never felt like this before. What does it mean?*

On her way to the truck, she glanced over at the remains of the general store. The building was completely ruined now, caved in on itself like a giant cracker box that had gotten caught in a trash compactor.

Mick had been inside that crushed mess.

He could have died.

He and Josh and Kathryn—they all could have died.

Her hands shaking, Lorna suddenly realized what the great fear clawing at her gut was really about.

She was falling in love with Mick Love.

She couldn't fall in love with Mick.

Because she couldn't bear to lose him.

Better to keep her distance, and keep things under control. Then she'd never have to suffer again—the way she'd suffered when her parents had been so brutally taken from her, the way she'd suffered during the raging storm, and the way she'd suffered this morning.

And that was it in a nutshell. That was why she'd always run away from a serious commitment. That was why she'd called off her so-called engagements. And ultimately, that was why she'd been left at the altar.

A blessing in disguise, no doubt.

If she refused to acknowledge how Mick made her feel, she'd never again have to stand over a pile of rubble and know that the man she was falling for could become buried deep inside, away from her touch, hurt and helpless in a small, dust-filled hole.

Long ago, Lorna had made a promise to herself that she'd never again be left alone in the dark.

If she fell for Mick, then lost him, that's exactly where she'd be—back in the dark. And she wouldn't go through that again. Ever.

Chapter Eight

$\sim$

"How can we ever repay you?"

Hilda Dorsette stood in the hospital lobby, her hand on Mick's arm, her eyes misty with gratitude. She was making him extremely nervous.

"You don't have to repay me, Miss Hilda. I just did what anyone would have done."

"You were very brave," Hilda replied, her wrinkled, bejeweled hand still clutching his. "How's your head?"

"Hard as a rock," Mick joked, embarrassed by all the fuss he'd received since he and Lorna had arrived at the bustling medical center in nearby Kenner.

The media had been there, asking a million redundant questions.

"*...Mr. Love, what went through your mind as you plunged down into that dark abyss?*"

"...Mr. Love, how did you manage to rescue two people without getting seriously hurt yourself?"

What did they expect him to say? What could he say? How could he explain? Now, Mick couldn't even remember what he'd told the excited reporters. It didn't matter, anyway.

He only wanted to find Lorna and go back to the peace and quiet of Bayou le Jardin. But it looked like that might not happen any time soon.

The family had all been here—all the Dorsettes and the Babineaux, even Kathryn's grateful mother Polly, cooing and aahing over him and embellishing his rescue efforts into a dramatic tale full of excitement and daring deeds—before they'd all scattered for lunch and visits with Kathryn.

Except for Lorna, of course. Since she'd brought him to the emergency room and been assured by several doctors that he wasn't seriously hurt, she'd managed to find all sorts of excuses for steering clear of Mick. Oh, she had to call to talk to the contractors about the restaurant repairs. She had to make sure her vendors wouldn't make deliveries until all was clear. She had to see that no guests were booked to stay at the mansion or in the cottages until the repairs and cleanup could be completed.... Mick had watched her, amused and disturbed, as she pushed buttons on her cell phone with all the buzzing energy of a honeybee, her gaze averted from his all the while.

Lorna was still stewing about that kiss, he reckoned.

He'd known better than to kiss the woman, but he couldn't help himself. He'd needed that kiss as much as he'd needed his next breath. And he intended to kiss her again, lots. But that particular goal would have to wait until all this excitement and praise settled down.

Mick didn't want any praise. He just wanted to make sure Josh and Kathryn were safe and well. But now, Hilda Dorsette herself was thanking Mick and promising him a key to the city, so he had to be polite and give her his undivided attention. Hilda Dorsette commanded that kind of respect, and Mick certainly had enough manners to give it to her. She was worried about her town, so she appreciated his efforts.

"Can't you see?" she said now, her eyes watering. "What you did gave new hope to all those who lost so much in this storm. We found a tiny bit of triumph in the midst of our despair. And for that, I will be eternally grateful."

Touched, Mick could only smile and nod. "Really, now, Miss Hilda, don't make me out to be something I'm not. We had a lot of help. Josh was much braver than me."

"He'll be rewarded as well, believe me." She tugged Mick to a nearby floral divan. "Have you noticed how Josh refuses to leave Kathryn's side? I think those two made a match down there in that rubble."

Mick sat back on the comfortable couch, then lifted a brow. "A match? Buried underneath a building?"

"The Lord works His ways, even in the darkness, Mr. Love."

He couldn't argue with that logic. Since he'd come to Bayou le Jardin, Mick had felt the Lord's presence all around him, both night and day. And it was making him crazy. In a good way, of course. For the first time in his life, Mick was beginning to understand what it meant to have a loving, supportive family gathered around you. And he liked that notion a whole lot, even if it did scare him. Even if he knew in his heart that he could never be a part of this particular family.

He liked Lorna Dorsette a whole lot, too. And that definitely scared him. He'd be leaving soon, so how was he supposed to continue things? Did he dare to hope that he might have a chance?

"You looked a bit confused," Hilda said, her appraising stare never wavering. "Are you sure you're feeling better?"

Mick touched the bandaged place on his head. "It still hurts, but I'm fine, really. Just a bit overwhelmed by all this attention, I reckon."

"Don't let it go to your head," Hilda said, her tone pragmatic. "Of course, you will stay at Bayou le Jardin as our guest until you are feeling better. Both you and Josh."

"That's mighty nice, but we're not invalids. And we do have to get back to work."

"Just for a few more days," Hilda replied, the words a statement, not a request. "We're going to have a special church service this coming Sunday to thank the good Lord for all His blessings. And I want you and Josh to attend as our very special guests.''

Mick couldn't turn down a request like that. ''Yes, ma'am,'' he said, smiling slightly at the petite but formidable woman seated next to him. Then, because he had been hit on the head and he was still feeling a bit tilted, he asked, ''Miss Hilda, do you believe in miracles, in divine intervention?''

''I most certainly do,'' she replied, tapping her elaborately carved cane against the linoleum floor. ''Don't you?''

Mick couldn't tell her that he'd always considered his faith lackluster—a haphazard, halfhearted attempt at grasping for something, someone to guide him. But he could tell her about what had happened down in that building—something he'd refused to share with a roomful of reporters. ''I don't know—I just felt this presence when I went in after Josh and Kathryn. It was almost as if someone were talking to me, guiding me. Whatever happened, it gave me the strength to come up out of there alive, and bring Josh and Kathryn with me.''

''God was there with you, Mr. Love,'' Hilda replied with complete confidence.

Mick nodded, lowered his head a bit. ''How can I be sure?''

''How can you doubt?'' Hilda retorted, but the words were gentle. ''You had no way of knowing this,

but we were all praying after you went down there.''
She smiled at him, took his hand in hers. "We held
hands—Lacey and Lorna and I—and we prayed. Then
when we opened our eyes, we saw others doing the
same thing.'' She let go of his hand and wagged a
finger at him. "Never underestimate the power of positive prayer, Mr. Love.''

"I won't,'' Mick told her, his words full of awe.
"Not ever again.''

Hilda patted his hand, then leaned on her cane to
get up. Mick helped her with a hand on her arm. Then
she turned to him, her smile a bit bemused. "You and
my niece seem to have hit it off quite well, Mr. Love.''

"Call me Mick,'' he said, wondering how to respond to her pointed comment.

"Then call me Aunt Hilda,'' she replied. "Everyone does.'' She leaned forward, propping her weight
on her cane. "And tell me what's brewing between
my Lorna and you.''

Mick glanced around, as hot and uncomfortable as
a crawfish about to hit a pot of boiling water. He didn't
really have the answer to that particular question yet.
But he was sure going to work on it. Yet what could
he tell Aunt Hilda, to assure her he had only the most
noble of intentions?

"I like Lorna a lot,'' he admitted. "She's...''

"Stubborn, opinionated, ornery, a challenge?''
Hilda finished the statement, then waited, a serene
smile on her peaches-and-cream face.

"All of the above," Mick said, laughing in spite of feeling like a trapped animal. "Lorna seems to have many layers—she's an independent woman who has a good career, and she loves her family. She works hard, that's for sure. And she seems to care deeply about the people she loves and the things she believes in."

"Sometimes too deeply," Hilda said, wagging her finger at him again. "I only ask that you remember that."

"I will," he said, nodding. "I wouldn't do anything to hurt Lorna, Aunt Hilda. You have my word on that."

"I'd expect nothing less," Hilda replied. "Now, what do you say we go and check on our patients? I'm anxious to talk to Kathryn and find out why she went into that building in the first place."

Mick offered his arm to Hilda. "Shall we?"

He was anxious, too. Anxious to find Lorna and get back to the unsettled business between them. Yet he couldn't put Aunt Hilda's warning out of his mind. Was that the reason Lorna seemed to be pushing him away, because she didn't want to care about him too much?

Was that the reason he saw that fear in her eyes each time he came near her?

Two days later, Mick's team had finished removing all the tree limbs and debris from the Bayou le Jardin property, and had managed to get the grounds back in shape enough to suit even the picky Mr. Justin Hayes. While Mick and Josh supervised from the sidelines— Hilda Dorsette and her two adorable nieces refused to let them actually do any work—Lucas and Justin both pitched in to help the men get the rest of the job done.

Then Claude Juneau, Mick's friend from the power company, came by to give Hilda a progress report on things in town, and to check on Mick and Josh. ''Well, the National Guard and the Red Cross will both be pulling out today,'' said Claude, a giant man with bright red hair and ruddy cheeks, as they sat on the gallery enjoying the gloaming at the end of a long, warm spring day.

''The National Guard arrived right after the cave-in the other day—too late to prevent that, but they did help remove most of the debris, and they gave us some much-needed relief in patrolling for looters. And the Red Cross has been great, but they've got other places to see about. Basically, now it's on to rebuilding and getting things back to normal, dealing with the insurance people, things such as that. Reckon we're on our own from here on out.''

Then he turned to Mick. ''Unless, of course, I could entice Mick here to keep his crew with us for a few more days. We could sure use some strong hands to finish the cleanup, and there's still some fallen trees that need to be removed mainly between here and town, just so we don't let them rot where they fell. We'd pay you for your efforts, of course.''

Mick glanced over at Josh, who sat on a cushioned wrought-iron love seat, right next to where Kathryn had her broken leg—straight from being set in the cast she'd have to wear for six weeks—propped on a pillow-laden footstool.

"Josh, what's on the agenda for the next week or so?"

Josh grinned, then squinted. "Well, boss, let's see. We've got the Duvall's pines to trim back—that'll be about a week's worth of hard time. You know how Mrs. Duvall likes to supervise things. Then after that, it's just some odds and ends. A few clearings here and there around Vicksburg. We did hire on to clear away some dead oaks right outside Battleground Park, but that's not scheduled until later in the summer." He waved a hand at Mick. "Besides, why am I telling you all of this? You know better than me what we've got on the agenda."

Mick grinned. "Just wanted to see if you'd jump right in and volunteer to stick around here for a few more days." He looked over at Kathryn, then shrugged.

Kathryn's smile gave him his answer, even if Josh didn't have the guts to say what was on his mind.

"That would be nice," she said, turning to glance over at Josh. "Especially since Aunt Hilda insisted I stay here until I'm feeling better."

"Only right," Hilda interjected. "Your momma has her hands full with your siblings and her grandchildren as it is. And besides, we can get some work done if you're handy.''

Kathryn only nodded, then giggled again. ''Leave it to you to be practical about all of this. But you're right, of course.''

Aunt Hilda had also been right about Kathryn and Josh. Since the accident, they'd stuck together like glue to paper. Josh had stayed near Kathryn while she rested in the hospital, then had insisted on going with Aunt Hilda and Lacey to pick her up this afternoon.

Mick couldn't blame his friend, since he himself wanted to stick around to be near Lorna. And Josh certainly deserved some happiness in his life.

Kathryn was a pretty woman, no doubt. Her cropped black curls complimented the classic lines of her dark face, and her big round brown eyes opened even wider each time Josh talked, as if she couldn't get enough of all his wisdom. Each time she giggled at some brilliant remark coming from Josh's mouth, her large silver hoop earrings swayed against her slender neck. Broken leg or not, the woman seemed in very good spirits since the hospital had released her this morning.

And so did his friend, in spite of the stitches lining his back and arm. Maybe love was the best medicine, after all.

Which again brought Mick to his own need to stay at Bayou le Jardin a while longer.

Lorna Dorsette.

She was missing from this little circle.

She was back at her restaurant—which had re-opened today—no doubt fussing over the *potée* (some sort of salad), the *soufflé au fromage,* (it was made with cheese, from what he could tell), her *baguette* and *petit Parisien* breads, and his favorite, *brioche,* not to mention the bouillabaisse, the *homard à l'Americaine* (lobster with a tasty sauce), or the *caneton aux navets* (roasted duck) or the plain ol' *boeuf à la mode* (stuffed shrimp and pot roast) that the Garden Restaurant offered as entrees.

In fact, Lorna had been so busy, Mick had hardly had two minutes alone with her since the accident, but he'd sure learned a lot about French cooking. Maybe because he'd gone in the restaurant each night to stare at the menu when he wasn't watching her. If he kept this up, he'd gain ten pounds.

Lorna only ignored him and attended her other customers.

But he intended to fix that little oversight.

"We'll be glad to stay on," he told Claude now. "Besides, we promised Aunt Hilda we'd be in church this Sunday, and I don't think she'd take it too well if we up and left before then."

"I certainly would not," Hilda said, her eyes twinkling. "Lacey has told everyone in town to be there, so we can celebrate together. And I know Lorna has been issuing orders to Rosie Lee about what foods to prepare. We're going to have an old-fashioned dinner right here on the grounds after the service."

"I'll be there myself," Claude said, rubbing his broad stomach. "I'm telling you, Mick, when the Dorsette women put on a spread, a man never walks away hungry."

"All the more reason to stick around," Mick told his friend. "Oh, and Claude, I'm only going to charge you half rates for the work."

Claude reached out to shake his hand. "You're a good man, Mick. But then, I always did know that for a fact."

"How'd you two meet, anyway?" Lucas asked. He was sitting off to the side, out underneath one of the towering oaks, in a wooden glider, a boot propped against one arm of the swing while he slowly rocked himself back and forth with the other foot.

Mick looked over at Lucas. Now, there was a man who was very hard to read. From all indications, Lucas took life easy, showing up now and then to do some hard work, then disappearing for hours on end—to fiddle and play, Lacey seemed to think. But Mick knew better.

Tobbie had confided in Mick just this morning, telling him how much Lucas had helped with the cleanup around Tobbie's own modest home—which had suffered severe damage in the storm. Then Lucas had gone into the swamp to check up on the other Cajun families living there—families, Tobbie had said under his breath, that didn't have two nickels to rub together.

"They depend on Lucas's good graces," Rosie Lee

had added. "But he don't like to brag about stuff like that."

Mick only knew Lucas always seemed to be around at the most crucial of times, like the other morning when he'd helped pull all three of them from the rubble. He'd pitched right in, taking over for Mick when the Dorsette women had insisted Mick and Josh take things easy. And Lucas had stepped in several times, intervening between Mick's crew and Justin Hayes, saving the day with some sort of humor to break the tension of too many chiefs trying to get things done.

Mick trusted Lucas. He didn't mind answering his question, either. "I met Claude when I used to work at the power company over in Jackson."

"He was young and hotheaded," Claude interjected, "so he didn't last very long."

Mick shrugged. "Long enough to know I liked working with trees. So I learned everything I could, took some college and technical courses, and I opened my own tree service—after a few years of false starts and several different jobs."

"We kept in touch," Claude said by way of an explanation. "I kinda had to look out for him, you know. Didn't want him to do anything stupid."

"He preached to me day and night," Mick said, laughing.

"Well, did any of it soak in?" Claude asked, his big hands on his hips.

"Some," Mick replied. "At least, you managed to get me to come here. And I don't regret that at all."

"Well, good. That's good." Claude raised a hand in the air. "Folks, I'd love to stay and chat, but I've got work to do, and since my wife and kids haven't seen me for three days, I'd better get home before the sun goes down."

"Thank you for coming out, Claude," Lacey said from the open doorway leading to the kitchen.

"No problem." Then Claude turned to Mick again. "See you first thing in the morning, then?"

"We'll be there," Mick told him. "Josh can supervise, while the rest of us work."

They followed Claude to his truck, then Josh punched Mick on the arm. "So, I guess this means we're all sticking around for a spell."

"I guess it does, at that," Mick replied. "I'll go down to the cottages and tell the rest of the crew, then I'll call our secretary back home and let her know to hold off on any more appointments."

They all looked up to see Lorna hurrying up the path from the restaurant, her blue linen dress kicking up with each quick step she took. She was wearing her white chef coat over the dress and a prim white kerchief scarf on her head, keeping her long hair away from her face.

"We keep blowing fuses," she said immediately. "The lights keep dimming, and the stove goes on and off." Lacey shot out the door. "But you're not in complete darkness, right."

Lorna held up a small flashlight. "No. It's okay." Mick noticed the long look passing between the sisters before Lorna said, "But I'm going to have that electrician's head on a platter. He assured me it was safe to go ahead and open up today."

Lucas let out a hoot of laughter. "You tell 'em, Sister Lorna."

Lorna whirled on her brother. "And you, just sitting there as if you don't have a care in the world—"

"I don't," Lucas replied, saluting her with one hand to his temple. "I'm sorry. Did you need something?"

"I could use some help," she replied, her green eyes flashing like heat lightning. "Believe it or not, we have a large crowd tonight, and one of my waiters couldn't make it in—he's still dealing with losing part of his roof to the storm."

Lucas hopped up, brushed his hands on his faded jeans. "Okay, I'll wait tables, but only if you let me play a few tunes when things settle down. I'm in a blues kinda mood."

"Fine, work first, then play that whining saxophone later—just so my customers are happy."

With that, she stomped right past Mick and into the kitchen, leaving a scent of fresh herbs and floral perfume to merge in his head.

But they could still hear her ranting, her hands in the air. "I had to go for a walk, or lose it in front of all my employees and the customers. Plus, in all of the clutter and confusion, we seem to have misplaced at least half of our measuring bowls. I'm going to borrow a couple from the kitchen."

"She is very precise about these things," Lucas said, before heading off in a lazy stroll toward the restaurant. Walking backward, he directed his next words to Mick.

"Has to have everything in order, just for good measure, of course, or so she tells us."

Lacey watched her brother grin, then pivot toward the lane with an eloquent parting shrug. "That man never gets in a hurry about anything. Honestly, I just don't get my brother at all."

Hilda hushed her. "Lucas knows his own mind, and he knows when he's needed and when he's not."

"So, leave him alone, right?" Lacey didn't look too pleased, but she quieted under her aunt's warning glance.

"Yes, leave him alone. He's never let any of us down, has he?"

"Well, no." Lacey lowered her head. "I guess we're just all a bit frazzled. This has been one long, busy week."

"All the more reason to rest and rejoice come Sunday," Hilda replied. "Now, children, I'm rather tired. I'm going to take my supper on a tray in my room, look over some files, then go to bed." She gave Kathryn a pointed look. "And I suggest you do the same, young lady. That pain medicine should be kicking in soon."

"Yes, ma'am," Kathryn said quietly. Then she added, "I'm sorry I caused everybody such a scare. But I could hear that little kitty meowing..."

Her voice trailed off as her eyes misted over with tears. Josh took her hand, his own eyes going soft. "You sure were brave."

Aunt Hilda nodded, her eyes misty, too. "Yes, and we're very glad the kitten, the child, and all of the rest of you are safe and sound."

Everyone fell silent for a minute, then Aunt Hilda said, "Now, I'm off to get to that paperwork."

Mick got up when Aunt Hilda rose. "Do you need help getting up those stairs?"

Hilda chuckled. "I have my own elevator in the back of the house, Mick. I didn't want the thing installed, but actually it's come in quite handy, especially since I have arthritis in my bad knee. It even has a nice bench seat, so I can sit as I ride up. But thanks for the gentlemanly offer, anyway."

"My pleasure," Mick said. "I don't remember seeing an elevator," he told Lacey, after Hilda had gone inside.

"It's hidden from the public," she explained. "It's behind the back stairway, near the kitchen. Guests never wander that far back, and it's rather nondescript so no one will notice it—it looks like another door."

"I see." Another of the many interesting stories surrounding this old house.

But Mick wasn't worried about elevators right now. He wanted to talk to Lorna. Glancing down at Josh, he asked, "Friend, will you be all right? I think I'll go for a walk before supper—get some of the kinks out of this sore body."

"We'll be just fine," Josh replied, his eyes on Kathryn. "I'll make sure Kat gets tucked in, then I'm going to bed myself. These stitches are starting to burn."

Kathryn slapped him playfully on his good arm, before batting her thick, dark lashes at him. "I'm gonna have to check in with my momma. She'll be worried if I don't call."

Mick pointed to Josh. "And she should be, if you're gonna keep hanging around with this one." But he grinned when he said it, and Kathryn only giggled again.

It was downright sickening to see Josh and Kathryn so wrapped up in each other, but Mick couldn't begrudge his friend this chance at love.

Only, he wanted that same chance with Lorna. And it didn't help matters one bit when he reminded himself that he'd vowed to steer clear of any binding relationships, that he'd learned his lesson with Melinda, that he wasn't worth the dirt underneath Lorna Dorsette's pretty feet.

None of those warnings or reminders could stop him

from achieving his purpose for being here. A purpose he somehow knew he'd regret in the long run.

But he needed to test that purpose, needed to find out if what he'd been feeling was real or imagined, if all of this disaster and drama had heightened the attraction, or if the attraction had been real from the first time he'd touched her.

Which is why he marched into the kitchen to find Lorna. She might be busy, but Mick intended to make his presence known.

And he intended to take up right where he'd left off yesterday. He wanted another kiss, just for good measure.

Chapter Nine

"You sure are making a lot of noise," Mick told Lorna a few minutes later.

She whirled around, inhaled deeply, then tried to ignore the feathering of butterflies hopelessly trapped in her stomach. But how could she ignore the effect this man had on her? Or the lasting impression his kiss had left in her heart and head?

She was certainly going to give it her best shot.

"Found them," she said, holding up two big glass mixing bowls. "Got to get back to the restaurant."

"Just hold on a minute," he said, reaching out to catch her arm, as she tried to slip by.

From her spot at the stove, Rosie Lee cast them an amused look, then quickly brought her gaze back to the pork roast she'd prepared for dinner.

But Lorna knew exactly what her friend was thinking. Not wanting to give Rosie Lee the satisfaction of witnessing one of her tirades, Lorna glanced down at Mick's hand. "I have to get back—"

"Okay, then, I'll walk with you."

He took the bowls right out of her arms. "Busy night, huh?"

"Ah, yes." She had no choice but to start walking. "Don't you want to stay and sample Rosie Lee's pork roast with lemon pepper?"

"Save me a bite, will you, Rosie Lee?" he said over his shoulder.

"Of course," Rosie Lee answered. Lorna didn't miss the slight smile curving the woman's lips.

"Really, Mick, I can carry those myself. Stay here and enjoy your dinner with the family."

"I'd rather walk with you. Nice night, don't you think?"

Lorna decided he wasn't going to take no for an answer, so she had to be polite, at least. She'd tried really hard to avoid him these past few days, but it hadn't been easy. He'd shown up at the restaurant every night, sitting there with a menu in front of him as his gaze followed her. Mick had become a loyal customer.

If she didn't at least talk to him, he'd probably spend another evening sampling way too much French cuisine. So she answered his question with politeness and grace, hoping those two attributes would hide her agitation and agony. "Yes, it's a bit warm, but nice.

The gardens are looking much better, though, thanks to your crew.''

''Yeah, the mud's dried up and everything is getting back into shape. We talked with the landscaper earlier today. He's already getting new flowers in place. Seems to have a lot of nervous energy, that one.''

''Justin is a hard worker,'' Lorna replied, glad to be talking about a safe, comfortable subject such as gardening. ''And he has a major crush on Lacey.''

''Oh, really?''

''They've known each other for years, since we came here. But I don't think she's interested. They're good friends, though.''

''You Dorsette women tend to have a lot of men friends, I do believe.''

They were nearing the summerhouse now, which only made Lorna remember being there with him the other morning. She also remembered how she'd lashed out at him. Obviously, he wasn't holding that against her anymore. But she didn't want to bring up their gentle truce or the kiss or anything else between them, so she decided to talk about her sister, instead.

''Lacey was married once.''

That turned his head. ''I didn't know.''

''She doesn't talk about it much. Neil was a pilot in the Air Force. His plane crashed on a routine training mission.''

Mick stopped her, a hand once again on her arm. ''I'm sorry to hear that.''

There was more to the story, but Lorna wouldn't share that with him. Lacey wouldn't want his pity. "Now, when people call her Lacey Dorsette, she doesn't bother to correct them. But her actual name is Lacey Dorsette York."

"How long ago did this happen?"

"Oh, it's been about six years. They were stationed up in Shreveport at Barksdale. She came home to Bayou le Jardin immediately after it happened. Neil is buried in our family plot at the chapel."

And my sister has retreated behind a wall of sadness and duty, she wanted to add.

"Well, that is a tragedy," Mick said, as they started back down the path toward the restaurant. "But who knows, maybe this friendship between her and Justin will turn into something more."

"Maybe, but I doubt it," Lorna replied. "Lacey is too afraid to let go of her heart again."

"And what about her little sister?"

The question threw her so off-kilter, she almost stumbled. "What do you mean?"

Mick halted again. Balancing the mixing bowls against his hip, he said, "I think you know what I mean, Lorna. What about you? What about us? Are we just friends, or did that kiss change things between us? Are *you* willing to let go of your heart?"

Too many questions, coming at her much too fast.

Lorna glanced down the path toward the noise and lights of her beloved restaurant. Longing to run to the safety of bubbling stews and hot ovens, she swallowed back the fear that choked at her, determined to be honest with Mick. Well, almost honest.

"There is no 'us,' Mick. We just got carried away the other day."

"Yeah, you could say that. And I guess I should say I won't let it happen again—only, I want it to happen again."

She wouldn't look at him. Couldn't. "It can't happen again."

But he made her look. He moved ahead of her until he was in her direct view, his face blocking out her escape route. "Why can't it?"

Lorna finally lifted her gaze to his face. "Because...I'm through wandering around. And you're apparently not. I came home to find some peace, some purpose in my life. And I'm content, living here, working here." The explanation sounded feeble, but it was the only one she could give him right now.

"What's that got to do with us?"

She threw up her hands, then let them drop to her sides. "Isn't that obvious? You like traveling around, doing your job. I can respect that, since I used to be filled with wanderlust myself. But I can't live like that anymore, and I won't ask you to become tied down— not when we've only just met and...this whole situation has gotten way out of hand."

"What situation?"

She moaned, expelled a breath. "Us."

"I thought you said there was no 'us.'"

"You known what I mean, Mick."

He lowered his head, bringing his face to within inches of hers. "I think I get it. You're afraid of what you're feeling for me because you think I'll be gone soon."

She shrugged, hoping to sound nonchalant. "Maybe."

"Is that what always happened before, in your other relationships?"

Lorna wanted to laugh. If he only knew. But she couldn't tell him that before, she'd always been the one to run away first—that is, until Cole had left her standing at the altar. Just when someone started getting close, or wanted more of a commitment, she got cold feet and broke things off, or worse, just up and left, like the coward she was. Cole had figured it all out, though. And he'd left her because he couldn't deal with her terrors in the night.

What if Mick reacted the same way?

This time, it was different. This time, she couldn't run. But Mick could easily walk away once he realized she was a coward, once he saw her for what she really was.

"Answer me, Lorna," he said, his hand settling on her hair. "Is that why you won't let me get any closer?"

"That's part of it," she replied, moving away to start toward the restaurant.

"And what's the other part?" he said behind her. "What's really going on here, Lorna?" When she hesitated, he asked, "Is it because of what I said the other day in the summerhouse? Because I grew up poor, living in a trailer park?"

She whirled around, shock filtering through her resistance. "Don't be ridiculous. Contrary to what you might think, I'm not a snob. And believe me, until Aunt Hilda took us in, we lived in much worse conditions than a trailer park. We lived in a hut in the jungle, with snakes and scorpions and spiders…" She stopped, dread and fear making her feel weak at the knees. Unable to look at him, she lowered her head. "I'm not that way, Mick."

Mick lifted her head with a finger under her chin, his face full of curiosity and questions. But thankfully, he didn't ask. Instead, he said, "I'm sorry. But I had to know. I'm not proud of my background, Lorna, and I could certainly understand if—"

"It's not that," she interrupted as she drew her chin away from his touch. "This is happening too fast, Mick. Can't you see that? Can't you understand that I've never—"

She paused, turned away again.

"Never what? Felt like this before?" he asked, following right on her heels. "'Cause that's the way I'm feeling. Like I've been hit by lightning."

"Or lived through a storm," she said, almost to herself. That's exactly what it felt like, being with him, being in his arms, as if she were reliving the storm all over again—helpless, frightened, alone in the dark.

"Lorna?"

They were at the door of the restaurant now. From inside, Lorna heard the sweet, sad notes of her brother's saxophone drifting out over the night. Lucas was such a paradox. Only her brother could play gospel songs on the saxophone and make people want to get down on their knees and praise the Lord, even if they felt the blues all the way to their toes. "Shall We Gather at the River" had never sounded so poignant, so clear.

Lorna wanted to sit down and cry. It was so tempting to do just that, to sit down and pour her heart out in a good old-fashioned sobbing fit.

But Mick was there, waiting. And she couldn't allow him to see her pain or her confusion. Or her tears.

"Lorna?" he asked again. "Can we talk about this?"

"I have to get back," she said, her head down.

"Then later. Meet me in the summerhouse after you're done here. Please?"

Her heart hammered a warning, reminding her of the beat of a drum somewhere in that faraway jungle. "We don't close until eleven."

"I'll wait."

Her head reeled at the prospect of walking back up the path alone to meet him there in the darkened summerhouse, causing her to close her eyes for just a second. "I could be awfully late."

"I don't care. I don't think I'll get much sleep, anyway."

You don't understand, she wanted to shout. *I can't meet you there. It's so very dark there late at night. How can I make you understand?*

But Lorna couldn't bring herself to confess her frightening secret to Mick. What if he, too, shunned her, laughed at her silliness the way so many others had done before? Walked away out of frustration the way Cole had done? No, she couldn't bear that. Not this time. And yet, this time she couldn't run away, either. But she had to convince him, somehow, that she wasn't worth his time or his energy.

"Don't wait for me, Mick. I have a lot to do tonight."

He leaned close, then shoved the bowls into her hands, his blue eyes turning to black in the growing dusk. "I said I don't care. I'll be there. And I expect you to show up."

Then he turned and left her standing at the door of the restaurant, while the notes of the saxophone filled the night around her with a misty fog of regret and rejoicing.

"Ready to go home now?" Lucas asked Lorna hours later.

Lorna lifted her tired eyes from the computer, then

hit the save button on the bookkeeping program. Glancing up at the clock, she was surprised to see that it was well after midnight. "I didn't realize how late it was," she told her brother as she pivoted in the swivel chair.

"I'm sorry I made you hang around all night."

Lucas gave her a grin, then reached out to pull her hair, just as he'd often done when they were growing up. "Didn't mind one bit, sis. It gave me a chance to play some of my tunes."

She got up, stretched, then laughed. "The customers always enjoy your impromptu shows. And I think they especially needed to hear some good music tonight."

Lucas ran a hand down his beard stubble, then did a little spin toward her. "And I think my baby sister needed to hear some good tunes herself. What's up with you and the tree expert, anyway?"

Knowing she couldn't hide anything from Lucas, Lorna sank back down in her chair. The little office off the back of the kitchen was quiet now. All the employees had gone home, and everything was neat and tidy, ready for tomorrow, just the way Lorna liked it. They'd had a fairly large crowd, considering the entire town was still dealing with the aftereffects of the tornado. But then, she reminded herself, the place always drew a large crowd from Kenner, too. Lots of folks had come just to see how much storm damage Bayou le Jardin had suffered.

Finally, she looked up at her brother. He waited

patiently, letting her take her time in answering his question. At times such as this, she loved that about Lucas. He never hurried anything.

''I don't know what's going on between Mick and me,'' she admitted. ''He kissed me the other day, after the cave-in.''

Lucas swung his lithe body up onto a nearby credenza, then settled back against the wall, his black eyes regarding her with a curious intensity.

''That cave-in must have been mighty powerful. First Josh and Kathryn, and now you and our Mr. Love. I guess a life-or-death experience can do that for a person.''

''We should know, right?'' Lorna replied softly.

''Yeah.'' Lucas looked away then, his eyes turning a shade of midnight that Lorna recognized. The memories of their parents' death always did that—made them turn away and retreat into their own nightmares. But Lucas didn't stay in that distant horror long. ''So, he kissed you? What's the big deal? You've been kissed before, right?''

''Right.'' Lorna pushed at the loose curls falling away from her braid. ''I don't know, Lucas. I don't know if it was all the excitement of the accident and the rescue, or if Mick and I really are attracted to each other. I only know that it scared me.''

''Different than the rest, hmm, *petite fleur?*''

''*Oui,*'' Lorna responded, lapsing into the French they sometimes used when they didn't want others to know what they were saying. Although they were very much alone, Lorna didn't want Mick to walk in and hear them discussing him. *"Mais, sa c'est fou!"*

"Now why is that so crazy?" Lucas asked, leaning his head down, his dark eyes widening. "Don't you deserve to feel some *joie de vie?"*

Lorna got up, started putting files away. "That's the crazy part. Kissing Mick did bring me joy—such immense joy that I don't know how to deal with it. I only just met the man—how can I feel this way? How?"

Lucas hopped off the credenza to stand in front of her. Looking down at her, he put a hand on each of her arms. "I don't have an answer for that, *chère.* But I do have some advice."

"I could use some of that."

"Go with it, love. Let it happen. Stop fighting against your heart. Lorna, you are a beautiful woman with a big heart and a soul that needs to be filled with love. Don't run from that."

Lorna groaned, then slapped him away. "Some help you are. You have a poet's soul, Lucas, and you fall in love at the drop of a hat. How am I supposed to trust anything you tell me?"

"Good point." His grin was full of the old charm. "But hey, I enjoy life to the fullest. I have fun. Why can't you and Lacey do that?"

"Because we have other things to consider," she told him as she turned out the lights and, flashlight in hand and on full blast, headed for the back door. "We have responsibilities, duties, obligations."

"I have all of those things, too," Lucas told her, turning to make sure everything was locked up tight before they headed up the path toward the mansion. "I know neither of you think that, but I am dedicated to this family."

"We understand that," Lorna replied. "It's just easier for you, I guess."

"Falling in love is never easy," he replied. "The hard part is falling out of love. When it's over, it's over. And it's sometimes hard to face."

"You don't seem to have a problem with that."

"I'm the shallow one, remember," he said, his voice going quiet again. "But let's get back to you. So what do you intend to do about Mr. Love?"

Lorna looked out at the night looming before them. Was Mick still there, waiting in the summerhouse?

"I don't know," she said on a whisper. "He wants me to meet him in the summerhouse. He told me he'd wait until I came up the path."

Lucas did a slow dance around her, smiling. "Well, that would be right about now, don't you think?"

"I'm frightened," she told him.

"You have your flashlight," Lucas said, coming close in an automatic gesture of protection. "And you have me. I'll escort you there myself."

They started toward the summerhouse together.

"It's not the dark so much—I'm afraid of my feelings for Mick."

"I can help there, too. If he gets too pushy."

Lorna tugged her brother close. "Don't worry, Mick is a perfect gentleman. But thanks for the chivalrous offer. I don't know what I'd do without you."

"Just remember that," he teased as he took her by the hand. "Right now, you need to find your suitor, though. Can't leave a man waiting too long, darlin'."

"I suppose that's an expert opinion."

"I am the expert on love," he replied, winking. "Even if my last name isn't Love."

They were approaching the summerhouse. Lorna could see the white outline of the building in the muted moonlight. The curtains billowed out in the wind, beckoning her to come inside.

"Full moon," Lucas commented, whistling low. "The gardens are shimmering with it."

"At least, I have that to be thankful about," she replied, her hands sweaty, her steps unsure.

"You have a lot to be thankful about, *belle.* Don't forget that."

"You're right," Lorna said, nodding. "Maybe I should take your advice and just enjoy myself for a change."

"There you go," Lucas said, pointing to a shadow inside the circular building. "Want me to check it out, make sure it's safe?"

But Lucas didn't get a chance to do that. Mick must

have heard them coming up the path. He came to one of the open doors, leaning a shoulder against the frame as he watched them—watched Lorna—approach.

Even in the muted light, Lorna knew it was him. She could see the stark white patch of his bandaged forehead, and she could feel his eyes on her.

"Mick, what a pleasant surprise," Lucas said, all exaggeration. "Enjoying the moonlight?"

"Very much," Mick answered, his hands tucked in the pockets of his jeans, his eyes still on Lorna.

Lorna turned to her brother. "Thanks for walking me home, Lucas. I'll see you in the morning."

"Are you sure?" Lucas waited, fully prepared to stick around if Lorna needed him.

"I'm sure. I'm okay, really," she said close to his ear. "The moonlight helps."

Lucas gave his sister a peck on the cheek, then turned to Mick. "Will you make sure she gets in the house safely?"

Lorna didn't miss the brotherly protection in that question, and apparently neither did Mick.

"I'll be glad to," Mick replied. "Don't worry."

Lucas shrugged. "Me, never." Then he turned, waved, and said, "Don't keep her out too late."

"I won't," Mick replied. Then after Lucas had strolled on up the path, he added, "Your brother sure is protective."

"That's what brothers are for," Lorna told him, her

nerves thrashing like loose bramble inside her body as she glanced over his clean T-shirt and faded jeans.

"I guess I don't blame him," Mick replied, still leaning against the door frame.

She couldn't explain that Lucas knew her deepest pain and her worst secrets, and that because he was her brother, he would hold both close to his heart unless she told him otherwise. And so would Lacey. Lorna returned their trust in the same way. It had always been that way among the three of them. She doubted Mick would understand that kind of bond, forged out of terror on a dark, storm-tossed night so long ago.

"I didn't think you would come," Mick told her, bringing her back to this fragrant, moon-washed summerhouse.

"I wasn't going to," she replied.

"Why did you?"

She shrugged, her voice lifting into a question. "It was on the way?"

"Not good enough." He tugged her close. "You came because you feel the same way I do. Because you know in your heart there is an 'us.'"

Lorna resisted his touch, resisted the soapy-clean smell of his hair, resisted the warmth that wrapped around her like a security blanket, blocking out the darkness and all her fears. "Maybe I came because I wanted to convince you that you're wrong."

"I'm not wrong—not this time."

And that was what she feared the most.

"How can you be so sure? You'll be gone in a few days. You'll probably leave right after church on Sunday."

Mick gathered her into his embrace, his face inches from hers. "Now that's where *you're* wrong. Claude Juneau came by today, asked me and the crew to hire on and help him clear up a few more trouble spots. I told him we'd stay."

Lorna felt the breath leaving her body, like a river tide being pulled away from the shore. "You're staying?"

"That's what I just told you."

His head dipped. His lips touched her cheekbone, making it extremely hard for her to focus, to concentrate. "For how long?"

He moved his mouth over her face in little feathery kisses that made her think of a soft field of clover. "Well, now, that just depends, don't you think?"

"Depends?" She tried to find her breath. Tried to find some reasoning thought. "On what?"

"On you," he said.

His lips cut off any kind of response she might have offered—except for the soft moan that escaped as she fell against him and gave in to his sweet, reassuring kiss.

Chapter Ten

Mick didn't want the kiss to end. But before he took this any further, he had to tell Lorna a few things. About him. About his past.

So he pulled away from her, then stood back to stare down at her. She looked so young and innocent, standing there, colored all lavender and blue in the moonlight. The scent of night-blooming jasmine and honeysuckle surrounded her as if she were a natural part of this garden. And he supposed she was.

Longing to ask her what had happened to her parents, why she'd lived in a jungle, why she and her siblings were so protective and close, he instead just stood there looking at her. He didn't want to frighten her away with too many probing questions. Not yet. Right now, he wanted to memorize her face, her lips, her smile.

Just in case she turned away from him.

"We need to talk," he said at last, his voice husky from need, his emotions lifting and scattering like the curtains that billowed out all around them.

He saw her nod, watched as she pushed a hand through the loose curls at her forehead.

"Lorna, I don't have a whole lot to offer a woman. I have a nice enough house back in Vicksburg. I built it on a bluff, thinking I'd get married and raise my children there. But my fiancée decided she didn't want to stay there waiting on me to come home after a long job. We were engaged, had been for about a year. I'd just finished the house, when she told me, standing in the middle of the empty living room, that she'd fallen in love with someone else. Someone who could provide her with a comfortable living, someone who could be there when she came home at night. Someone who didn't like to wander around the way I did."

Mick saw the surprise rushing like the humid wind over Lorna's face.

"You were engaged?" The question held a hint of hurt, of regret.

"Yep. Didn't work out, though. And I've been traveling ever since. I decided maybe she was right, maybe I didn't need to settle down, after all."

"She...she married someone else?"

He nodded, his laughter low and harsh. "My best friend."

"What?"

"The man who helped me build the house. While I was out making a living to pay for the thing, he and Melinda got very close. I can't say that I blame them. They were together so much, going over the plans, working on the house day and night. It was bound to happen, I guess."

"Not if she really loved you."

Mick heard the soft, fierce tenderness in that declaration. It went straight to his heart. "Then I guess she didn't really love me. And I guess I didn't love her enough to go back and fight for her."

"So you just walked away, let your friend take her?"

"Yes, that's exactly what I did. I didn't have much faith in anything back then. Not her, certainly not myself."

"And what about your faith in God?"

That wasn't what he'd expected, but then, this was Lorna, after all. He smiled, then shrugged. "I guess that was pretty weak, too. In fact, it's been that way for a while now. Until I came here."

"Here?" She lifted her chin a notch, her green eyes shimmering like forbidden emeralds caught in a beam of moonlight. "You mean, Bayou le Jardin has strengthened your faith in God?"

He wanted her to understand that he'd never felt this way before. But how did he explain something so elusive? "From the first moment, I think," he began, his hands touching hers. "When you told me that God had sent me, I took it seriously."

"I believed it, too," she said, her fingers curling around his, warm and reassuring. "I was so frightened that night, during the storm. And when it was all over, I was so very thankful. I had to get away from all the noise, all the confusion, just to talk to God. And I did ask Him to send us help—not just for this place, but the whole town." Her expression was full of amazement. "And then you came."

"And then—"

"You saved me from that tree limb."

"I thought you were a little boy."

"I always was the tomboy."

"You're not a tomboy now, that's for sure, Lorna. You're all woman."

She laughed. "Maybe we'd better get back to your faith."

Mick wanted to get back to kissing her and holding her, but he needed to talk about this. It had been a very long time since he'd wanted to discuss religion with anyone. "It just seemed as if this peace came over me, holding you there in my arms. As if I'd finally come home." He shifted, pulled her with him to lean back against a support column. "Then when the building caved in, and I went in after Josh and Kathryn, I just knew—I was meant to be here, right here, for some reason."

"To save us."

"But I didn't save anyone. I just did what had to be done."

Lorna reached up to touch the bandage on his forehead. "But, Mick, think about it. What if you hadn't been here? You and Josh both? I might not be standing here right now, and Kathryn might be dead."

"I don't understand any of it," he admitted, "but I do know that something inside me changed when I went down in that building. I heard…I heard something, someone, telling me not to give up."

"So you felt closer to God?"

"Yes. And I still do. You know, my momma taught me the word of God, but I kinda just let it wash right over me."

Lorna moved her fingers down his face, making his heart hurt with need.

"Mick, when you thought God's word was washing right over you, it was really washing through you. You had the foundation and the knowledge—you just didn't know how to apply it."

Trust Lorna to make it all seem so simple. But it wasn't that simple. His life was changing right before his eyes, and Mick wasn't sure how to deal with that.

"Maybe you're right. I mean, you and your family have such a strong faith. It's impressive."

"We don't mean to impress. It's just the way we feel. It's the way we view the world."

"So you're completely confident in your faith?"

She dropped her hand, then moved away. Mick saw

the defensiveness in her gestures, in the way she put her arms against her stomach. "Most of the time, yes."

"But?"

"We all struggle with our faith at times, I suppose. But Aunt Hilda has taught us to trust in the Lord, to depend on Him in all things. When she's worried, she goes out into the garden and talks to God."

"That's not always easy."

"No, it's not. But my family and I know He's there. And He's here—" She reached a hand up to her heart.

"Do you think he brought us together?"

Mick saw her smile. It radiated from her face, lighting up the night. "I sure hope so."

"But you still have doubts?"

"Yes, I have to admit, I do. Especially after what you just told me about Melinda and your friend. I don't think you want to trust me, Mick."

"It's hard to trust after that, but it was my fault. I couldn't give Melinda what she wanted."

"A big house and lots of charge cards?"

"Yeah, and security. That's what she really wanted. She wanted someone she could count on."

"Don't we all?"

"And what if I can't give that to you, either? Do you think you can count on me? Do you think I can give you that kind of security?"

Lorna moved close again, then reached out a hand to him. "Maybe it's not up to you to give me security.

Maybe *I* just need to be secure enough to accept what you can offer me.''

Mick held her hand up to his lips, kissing the delicate, slender fingers. ''I told you, I don't *have* much to offer. At least, not compared to the life you have here.''

''That's where you're wrong,'' she whispered.

Mick's lips moved from her hand to her mouth. He kissed her again, putting everything he wanted to give her into that one intimate gesture.

When he lifted his head, he said, ''So...there is an 'us'? I mean, are you willing to explore the possibilities?''

She laid her head on his shoulder, then let out a deep sigh. ''I don't know. I've had a lot of false starts, Mick. I've hurt people, and I've been hurt. And there's so much about me that you don't know, that I'm not ready to tell you.'' Raising her head, she glanced back up at him. ''The Dorsettes are famous for falling in love too quickly, so I want to be very cautious with you.''

''Why? Why not just go with how you feel?''

''I've done that before, and it's backfired. This time, I want to be completely sure.''

Mick thought he knew why she was being so careful. ''Maybe because of what I just told you? You said earlier that you're done with traveling around. You're settled here. But with me, well, you'd have to deal with my job, my long hours, lots of time away from home.''

"That's part of it," she told him. "But I can live with that, I think. Right now, I just want to be sure about what I'm feeling. What it really means.''

Mick knew what it meant to him, having her in his arms. But he understood her doubts. He pulled her close again. "We've got some time to consider all of that. Right now, *this* feels right.''

He held her there as they leaned against the ornate column, the moonlight and night breezes playing all around them, the scent of magnolias mixed with the rich distinct loam of the swamp surrounding them in a humid mist. Just outside the door, the white blossoms of a moon vine glistened and swayed, opening to follow the night.

Finally, Lorna shifted in his arms. "It's getting late. And you promised to walk me to the door.''

"Do you have to go?''

"Yes. Tomorrow is another busy day. The restaurant really fills up.''

Reluctantly, he guided her through the dark, shadowy garden. He noticed that she kept her flashlight on and pointed ahead of them until they'd reached the lighted back gallery of the imposing house. "Will you be okay from here, or do you want me to make sure you get to your room?''

"No, this is fine." She glanced toward the well-lit staircase, then turned the flashlight off. "Mick, thank you for being honest with me. About your past, I mean.''

"I just wanted you to know."

And he wanted to know all about her, too. When she was ready to tell him.

"Well, good night," she said, her tone making her sound shy.

"Lorna—" He couldn't resist pulling her back into his arms for one more kiss.

"This is crazy," she said on a breathless whisper.

"We don't have to rush," he told her. "I'll be around for a while longer. We can take it slow, get to know each other."

"That would be nice."

Then she slipped away from him like a dancer and moved inside. Mick watched through the glass doors as she headed upstairs.

For a very long time after that, he waited inside the summerhouse, remembering the feel of her in his arms, his gaze riveted on the light from her bedroom.

The light that never went out.

The next morning at dawn, Mick woke up in the cottage to that same light shining down from her window. Did Lorna stay up later than everyone else, then get up before the rest of the family? Or did she simply keep a light burning all night long? Sitting up in bed, he said, ''That's got to be it.''

Mick suddenly realized why he'd seen that fear and dread in Lorna's eyes so many times, and why Lucas had seemed so protective, why Lacey always asked if Lorna was all right. Why Lorna always carried a flashlight at night.

Quietly, so he wouldn't wake Josh and David, Mick got up and went outside to stand on the small cottage porch, his eyes never leaving Lorna's bedroom window.

"Lorna, are you afraid of the dark?"

That had to be it. She didn't like the darkness, didn't like being alone in the night.

If that was the truth, then Mick knew all of her insecurities had to be tied up in that one fear.

But why? What had caused her to be so afraid?

Lorna stood beside Mick in the tiny cedar-walled chapel located on the edge of the plantation grounds. Famous for the many weddings and christenings that were held here annually, the Chapel in the Garden was a quiet retreat that offered the Dorsette family and the entire community a place to worship in a peaceful, country setting.

The outside walls of the chapel had been built in 1850 out of cypress logs pulled from the nearby swamp, but it was now remodeled and painted a stark, glistening white. Square and compact with an ornate steeple complete with a brass bell, the small building couldn't hold a lot of people. But today it looked as if most of the townspeople had come to give thanks to God and celebrate with a dinner on the grounds back at the mansion.

Lorna was glad to see so many friends turning out for this special service. The town had survived the storm without any lives lost. Those who'd been injured were slowly recovering, and most of the cleanup was under control.

Now would come the rebuilding and the rejoicing.

She turned to look up at Mick. He was still here, but she knew he'd have to leave soon. He had worked so hard over the past few days, helping Claude to clear away the remaining debris and trees, helping Lucas and Justin get the gardens back in shape for the rest of the spring tourist season, doing whatever needed to be done, whether or not it involved his particular expertise. He'd sent some of his crew back to Vicksburg, but a couple of the men, along with Josh as supervisor while he was still recuperating from his wounds, had stayed to help out. Lorna would never forget their willingness to get the job done. Nor would she forget Mick's patience and understanding.

He'd gone out and worked each day, then returned to her each night. Their late-night meetings in the summerhouse had fueled the curiosity of both her family and the Babineaux.

Everyone wanted to know what was going on between Lorna and Mick.

She wished she could answer that particular question. After everything Mick had told her about his past, she now understood that he had come a long way. He'd found his way back to God, here in her gardens. He'd shared his journey with her, making her see that this hadn't been easy for him. Not after what had happened with Melinda and his friend. The woman he'd loved was now married to someone else; that had left Mick distrustful and doubtful.

Lorna knew that feeling, at least. And while she appreciated Mick's ability to open up and tell her the truth about his past, Lorna didn't know if she'd ever be able to do the same. And yet, she sensed Mick was waiting for just that. How long would he be willing to wait?

Lacey poked her, bringing Lorna's mind back to the song they were singing. As they finished the last verse of "Standing on the Promise," Lacey leaned over. "Where were you just then? Your lips weren't even moving to the music."

"Just thinking," Lorna replied, as they all settled back on the polished wooden church pews to listen to Reverend Mahoney's sermon.

"About *him?*" Lacey lifted a pink-polished fingernail toward Mick, her gaze on Lorna's face.

"Would you please stop pointing. It's rude," Lorna hissed back, hoping Mick hadn't seen Lacey.

"I'm not pointing, merely indicating," Lacey replied as she straightened the skirt of her light yellow cotton dress. "Aunt Hilda is concerned that you two are getting mighty close, mighty fast."

Lorna glanced up to where her aunt was sitting in front of them, wearing a white hat with a large yellow sunflower on its brim, Lucas right beside her in his tan summer suit and tie. Josh sat next to Lucas with Kathryn, who had her broken leg, cast and all, out in the aisle, while Kathryn's mother sat behind them next to Mick, keeping a close watch on her lovesick daughter.

Lorna studied her aunt, then put a hand over her mouth to talk to her sister. "She doesn't look concerned to me. In fact, she looks downright joyful."

"She's in church," Lacey retorted. "She always looks that way in church, whether she's worried or not."

"Well, she doesn't have to worry about me," Lorna said, her whisper lifting up in a muffled echo.

Lucas looked around, turned his head sideways, then brought a tanned finger to his smiling lips. "Shh."

Lorna gave her brother a nasty glare, then pushed at Lacey's hand on her arm. "Can we talk about this later?"

"Sure." Lacey settled back, her porcelain face all innocence, her glance cutting over Lorna to Mick. When he looked around, she smiled prettily, then pretended to be shuffling through the church bulletin in her hand.

"Everything okay?" Mick said in Lorna's ear, his warm breath reminding her of moonlight and kisses.

"Fine," she said, her breath hitching at his nearness. Oh, he smelled so good—like a forest just after a soft rain, like exotic spices mixing with warm butter, like...

She stopped thinking about Mick, determined to listen to the sermon. But somehow, now that they were all quiet and still, Mick managed to find her hand and hold it tightly to his. Somehow, she managed to steady her heart rate, sure that the entire congregation could hear it beating and flailing against the shiny cotton of her green-and-blue floral sheath. Somehow, a curling wisp of her long hair got caught against the crisp cotton of Mick's white button-up shirt, the curls holding to the fabric, pulling her to him each time either one of them took a breath. It seemed as if they were breathing in a rhythm meant only for them, a bit shaky, but steady and sure, measure for measure, as if their very breaths were dancing with each other.

Mick looked over at her and smiled.

Lorna knew she was in big trouble.

So she prayed while the preacher preached.

Dear Lord, what has come over me? Why am I acting as though I've never been around a man before? Why does Mick seem to affect me so strongly? I've never felt this way before, Lord. Remember Paris, when I thought I was so in love with Cole? And then he left, and now I don't think I even knew what love really was. Not even close. But my pride hurt all the same. Remember Italy, when I thought Dion was the

only one for me? Can't even remember his face. Re-
member Ireland and Weylin? What was I thinking?

Didn't I learn anything from Cole's cruelty?

Oh, Lord, this is Mick, not Cole. This is the one who
showed up when I asked you to send someone. I
wanted someone strong, someone who could make me
feel safe after the storm. And he does, Lord. He does.
I'm so frightened, though. I can't let go. I'm afraid,
Lord. So afraid. Help me to find peace. Help me to
find the answers. Help me to feel safe in the dark,
Lord. Show me what to do.

Lorna felt Mick's fingers tighten on hers, then she
glanced down at his hand covering her own against
the glowing brown wood of the pew. She chanced a
look at his face, marveling in his little-boy features,
marveling in the strength behind that innocent, lazy
expression.

Mick's gaze found hers, held her there. Then he
smiled and turned his attention back to the preacher.

Lorna went back to praying. She had to find some
way of understanding the enormous emotions swirling
like murky river water through her mind. She had to
get a grip on the enticing, yet frightening feelings blos-
soming inside her each time she was with Mick. She
couldn't rush this, couldn't give in completely. And
yet, she felt as if she were falling down a dark, narrow
tunnel. She had to shut her eyes to that particular fear.
Mick wouldn't leave her stranded—not like the others.

Not the way she always sabotaged herself and left herself stranded.

She'd been completely stranded and alone once. And since then, she'd never allowed anyone to get close enough to see the fear, the pain of that abandonment. How could she keep all of this from Mick? *How, Lord?*

Reverend Mahoney finished the sermon. "God is indeed our refuge and our strength. Even in times of trouble. Even when we don't see His hand reaching down to us. God was there with us during this terrible storm. Now it's up to us to rebuild and rededicate our lives to this town, and to His everlasting love."

Lorna wanted to feel God's hand reaching down to her, wanted to know God was with her, even in the dark. She knew inside her heart that she'd have to accept that, have to trust in God's guiding hand, before she could overcome her fears and make a firm commitment to any man.

She also knew that she wanted that man to be Mick Love. He hadn't let go of her hand—not once during the entire sermon.

He'd held on to her the whole time she'd been praying for God to send her a sign.

Chapter Eleven

"**M**ick, thanks for stopping that near-disaster with the cypress tree the other day," Justin Hayes said, as they made their way through the covered dish buffet set out underneath the great oaks.

"No problem," Mick replied, his gaze zooming in on a large crispy chicken breast.

"You saved a cypress tree?" Lorna asked, curious. "What was the problem?"

Justin spoke up before Mick could. "Storm got it—you know that big one down by the water?"

"Of course," Lorna replied. "It's a favorite among the tourists. I didn't realize it'd been damaged."

"One of Mick's men found it and decided to just whack it up," Justin said, squinting as he spiked a drumstick and a sliver of honey-baked ham. "I was trying to stop him when Mick intervened and...settled things between us."

Lorna lifted a brow toward Mick, then studied Justin's face. Tall and lanky, he had reddish-blond hair and a temper to match. She wasn't surprised that he'd jumped on one of Mick's men for infringing on his territory. Justin protected the gardens like the keeper of the gate. And tried to protect Lacey in much the same way, in spite of her sister's gentle rebuttals and sometimes distant demeanor.

"We thought we were going to have to cut part of the main trunk down," Mick explained. "At least, David—our young and eager new team member—wanted to do that."

"Thing was split near in two at the top." Justin chewed a piping-hot yeast roll as he tried to talk. Waving a handful of roll in the air, he added, "That David boy was just about to take a chain saw to it—figured it would become an eyesore—right there at the water's edge, but Mick halted the young fellow just in time." He shot Mick an almost relieved look, then glanced around, no doubt searching for the trigger-happy David.

"David thought he was doing the right thing," Mick explained. "I'm just glad I found him in time to save the tree, and in time to save David from getting into a fistfight with Justin."

Justin didn't seem to mind any of that now, though, Lorna noticed. He just kept on talking.

"We reshaped it so that when it does grow back out, it'll probably be just fine. That tree's so old, but the roots and knees are intact and so peggy, it's almost completely hollow at the base. Time will tell about the top growing back in straight, though.''

This time, he gave Mick a determined look, as if daring him to question this opinion. Then he marched away, obviously headed to find Lacey, his plate full of chicken, turnip greens, potato salad and rolls.

Lorna let out a hoot of laughter. ''So you came up against the mighty Justin Hayes. Poor David. I'm so glad you came to that kid's rescue in time. I suppose no one bothered to tell sweet David that Justin rules the roost around here, as far as the landscaping goes. He's a royal pain, but very good at his work, and he's fiercely protective of these gardens.''

''I don't blame him for that,'' Mick said, as they took their plates and headed for the summerhouse. ''And I gave David a gentle but firm talking-to. He just got a little bit too ambitious. And as for Justin, I think he's tolerated *me* being here this past week because he knows I've got a hankering for the younger of the two lovely Dorsette women. Lacey is safe.''

''But I'm not?'' She grinned at him.

''A mighty strong hankering,'' he told her, his eyes holding hers.

A hankering? Was that what this was? She sure had a yearning inside her, too. But she kept that to herself as they strolled past where Lucas sweated and toiled, flushed and grinning, over a huge aluminum pot filled to the brim with steaming freshly boiled crawfish.

"Hey, Mick?" Lucas called, waving to them as he wiped his face and curling, humidity-soaked hair with the colorful bandanna he'd tied around his neck. "C'mon, man, and get some of these mudbugs while they're hot and spicy."

With that, he pulled on the handle of a large steaming colander full of spicy, bright-red crawfish, then dumped the whole thing unceremoniously across a long table covered with a white plastic cloth.

"Maybe later, friend," Mick called back, watching as people rushed to eat the mudbugs right off the pile in the middle of the table. "They do smell good, though."

Lucas winked and went right back to flirting with a leggy blonde who seemed extremely interested in getting a plateful of the little critters for herself.

"I see my brother has anxious customers lining up for his specialty," Lorna said on a droll note.

"And would that specialty be crawfish or that killer smile he's beaming out to all the single women here today?"

"You've figured him out, I see."

"It didn't take long. But I like your brother."

She only smiled and shook her head.

They stopped at the summerhouse. Mick glanced over at her and indicated a table just inside the cool shade of the open room.

Lorna wondered why they were automatically drawn to the rounded, octagon-shaped building, but at least today there were several other diners already there enjoying the breezes off the nearby bayou waters.

After they settled at a bistro table in a quiet corner, Mick straddled a chair, then glanced over at her. "Justin has every right to be protective, you know. This place is beautiful—that's why people come here. It's understandable that he wants everything to be perfect."

"So how did you manage to prevent him from throttling David?"

He took a bite of fluffy corn bread, closed his eyes in a moment of pure eating pleasure, then looked across the table at her. "First, I explained to David that the whole tree wasn't damaged. The tree was actually split about halfway up into two trunks—apparently happened when it was very young. David just thought the damage would eventually kill the whole tree, so he decided—without consulting anyone—to whack both trunks off about midway and leave it at that. But after I calmed Justin down, all we had to do was cut and shave the damaged trunk, then reshape the other trunk so it looked like a complete tree. I think with a little growth, it'll fill out just fine."

Lorna sat back on her chair, her food forgotten. "You've done it again."

"Done what?"

She watched as he sopped up turnip juice with his corn bread in typical Southern fashion. "Helped us out, saved us yet again. And this time, you saved poor shy David, too.''

''David will toughen up eventually and...it was just a tree, Lorna.''

''That tree has been at the edge of that swamp for well over one hundred-fifty years, Mick. It's more than just a tree. Don't you see, that's why we put up with Justin's temper around here. He loves each of these great oaks, and the magnolias and camellias and the cypress trees—they're like his children.''

''He didn't have a problem about jumping on that boy, though.''

''His temper will get the better of him one day, I'm afraid. I'm just sorry...and I apologize on his behalf. I'll be glad to talk to David, too.''

''No, now, don't go and make matters worse by embarrassing David. He learned his lesson. And to his credit, Justin did apologize—grudgingly.''

''That's good. And he should have, since you did save the tree in the end.''

''Well, he was relieved when I came up with a solution. And just a tad irritated that he didn't figure out the process himself.''

She gestured to indicate their surroundings. ''There, you see. The trees, the grounds, the flowers—they're such an important part of this place. We're probably all a bit too protective—''

Mick grabbed her hand. ''Lorna, I understand. Really, I do. Remember, I'm a tree person myself. That's why I wanted to save the cypress.''

Groaning, Lorna sank back against her chair. ''I'm sorry. You of all people, of course, understand.''

''Tell me about the oaks,'' he said, his eyes bright with amusement. ''That is, if you can keep calm while you're doing it.''

''I'll try.'' She took a bite of fruit salad, sighed, then tried to relax. ''A trapper planted them almost two hundred years ago. They were just saplings then, but somehow he must have known that they'd grow to be strong and tall one day. He planted them far enough apart that today they form that incredible canopy leading up to the house.''

''Was the trapper your ancestor?''

''No. He moved on after selling the land to my family. The Dorsettes have lived on this bayou almost as long as those trees have been here.''

Lorna saw the confusion mixed with regret in Mick's eyes.

''I've never had those kind of roots,'' he said, his voice low and edgy. ''Seems as if I don't really have a family tree to call my own.''

''Don't you have any relatives back in Mississippi?''

''None to brag about,'' he admitted. ''My daddy's family was always scattered and feuding. I've lost touch with all of them. My grandparents died when I was real young, so I never really had that kind of security. It was just my momma and me for a long time.''

She nodded her understanding. "We lost both sets of our grandparents early. I have vague memories of my father's parents, but my mother's parents passed away before I was even born.''

She waited for him to ask more about her parents, but he didn't.

"So Aunt Hilda's it for you?''

"She's it. And I do mean *it*. She has always been our link to the past and our link to our faith.''

"What about your uncle, her husband?''

"He died of a heart attack years ago. But she never remarried. After our grandfather died, she just naturally took over this place and the town. She's been the mayor for close to twenty years.''

"No one ever runs against her?''

"Why would anyone want to?''

"Good point.''

They ate in silence for a while. Lorna listened to the laughter of the many children running through the gardens. She loved having people here again. Justin had done a wonderful job of replacing and pruning the damaged flowers and shrubs. And Mick and Josh had both pitched in way beyond the call of duty.

"When will you be leaving?'' she asked now, her gaze lifting to his, memories of their time here together so bright that she wanted to close her eyes.

Mick leaned forward, took her hand. "I guess we'll

be moving out, day after tomorrow. Claude had one last trouble spot he wanted me to look at, then…''

He didn't finish the sentence. Lorna felt his eyes move over her hair, her face, her lips. His eyes held such a mystery, such a challenge.

''Where do we go from here, Lorna?''

''I don't know,'' she said, honest in spite of the pain. ''We always knew you'd have to leave. And we're not kids on spring break. We're adults, Mick. But I honestly don't know what's going to happen with us now.''

''Vicksburg isn't that far away.''

''Might as well be a million miles,'' she stated, her heart longing to find a spot on one of those utility trucks of his and hang on for dear life.

''What does that mean?''

''It means that I can't leave Bayou le Jardin, and you obviously can't stay. I have responsibilities here, and you have to get back to your own work.''

''Then we do have a problem.''

''And no solution in sight.''

''Not if you refuse to even consider just coming to visit me.''

''I can't, Mick. What would be the point?''

He reached across the table, touched her chin. ''The point is that I don't know how I'm supposed to go on with life the way it was before I met you. The point is that I'm not nearly finished with you, Lorna. I want more. I want you to come and see me, to see how I live and work, to be sure.''

"Sure of what? That I like being with you, that I'm attracted to you? I already know all of that, but it's useless to think we can keep this going.''

"It's not useless,'' he replied, his anger snapping the words like twigs. "*We're* not useless. Something has happened here, Lorna, between us. You can't deny that.''

"I'm not denying it,'' she said, her voice low and strained. "I'm just saying that I have to accept that you have a life back home that does not include me.''

"But why can't it?''

She pulled away, threw up both hands. "Because when I came back here, I promised myself no more roaming, no more wandering. I'm secure here, I'm safe. I have a career I enjoy, and I have family around me. That's important to me, Mick. It wasn't before, but it is now.''

"As it should be,'' he retorted. "But isn't having someone in your life, to share your life *with*, important, too?''

"Of course it is.'' She looked away, aware that the few other people in the room were watching them with curious expressions. "Let's drop this for now, all right? I don't want to spoil Aunt Hilda's celebration.''

He got up, grabbed his empty plate. "Sure. I understand. I wouldn't do anything to upset your aunt. But this conversation is not over, Lorna.''

With that, he stomped away, leaving Lorna to stare down into her own forgotten plate of food.

"But it is over, Mick," she whispered to herself. "I don't see any other way."

She wasn't ready to leave the sanctuary of this safe haven. Not even for the man with whom she'd fallen in love.

A couple of hours later, however, the decision was made for her. And for Mick.

Most of the churchgoers and townspeople had gone home to rest underneath fans and air conditioners that would hum them into a nice Sunday afternoon nap. The family and the Babineaux were busy cleaning away the trash and leftovers from the day's events, Mick included.

Josh came hurrying up the path from the guest cottages. "Hey, boss, we got trouble," he said, his breath huffing out with each word.

Mick turned from a nearby trash can. "What's up?"

"That storm that ripped through Shreveport and Monroe last night went straight for home, too," Josh told him, a cell phone in his hand. "A big pine fell right across one of the access roads into Battlefield Park. The power company cleared the road, but they want us to come on back to finish up the job. Seems there's several trees down around Vicksburg. We gotta get back."

When Mick hesitated, looking at Lorna, Josh added, "Today, boss."

"I get it," Mick told Josh. "Do the other men know?"

"They're gathering their gear right now. Want me to call Claude?"

Mick nodded, looking down at the ground. "Yeah, tell him we can't finish that one spot we had pegged for tomorrow morning. And Josh, tell him we'll settle up the bill just as soon as I can process the paperwork. No hurry."

"Right." Josh pivoted to head back to the cottages.

Mick turned to find Lorna standing there with a stack of paper plates in her hands, her eyes on his face.

"You have to leave," she said evenly.

"Yes."

The word hung in the still, humid air between them.

"I don't have any other choice. They need us back home."

"Of course. I understand."

Mick wanted to grab her and make her admit that she didn't understand. How could she stand there, so cool and collected, her green eyes as unreadable as the murky waters of the swamp? How could she do that, when his heart was pounding and his head felt as if someone had hit him with a two-by-four?

"I thought we had more time," he finally said, turning to finish tying up the black trash bag.

When he turned back around, she was handing the

plates to Rosie Lee. Then they were alone again. And yet she stayed silent and still.

"Well, say something," he finally said.

She shrugged, looked off into the bayou. "What's there to say? We knew this was coming. But I thought we had a couple more days, too. I guess it doesn't really matter, anyway."

Mick ran a hand through his hair in frustration. "It doesn't matter? Is that how you really feel? That we don't matter?"

She looked up at him, her eyes burning a bright angry green. "You have no idea how I feel, Mick."

"Oh, you're right about that. You don't want me to see how you really feel. And you'll just let me go, because you're too afraid to admit anything."

He saw that fear in her eyes, in the lifting of her chin, in the way her lips trembled in spite of her clenched jaw. He also saw a distant need in her eyes, the same need he felt in his heart.

So he reached for her—but she turned away.

"No, just go," she said in a whisper. "I told you there could be no 'us.' I told you we shouldn't get too involved."

"Yeah, well, I've never been good at listening to other people's advice."

Her head still down, she said, "Well, listen to me now. Just go back home, Mick. And forget about all of this. Forget about me. It's the best advice I can give you."

She started walking toward the house.

"Lorna—?" He took two long strides to catch up with her, and pulled her back around. "Don't walk away from me, Lorna. We can work this out."

She stared up at him, her eyes open and misty now. "How? Long distance? With me here, working at the restaurant, and you there, doing your own job? I don't want to leave this bayou, Mick. I can't."

"I wouldn't make you do that."

"Then I don't see how we can resolve this."

Needing to make her see reason, Mick took her hands in his. "Lorna, we found in one week what most people never have in a lifetime. I don't want to lose that."

But he could tell in her eyes, in her touch, that he already had. She went stiff in his arms.

"I've had other weeks, with other men, Mick. And they all managed to survive without me just fine. So will you."

That made him so mad, he could see little sparks of red rage flashing in front of his eyes. "And I guess you'll survive just fine without me, too, huh?"

"I've managed for this long," she said, her tone level and calm. "I'm really quite used to it."

He let her go, standing back to glare at her. "I never took you for a quitter, Lorna. Nor a liar. I guess I was wrong about us, after all."

With that, he turned and stalked toward the cottages.

Away from the harsh glare of her green eyes. Away from the resolved lift of her stubborn, trembling chin.

Away from the love he knew she felt inside her heart.

The same love he could never have denied her, the way she'd just denied him.

Chapter Twelve

The rain that the weatherman had predicted all week had finally arrived, and it seemed to be settling in for a good long stay.

Lorna stood at one of the large work tables in the restaurant, worrying over a *crème Chantilly* for tonight's dessert of *fraises des bois*—wild strawberries. She would delight her guests by telling them of the French custom of making a wish over the tiny delicate strawberries.

And maybe she'd make a few wishes of her own.

The *baron d'agneau Armenonville*—roast baron of lamb—was ready for tonight's crowd. The *canard à l'orange*—duck with orange sauce, served with wild rice and julienned vegetables, would be a hit, she was sure.

Everything was as it should be.

Except her broken heart.

She missed Mick with a knife-edged sharpness that cut into her very soul.

Had he really been gone a whole week?

It seemed like an eternity.

Lorna turned away from the rich fluffy cream. Hurrying to a huge wooden table in the middle of the restaurant's kitchen, she halfheartedly smiled at one of the Babineaux girls who worked with her and wanted to become a chef herself one day. Emily helped with the standard American and Cajun dishes. Right now, she had the beginnings of a rich, brown roux going for Lorna's famous Gumbo le Jardin—called that because most of the ingredients came right from the vegetable garden and swamp out back.

"You okay, Miss Lorna?" sixteen-year-old Emily asked as she stood beside Lorna and began helping her chop the onions, celery and bell peppers that formed the trinity of true Louisiana cooking. "Or are those onions getting to you?"

"It's not the onions," Lorna said, pushing with the back of her hand at the white chef hat planted atop her head.

"It's that man, then," Emily said with all the wisdom of a teenager, her thick Cajun accent becoming sharp with disapproval. "He ought not to have left you like that."

"I sent him away, Em," Lorna said, too tired and disillusioned to argue with the girl or deny the truth.

"You sure did," Lacey said from the doorway, an umbrella in one hand and a beige raincoat thrown over her shoulders.

Emily looked with wide-eyed fascination from one sister to the other, then quickly found work to occupy her across the long room.

"You're dripping water all over my floor," Lorna said to her sister with a sniff.

"Well, better get used to it," Lacey replied. "There's a flash flood warning out, and the forecast calls for even more rain. I don't think it's going to clear up anytime soon."

"Thanks for the update," Lorna retorted, angry at this intrusion. Her kitchen was her sanctuary, and she didn't need Lacey hovering over her like a mother hen, telling her she was making a huge mistake by letting Mick walk out of her life. "Now what do you really want?"

Lacey propped her umbrella out of the way against the wall, then shook out her raincoat before tossing it on a nearby chair. "I want to see my sister's pretty smile again. I want to laugh with you, talk with you. I want…"

She stopped, looked out the window where rain splattered on the green wrought-iron tables and chairs of the plant-filled courtyard.

"I want a lot of things," she finally said, coming to stand by Lorna.

"Well, we can't always get what we want," Lorna

snapped. Then because the onions *were* getting to her, she rushed to the sink to wash her hands and face.

Humiliated, she leaned over the running water, her shoulders shaking beneath her crisp white chef coat. Leave it to Lacey to make her feel even worse.

And leave it to Lacey to come rushing to her side to pull her into her arms. "Oh, honey, I'm so sorry. I didn't mean to upset you."

"It's not you," Lorna said into the floral print of her sister's flowing dress. She couldn't blame this discontent on her sister, and in spite of her harsh words, she was glad to have the shelter of Lacey's comforting arms. "I don't know, maybe it's the rain. I just miss him so much. Lacey, what's the matter with me? I've never missed anyone in such an awful way—not like this."

"You're in love," Lacey told her as she lifted Lorna's face and wiped at the tears trailing down her cheeks. "It's the best feeling in the world and also the most painful."

"Did you feel this way with Neil?"

"Every day of my life."

"Even now?"

"Even now."

Lorna pulled away, rubbing at her tears. "You see, that's why I can't do this. I can't love Mick. It just hurts too much."

"Only if you lose him—no, make that, only if you let him get away," Lacey pointed out. "But Lorna, you have to remember, like that old song says, it's better to have a little bit of love than to never know what love feels like at all.''

"Is that how you sleep at night?'' Lorna said, her words harsh again. "By telling yourself that you had one great love?''

The shock on Lacey's face made Lorna instantly regret that horrible remark. "Oh, Lacey, I'm so sorry. Please, just ignore me. Let me get through this in my own time and way. I'll be all right.''

But from the tormented look on Lacey's face, she wasn't finished with her little sister.

"You want to know how I go to sleep each night, Lorna? I curl up in that big bed and turn to the empty pillow at my side, and I remember…I remember the feel of Neil's hair underneath my fingertips. I remember the touch of his lips to mine. I remember the warmth of his arms, and the way he'd tell me he loved me as we drifted off to sleep.'' She stopped, took a breath, then held up a hand when Lorna tried to speak. "And it hurts. It hurts worse than anything you can imagine. But in spite of that awful pain, I always thank God for the time I had with Neil. I cherish those memories because they were the happiest times of my life. And I guard them, because I know I won't ever have that kind of love in my life again.''

"I'm sorry,'' Lorna said again, her eyes welling with fresh tears. "And I truly wish I could have what you and Neil had. You two loved each other so much, and I'm so sorry that you lost everything when he died. Honestly, I'd love to have some cherished memories of my own, even if it does scare me to pieces.''

"Then, do something about it. Go to Mick and tell him you love him. Work this out—whatever it takes—long distance or not. Don't punish yourself out of some sense of nobility or fear.''

Lorna headed back to the chopping table. ''But he's there and I'm here, and…this just happened too fast. There's nothing to be done about it.''

"There's lots to be done,'' Lacey said as she walked toward the door. ''Don't wait until it's too late.''

"Maybe it's already too late,'' Lorna replied.

"Just as water mirrors your face, your face mirrors your heart,'' Lacey said, paraphrasing Proverbs. ''Stop denying it.''

Lorna watched as her sister silently left the room.

And outside, the rain came down in soft blue-gray sheets, the exact color of Mick's eyes the last time she'd seen him.

The rain hadn't let up for three days.

Mick stared out his kitchen window, down the bluff toward the dark, swirling Mississippi River below. And once again thought of Lorna.

Had this same rain washed over her? Had this same rain made her stop and think of him? Had this same rain made her feel gloomy and melancholy, edgy and full of discontent?

"Must be raining all over the world," he said aloud, turning to pour yet another cup of coffee. He'd learned how to make it strong now, just the way Lorna made it.

He looked down into the black brew, only to see his distorted reflection mirroring his innermost thoughts—and missed her all over again.

"I need to get back to work," he told the talking head on the blaring television set. "I need for this rain to go away."

But the weatherman on television was predicting even more rain all across the South. Leftovers from yet another big storm out in the Gulf. Mick was tired of fighting storms.

After taking care of the fallen trees he'd been called back to clear, he'd been shut up here for days, and he was running out of things to keep him occupied. He'd caught up on the mail, paid the bills, done all the necessary paperwork, talked to his accountants, harassed the bookkeepers, and growled and snarled whenever anyone called to check on him.

And to make matters worse, Josh had been going around grinning like an idiot because the man was so slap-happy in love with Kathryn that he couldn't contain himself.

Josh didn't mind telling Mick that he and Kathryn talked on the phone each night, and that he'd already made plans to go back to Bayou le Jardin come vacation time. Once Kathryn's cast was off, Josh and Kathryn planned to take a day-trip to New Orleans, to explore the sights and to continue getting to know each other.

"And after that, we'll see," his friend had said yesterday, that big grin conveying everything. "I think this is the one, Mick, my man."

"Sickening," Mick said now, as he slammed his empty coffee cup into the sink. He'd downed the coffee so fast, it had probably burned a hole right to his stomach.

That brought the question burning a hole through his heart right to the surface. Why couldn't he just pick up the phone and have a nice, normal conversation with the woman *he'd* left behind? Why couldn't he and Lorna have the same kind of happiness his friend and Kathryn were experiencing?

Mick looked at the phone, imagined picking it up, dialing the number for Bayou le Jardin, asking for Lorna. *Asking for Lorna.*

But, he reminded himself with a bitter groan, Lorna didn't want to be asked for, Lorna didn't want to take things any farther with him. She was afraid.

Did she think he'd hurt her, desert her?

Didn't she know him better than that?

The rain picked up, as if to answer his question with its constant pounding on his roof.

She *didn't* know him better than that. She didn't

know him at all. And right now, Mick couldn't blame her for sending him away. They'd had so little time together.

But that didn't mean a whole lot right now. He'd fallen in love, swiftly and surely. And he didn't know how to deal with that. And he certainly didn't know how to deal with her fears—of both the dark and him.

Maybe if he'd told her that he'd figured her out, that he'd seen her fear and wanted to help her get through it—maybe then, she would have trusted him. But he'd been a coward, afraid she'd turn away if he questioned her about her phobia. Mick had thought he could gain her trust by just being there with her. In the end, she'd simply given up and sent him away. She'd let him go without so much as a fight. And no faith in what might have been.

A commercial for a nearby church came on the television. Mick knew the church well. His mother had attended before her death, had insisted he attend with her at times, and Josh's whole family still went there.

Suddenly, it occurred to Mick that maybe Josh had something in his joyous smile, in his whole mind-set, that Mick had been missing. Josh had faith—in himself, in his budding relationship with Kathryn, and in God.

And in that instant, Mick realized he wanted that kind of faith. He needed it to make Lorna see that they could have a life together. He needed it to show her that she, too, had to have faith, that somehow God would see them through.

With a shaking hand, Mick turned off the television set and headed for the front door. He needed to talk to someone. He needed to turn back to God. Because in his own way, he was just as afraid as Lorna.

"Mick, I can't tell you how glad I am that you came by to see me today," Reverend Butler said as he got up to shake Mick's hand. "I hope I've helped answer some of your questions."

"You've helped a great deal," Mick replied, taking the older man's hand in his own. "I appreciate your taking the time to listen."

"That's part of my job," the reverend told him as he guided Mick out of his office. "You know you're welcome here anytime."

"Thanks," Mick said. Then he stopped and looked down the hall toward the sanctuary. "Would you mind if—"

"That's what it's there for," the reverend said, gesturing toward the sanctuary. "Go on in. God's been waiting for you."

Nodding, Mick slowly walked toward the darkened sanctuary. The rain was still falling, and the long silent room basked in shadows. But somehow, those shadows were comforting to him.

He entered, then stopped to look down toward the altar. His mother had forced him to come here. Had wanted him to have a church home in times of need, and in times of joy. But he'd turned away from all of that, simply because he'd blamed God for the sorry life his mother and he had had to endure.

This talk with God was long overdue.

"Hello, it's me," he said on a low whisper as he settled down on a pew in the middle of the high-ceilinged room. The pitter-patter of rain answered him as it hit the wide skylights over the altar. *"I know it's been a while. But I've talked to the preacher, and he says You don't mind that. Says You'll forgive me for staying away. He explained things to me. All this time I thought You deserted us, but You didn't. You gave my mother the strength to carry on, to become a self-sufficient person. You gave her courage, and for that, I thank You. I'm not so bitter about her death now. You took her home because she was a good and faithful servant, and she deserved some glory. The preacher explained that to me, too."*

He stopped, looked toward the skylights. Light seemed to be shining down on the altar, despite the rain and clouds. *"And I guess I have to forgive my old man, too. The preacher says I can't get on with my life until I let go of the bitterness toward my father. Will You help me let go of that, Lord? Will You teach me to forgive, to understand?"*

Mick listened to the rain, thinking it sounded very close to a melody.

"I need Your help here, Lord. I need to make Lorna

see that I *won't desert* her. *She has such a sure faith in You, but she's afraid to let go and trust in me. Somewhere, somehow, she was hurt deeply, and now she's afraid of the darkness, afraid of being alone. Help me to show her that I won't leave her. And help me to see that You will never desert either of us.''*

Mick stopped praying and sat for a while in the comforting enclosure of the church. He continued to listen. Really listen. There was a strange peace in just being still.

The rain kept on falling, like a great purge that at last released him from all the past hurts, from the yoke that he'd carried for so many years.

"I can make her a good husband, Lord. I have to believe that, before I can love her completely. I failed once. I didn't love Melinda enough to fight, because I think I was afraid that I'd fail—the way my daddy failed. I gave up, just like I gave up on You.'' He paused, took a deep breath, lifted his head to the sky-lights. *"I'm going to fight for Lorna. I need You on my side in that fight. And I promise, I will never give up on myself or You again.''*

Mick sat there for a few more minutes as the rain settled down to a gentle misting. A sense of complete peace came over him as he cast off all the guilt and pain of the past. He felt light, cleansed, content, at last.

He got up, then glanced back up at the skylight. The rain had stopped, and for one brief moment, he thought he saw a ray of brilliant sunlight pushing through the dark clouds.

He smiled then, and knew the same joy that he'd always seen in his friend Josh's smile. Knew that at long last he, too, could find that certain joy.

He intended to share that joy with the woman he loved.

He intended to go back to Bayou le Jardin.

And this time, he wasn't leaving without Lorna.

Even if it meant he'd have to stay there for the rest of his life.

Chapter Thirteen

"**I**'m not gonna lie to you. It looks bad."

Claude Juneau sat across from Hilda Dorsette in the spacious parlor of Bayou le Jardin, surrounded by opulent antiques and freshly cut flowers. Lorna and Lacey stood behind their aunt.

It was Saturday, and because of that, Lorna and Lacey had convinced their aunt to stay home this morning. But already, Lorna could see the agitation and nervous energy radiating from her aunt's worried face.

"I can believe it," Lorna stated with a sigh. "For three weeks, either we've had to turn guests away or we've had them canceling out on us because of these spring storms. First the tornado, and now the possibility of flooding."

This turn of events didn't suit her already dark mood, nor did it bode well for the already battered town or Bayou le Jardin's tourist traffic. Of course, knowing she couldn't control that only added to her dismal reckonings. Surely things would get better soon.

"How bad?" Hilda asked, a hand on Lorna's arm, no doubt to calm her niece as well as herself.

"Flash flooding of the roads," Claude said, shifting his big bulk as he tugged at his red suspenders. "More power outages from downed trees—their roots can't hold up in that soggy ground out there. I've got my men working, and, of course, we've got volunteers watching and waiting, too." He paused, then added, "And...we might have some problems with the levee."

"The river?" Lacey said, worry clouding her eyes. "We've never had trouble with the river—not too much, anyway. What are you saying, Claude?"

"I'm saying that we're gonna have to sandbag the levee. That water's rising mighty fast, and in some of them low spots, it's gonna spill over. I expect we'll see some homes and property get flooded. Which is why I came by. I wanted to warn y'all. This place might be knee-deep in water in a few hours."

"Bayou le Jardin?" Hilda asked, her eyes drawn to the ceiling-to-floor French windows that gave a clear view of the great oaks outside, and beyond that the levee. "The last time this place flooded was well over seventy years ago—the great flood of 1927."

Lorna looked outside, too. The flat, sloping yard

was already standing in water. "Well, this could be the next great flood."

"That's what I'm telling y'all," Claude replied, a frown marring his ruddy complexion. "The city workers are up to their eyeballs trying to contain this thing, and the parish experts are predicting a big flood. Miss Hilda, we might have to call in the National Guard again. And we're gonna need everyone—every able body—to help with the sandbagging and the evacuation."

"If it comes to that," Hilda replied, her voice steady, her demeanor calm.

"It might," Claude said, standing to leave. "I knew you'd want the latest information so we could form a plan."

"Then, we'll be prepared," she told him, rising with the help of her cane and Lacey's arm on hers. "I'm going into town right away, to make sure everything's in place. Meantime, Claude, do whatever it takes to spare lives—that's foremost in my concerns. Then we'll worry about the property. I'll call City Hall right now and tell them the same thing."

"You'd certainly be safer there," Lacey told her.

"Lacey's right," the big man agreed. "You know I'll do whatever I can, and so will everyone else. But my advice to all of you is to get to higher ground before nightfall."

"Thank you, Claude," Lacey said as she escorted him to the double doors at the back of the house, where he'd parked his truck in the driveway. "And please keep us posted until we can get there."

Lorna waited at the doors to the parlor for her sister. "What do you think? She's going to insist on going into town, but she's also worried about her home. Of course, she thinks this place is a fortress. And she certainly won't let us pamper her—not when she thinks others are in danger."

Lacey nodded, then whispered, "We'll just have to take matters into our own hands. We'll make sure she's safe." Then with a low rumble, she added, "Oh, it's just like Lucas to be off on some great adventure, when we need him here."

"Last I heard, he was headed out into the bayou. You realize we could get flooding from the swamp, too."

"Yes." Lacey nodded, frowning. "I just hope Lucas will have the good sense to come on home and help us persuade Aunt Hilda to leave before we get trapped in here."

"Children, come on back inside the parlor," Hilda called. "I'm not as deaf as you seem to think, and I don't cotton to whispering outside doorways when we've got so much work ahead of us."

Lorna walked back into the room. "We're just concerned, Aunt Hilda. We're thinking maybe you're smart to leave now—go on into town where it's safer."

Lacey nodded in agreement. "Or we could drive

you up to Shreveport to see your friend, Cindy. You haven't had a good visit with her in such a long time, and you'd be safe up there."

Hilda stared at them through her bifocals, her lips pursed in a stubborn tilt. "Last I heard, it was raining upstate, too."

Lorna tried again, coming to stand by her aunt. "We just want you to be away from this mess. There's no need for you to be right in the thick of things."

"I'll go when I decide it's time," her aunt replied, her hand firm on the tip of her cane. But she turned to Lorna and placed her other hand gently underneath Lorna's chin. "And not one minute sooner." Then she dropped her hand and started out the parlor door. "I've got to find Tobbie and Rosie Lee. We've got to get busy salvaging what we can, in case the water makes it up to the house. I'll keep my phone near, so I can receive updates. But as soon as we have this place somewhat secure, I'm going to the office to oversee this problem."

Lorna gave her sister a knowing glance, then looked back out the wide windows. If they didn't make a decision soon, they might not have a minute to spare.

Checking the clock, Mick threw some clothes into his old, battered suitcase, then grabbed his cell phone. Not wanting to waste precious minutes, he decided he'd call Josh from the road.

But he didn't have to make that call. The house

phone rang even as he was heading for the back door. Debating whether to answer it, Mick looked at the caller identification number. It was Josh.

Mick picked up the phone. "Hello?"

"Boss, we got problems."

Groaning, Mick let out a sigh. "What now?"

"We gotta get back to Louisiana," Josh explained, his voice edged with worry. "They say there's been some major flooding around New Orleans and along the Mississippi, and they're expecting it to get even worse before nightfall."

Mick's heart stopped. "Bayou le Jardin?"

"Yeah, that's the word I'm getting," Josh said. "I...I have to go, Mick. Kathryn needs me—her momma won't be able to get all those children out in time if I don't go and help."

"I'm with you, man," Mick told his friend. "I'm on my way out the door right now. In fact, I was just about to call you to let you know I was headed back to see Lorna. But I didn't know there was a chance of flooding."

"C'mon by and get me," Josh said. "We'll have to drive it. The airports are booked solid, and every flight out is delayed because of this storm."

"We'll make it, Josh," Mick told him. "Just hold tight until I get there."

"Hurry," Josh said, before he hung up.

Mick did exactly that.

He had to get back to Lorna. He had to make sure her family was safe.

And he had to make sure that he told her how much he really loved her.

Lacey huddled with Lorna on the back gallery, watching as the rain continued to fall in angry, slashing sheets.

They'd worked steadily for the past couple of hours, securing the mansion as much as possible. Along with Tobbie, Rosie Lee and their daughter Emily, Lorna and Lacey had moved furniture and fixtures up to the second-floor landing.

But Rosie Lee was worried about her other children. "Little Tobbie is with his big brothers," she'd told Lorna, sounding worried. "I sure hope they're watching him."

"We'll get you home to them, I promise," Lorna had replied.

Because of Rosie Lee's worry, Lorna had paged Lucas to go and make sure the children were safe. When Lucas had come home, stating the family was fine for now, she'd sent him back out to take Tobbie and his wife home. There wasn't much else anyone could do now.

Aunt Hilda had pitched in, too, refusing to listen to her nieces' pleas. Even now, she was in her office, on the phone with a state trooper, getting the latest report on the flood conditions.

"I wish Lucas would come on back," Lorna said.

"Oh, I forgot to tell you," Lacey replied. "He insisted on taking Emily and Rosie Lee home himself, while Tobbie stayed behind to secure the outbuildings. He's probably holed up with the Babineaux clan, trying to keep them calm while they wait it out."

"Well, then, they might be in for a very long wait. Maybe he can convince them to get off that bayou while there's still time."

Lorna didn't think Lucas would be much help to them, anyway. The storm wasn't letting up. The restaurant was once again closed, the bed-and-breakfast shut down until the waters receded. She'd never seen her beloved gardens looking so lonely.

Which was exactly how she felt.

Preparing for the worse had taken her mind off Mick for a while, at least. But now as she stood here with her sister, wondering if they should stay or go, she longed for Mick to come around the corner in his hard hat with that wonderful grin on his face. She longed to hear his voice, reassuring her that everything would be all right.

But he's gone, she reminded herself. *You let him go. You told him not to come back.*

Shivering, Lorna placed her arms across her chest to ward off the wet chill. She couldn't think about Mick now. She had to take care of her home and her family.

"We have to get Aunt Hilda out of here. She's

champing at the bit to get into town. And if we don't do something soon, we're going to be trapped between the bayou and the river.''

"Good thing Lucas has a boat."

"I'm serious, Lacey. Let's just go inside and tell her we've done everything we can here, and we'll take her to town."

"That means we have to leave, not knowing what will happen here."

"Well, what else can we do? I think everyone would be a lot calmer just having her there to lead them in prayer and keep them focused. And we do need to get her off this bayou."

Lacey gave her sister a long look. "Are you all right?"

Lorna knew what Lacey was thinking. "I'm okay with the rain, really. At least, there's no thunder and lightning."

"And no tornadoes this time."

"Just a lot of water." Lorna couldn't tell her sister about her intense loneliness. That would be admitting that she'd made a mistake in sending Mick away. Instead, she said, "So, do you want to tell Aunt Hilda we're ready, or shall I?"

Lacey thought about it, then nodded. "Why don't I talk to Claude first—see where things stand in town. If they're already sandbagging, she'll want to be there. And she'll listen to Claude. That might get her mind off worrying about this place."

Lorna whirled around. "Okay, but why don't you drive her in—and to keep her from worrying about Bayou le Jardin, I'll stay behind with Tobbie and wait for Lucas. He should be home soon, and he can help me with any last minute problems."

"Did he take a cell phone or walkie-talkie with him?"

Lorna was already heading for the open hallway. "Who knows? I'll try to page him, but half the time he doesn't answer, anyway."

Lacey was right behind her. "Well, keep trying. Tobbie is down in the far gardens near the bayou, so he won't be much help—and you don't want to stay here by yourself, either."

Lorna hurried up the winding staircase, then turned at the curve. "I promise if I can't reach Lucas in an hour, I'll come on into town. We can spend the night in the school gym."

Lacey looked skeptical. "I'll find out from Claude if we can even make it into town."

"Okay. I'll meet you back down here."

Lorna rushed up the winding stairs and into her room, determined to page her brother. She tried Lucas's cell phone first, leaving a message for him to call her cell phone. Then she dialed his pager number and waited for him to respond.

Glancing around, she wondered what she should take if there was a flood. This bedroom was full of priceless artifacts and antiques. As was the whole house, for that matter.

"I can't let this storm destroy our home," she said, wishing Lucas would call.

The four-poster bed was bright and cheery, its comforter and pillows done in vivid shades of blue and yellow. She'd wanted it that way, to reflect the gardens outside. The pictures on the walls told the tale of her travels—some prints, some originals.

Monet. Picasso. Van Gogh. Wyeth.

Her vanity held exotic jars and bottles from various parts of the world. Her armoire held sundresses, and ball gowns, and faded blue jeans, and soft, worn sweaters and shirts. And hats—lots of hats.

"I need to wear my hats more often," she told herself, her nerves tearing at the calm she was trying so hard to hold on to. Crossing her arms in front of her, she stared at her reflection in the gilt-edged mirror over the vanity. "I need to do a lot of things."

Her cell phone rang, causing her to jump.

"Start talking, *belle,*" Lucas said, his voice coming in and out over a heavy static.

"Lucas, we need to get Aunt Hilda to town. The water is rising."

"Don't I know it. I'm down at the boathouse with Tobbie. They didn't come to sandbag?"

"Not yet. Aunt Hilda insisted that the main road into town be taken care of first. All the houses there—"

"I get it. Where are you now?"

"In my room."

"How's the river?"

"It didn't look so good last time Lacey and I checked. It's mighty close to coming over the levee. What about you?"

"The bayou is full, sugar. Rosie Lee was frantic about Tobbie being out here by himself, so I headed out to look for him—ran into him in his pirogue. He's checking the marsh, and I'm just helping him secure a few things around the boathouse. Then he's gonna go get his family, and we'll be outta here. You need me home?"

"I need you home."

"I'm on my way. Are you all right?"

"I will be when you get here. Lacey is going to drive Aunt Hilda in. But I'll wait for you. Maybe together, we can do something to hold back the water, or at least move some more things to higher ground."

"I'm coming, darlin'. You hang on."

"Okay."

Lorna hung up the phone, then hurried back downstairs. "I got in touch with Lucas," she told Lacey. "He's down at the boathouse with Tobbie. But he'll be here soon. What did Claude say?"

Lacey pulled her close. "He said to get her out of here, and if that means bringing her to town to keep her occupied, then so be it. And us, too. They've sandbagged the main area of town, but the road into Jardin is almost impassable.''

"Then take her. I told Lucas I'd wait here for him.''

"I won't leave you alone,'' Lacey replied. "Rosie Lee isn't here, remember? No one is here.''

Lorna put her hands on her sister's slender shoulders. "It's still light out. I'll be fine for another hour or so. Lucas is just down the bayou at the boathouse helping Tobbie. He'll be here in a few minutes, and in the meantime, I can move more things upstairs.''

"But—''

"You have to get Aunt Hilda to the shelter.''

"I don't like this. You don't have to prove anything to me, Lorna. Don't be foolish.''

This was an old argument. And one Lorna didn't have time for today. "I'm not trying to prove anything. I'm just worried about Aunt Hilda, and I won't leave without Lucas.''

Lorna watched her sister's concerned face, thinking she did need to prove something—to herself. It was time she quit depending on her family to hold her hand. It was time they learned that they could depend on her, too. She refused to remind herself that due to the years she'd tried to strike out on her own, she'd wound up coming home in a broken heap. She was tired of being broken. And she was tired of being afraid. Because of that, she'd lost Mick forever.

"I'll be all right, Lacey. Please don't worry. Lucas is on his way.''

"I still don't like this."

Wanting to take Lacey's mind off *her* inadequacies, Lorna asked, "Is Aunt Hilda ready to go?"

"Yes, of course. She was ready two hours ago, but she knew we needed to do some things here, too. She's torn between staying to protect her home and going into town to protect the village." She paused, sighed. "I was very…elaborate with Claude's report. And I told her Lucas and you were taking care of things here, so that eased her mind some." She shrugged. "She thinks Lucas is close by."

"Well, he is, so get her in the truck and go. I promise I'll be fine. I'll get my flashlight and wait for Lucas."

She lifted a hand to wave away Lacey's still-obvious fears. "Look, it's midafternoon. And in spite of the rain, I have plenty of light yet."

"Oh, all right," Lacey said finally. "I can't fight both you *and* Aunt Hilda."

"I'll see you in a couple of hours," Lorna said.

A few minutes later, she watched at the back door as Lacey guided Aunt Hilda into the truck. Waving goodbye, she turned around, holding her flashlight securely close, just in case she needed it.

She'd make a strong pot of coffee and listen to the weather report, while she waited for Lucas. He'd probably be hungry. She'd make him a turkey sandwich. Then she'd start in the parlor, moving the rest of the odds and ends to the upstairs landing, at least. There was lots to do, lots to keep her busy.

Standing there alone in the kitchen, she said a prayer. *"Give me the strength, Lord. The strength I've been missing. I've been so afraid, of many things. I don't want to be afraid anymore."*

Everything would be okay. Lucas would soon be here to help her, and Lacey would take care of Aunt Hilda. They'd make it. They'd been through much worse, after all.

Except that Lorna had never before faced anything they'd been through completely on her own.

Chapter Fourteen

"**H**ow much farther?" Josh asked for the tenth time, as Mick's four-wheel drive truck zoomed down the interstate.

"An hour at most," Mick replied, watching the rain-slick roads while he pushed the gas pedal to the floor. "We'll make it, Josh. And when we get there, we'll probably find all of them safe and sound."

They'd tried calling every number they had between the two of them, but the phone lines were either messed up or completely down. They couldn't get through.

"Yeah, I know," Josh replied, leaning against the passenger door. "The Dorsettes can take care of each other. And they watch out for all the rest, too."

Mick had to smile at that. "Yeah, you know, I think that's what drew me to them. They are so tight-knit and close, but they don't exclude others because of that.''

Josh laughed. ''Nah, they just invite you right on in.''

They drove in silence for a few minutes, then Josh said, ''You're in love, too, aren't you, boss.''

Mick glanced over at his friend. ''Yeah, I'm afraid I am.''

''Nothing to be afraid of,'' Josh retorted, grinning. ''I knew it the minute I saw you and Lorna together. It just seemed...right.''

''Tell that to Lorna.''

''No, man. You gotta be the one to do the telling.''

Mick nodded. ''That's why I'm headed down the interstate, friend.'' Then he reached over to punch Josh's muscular forearm. ''And what about you? When did you know it was 'right' between Kathryn and you?''

Josh chuckled. ''The minute I went down into that crumpled building to find her. Or I should say, the minute I laid eyes on her.''

''But it was dark down there,'' Mick pointed out. ''How could you fall in love with her without even seeing her?''

Josh touched a big hand to his heart. ''I saw her inside here, man. I saw her heart, her soul. That woman has spunk. I felt her strength.'' He shook his head, his tone full of awe. ''Even trapped in a collapsed building, with a broken leg, she still had more courage than I'll ever have. I didn't need a spotlight to show me what Kathryn's all about.''

Mick couldn't respond to that. He didn't have the words for a snappy comeback. But he did know what Josh was saying. "I guess that's why I love Lorna," he said at last. "I saw her courage that day when I pushed her away from that falling limb." He smiled again. "I saw so much in her eyes—bravery and defiance—but I guess what really caught me was her wariness.''

Josh lifted two dark brows. "Wariness? That's a new one. Most women aren't in the least wary when it comes to being around Mick Love.''

"Exactly," Mick replied with a wry grin. "Lorna didn't fall for my earth-shattering good looks and glowing smile.''

Josh sat up, laughing. "Get outta here. She fell all right, and fell hard.''

"But she had my number." Mick tried to explain. "She didn't want to rush into anything.''

"And that's how you two left it—just hanging out there? Y'all couldn't reach a compromise, at least?''

"Lorna doesn't want a compromise. That wariness has her running scared." He shrugged. "And she won't tell me what she's really afraid of, even though I think I have that figured out. It's complicated. *She's* complicated.''

"So…she loves you, though, right?''

"I think she does. At least, I intend to find out if she does."

Josh shook his head. "Sounds like you're gonna be bailing a big bucket of water in this flood, my friend."

"Let's hope I don't wind up drowning in regret," Mick replied.

They both groaned at their attempt at symbolism.

"Let's just get there and make sure they're all safe," Josh said, his tone serious. "Then we'll worry about all the rest."

Mick nodded in agreement. "A few more minutes. We'll be at Bayou le Jardin before nightfall."

Lorna glanced out the back door again. It would be nightfall in about an hour. And Lucas wasn't home yet.

"Lucas, where are you?" she asked as she tried his phone again, irritation covering the shiver of fear running through her voice.

She moved away from the window, then looked around the kitchen. She'd done what she could to prepare the room. All the food was up on the counters and in the higher cabinets. She'd moved pots and pans into the big pantry.

The place looked as if she were getting ready to move permanently.

After organizing the kitchen, she'd gone through the downstairs rooms, removing antique knickknacks and priceless artifacts, taking them one by one upstairs to the highest level of the house. All the upstairs bedrooms now were full of portraits, porcelain figurines, valuable vases, rococo candlesticks, and what few Chippendale dining chairs she'd managed to lug up the winding stairs. There was little else she could do on her own.

So she walked the long central hallway, checking yet again for anything that might be damaged if the water kept rising. She knew the heavy Hepplewhite secretary in the hallway would be ruined—

"Stop thinking about that," Lorna said aloud, her voice echoing eerily down the empty hallway. "These are just things. Just things." And yet, she knew she'd fight the flood to keep these precious "things" intact. They were part of her heritage, after all.

Maybe that explained the sense of calm falling over her. That, and her thoughts of Mick. Whenever she felt the fear creeping in like a wave of relentless water, she remembered how safe she'd felt with Mick out on the levee. She thought about his touch, his kisses, the security that being in his arms had given her.

"We had so little time together," she whispered. Yet, somehow, her time with Mick had begun a healing process inside her. She would be all right. She would survive this, just as she'd survived so many crises in her life. If nothing else, she had Mick to thank for that.

Her cell phone rang, the singsong noise snatching her back from her thoughts. "Hello?"

"*Chère,* we've got problems."

"Lucas, where are you? What's happened?"

"Tobbie got a call from home. One of the children—" Static cut him off.

"What? I can't hear you, Lucas."

"...missing."

Lorna heard that one word loud and clear.

"...got to help them...looking for the baby—Tobias. He ran off—said he was going to climb high up in a tree."

"Go, go!" she shouted into the phone. "Lucas, don't worry about me. Find him, find Tobias."

Lucas said something else, but she couldn't make it out. Then the phone went dead.

Little Tobbie—out there alone in the rain.

Little Tobbie was only eight years old, the baby of the Babineaux clan. Lucas had to find him. Lucas *would* find him. After all, *he* knew what it felt like to be alone in the rain and dark.

With water everywhere.

And so did she.

Lorna looked out onto the back gallery. Already the flat green stone was covered with about six inches of water. Already that same water was slowly rising up the couple of inches to the door frame.

The flood was coming.

She was still very much alone.

And darkness was beginning to fall.

Lorna automatically headed back into the kitchen to

find her flashlight. Then she went around flipping on lights and turning on lamps. Lucas wouldn't be here for a long, long time. She'd have to leave without him, hoping that he found Little Tobbie, hoping that they'd all be safe.

She decided to go to the upstairs gallery facing the river to see how well the levee was holding. Then she'd come around to the other side, toward the back gardens and the bayou. Maybe she'd be able to see how high the water was from there.

If not, she'd have to go ahead and drive out on her own. Her little second-hand sportscar wouldn't be too safe in a raging flood, but that was her only choice.

Lorna stopped on the second-floor landing, surveying the scattered possessions she'd hurriedly assembled there earlier. Among them was the portrait of her parents that had been hanging in the downstairs parlor. She wouldn't let the flood waters damage that. She would carry it out of here on her back, if she had to.

Pushing back memories of another night and another raging storm, Lorna moved toward the French doors to the gallery, then opened them to stand on the porch.

The rain kept falling, softly now, but with a cadence that had an almost soothing quality. She looked through the dusky, gray light to the river.

And her heart stopped.

The water was beginning to tip the levee. She could see it gleaming blue-black against the approaching night. The saplings and reeds nestled on the other side of the levee were now under a murky wall of water.

Panic seizing her body, she spun around to head up the hallway toward the back of the house. She wanted to see the bayou, to find her brother.

What she saw there terrified her even more.

More water. It was hard in the dim to distinguish where the bayou left off and the yard began. The restaurant was slowly becoming submerged. She was glad that she and Lacey had earlier tried to secure some of its furnishings and supplies; she could see the water lapping hungrily at the seats of the wrought-iron chairs on the low back patio. In another few minutes, the water would be inside her beloved restaurant kitchen.

And there was absolutely nothing she could do about it.

"Stay calm, Lorna," she told herself. Reaching for her cell phone nestled in the pocket of her baggy walking shorts, she dialed Lucas's number again. And got no response.

Then she tried Lacey. Her sister answered on the second ring.

Through the static, Lacey asked, "Lorna, where… you? I thought you and Lucas…behind us."

"I'm still waiting for him, but I don't think he's coming anytime soon. Lacey, he hasn't made it in from the swamp. Tobias is missing. Lucas had to go look for him."

"Oh, no. Oh…Little Tobbie?"

She heard the panic in her sister's voice, felt that same panic lifting like a fierce, fast-moving wind over her body.

"Listen to me, Lorna. Just get…car and come into town. You've still got time. The sandbags are holding so far…road…passable. But…different story in a few hours. Just come on, honey."

"I can't leave without Lucas—he's got to find that child. I can't leave until I know they're both safe."

"Yes, you can." Impatiently, Lacey snapped, "Why did you have to pick a flood to try and prove your courage?"

Tears sprang to Lorna's eyes. Tears of longing, tears of regret. "I don't know. I guess because of Mick."

"Mick? What's he got to do with this?"

"I…I wouldn't give him a chance, because I was afraid…afraid he'd leave me. You know I always have to be the first one to leave, right?"

"Yes, I know that. But…you're still smarting from being jilted by Cole. I don't think Mick is anything like Cole Watson."

"But what if he can't deal with me?" Lorna asked, her eyes watching the water. "What if he can't understand my…fear?"

"Can't we talk about this later?" Lacey said gently. "Just come into town, Lorna. Now."

"Okay. I'm coming," Lorna finally said. "But I'm so worried about Lucas."

"Lucas knows that swamp like the back of his hand," Lacey reminded her. "I'm sure he's going to find Little Tobbie safe and sound. But *you* can't wait. We'll just have to send some of the men out to find all of them. And you, too, if you don't hurry."

"What if…" Lorna couldn't finish the thought.

"He'll be fine," Lacey replied, but the words sounded hollow and dull. "Now, come on, before we have to send someone to rescue you."

Lorna hung up the phone and looked out toward the trees.

No sign of Lucas.

She turned back inside. She'd just grab her raincoat and go. Her hands shaking, she found her car keys and donned a long beige trench coat. Sending up prayers for her brother, for her family, she started down the stairs, her flashlight in her hand even though lights were blazing throughout the house. At the bottom, she stopped.

"My parents' portrait." She ran back up the stairs to grab the rectangular picture, its gold-etched frame shining like fire in the lights from the chandelier over her head.

Glancing around one last time, she turned to rush back down the stairs.

And that's when the lights went out.

Mick pulled the truck up to the town square in Jardin, then turned off the motor. He was dog-tired and worried, but at least he was here now. He'd find Lorna, and everything would be all right between them.

"Looks like the town's safe so far," Josh said as he rounded the truck, stretching his sore body in the process.

"Let's go find them."

They headed to the mayor's office. And came face to face with Lacey.

Mick took one look at her and knew something wasn't right.

"Mick," she said, grabbing his arms with white-knuckled fingers. "I'm so very glad to see you. And you, too, Josh." She touched Josh's arm. "Kathryn is in the back conference room with Aunt Hilda. She's safe, but they're still trying to round up her family."

Josh nodded and took off down the hallway.

That left Lacey staring up at Mick, a fear brightening her blue eyes.

"What is it?" Mick asked, scanning the hallway behind her. "Where's Lorna?"

Lacey lowered her head. "She's at the house. She was waiting for Lucas to come in from the bayou."

Mick swallowed the lump of cold dread that had formed in his throat. "And?"

Lacey looked up then, and he saw that same dread on her face. "Lucas never made it home—Little Tobbie is missing, and Lucas had to go back out and help search the bayou...to find him. Lorna is still there, alone. She was supposed to be on her way here, but that was over an hour ago. And we just got word that the power's out in some parts of the parish.''

''What?'' He pushed Lacey away, then dropped his hands to his side. ''You left her there alone, knowing...knowing how things are with her?''

Lacey gasped, her hand coming up to her mouth. ''You mean, *you* know?''

''That she's afraid of the dark?'' He nodded. ''It didn't take a whole lot to figure it out.'' Then he whirled around and headed to the door. ''I have to get to her. She must be terrified. Why did you leave her like that?''

Lacey blinked back tears. ''I didn't want to. But Lorna insisted that Lucas was on the way, and we had to get Aunt Hilda to safety. Oh, Mick, I'm so sorry. You have to get her.''

Mick didn't bother answering. He only knew that his heart felt like a lead weight bobbing against his chest. He only knew that the courage he'd seen in Lorna's eyes the first time he'd met her had been a big front.

He had to reach her.

He went back out into the darkness and got into his truck. Water rushed all around the vehicle as he backed it out into the street.

''Lord, I need You now. Lorna needs You. Help her to hang on until I can get there, Lord. Help all of us.''

Chapter Fifteen

～

Mick made it to within sight of the house. Just as he rounded the curve leading to the gate, the road became impassable. There was a low spot in the levee, and through the beam of his truck's headlights he could see the river water rushing over the spot in swirling urgency.

He got out of the truck, stared down into the water, and decided it was too risky to try to drive through it. If he got stuck—or worse, carried off on the river currents—that wouldn't help Lorna.

He'd have to go the rest of the way on foot. Which meant he'd be tracking through knee-high water.

Quickly, he went back to the truck and managed to pull it over to the side of the road, up onto the levee. Then he got a flashlight and a first-aid kit out of the big toolbox on the back of the truck. He didn't want to think about having to use the kit.

After securing the truck, he started trudging through the water, his hard hat and yellow slicker his only protection against the pounding rain. Once he was away from the beam of light the truck had provided, he realized just how dark it had become. Lorna would be terrified if she was alone in this blackness.

Then he saw the silhouette of the big house up ahead. It was completely dark, too.

Mick ran the rest of the distance to the front gate, and with shaking hands managed to get it open despite the rushing water pushing it back. Then he was in the front gardens, underneath the cloying dark canopy of the great oaks.

"Hang on, baby," he said into the wind and water washing over his face. "I'm coming."

He followed the bouncing beam of his powerful flashlight, hoping Lorna would at least see it and come out to find him. But as he got closer to the house, a solid wall of fear slammed into him.

The entire bottom floor of the mansion was covered in at least six inches of water.

Mick sloshed through the water, his jeans now completely soaked. "Lorna?" He shouted her name above the din of rain and wind. "Lorna, it's Mick. Can you hear me? Lorna, are you in there?"

Figuring she probably couldn't hear him, anyway, he tried the front door. It was locked. Mick hurried around the first-floor gallery, his heavy work boots pushing at the dark water. He reached the kitchen, then tugged at the French doors. They opened with a groan against the surging waters.

"Lorna?" He beamed his flashlight over the room but didn't see anyone. He did see, however, that Lorna had managed to stay busy. Everything was up high, away from the floor. She'd even turned the high-backed chairs up onto the long, butcher-block table.

He moved toward the central hallway, his wet clothes and shoes hindering each step as he pressed against the current of the flowing water. "Lorna?"

The flashlight's single beam showed someone had worked hard here, too. The hallway was practically stripped: no rugs, no potted plants, no artifacts. Whoever had moved things had only left the things that couldn't be lifted.

He came to the front parlor and searched across the hall in the formal dining room, doing a quick once-over with the flashlight. Again, the rooms looked as though someone had robbed the place, with portraits and paintings missing, and all the furnishings stripped of their ornaments and decorations—even the chairs turned up on top of the table.

He quickly turned from the dining room to the parlor. Most of the furnishings here were bare, too. And the portrait of Lorna's parents was gone from its place of honor over the fireplace.

"Lorna," he said, whispering to himself now. "Where are you? Why did you pick today to stay here on your own?"

Mick supposed her fear had driven her to stay busy. His heart ached to comfort her, to hold her and tell her she was safe now. But first, he had to find her.

He started up the stairs.

Glad to be away from the water's strengthening current below, he stopped on the third stair to move his light up to the landing, hoping to find her there. Instead, he found most of the missing things from downstairs.

Shaking his head, Mick put down the first-aid kit, then took off his heavy, dripping wet slicker. He slowly made his way around the winding staircase. "Lorna? Honey, are you up here? Where are you?"

No answer.

She had to be somewhere upstairs. It was the safest, most logical place to get away from the rising waters. But then, in her state of mind she might not be thinking logically.

"Lorna? he called, sharper this time. "It's Mick. I'm here, Lorna. I'm here."

They were coming for her. She had to hide, had to stay still, just as Lucas had warned her to do. She had to find Lacey. Lacey would hug her close and keep her safe. Lacey on one side and Lucas on the other, here away from the rain and the storm, away from the water and the darkness. That's the way it had always been.

Away from those horrible, bad men who'd killed their parents.

"Just stay still and quiet," she told herself. The same words Lucas had repeated to her over and over again as they'd hidden there in the darkness, his hand sometimes clamping down on her mouth to keep her from screaming or moving.

If I move, they'll find me.

She didn't dare breathe, didn't dare call out. The darkness moved over her like a hot, wool blanket, thick and suffocating. But if she tried to push at it, tried to breathe, they would find her and kill her, the same way they'd killed Mommy and Daddy.

Where was Lucas? Where was Lacey? Why had they left her here all alone? Weren't they supposed to be here, too? They'd always, always been here with her. She remembered them being here, could almost feel them on each side of her, protecting her.

That's the way it had been.

But then she remembered how she'd tried to outrun the fear. How she'd left her family behind to strike out on her own. And for a while, it had worked. She'd taken off to Europe, always running, trying to escape the great fear that chased through her dreams and taunted her even in her waking hours.

But, that had to be it—she must be dreaming again. That was why Lucas and Lacey weren't here. They would never leave her alone in the dark. Never.

Yes, that was it. She was having that same horri-

fying, familiar nightmare. The one she'd fought
against for so very long. The one she'd paid countless
therapists to help her cure. And for a while, it had
been dormant. Until the tornado had brought it all
crashing back.

Tired. She was so tired. But she couldn't sleep. The
men might find her and kill her. She had to stay awake,
had to stay calm.

The darkness trapped her. She couldn't move. She
could hear the rain falling, falling, never stopping. She
could almost reach out and touch the water creeping
ever closer to her hiding place, here underneath the
house on the hill.

But she wasn't underneath the house on the hill, she
reminded herself. For a brief instant, that gave her a
measure of calm and relief. She was at Bayou le Jardin. Safe. She'd always been safe here. God had
watched over her here. Was He watching over her
now?

Lorna tried to focus, tried to remember what had
happened to her flashlight. Had she dropped it, or had
the batteries burned out? *Can't remember. Must not
remember.*

She held the memories at bay, along with the fear.
She pushed at the horrible, clinging fear, fought it,
refused to acknowledge it.

But she could hear *them* coming. She could hear the
footsteps, the movement of man against water, the rip-
ple of waves as the dark water lapped ever closer to

her hiding place here amid the tangled vines and undergrowth behind the house on the hill.

You're not there, she silently shouted to herself. *Lorna, get a grip. You're at Bayou le Jardin. Don't panic.*

But she'd already reached that point.

She tried to speak. "Lucas?" But the word, his name, had no sound. "Lacey?" Why wouldn't her throat cooperate?

The footsteps were getting closer now.

Her heart was beating so loud, so fast, she knew it would give her away. It sounded so much like the beating of the drums.

This time, they'd find her.

But this wasn't how it was supposed to end. Lucas and Lacey were supposed to be here with her, and they'd stay here just like this until morning, when the authorities would come and get them.

And then, they'd be sent home to Aunt Hilda.

And Mommy and Daddy would be sent home, too. In their coffins. They would be buried by the Chapel in the Garden.

Home.

But she *was* home. She was safe. Why was it so dark? Where was everyone?

Lorna shook her head, tried to focus in the darkness, tried to find air. Somewhere in the center of her being, she felt a core of steel giving her the strength to hang on. And somewhere, deep in her soul, she heard a voice.

Be still, child. You will survive. Trust in the Lord with all of your heart.

Then she heard the footsteps again. With a gasp, she realized they were near—right outside her hiding place.

They'd found her. The bad men had found her.

And she was all alone.

Then all the memories came rushing toward her like the great raging river bursting through the levee. And she knew this was no dream. This was real, and she was once again alone in the dark.

Giving in to sheer terror, Lorna opened her mouth and screamed. The fear that had chased her for so long had become a real and tangible thing, gripping her like a twisting vine as she thrashed against the cloying black night.

Mick heard the scream.

It was a sound he would never forget.

He shouted her name. "Lorna!"

He was just outside the door to her bedroom. Not bothering to stop and think, he kicked with his boot at the locked door, shattering the frame, sending wood flying out before him.

"Lorna?" He called her name over the scream, then sent the beam of his flashlight around the big square room.

No sight of her. Yet the scream was echoing all around him.

Taking a breath to regain control, Mick stood still. Then he put the flashlight on a nearby table, and waited until the screams subsided.

The silence was just as loud. It was filled with her fear.

Dear God, what caused her to come to this?

Mick understood so much now. He understood why Lorna had run away from every relationship she'd ever had. And he certainly understood why she'd pushed him away.

But he had to show her that he wasn't like the others. He wouldn't leave her again. Ever. He waited in the silence, a cold, shivering sweat mixing with the rainwater covering his body. And he listened.

God, help me. Guide me to her.

He heard a sniff, a sob, and then he heard her labored breathing, as if she couldn't get enough air.

"Lorna?" He said her name softly this time, then he moved a step closer to the sound of the sobs.

She was in the closet.

Mick heard the shuffling of her body. She was trying to move away. "Lorna, listen to me," he said, his voice firm in spite of his shaking insides. "Lorna, it's Mick. Honey, it's all right. Do you understand? I've come to help you. I'm going to get you out of here, okay?"

Mick listened again, straining to hear over the sound of rainfall.

He didn't know how to help her. He'd never encountered this kind of deep-seated terror. So he prayed, silently and with total dependence on God to guide him.

And then he started talking.

"Lorna, remember our nights out in the summerhouse? Did you feel safe with me there?" When she didn't answer, he continued, his voice soft and soothing. "You must have. You stayed there with me long after the moon had come up. Think about that, honey. Think about how we laughed and talked and cuddled. Remember? I held you in my arms, and we listened to the frogs croaking out in the bayou. We listened to the crickets singing and those pesky mosquitoes humming around our ears. Lorna, that was magic for me. You brought me such a sense of peace, such a sense of belonging. You taught me how to have faith again."

He stopped, waited. Prayed.

"Lorna, you can trust me. You can tell me anything. I'm not going to judge you or condemn you. I understand everything now. I know what you've been fighting against."

Again he stopped. Hoped. Listened.

And all the while, he knew the water was rising.

He had to get her out of here.

So he tried one more time, based on a hunch and

sheer desperation. "Do you want to tell me about that night? The night your parents died?"

He thought he heard a sob. He stopped breathing just to hear it again.

And then he heard her voice.

"They...they came to our camp in the middle of the night."

She sounded so small, so lost, that it took every ounce of strength he had left to keep from rushing into the closet to pull her close.

But he held back. "Who came to your camp?"

"The rebels," she said, her voice growing stronger. "They didn't like us being there. They...didn't want missionaries in their village."

Missionaries. Mick swallowed that bit of information right along with the knot in his throat.

"Where was your camp, Lorna?"

"Africa," she said. She was silent for a minute. "Somewhere far away—a very remote spot in Africa. Mommy and Daddy wanted to help...they wanted to take care of people. God sent them there, you know."

He heard another sob. Pushed at the tears burning his own eyes. "But the rebels...they hurt your mommy and daddy?"

"They murdered them," she said at last.

Then Mick heard the sobs coming as softly and surely as the rain falling outside the open French doors. And he wondered if she'd ever allowed herself to cry like this before.

"And what about you? How did you get away?"

"We hid. Lacey and Lucas pulled me out of my bed and we ran and ran. Daddy told them—get away—run—run."

Mick swallowed again, closed his eyes to the horror she must have suffered. They'd all suffered.

"Where did you hide?"

"Underneath the house on the hill. The hut. It was round and open." She stopped. Took a shuddering breath. "Like the summerhouse, only it was dark and…it was up on stilts. There were snakes underneath there—and spiders, big spiders. But the storm was coming. Rain. So much rain. And wind. A big storm. And the men who'd hurt my parents were still in our compound."

She was talking now, her voice growing stronger with each word, sounding more like herself. Mick didn't interrupt. He knew deep within his soul that she needed to tell this story.

"But Lucas held my mouth shut so I wouldn't scream, and he pushed me under there. Lacey came in with me. She held me in her lap and rocked me. She was crying. Then Lucas came in and pulled the vines back around us. So many vines. They held me there, in the dark. We waited. We heard the men roaming around, walking past us, running in the rain and mud. They came up inside the round house, above our heads. We heard them talking as they searched."

She stopped, sighed.

Mick stepped toward the closed door separating them. "What happened then?"

"The storm," she said, her voice edged with fatigue.

"The storm was getting worse. Flooding. Water. We were safe up on the hill. Dry behind the vines. But the water was coming, so they…they finally left."

Mick didn't ask what happened next. Instead, he held his breath. Hoping she'd keep talking.

She did. "We stayed there until morning. The rain finally stopped and daylight came. Then Lucas told Lacey and me to stay put. He was going out to find help. We didn't want him to go out there, but Lucas told us to be still. Then he left us there."

"Was he able to find someone?"

"Yes, he ran to a nearby village. A friendly village. Then the authorities came and…told us our parents were gone…dead. But we knew that already." She paused again, then said, "We stayed at another compound for a few days, and then we came to live with Aunt Hilda."

Mick took off his forgotten hard hat and ran a hand over his hair. He couldn't imagine the terror the sisters and their brother must have suffered that night. Alone in the dark, in a remote jungle, caught in the middle of a raging storm, with rebels and poisonous creatures lurking about. Alone for hours on end. They must have thought everyone had abandoned them.

Even their God.

But then Mick realized something that the three never had. *The storm had saved them*. It had caused the rebels to flee.

He wiped away tears that he hadn't even known were falling. No wonder this incredible woman was so afraid of the dark. And no wonder her family had protected her. Lacey and Lucas had taken care of their little sister on that horrible night, and they were still trying to take care of the woman she'd become. In her own way, Lorna had rebelled against all of it—running away across the world to prove she could do things her way. Only to return home to the sanctuary of her family and Bayou le Jardin.

Mick wanted her to find comfort and sanctuary in his arms. He'd make her see that she could trust him. And he'd make her see, just as he'd had to see, that God had not abandoned her.

"Lorna, listen to me, okay?"

"Okay," she said on a whisper. "Mick?"

The hope in her voice, in the way she said his name, made him want to cry all over again. He shut his eyes to the tears. She knew who he was, at least.

"It's me, honey. I'm here and I'm not going to leave you. Can you see the light? Can you see my flashlight?"

"Yes. Mine…quit on me. I…lost it, and I got scared. I wanted to show them I could do this—but I guess I'm still scared, after all."

In spite of her confession, she sounded stronger now, more coherent.

"It's all right to be scared, Lorna. I was scared myself. Scared of loving you, scared of giving up my pride. I was scared of turning back to God, of giving Him control."

"Really?"

"Really. But I had a long talk with my pastor, and then I had a long talk with God. I'm not scared anymore."

"Is that why you came back here?"

"I came back for you," he told her, his voice low but clear. "I had to see you again. I had to be here with you."

"God sent you." The statement was both solemn and full of awe.

"Maybe He did," Mick replied, closing his eyes in thankfulness. "I'm here now, honey, and I'm not going anywhere."

She was silent for a minute, then she said, "Even though I'm a coward?"

"You are no coward, Lorna Dorsette. You are one of the bravest women I've ever known. Now, stop this foolishness and come on out here so I can hold you in my arms."

She became silent again. Mick felt the tension in his neck, twisting him like a vice. "Lorna, please."

"I'm not…sure. I'm still…afraid."

"Lorna, you don't have to be afraid anymore. You know why?"

"Why?"

He sighed, fell to his knees right by the closed door. "I think I've figured this out, baby. Even though the rebels killed your parents, God didn't abandon you that night. Do you hear me?"

"I hear you."

He took another breath, closed his eyes. "The rain came, remember? That raging storm saved you and Lacey and Lucas. Those men went away because of the water. It scared them away."

Silence.

Mick breathed, knowing that they were breathing together—a slow, steady rhythm of hope in the midst of so much darkness.

"I never thought of it like that," she said at last. And then she added, "Why didn't the rain come sooner? Why didn't God send it to save my parents?"

He surely didn't have an answer for that one. Except the one the preacher had given him. "Maybe God had a different plan for them. Maybe they had to die in order for you to have a different life. God needed them in heaven, Lorna."

Then he heard the anger.

"Yes, and He took them and left us all alone."

Mick edged closer to the door, touched the knob. "No, Lorna. It's horrible that your parents had to die, but God didn't desert you that night."

"I don't believe you."

Slowly, Mick turned the knob. "Lorna, listen to me. I'm going to open this door so you can see the light."

"No!"

He stopped, then tried again. "Yes, I'm going to come in there and get you. And I promise you, I will never leave you again. And neither will God."

"How can I be sure? Cole left me standing at the altar. He was afraid of living with me. He thought I was crazy."

Surprised, Mick asked, "Now why would he think that?"

"The nightmares," she explained. "The horrible dreams. He laughed at me when I told him. Laughed at me because I had to sleep with the lights on. The night before our wedding, I was asleep in a guest bedroom at his parents' house, and I had a nightmare. He got angry with me and...he was embarrassed, so the next day he left me."

"I'm not Cole," Mick said, wishing he could find the man and throttle him. "You can trust me, Lorna." Then he tried another tactic. "And because of you, *I've* learned to trust God again. I want to thank you for that."

She didn't speak for a while. Then she said, "You came back here, for me?"

"Yes, I sure did. I drove for hours and then walked through all that water, just to find you."

"God sent you." She said it again, as if to reassure herself that this was real.

Mick closed his eyes again, thanked God. "That's what you told me that first day, remember? You have to believe that, Lorna. God brought us together, to heal each other."

He heard her sobs again, this time soft and muffled. "Can I come in now, Lorna?"

He didn't wait for an answer. Instead, he opened the door and saw her there in the corner, huddled beneath clothes and blankets, her green eyes wide with fear and doubt, her long hair flowing out around her face as she held her parents' portrait tightly in her arms. The sight tore through him with a delicate clarity, like shards of tattered lace moving through a rainstorm.

Mick stayed on his knees, one hand on the door. With his other hand, he reached out to her, the light behind him guiding him. "Lorna, take my hand."

"I...I don't think I can."

"Yes, you can. I love you, Lorna. I love you, and I want to marry you. And if you want to sleep with every light in the house on, that's okay by me. But I will always be there by your side. You'll never be alone in the dark again."

"How can I be sure of that?"

Mick held his hand out, almost touching her. "You're just going to have to trust me on this. Trust me and trust God."

"He sent the rain?"

"I believe he did."

"He sent you?"

"I sure hope so. I know because of Him we found each other." He inched closer. "And I fell in love with you."

She stared at him, her gaze locking with his. "I fell in love with you, too." Then she lifted her hand toward his. "Help me," she said, a single sob shuddering down her body.

Mick closed the space between them, took the portrait away and pulled her into his arms. "Lorna, I love you so much."

"I love you, too," she whispered, tears falling down her face as she clung to him.

Mick held her there for a while, then gently lifted her body away from his. "We have to get out of here now. Are you all right?"

Lorna nodded. "I am now."

Mick helped her up, then turned to the open French doors. "Listen. The rain's stopped."

The beautiful silence fell over them like a soft chenille blanket, warm and reassuring.

"I think we're gonna make it," Mick told her.

Together, they went out onto the upstairs gallery. Then they heard a shout from below.

"Lorna, are you in there? Are you all right?"

"Lucas, is that you?"

"Yes. I'm here now, love. We found Tobias high up in a tree. He's safe and sound with his momma."

"Lucas?" Lorna called to her brother again, watching as he pushed through the foot-deep waters below. "We're up here. Mick's with me."

Lucas stopped, a shadowy silhouette there in the center of the garden. "Thank God for that."

Lorna turned to Mick. "Yes, thank God for that."

Mick pulled her close and kissed her. And again promised God that he would love her and stay by her side, always.

Through sunshine and rainstorms.

And all through the night.

Epilogue

Three months later

"It was a beautiful wedding, love."

Lorna stood with her new husband, smiling over at her brother. "Thank you, Lucas." Then she reached up to touch Lucas's cheek. "Why so sad?"

His dark eyes searched her face. "I wasn't there, *belle*. I let you down the night of the flood."

Glancing up at Mick, Lorna pulled out of his embrace to tug her handsome brother close. "Don't be silly. You saved Little Tobbie's life. Doesn't that count for something?"

Lucas nodded, then let out a sigh. "I'm thankful for that, but…we made a promise. You, me and Lacey. And I didn't live up to that promise."

"Hey, man, that was a long time ago," Mick interjected, a hand on Lorna's arm. "You can't be every-where at once, Lucas. You did the only thing you could do. You had to find Tobias."

Lorna sent her husband a loving look. "Mick is right. For a very long time, we depended on each other so much. We forgot that God is the one in control. Lucas, we have to let go. We have to keep the faith."

Lucas nodded, then lifted a tanned hand to the white bow tie at his neck. With a grimace, he unlaced the knot. "Maybe you're right. But...something shifted inside me the night of the flood. I think I finally re-alized...I'm tired of remembering." He gave an elo-quent shrug. "And yet, how do I forget?"

Lorna's heart went out to her brother. Ever since the flood in the early spring, Lucas had blamed himself for leaving her alone in the mansion. Now, as he stood here in his cream-colored linen suit—the one she'd insisted he wear to give her away—she could tell that he was still suffering. And not just from that flood.

He had changed. Despite his lighthearted banter, there was a melancholy surrounding him like a dark aura each time he stopped smiling.

She had to make him see that everything had hap-pened for a reason.

Looking around, she saw Lacey talking quietly to Aunt Hilda and Justin. Although her sister looked as serene as ever in her sky-blue bridesmaid dress, Lacey, too, seemed different since the last storm.

They all had changed.

Or maybe Lorna was the one who'd changed; maybe she was just imagining things in her newfound glee. Her sister had been so relieved to find Lorna safe and sound in Mick's arms the night of the flood, but now they'd all have to adjust to Lorna's marriage. And Lacey had been so busy helping to prepare for the wedding, she probably hadn't even seen that Lucas was still worried about not being able to get to Lorna that night.

Well, Lorna wouldn't bring that up to Lacey today. Today was her wedding day, and she only wanted those around her to feel as wonderful as she did right this minute.

Pulling away from her brother, the gathered skirt of her stark white linen wedding dress rustling as she moved, Lorna stared up at him. "Listen to me. All this time, I thought I was afraid of the dark. I was terrified of things I couldn't see. But it was the memories, Lucas. It was the memories of things I *had* seen, that haunted me." She turned to Mick, reaching out a hand to take his. "In reality, it wasn't so much the darkness I feared." She stopped, took a deep breath, smiled at the two men she loved. "It was the light, Lucas. I was afraid to live in the light."

Lucas's eyes, midnight deep and just as mysterious, held hers. "And now you've found the light with our Mr. Love?"

"Yes." Lorna laughed, then threw her arms around her brother. "Yes, I've found the light."

Mick watched as his wife hugged her brother tightly. She looked like something out of a dream in her sleeveless wedding gown, with her hair cascading from underneath her mother's perky white straw hat—the "something old" Lacey had found in the attic and cleaned up for Lorna to wear.

But she was real. This was real. Today, Lorna Dorsette had become Lorna Dorsette Love. Lorna Love. He liked the sound of that. He loved her.

"We love each other," he told Lucas. "And...I can promise you this, friend. I will never leave her alone, night or day."

Lorna nodded. "I'm all right now. I know I've still got some issues to work through, but...I'm so very happy."

"Okay, okay," Lucas said, raising a hand in defeat. "Then I'm happy for you. And I'm happy for that sap Josh, too."

They all laughed as they glanced over at the other bride and groom standing in the still-recovering summer garden of Bayou le Jardin. Josh had married his Kathryn.

The double wedding in the chapel had been Lorna's idea. And Aunt Hilda had insisted on having the reception in the garden, in spite of the continuing cleanup and replanting.

"That 'sap,' as you called him, can't be any happier than I am right now," Mick told his new brother-in-law. "And to think, he's going to train to become a real fireman, too."

"Maybe chief one day," Lucas said with a nod of approval. "The village needs a good strong, willing soul to take on the new fire department."

"I'm losing a good man," Mick confessed.

"And you're moving to a new location," Lucas countered, pointing to the big house behind them.

"No, I'm moving home," Lucas told him, his gaze scanning the gardens. "I didn't have anything holding me back in Mississippi, and I can get back there anytime if they need me."

"Right now, *I* need you," his wife told him. "I'm ready to start our honeymoon."

Lucas chuckled, then winked at Mick. "Can't turn that request down, now can you, brother?"

Hours later, as the moon glowed a creamy yellow over Bayou le Jardin, Mick stood at the foot of the four-poster bed in Lorna's room. "I'm glad we stayed here for our first night. It seems right."

She was all dolled up in something long and silky, with just a breath of the lightest shade of green in the shimmering material, to match her eyes.

Those eyes held his as she smiled up at him. "And tomorrow, we'll be on our way to our new life. New Orleans…and then I get to show you Paris."

"I've always had a hankering to see Paris."

"But not tonight."

"No, not tonight."

"Mick, turn out the light and come to bed."

"Are you sure? We can leave a lamp on."

"I'm sure. I know I'm safe with you. Safe at last."

"I'm glad you feel that way." He stood there, feeling a sense of awe. "And I'm glad you decided to become my wife."

"I didn't have a choice there," she replied. "Remember, God sent you." Then she reached out to him.

Mick took her hand, then turned out the bedside lamp.

And moved toward the light of her smile shining through the shadows.

*   *   *   *   *

Dear Reader,

Have you ever been afraid and alone in the dark? As children, we often had bad dreams that sent us running to our parents for comfort. That's the way it is with the Father. He is always there to offer comfort, if only we look for the light of His love.

Lorna Dorsette had forgotten that even in her darkest moments God was still there with her, acting as her guiding light. Her fears became insurmountable, so she was afraid of the darkness. Then along came Mick Love, a simple, hardworking man who saved her not only from physical harm, but also from the dark fear deep inside her soul.

Together, Mick and Lorna had to rediscover God's guiding love and His everlasting protection. They found their own secret pavilion, and there in the moonlight they regained their trust in God and found a love that would carry them through even the darkest moments.

Until next time, may the angels watch over you while you sleep.

Lenora Worth

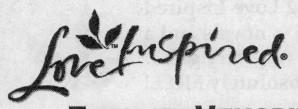

TANGLED MEMORIES

BY
MARTA PERRY

Finally meeting the
wealthy family she'd
never known should have
given Corrie Grant the
information she'd always
craved about her father.
But the relatives were
a secretive bunch, and
though Lucas Santee was
there to stand beside her,
Corrie soon found herself
in danger....

**Available August 2006
wherever you buy books.**

Steeple
Hill®

www.SteepleHill.com

LISTM

A SHELTERING HEART

BY
TERRI REED

Showing handsome Derek Harper that Healing Missions International healed hearts, not just bodies, was the promise Gwen Yates had made to her boss, because Derek was more interested in the organization's numbers. That her own heart was vulnerable to Derek had somehow escaped Gwen's notice.

Available August 2006 wherever you buy books.

Steeple Hill®

LIASH

Love Inspired.

CLASSICS

TITLES AVAILABLE NEXT MONTH

Don't miss these stories in August

A BRIDE AT LAST
AND
A MOTHER AT HEART
by Carolyne Aarsen

Two couples share their journeys of love and
homecoming in the Canadian heartland.

THE FORGIVING HEART
AND
A DADDY AT HEART
by Deb Kastner

A pair of single dads each get a second chance
at love in two unforgettable stories.